Wish I May, Wish I Might...

Best Wishes —
Barbara Elliott Carpenter

By

Barbara Elliott Carpenter

1663 LIBERTY DRIVE, SUITE 200
BLOOMINGTON, INDIANA 47403
(800) 839-8640
WWW.AUTHORHOUSE.COM

© 2005 Barbara Elliott Carpenter. All Rights Reserved.

No part of this book may be reproduced, stored in a retrieval system, or transmitted by any means without the written permission of the author.

First published by AuthorHouse 07/26/05

ISBN: 1-4208-6010-0 (sc)
ISBN: 1-4208-6009-7 (dj)

Library of Congress Control Number: 2005904710

Printed in the United States of America
Bloomington, Indiana

This book is printed on acid-free paper.

Dedication

To Glenn...always and forever

To the Classes of 1958 who attended schools in Dix, Arcola, Salem and Mattoon, Illinois, I dedicate this book. Many thanks to the teachers in those schools who were tireless in their efforts to turn out students who could read, write, and 'rithmetic with the best.

To some of the teachers in the order I knew them: Carrie Freeman, Frances Holterman, Fern Covalt Knauss, Katherine Cox, Robert Brehm, Mary Jane Saunders, Gretta Osborne, Grace Quarterman, Lloyd Esmon, Ivan Gibbs, Blanche Stoafer, Anna Jane Wham, Mary Ruth Turnbull, Winifred Jones, Herbert Davis, Dwaine Crane, Mary Peace, Mr. B. E. Gum, Esther Grimes, Henrietta Worrell, and James Stewart, thank you.

To good teachers everywhere...God Bless You!

Kathy Baker and Ginger Boda, two of my wonderful online friends, proofread the manuscript and caught typos and some errors that the computer missed. Their support and encouragement were a tremendous help. Writers themselves, each lady has a wacky, witty, quick sense of humor and an ability to make me laugh that kept me halfway sane throughout the writing process.

Thanks, Kathy and Ginger!

To Laura

From the bottom of my heart, a cliché that is appropriate here, I thank my editor, **Laura Berry Bengelsdorf**. Laura spent untold hours pouring over the manuscript, and her suggestions and "red marks" on the pages were right on target. She helped make this continuance of Sissy's story a book that I am proud to present to new readers and to fans of the first book, <u>Starlight, Starbright</u>.... Her encouragement was a major influence in the decision to continue the saga with a third book in the series, to be released in 2006. That book will be titled <u>THE WISH I WISH TONIGHT</u>....

Thank you, Laura, for making a difference in the book and in my life!

Special Acknowledgement

With gratitude and appreciation, I wish to thank **General Chuck Yeager** for graciously allowing me to share memories of an airman under his command at Seymour-Johnson Air Force Base in North Carolina during 1967-68. While the book is fiction, bits of fact and a few real people appear within the pages, one being a former classmate and long-time friend of mine, **Jerry W. Davis, Colonel, USAF (Retired)**, whose experiences with then Colonel Yeager, as his wing commander, are briefly related.

On the official web site, **www.ChuckYeager.com,** can be found the history of General Chuck Yeager, one of our national heroes. I urge readers to access that website to learn more about the man behind the legend. Many pictures and articles tell the story of General Yeager, who spent a large part of his life in service to his country in the United States Air Force. Beginning even before he became the first pilot to break the sound barrier, his contribution to the world in the field of aviation is well known; and he is still involved in numerous endeavors, one of which is his own foundation. The following paragraphs are taken from a page on his web site:

Mission Statement

"The General Chuck Yeager Foundation supports programs which teach the ideals by which General Yeager has lived his life: honor, integrity and courage in our daily conduct, a strong sense of public service and duty to our country, and an intellectual curiosity.

What We Do

"**General Yeager flies Young Eagles and Make-A-Wish Foundation children, participates in fundraisers for Down Syndrome and Autistic Folks in Abilene, Texas, schools; conservation; Women In Aviation International, Paralyzed American Veterans, Disabled Veterans, and other programs."**

The above paragraphs merely touch the surface of what the Chuck Yeager Foundation represents. Its endeavors benefit many, many people and worthy organizations. Donations to the foundation are accepted and appreciated, as explained on the ChuckYeager.com web site. The world needs more men of General Yeager's caliber in roles of leadership. He has provided an example that merits emulation.

......Barbara Elliott Carpenter

Author's Note

This book is a work of fiction. Some liberties have been taken with the timeline of a deceased entertainer's life and concerts, to coincide with the storyline.

Table of Contents

Dedication   v

Special Acknowledgement   vii

Author's Note   ix

Prologue   xiii

Poetic Justice   1

Shades of Crazy   15

Summer's Child   53

Feuds   81

Sally's Mountain   103

Diane   125

Chains   145

Heroes   163

Love and Other Insanities   179

Broken Pieces   201

Still Waters   217

Dad   231

Through A Glass, Darkly   261

Epilogue   287

Readers' Reviews of Starlight, Starbright...   291

Prologue

When my father returned from Italy, where he had spent the last several months of World War II, my six-year-old heart beat with joy. The prospect of having a daddy in our house again filled me with excitement and anticipation. His return took place only a few weeks before the birth of my baby sister, two events that made our little family complete. Life was good.

Midway through my first year in grade school, my dad took a job in Redbud Grove, Illinois, one hundred miles north of the village in southern Illinois where we lived. We arrived at our new home during one of the coldest winters on record. January held a firm, frigid grip upon the little prairie town. The community cowered beneath the bitterly cold winds that rushed across the open plains, bringing Arctic blasts from Canada.

I remember those first days in Redbud Grove as a time I could never seem to get warm. I recall the sensations of teeth that chattered, legs that trembled, and chills that traveled up and down my body. Scared, lonely and cold on those long walks to and from school that winter, I was miserable. For days, fear was my constant companion: fear that I would never find friends like Becky and Jerry and all those I left behind, fear that no one would want or like me, fear of the unknown. I thought that my heart would break.

It didn't.

I made many wonderful new friends, and I was certain that the relationships we formed would last forever. When my father was transferred to Dixon, West Virginia, only days after my eighth-grade graduation, I was shattered. Once again I had to leave a home I loved and friends I adored. I was older, and the pain was greater. This time,

I understood how difficult it was going to be to make new friends. I knew how hard it would be to establish my own niche among teen-agers whose friendships had been formed for years. I think, for a time, that I really did hate my dad.

I got over it.

When we drove away from Redbud Grove, the town that held my home and dear friends of all ages, it felt as if I had left a major part of myself within the city limits. I missed the companionship and the long conversations with those friends. I missed Saturday matinees at the Ritz Theater, followed by sodas at The Sweet Shoppe. I longed for letters to keep me abreast of everything that happened back in Redbud Grove, both in the neighborhood where we had lived, and in the lives of my friends and their families. I missed Mrs. East, my surrogate grandmother. I missed the sound of the creaking swing cables in the park beside our house. I couldn't bear to think that life in Redbud Grove was going on as usual, without me.

I got over that, too.

Contrary to an old cliché, absence doesn't necessarily make the heart grow fonder. I discovered that it wasn't possible to keep one foot in Redbud Grove, Illinois, and the other in Dixon, West Virginia. For a while, letters flowed back and forth between my friends and me. Eventually, however, the number of letters dwindled; and the paper connection thinned until it finally broke. The flesh and blood people I saw every day became the ones who journeyed with me through the teen-age years of raging hormones, frustrations, dances, tragedy, frolicking fun, old and new loves, and beyond.

One day I realized that I had left my old friends behind.

They, predictably, had let me go.

Oh, but only for a time.

Poetic Justice

I felt as if I were going to drown.
A sea of teenagers spilled out the heavy front doors of the Dixon Community High School. They flowed down the concrete steps and onto the landing. My new friend and uphill neighbor, Karen Courtney, and I maneuvered our way to the registrar's office. I looked for Jerry Davis, the one other person that was at least somewhat familiar; but he was nowhere in sight. I was grateful for Karen's presence among all these strangers.

I experienced a sense of déjà vu, for once again I was the new kid. The main difference was that I was not the *only* new kid. I knew that there were others who were as disoriented as I. The hall reverberated with the sounds of voices, laughter, metal lockers slamming shut and books slapping against the tiled floor. The sounds were familiar, but Dixon High School was newer and much larger than the one in Redbud Grove.

I felt a tingle of excitement, mingled with a touch of anxiety. At the moment, anxiety held a distinct edge. If registration day created such pandemonium, it must be chaotic when classes actually started.

"Y'all register here," Karen said. She indicated the door I should enter. "Y'all go on in. I'll be back in a little while. 'Bye." Karen disappeared into the crowd. I took a big breath and grasped the doorknob. I paused for a moment, while old memories took a lightning flash trip through my mind.

I thought about my first day at school, midterm, back in Redbud Grove. The weather had been bitterly cold. My desperate mother had ambushed a neighbor boy as he passed our house, giving him no choice but to take me to school. Pressed into service as my escort, he had spoken to me only once during the cold, nine-block trek along unfamiliar streets. He had been all of eleven years old, five years my senior.

Today the weather was warm, and my companion had talked to me as we walked together. Although she was pre-registered, Karen had volunteered to accompany me. Apparently, many students had come simply to socialize. I was one of only a few who had not yet registered, but the corridors were crowded.

Registration complete, I plunged into the maelstrom in the hall, just in time to meet Karen. I followed her outside, where she led the way to a stone bench that circled one of the tall oak trees on the campus. Karen seemed to know everyone. Although she introduced me to each one, I couldn't begin to remember the names of all the boys and girls who stopped to speak to her. I smiled a lot, but I knew that it would be a long time before I connected their names with their faces.

"Let me see your schedule," Karen commanded. I gave the folded paper to her, and we scanned it together. "Oh, look, we have Miss Porter's first hour English class together. My sister, Nancy, says that she's really tough, but a good teacher. Miss Porter's a Yankee, like y'all; and she still talks like one." I grinned at Karen.

"How does a Yankee talk?" I asked.

"Like y'all do," she replied.

"Wait a minute. I'm not a Yankee. Illinois is in the Midwest, and I was born in Missouri. I *can't* be a Yankee."

"Well, y'all sound like one."

"When you say 'y'all', do you mean just me, or my whole family? I'm just one person, so why would you say 'you all' if you mean only me?"

"Huh?" Karen looked puzzled.

"Never mind," I laughed. "I'm just teasing you. I love the way you talk."

"I talk like everyone else around here," Karen said, "except the hillbillies. Now *those* people come from so far back in the mountains that even I have a hard time understanding them. Not many of them go to high school. You won't have any trouble spotting them." Karen returned to the schedule.

"You're taking art? I don't know *anyone* that takes art. The teacher is Mr. Boudreaux, and he's kinda weird. He doesn't hang out with the other teachers much, and he isn't married. People think he may be-- you know." Karen held up her hand, fingers outstretched, and waved it gently back and forth. I didn't know what she meant.

"Be what?" I asked. Karen slanted a look at me.

"Queer," she whispered.

"What's queer about him; and why are you whispering?"

"Don't y'all have queers up north?" Karen demanded. "Oh, *excuse me*! I mean in the *Midwest*." I was dumbfounded, and my expression must have indicated so. "Sissy, don't you know about boys that like boys and girls that like girls? You know, like *boyfriends and girlfriends*?" I blinked stupidly. Evidently my education in Redbud Grove had not covered this particular issue.

"Oh, that," I shrugged, hesitant to reveal my total ignorance. "I thought you were talking about something else." I pointed to the schedule. "Do you think you could walk me through this schedule? This school is at least five times bigger than the high school where I used to live. I don't want to get lost my first day."

"Sure." Karen agreed. I slipped the "queer" business into a file inside my head, where it took up residence with all the other things I needed to investigate. Occasionally I discovered answers to questions in that file, sometimes when I wasn't looking for them. Instead of becoming smaller as I grew older, the file of questions that needed answers seemed to grow larger.

An interesting thing happened as I listened to Karen that day and all the days that followed. At some point, I stopped noticing how different her accent was from mine. Without meaning to, I began to sound just like her. I was unaware of the change in my speech, until a visiting cousin pointed it out to me.

"You have a southern accent!" she accused.

"I do not!" I retaliated. I immediately thought of the night I had reconnected with Jerry Davis, at Karen's house. I had made the same accusation to him.

I suppose that I had become acclimated.

Karen's sister, Nancy, had told the truth about Miss Blanche Porter, the English teacher. "Tough" was a good word to describe the lady. The first day I sat in her English 101 class, there were many more descriptive words for her that came to mind: firm, aloof, majestic, merciless, even somewhat menacing when she tightened her mouth in stony silence.

Miss Porter's age was probably in the vicinity of forty years. She had a pronounced limp, and she walked with a cane. She moved slowly, but with dignity, and without a trace of self-pity or complaint. During the next year, I heard various versions of the accident that had injured Miss Porter. The most often repeated and the most believable, was also the saddest.

Miss Porter and her fiancé had been involved in a car accident. A drunk driver had hit them, killing Miss Porter's fiancé and leaving her permanently handicapped. After months of physical rehabilitation, she had become able to walk with the help of a cane; and she resumed her career as a teacher.

She looked like the actress, Ava Gardner, just not quite as glamorous. Her hair was dark, sprinkled with a few strands of silver; and her eyes were an indeterminate shade, sometimes gray, sometimes blue or green.

Miss Porter dressed impeccably, usually in two-pieced suits, with blouses that either contrasted or matched perfectly. She often wore a single strand of pearls that hung, just so, beneath her collar. The pearls would never have dared to move, not on Miss Porter's throat. Something in her manner, perhaps self-containment, reminded me of my first grade teacher, Miss Kate; but there was no physical resemblance.

Back in Redbud Grove, I had been under the tutelage of some very demanding teachers. My sixth grade teacher, Mary Jane Saunders, had stressed grammar and spelling. My seventh grade teacher, Mrs. Sylvester, had made the remark that she didn't want high school English teachers thinking that she had not done her job well. She had drilled grammar into us with the determination of an infantry sergeant.

While Miss Porter's demeanor may have intimidated me just a little, I felt that I would do fine academically under her sometimes baleful gaze. Except for roll call, I think that the woman was unaware of my presence in her classroom, until a few weeks into the semester. After she had given a pop quiz on the eight parts of speech, just to "see what kind of task" was ahead of her, as Miss Porter put it, I was reasonably certain that I had done well on the test.

After grading the papers, Miss Porter delivered her opinion of our knowledge, or lack thereof, of the English language. Her scathing words and disgusted demeanor assumed the proportions of a tidal wave. No one dared lift their eyes from their desktops. I began to wonder if I had absorbed one iota of Mrs. Sylvester's instruction.

"Only one person in this classroom has shown that she actually *retained* some of the instruction she received, during the past eight years," Miss Porter continued. My heart skipped a beat. I lifted my head, and Miss Porter was looking directly at me. I sank down a little more into my seat, knowing that I couldn't become invisible, but still trying. I *knew* she meant me. *Oh, please, please, puh-lease don't call my name!* I silently begged.

"Miss Sissy Bannister has a score of ninety-eight. Not one other person scored over eighty. I promise you, Ladies and Gentlemen, that before the year is over, you *will* know the parts of speech and how to use them." I wanted to die! Now no one would want to be seen with me, much less want to be my friend! It was one thing to grow up with people who knew me, knew my grades, knew the *person* I was. It was entirely different to be a new kid, to have the toughest teacher in the school single me out as an *example*! *For cryin' out loud!*

I endured the rest of the class. I didn't look at Miss Porter. I just wanted out of there! When the bell rang, I was the first to stand. I gathered my books and headed for the door.

"Sissy, wait!" Karen called to me, so I waited in the corridor. "How did you do that?" she demanded. "How did you get such a good grade on that test?" I shrugged.

"I had good teachers, I guess."

"I don't think the problem with *my* grades was my teachers' fault. I just don't like English! Maybe you can help me." Karen grinned.

"Sure," I replied, feeling a little better.

"Hey, Sissy, good job." Rick Endicott, the tall, blond center on the freshman basketball team, tapped my shoulder as he spoke. I felt a *lot* better! I agreed to meet Karen on the front steps after school, and we went to our separate classes. A tiny warm sense of acceptance began to grow inside me. It felt good.

When the trees on the hillsides began to turn from green to various shades of autumn colors, I fell helplessly in love with Dixon, West Virginia. I had thought that nothing could be more beautiful than the rows of bright maples and the yellow-leafed redbud trees along the brick-paved streets of Redbud Grove, Illinois; but I was wrong. Here in Dixon, the vivid colors shimmered behind early morning mists. I enjoyed the crisp mountain air as I walked to school with Karen and other friends who joined us along the way. I wrote a poem about the intensity of the colors and its effect on me.

Poetry had always held a fascination for me. Something about the rhythm, the meter caught my imagination, especially iambic pentameter. I had notebooks filled with little jingles and rhymes I had written over the years. I had even penned some dark thoughts about leaving Redbud Grove, and the sorrow of losing old friends. Some of the stuff I wrote was pitifully maudlin.

Before Thanksgiving, Miss Porter introduced us to great American writers. Our literature book included poetry by some of the more famous poets: Edna St.Vincent Millay, Dorothy Parker, Alan Seeger, T.S. Eliot, Emily Dickinson, Robert Frost, who was my favorite, and other notables who touched my heart with their words and sentiments.

The first creative writing assignment thrilled me, but I was one of very few in the class who wasn't horror-struck. Moans and groans erupted throughout the classroom. One scathing look from Miss Porter quickly diminished the sound to a sigh.

"Write a poem?!" Karen shrieked, after we were well out of the teacher's range of hearing. "Is she *crazy*?! I can't write a stupid *poem*!"

"Oh, come on, Karen. It's not that hard." I soothed. "I'll help you."

"Help me, my foot! The only way you could help me is to write the darn thing!" Karen sputtered and complained all the way home, but I was already planning the epic ballad that I hoped would win the respect of Miss Porter. I already knew what the subject would be.

"Mom, would you tell that story about the crazy old man, the one that shot his mule, back in Missouri where you and Dad lived?" I asked. Supper was over; and my little sister, Beth, and I washed dishes, while Mom put things away. The newness had not yet worn off our house, and I actually enjoyed working in the roomy kitchen with my mother.

"You've heard it so many times, you could probably tell it to me," Mom replied.

"Yes, but I need to hear it again. I'm going to write a poem about it."

"A poem? About Crazy Jessie?" Mom laughed.

"I have to write a poem for English class," I explained; so she told the story once more. It was sad and funny at the same time.

We had two weeks to finish our poems, and I worked on mine every night. One evening during the second week, I read what I had written to my family. When they laughed in the right places, I knew that I had a good thing.

"I don't know how to end it," I complained. My brother, Bill, began to laugh.

"I know what you can do," he chortled. He whispered in my ear, and I laughed out loud.

"That's *perfect*!" I shouted with glee. I hurried up to my room and wrote the final draft. "Bill, come listen." My brother came into my room. I closed the door and quietly read all nine stanzas to him. It was all I could do not to burst into laughter at the last line, but Bill did it for me. He fell back onto the bed in a fit of mirth; and we shared a brief moment of appreciation for each other, without rancor of any kind. It was a rare occasion.

I was eager to turn in my poem. On the day it was due, I was more than ready. Miss Porter had not assigned additional homework the preceding day, so I had assumed that she would lecture or spring another pop quiz. I was so wrong.

"We will spend the next few days hearing the poems you have written," Miss Porter announced. "When I call your name, you will bring your poem to the front of the room, read the title, and then read your poem aloud to your classmates. Then you will place the poem upon my desk and sit down."

Amid the muted groans, I sat as though carved in stone. I think my face must have paled. There was no way I could read my poem aloud! I had thought that only Miss Porter would see it. I might have let Karen read it, but certainly I had no intentions of reading it aloud to a room full of my peers.

Miss Porter began calling students alphabetically. I counted them off: Adams, Adcock, Akes, Amos, Anderson, Atkins, Bailey, Bains. Each person read two to four lines, filled with convoluted rhyme and rhythm patterns. I hoped that we would run out of time before she got to me, which would give me time to change the ending of my poem; but I knew that wasn't likely.

"Sissy Bannister," Miss Porter called. I moved very slowly. "Today, please, Sissy."

"Miss Porter, I really don't want to read this," I said. The teacher looked at me, pursed her mouth slightly, and raised an eyebrow.

"Really," she said. Her voice was very soft.

"Yes, Ma'am," I answered.

"You will read your poem, or you will take an F on the assignment." She continued to look at me. "It is a good percentage of your grade for the quarter," she added. I swallowed. I had never received an F in my life, and I wasn't about to get my first one in this class.

I stood, slowly went to the front of the room, and began to read:

"The Ballad Of Jessie's Mule

My mother tells the story, and she swears that it is so,
Of an Ozark mountain hermit, who lived many years ago.
He was quite a shaggy creature, never shorn and never shaved,
With a most distinctive odor, for he never, ever bathed.

He was known as Crazy Jessie, and his home was just a shack,
With a single door and window and a lean-to on the back.
He had never had a girlfriend and had never gone to school,
And the only thing he cared for was a sway-backed, flop-eared mule.

Now old Jessie's mule was ancient and was showing signs of wear,
For its eyes were nearly sightless and its ears could hardly hear.
But old Crazy Jessie loved him, sharing with him all he had,
Even down to sleeping quarters, when the weather turned off bad.

In the woods near Jessie's cabin, many forest creatures roamed,
But only one struck terror to the marrow of his bones.
So he always took his shotgun, for he fully understood
That hiding somewhere in the shadows, roamed a bear deep in those woods!

On one brisk October morning, Jessie led the mule outside,
Then went back into the cabin, to scoop out what had not dried,
When he heard the fiercest growling ever underneath the sun;
So he quickly dropped the shovel and grabbed up his loaded gun.

By the time old Jessie reached the brush where all the noise was made,
Everything was deathly quiet. Nothing moved within the glade.
Then suddenly, a movement, and a muffled grunting sound
Had poor Jessie stopped in horror, his feet frozen to the ground.

He was sure behind the bushes he would see the monstrous head
Of the creature that he hated, that had filled his heart with dread.
His eyes were dimmed with sweat, as he took trembling, shaky aim,
And though he couldn't see that bear, he'd kill him, just the same!

The gun went off! Both barrels fired, and Jessie heard a crash.
"I got 'im!" yelled the old man, and ran quicker than a flash,
For he couldn't wait to see the creature, dead upon the ground;
But, sad to say, a dying mule was what poor Jessie found.

The seasons come. The seasons go. And still the tale is told,
In the peaceful Ozark Mountains, of that day so long ago:
Crazy Jessie was a legend and was laughed at everywhere—
For the old man shot his own ass and completely missed that bear!"

    I placed the paper on Miss Porter's desk and sat down. For the space of five or six seconds there was utter silence, and then the class erupted with applause and laughter. I looked to my right and met the twinkling eyes of Laurie Adcock.
    "That was great," she whispered, under cover of the laughter. The bell rang. I was afraid to look at Miss Porter. I thought there might be safety in numbers, so I quickly merged with the body of the class and exited the room.
    "I think you're disgusting, and you're going to *hell*!" Shouted into my right ear, the words certainly got my attention. Someone grabbed my arm and spun me around. I had seen the girl in class, but we had never spoken to each other. Her name was Lillie Faye Snodgrass, and she sat near the back of the classroom. Sitting in the front row as I did, I was always one of the first out the door when the bell rang.
    "What are you talking about?" I asked.
    "You heard me! You really thought your poem was funny, didn't you? You'll go to hell for talking like that! Any girl that dresses like you do..." she dragged her angry eyes up and down my body "...and uses profanity and goes to those nasty ballgames is going to *hell*! I know how

you and all your friends live! God will punish you!" I looked down at my straight, brown wool skirt and white cardigan-pullover sweater set, and wondered what was wrong with the way I was dressed. Profanity? I hadn't used profanity. I had simply substituted a good, old biblical word for mule! At least, I hoped that was the way Miss Porter would see it.

Lillie Faye's cheeks flushed, and her blue eyes blazed with fervor. With just a little effort, she could have been a pretty girl. Her long, dark brown hair looked clean; but it was parted in the middle, pulled back from her ears, and held with two big, ugly bobby pins. Lillie Faye's dress looked like something her mother or grandmother might have worn. It hung like a sack on her slender body. The fabric, a dark olive green calico, made her clear skin look sallow.

"Hurry up, Sissy; you'll be late for your next class." Karen pulled my other arm, and we hurried down the corridor. I looked over my shoulder at the angry girl who had confronted me.

"What's wrong with her?" I asked Karen.

"Oh, don't pay any attention to Lillie Faye. Her daddy's a holy-roller preacher; and the whole bunch is crazy, if you ask *me*. They think everything is a sin, even basketball and football games and movies and television, just about everything that's *fun*. I thought your poem was really good. Don't worry about Lillie Faye."

I wasn't worried about that girl, but Miss Porter was another matter. I must have been out of my mind to follow my brother's suggestion. I thought about his whispered words to me: *"Say that he shot his own ass!"*

Well, I had; and now it looked like I might get mine handed to me. It was Friday, so I had two days before I had to deal with any repercussions. On the other hand, I had two days to *worry* about said repercussions.

When I got home from school, a letter from Sharon Bennett, one of my best friends back in Redbud Grove, was waiting for me. I grabbed it and ran upstairs to my room. I tore open the envelope.

A school photo of Sharon fell from inside the pages of a big, fat newsy letter. She looked so good. Her hair was longer, and her lips were parted in a beautiful smile. I was immediately so homesick that tears formed in my eyes.

I blinked them away and began to read the letter. It was full of details and word-by-word conversations she had shared with Melissa and Shirley and Cathy. She told me about her classes and teachers; about which girl was dating what boy and vice versa; about Redbud Grove's winning football team, the Purple Riders; about the Homecoming Dance

Wish I May, Wish I Might...

and about her being elected freshman attendant to the Homecoming queen.

Sharon wrote that Joe Bob Brady, although he was just a freshman, had played junior varsity football. He had been allowed to dress for the varsity games, too, something practically unheard of for a freshman. She said that Joe Bob had replaced the injured quarterback, and had scored the touchdown that not only won the game for the Purple Riders, but also the regional championship.

"Joe Bob is really, really good looking, Sissy! He just gets cuter every day! Whoever would have thought it?" Sharon had underlined the whole passage about Joe Bob. I thought about my last conversation with Joe Bob Brady, but quickly pushed it from my mind. He had told me to forget about that horrible night, and I seldom thought about it. Some things were better left alone.

I skimmed through the letter quickly, then went back to the first page and read it again, slowly, so I wouldn't miss a detail. I kicked off my shoes and tucked my feet beneath me. After I had finished reading the letter a second time, I lay back against the pillows and stared up at the ceiling. *What in the world was I doing here, in this town, while life in Redbud Grove, Illinois, just went on as usual? How dare my friends back there live my life without me? How could they?!*

Quite easily, apparently. I don't know where the thought came from, but there it was. The image of my new friend, Karen Courtney, popped into my mind. I put Sharon's letter on my desk, propped the photograph against the lamp, and went downstairs. My life was no longer in Redbud Grove. My life was here, and I was going to make it a good one. I paused on the bottom step. That is, I thought, unless Miss Porter or that crazy Lillie Faye snuffs it out!

On Monday morning the English class continued with the reading of students' poems. Miss Porter said nothing about my literary endeavor, so I began to breathe a little easier. Perhaps I had done nothing to merit her wrath, a force of nature that, my new acquaintances assured me, should be avoided at all costs.

Tuesday morning, following the principal's daily announcements over the intercom, Mr. Sheffield added a single command. It seemed impossible that such a simple phrase could send a chill down my back. That is, however, what happened.

"Sissy Bannister, to the office, please." The fact that he had tacked "please" onto the request did not alter the fact that his words conveyed a summons, not an invitation. My eyes flew to Miss Porter's face. The woman merely nodded briefly to me.

"You are excused, Sissy." Her tone told me nothing. A soft murmur of mirth emanated from the boys in the back of the classroom. I gathered my books and swished my skirted crinolines out the door. A trip to Mr. Sheffield's office was usually the result of an infraction of a rule, a misdemeanor calling for a reprimand, an act calling for suspension, or a total disaster that resulted in expulsion.

Mr. Sheffield's office was on the ground floor, one flight of stairs directly below Miss Porter's classroom. It took me no longer than a full minute to enter the anteroom, where one of the two secretaries greeted me.

"Just have a seat, Sissy. Mr. Sheffield will see you in a few minutes. He had to take a phone call."

I sank onto a bench against the wall. My mind floundered, failing to find a reason why I had been summoned to this office. I couldn't think of a thing, other than that stupid poem. Perhaps Miss Porter had turned me in to the principal for inappropriate language or vulgarity or—who knew what?

"Sissy Bannister?" I jerked to attention at the sound of Mr. Sheffield's voice. "Come in, please." I picked up my books and walked past the principal, as he indicated I should, into his office. "Sit down, Sissy." I sat. Mr. Sheffield made himself comfortable in his big leather chair and shuffled some papers atop his desk. He picked up one sheet and glanced down its length.

"A complaint has been made against you, Sissy," he said. I blinked. I didn't think that I had lived in Dixon long enough to have enemies. "Do you have any idea why this complaint has come to me?" he asked.

"No, Sir, I don't," I replied. One thing I had quickly learned in Dixon was that all adults were to be addressed as "Sir" or "Ma'am," regardless of their age.

"This letter was sent to me by the minister of a church that's located a few miles outside Dixon. It seems that you have mightily offended his daughter, Lillie Faye Snodgrass, with a poem you read in English class last week." I felt the blush begin at my neck and creep all the way up to my hairline. "Why did Lillie Faye find the poem so offensive?"

"I, uh, well, I guess it's, uh, uh…" I stuttered.

"Do you have a copy with you?"

"Uh, uh, yes, Sir." There was no point in lying. Miss Porter had one, too.

"May I please see it?" I opened my loose-leaf notebook and extracted the original copy of my poem. I bit my lower lip and handed the paper across the desk to my jury, judge, and executioner. "Thank you, Sissy."

I stared at Mr. Sheffield while he read the incriminating paper. The principal was only a few inches taller than I, and more than a little rotund. His pleasant round face framed a double chin that jiggled when he spoke. He always wore white shirts with his suits and ties. His collar was so tight that it cut into his double chin, spilling a bit of soft flesh onto the fabric. I wondered how he could breathe.

Mr. Sheffield's sandy-red hair grew sparsely. He combed long strands from the side, up and over his balding scalp, which did nothing to disguise the fact that he was losing his hair. Little pouches hung beneath his non-threatening, light blue eyes. Mr. Sheffield's lips were full and a bit pursed, somewhat like a fish. He looked deceptively benign.

With no change of expression, Mr. Sheffield lowered the paper, folded his hands upon it, and raised his eyes to look directly at me. I felt the blush begin to rise again.

"Where did you get this story?" he asked. I was surprised. Curiosity was not the response I expected.

"Well, it's something my mom has told, ever since I was little," I explained.

"Did she help you write this poem?"

"No, Sir. She hasn't even read it."

"Do you intend to let her read it?" he asked. I had to think about that for a minute. I dropped my eyes.

"No, Sir, I don't, at least, not yet."

"What would be her reaction?" he continued.

"She wouldn't be very happy with the ending," I murmured.

"Then perhaps you should have anticipated that others would be equally unhappy," Mr. Sheffield suggested. I remained silent.

"Well, Sissy, this is what we are going to do. Since you have a way with words, you will draft a letter of apology to Lillie Snodgrass and her father. You will bring the letter to me; and if it is suitably contrite, I will send it. You will rewrite the last line of this poem, making it more appropriate as a classroom assignment; and you will also bring a copy of that to me. Do you have any questions?"

"No, Sir," I answered. "Well, one. May I have my poem back?"

"No, Sissy, I will keep this copy. You may go back to class."

I stood up and left Mr. Sheffield's office. After I closed the door, I leaned against it for a moment and took a deep breath. From inside the office I heard muted laughter and the principal's voice. I could just distinguish his words. *"Delightful!"* Mr. Sheffield said, and he chuckled again. *He was laughing at my poem! The old hypocrite was laughing at the last line of my poem!*

I couldn't help the slightly jaunty air in my step when I left the anteroom and ventured into the corridor. I loved the way my skirt and crinoline petticoats swished from side to side. I be-bopped confidently down the hall and skipped up the stairs to Miss Porter's room. I had inside knowledge about a superior. I couldn't wait to tell the gang about Mr. Sheffield's reaction to my poem.

I had always known that there were definite, different codes of conduct for people under the age of eighteen and those adults who were in charge of them. However, the day would come when I could write anything I wanted, without reproach. Well, perhaps not *totally*; but it wouldn't matter, because I would be on the other side of eighteen.

Miss Porter gave me an A for the poem, and she said not one word of criticism. She actually smiled when she returned it to me. During the year I spent in her classroom, I learned how to listen, how to discern what I read, how to think more critically about subject matter, and not always to rely upon first impressions. My respect for her deepened with every year that I knew her. I wish that she could have known what an impact she had on my life.

I rewrote the last line of the poem and left a copy with the secretary in the office, to be given to Mr. Sheffield. I wrote the letter of apology. It was accepted, and Mr. Sheffield sent it to the Snodgrass residence. The rewritten stanza read:

The seasons come. The seasons go. And still the tale is told
In the peaceful Ozark Mountains of that day so long ago:
Crazy Jessie was a legend and was laughed at everywhere--
For the old man shot his *donkey* and completely missed that bear.

Somehow, it lost something in the changing; but if it made Mr. Sheffield happy, everybody was happy. I vowed, thereafter, never to change a word of any creative endeavor I wrote, unless it was of my own volition and would improve the final draft.

For the most part, I never have.

#

Shades of Crazy

Basking in the glow of my success with the poem was short-lived. As it turned out, I needn't have worried about my mother's reaction to the last line, my grand finale. Two telephone calls on the same evening, about two events in the same little Missouri town, called for my parents' immediate attention.

The first call came just as we sat down to supper. Dad's sister called to tell him that Grandpa Bannister had suffered a stroke, and the prognosis was not good. Grandpa's right side showed some paralysis, and he had difficulty speaking.

My dad was quiet as we ate, and the rest of us were just as subdued. We all loved Grandpa Bannister. Mom began to outline plans.

"We can leave early tomorrow morning, Will. It won't take long to pack. Can't you call someone at the foundry tonight?" Dad nodded.

"I think so," he said. Worry created two deep lines across his forehead. He put down his fork and pushed his plate aside. None of us had much appetite left.

"Will Grandpa be okay?" Beth asked the question that hovered in the air.

"We hope so, Honey." Dad smiled at her. When the phone rang again, five pairs of eyes sought reassurance from each other. Mom got up to answer it.

"Oh," she said. "Oh. Oh, my." Dad quickly pushed his chair away from the table and hurried to the living room. Mom covered the mouthpiece with her hand and whispered to him. "It's not about your dad, Will." She continued to listen. "We were coming down anyway," she said. "Will's sister just called to tell us about Grandpa Bannister. You didn't know? He had a stroke this morning."

Mom spoke to the caller for a few more minutes before she slowly replaced the receiver. She looked at Dad. Her shoulders slumped.

"What?" Dad demanded.

"It's my half-brother, Homer," Mom answered. "I think he's lost his mind. That was my cousin, Molly. Homer showed up at Aunt Rosa's house, and he's acting crazy, hearing voices. They need help." Mom and Dad stared at each other for a long moment before Dad opened his arms; and Mom went into them.

It didn't take long to pack. My parents planned a short stay, at least initially. Dad couldn't afford to be gone from his job over two or three days, and missing more than a few days of school was not an option for my siblings and me.

I asked for permission to stay with Karen Courtney, but my mother wouldn't even discuss the possibility. It would have made more sense to me. Going back to the place of my birth, to see a sick grandpa and a crazy uncle, were not my first choices; but then I was only a fourteen-year-old girl.

After I went to bed, I thought about the last time I had seen my mom's youngest brother. Homer Loring, my mother's half-brother, who had been lucky enough to grow up in his Aunt Rosa's home, had been emotionally troubled since his mid-teens. He was the son of my grandfather Loring and his third wife, who had died a month after Homer's birth.

Grandpa's wife had brought her two-year-old daughter to the marriage, followed quickly by another little girl and even more quickly by Homer, which made a total of eight children in the small, rural house during the worst depression in the country's history.

Homer's mother had been less than kind to her stepchildren. Some of the stories my mother had told us made Cinderella's stepmother look like the fairy godmother. Hideous, unspeakable things had occurred in that house.

Still, the poor woman's lot, living with Arthur Loring, could have driven anyone to distraction, if not to lunacy. Three children in less than five years, five stepchildren and a sexual predator for a husband could not have been conducive to health and sanity. One could hardly blame the poor woman for escaping through death.

My mother, who was nine when Homer was born, and her eleven-year-old sister were not equipped to care for a baby; so Homer was placed with Grandpa Loring's sister, Rosa, one of the sweetest, kindest women who ever breathed. Her older daughter, Molly, was newly married. Maria, the younger girl, was fourteen. Homer became the son that Aunt Rosa and her husband had longed to have. At that time, he was the most fortunate member of the family. The rest of the children had to remain under the roof of Arthur Loring

Unable to sleep, I re-played some of the dozens of stories my mother had told me about growing up during the depression in Southeastern Missouri. I had heard them so many times that they seemed more like memories to me than stories told by someone else. She often seemed on the verge of telling me something important, something that weighed heavily upon her; but she always changed her mind.

I drifted to thoughts of my half-uncle. He hadn't been close to our family for several years, and I hadn't thought about him for a long time. I had a vague memory of him from when I was five years old. My mother had taken my brother and me to visit with Missouri relatives while Dad was in the army. Homer was sixteen then, and we hadn't seen him again until he'd come to visit in Redbud Grove.

Homer had lived with us during the winter of nineteen forty-nine, when I was nine years old. He had been twenty, a tall, handsome young man with black hair, black eyes, and a wide mouth that covered straight, white teeth. My dad got him a job at the foundry, where Homer had worked hard but made no effort to make friends.

"Sissy, who's that gorgeous guy that lives in your house?" I had shrugged at the question from the high school girl who had been baby-sitting at my friend's house one Saturday afternoon. My friend and I had been busy with her new coloring book and crayons. I had no interest in boys or in anyone else's interest in boys. I had shrugged.

"My Uncle Homer is living with us," I had stated.

"Does he have a girlfriend?" she had asked.

"Nope."

"Would he like one?" I had shrugged again. "Why don't you tell him that Mary Walsh would like to have a date?" Mary had laughed.

"Okay," I had answered. I'd kept my word. I'd told Homer what Mary had said, but he had given no indication that he even heard me. He hadn't looked up from the newspaper. So I'd shrugged again, and gone about my own life.

I tossed and turned, trying to find the right spot in my bed. Thoughts and memories tumbled inside my head like marbles dropped upon a sidewalk, bouncing from one angle to another. A quiet picture came into focus, somewhat like standing outside myself, watching Homer teach me how to play checkers.

"Move there." "Don't move there!" "Move this one." "No, move that one!" I could hear Homer's voice as clearly as if he'd just uttered the words. What a fascinating, troubling thing is memory.

We left Dixon at four o'clock the next morning. During the long trip, Dad stopped the car only to fill the gas tank, at which times we used the restrooms. I didn't mind. I'd scarcely slept the night before, so I napped easily in the car. We ate sandwiches and drank jugs of ice water that my mother had prepared. Dad ate while he drove. Less than an hour from our destination, rain began to fall in torrents. Visibility was near zero.

"What the...?" Dad muttered. I thought that he was preparing to stop, but the car had stalled. He barely managed to steer it off the highway before the engine died completely.

"Will, what's wrong?" my mother asked.

"I don't know! The stupid car just stopped!" Dad threw open the car door and stepped into the downpour. He lifted the hood and bent over the front of the engine. We could hear him yelling in frustration. In a few minutes, he hurried back into the front seat. He was soaked to the skin, coat and all.

"I'll have to walk back to the last town and get a part," he said.

"You can't do that, Will! You'll catch your death out there in that cold rain!" Mom told him. "You're already dripping wet!"

"We don't have a choice, Jackie!" Dad said. He beat his hands on the steering wheel. "I'll be back as soon as I can. You all stay in the car." With that, my dad ventured into the rainy, cold, dark evening.

I don't know how long we sat there. I'm sure that it seemed much longer than it really was. Mom distributed more sandwiches, but no one seemed hungry. We were worried about Dad.

It was a relief to see car lights pull up right behind us. We heard Dad and the answering voice of a stranger. Just then, the rain stopped as suddenly as it had begun. Early darkness had fallen, but an afterglow could be seen in the western sky.

As the other car pulled slowly onto the highway, the driver called out to my dad. "The Lord told me to stop and pick you up, Young Man!" My dad raised his hand in farewell to his Good Samaritan.

"I'm sure glad He did!" Dad called. "Thanks!" Dad didn't talk to us until he had the car running. In spite of his protests, Mom demanded that he remove his wet jacket and shirt while the car warmed up again. She took dry clothes from a suitcase in the trunk and shielded Dad while he changed.

Wish I May, Wish I Might...

In spite of the somber reason for the trip, my brother, sister and I laughed helplessly at the sight of our father. The impending darkness helped to hide his predicament, but two or three cars honked as they passed, whether in humor or disgust we couldn't tell. I suspect the former.

The car was warm by the time Mom and Dad reentered it. Dad shivered with the delicious warmth, choosing to ignore the smothered laughter from the back seat. Mom glanced at us briefly, but the expression on her face was all the warning we needed. Without words, she conveyed the message that she and Dad were tired, worried, and that there was no room in the car for foolishness.

The next morning we woke to the aroma and sizzle of home-cured bacon. Aunt Berniece, my dad's youngest sister, had allowed us to sleep as long as we wished; but the wonderful smell of breakfast seeped into our subconscious state. Beth and I, warm and cozy beneath a mound of our aunt's handmade quilts, were reluctant to step onto the cold linoleum; but hunger called and must be answered.

I couldn't recall another time when we had come to the area during winter. More than anything, except baseball, my dad loved to hunt; so our visits had taken place on summer holidays and during hunting season. Several cousins, on both sides of our family, resided within a ten-mile radius; but they were all in school. This trip would include no time or opportunity to see them.

"You girls better come on and eat now!" Aunt Berniece called from the kitchen, just on the other side of the bedroom door. Within minutes, Beth and I obeyed. The long table, laden with platters of eggs and bacon, homemade biscuits with jars of strawberry jam and fresh butter, was lined with hungry people. While we ate, Aunt Berniece, her soft, Missouri drawl sometimes filled with tears, gave us details of Grandpa's stroke and condition.

The longer she spoke, the more somber I felt. It sounded as if our grandfather, adored by his many grandchildren, would not long survive the stroke that had stopped him in his seventieth year. Talk then turned to the subject of Homer and speculation about what we would find when we went to Aunt Rosa's house. I felt as if we had been dropped into the midst of two dramas, neither of which had been written with a happy ending.

Although only a few miles lay between the location of my mother's birthplace and Aunt Rosa's house, there was a marked difference in the landscape. Grandpa Loring's small farm lay in the hills, where the red-hued soil was rocky and difficult to farm.

His sister's farm was in one of the sandy river bottoms, where low, swampy areas, filled with ancient trees and copperhead snakes lay next to fields of what appeared to be pure sand. Cotton, corn, watermelons and rattlesnakes thrived in the moist, hot earth. Not much grass grew in the small yards, but Aunt Rosa's garden and flowers were bountiful every summer.

Aunt Rosa's house stood a few hundred feet down a soft slope from her daughter's home. A widow for several years, Aunt Rosa maintained her own household, although she lived near her daughter, Molly. The younger daughter had died, tragically, during a pregnancy that went terribly wrong in her first year of marriage. Aunt Rosa and Molly grew closer with each passing year.

Bill, Beth and I always enjoyed our summer days at the home of Molly and her husband, Owen. Five gregarious children, a slow-talking, happy husband and a bustling, energetic wife made for an interesting, household. The three older children, two boys and one girl, came home from college every summer to help with the farming. A younger boy, who was my age, and another daughter, a little younger than Beth, completed the family. We would see only the younger two this trip.

The afternoon sun hung low in the skies before we arrived at Molly's house. The day had been spent at the hospital in Poplar Bluff, where Grandpa Bannister lay recovering. Bill, Beth and I had looked at old magazines and newspapers in the waiting room, since none of us were old enough to see Grandpa, while Dad and his two sisters took turns sitting with him. It had been a long day, but Grandpa appeared to be a little better.

Molly's house seemed empty. The three older children, away at school, left a big hole. Supper was as good as always at Molly's table, but tension filled the kitchen. We listened while Molly and Owen spoke of Homer's sudden appearance and his erratic behavior during the last few days.

"We don't know what to do, Jackie," Molly said. "We thought that you could probably deal with him better, since you're his sister. We've got to do *something*!"

"When did he get here?" Dad asked.

"Three days ago," Owen replied. "Someone from the boarding house in Saint Louis called to tell us that he had disappeared. They found Rosa's number in Homer's room, and they thought that he would probably come here."

"I'm afraid he's going to hurt Mom!" Molly said. "She told us yesterday that he took a stick of stove wood and banged against his

Wish I May, Wish I Might...

bedroom walls. He said that the voices had told him to kill the big mice that were hiding there." Tears filled her eyes. I looked at my plate.

The kitchen door opened, and suddenly I was looking into the troubled black eyes of my uncle. I knew that the young man with the deep lines in his face had to be Homer Loring; but he was much thinner than I remembered. He was freshly scrubbed and clean-shaven, but his skin looked wind-burned, dark and red. A light jacket hung loosely from his shoulders, too big for him, like the rest of his clothing.

He stared at me, but I don't know that he recognized me. I was no longer the child he would remember, if he had any recollection of me at all. A strange, wild something stared from his eyes. Chills swept from the top of my head to the bottoms of my feet. I was very afraid.

"Well, hello, Homer." My dad stood up and walked toward him. Dad extended his hand, waiting for Homer to take it. For a moment, I didn't think that Homer was going to grasp Dad's hand; then, slowly, he did.

"Kids, go into the living room," my mother softly instructed. None of us had to be told twice. For the next hour, we listened to the conversation that took place between the two men, mostly. Occasionally, my mother's soft answers could be heard; but her voice seemed to antagonize her brother.

"What do *you* know!" he shouted. "You're not a Christian!"

"Homer," my mother said, "I want to help you."

"You can't! You don't know anything!"

"Homer, Jackie's your sister. She cares about you, and she wants you to get help," Dad said.

"She can't help! She's just like my mom, trying to tell me what to do; and they don't know anything about me or about the voices or what I'm supposed to do! They're just women, always telling me what to do! Mom says I need to go to a hospital somewhere!" Homer shouted. "But I ain't going! I've heard about places like that! They do things to people—things that hurt you, and they lock you up. You all just need to leave me alone...."

"Why not let us call and make an appointment with a doctor, Homer? You may be just fine. What's the matter, Homer? Does your head hurt?" Silence filled the house. "Does your head hurt where you're rubbing it?" Dad continued.

"All this foolish talk hurts it," Homer said.

"How about it, Homer? Why don't you let us try to get someone to help you?" my dad asked. "Molly and Owen and Rosa only want to help you, too." He sounded so reasonable, so *sane*.

"Would *you* go?" Homer demanded.

"Absolutely! If I got sick and needed help, I'd go!" Dad answered.

"I'm not sick! I don't have to go! None of you can make me go! I could come up here tonight and kill all of you with a knife while you sleep, if I want to! You couldn't stop me! And you can't make me go to that hospital!" Rage filled Homer's voice.

"You're right, Homer, you could; but why would you want to? We're your family, and we care about you." My dad's soft reply seemed to puzzle the other man.

"I didn't say I wanted to," he muttered. "I said that I could."

I looked at the two little girls on either side of me. The louder Homer's voice, the closer they drew to me. I hugged them.

"Let's go in there." I stood and pointed to the room of Tina, the older daughter. I had slept many nights in that room, laughing and talking with Tina, who had treated me as an equal, although I was five years younger. I knew that high school annuals, books and magazines were on shelves there; and I could use them to distract the girls. Bill and Wayne went out the front door, quietly closing it behind them.

I closed the bedroom door, effectively muting the sound of the confrontation in the kitchen. Beth, eight, and Sarah, who was seven, relaxed a little; but they often cast worried glances toward the door. We stayed inside the room for another hour before Homer went back to Aunt Rosa's house. Sarah's mother opened the bedroom door.

"Sissy, you and Beth will sleep here in Tina's room," Molly announced. "Bill and Wayne will sleep in the boys' room. Sarah will sleep with her dad and me. It's getting late, so get your clothes off and climb into bed." Her brisk, no-nonsense manner was reassuring.

"Where will Mom and Dad sleep?" Beth asked. My mother appeared in the doorway, Dad close behind her.

"We're going to stay at Aunt Rosa's house, Honey," Mom said. She hugged Beth, kissed her forehead and smiled at me. I frowned. I wasn't very happy with the thought that they would be in the same house as my uncle, not after what he had said about killing us. I didn't feel much safer in Molly's house.

"Everything is going to be all right," Dad reassured us. "Good night. You all get some sleep. It's been a long day." He sounded exhausted, too.

Beth wanted the wall side of the bed. I think that she felt safer there. It didn't matter which side of the bed I had, because I was sure that I wouldn't sleep anyway. The house grew quiet; but there were unfamiliar pops and creaks, like in every house. I had just begun to doze when I heard a noise that caused me to hold my breath.

My eyes popped open in the darkness. We hadn't closed the bedroom door, and I could make out the faint shape of the sofa and a chair in the adjacent living room. There was a swoosh, swoosh sound, like the legs of denim blue jeans brushing together. The movement ceased, but I couldn't close my eyes.

The beat of my own heart threatened to choke me. I pictured my uncle, butcher knife in hand, creeping through the house, trying to decide who would be his first victim. Intently, I listened. I strained to focus upon any movement, ready to scream should a form appear in the doorway.

I stayed awake for hours; but eventually, my eyes closed. I was too tired to hold them open forever. Sometime in the night, Beth snuggled close to my back, whether to seek extra warmth or reassurance, I couldn't tell. The closeness of her little body filled me with a sense of responsibility for her safety.

I got up, closed the door, and wedged a straight-backed chair under the knob, like I had seen done in the movies. Should anyone try to open that door, there would be a terrible commotion. I went to sleep and didn't awaken again until dawn filled the sky with the promise of a beautiful autumn day.

After breakfast, I made our bed and then sat upon it, wondering what the day would hold. The little girls seemed relaxed, unaffected by the previous evening's events. Suddenly I heard the stealthy sound of brushing denim, the same as I'd heard during the night; but no one else was in the room. Slowly, I looked all around the room; and I discovered the source of my torment.

The living room window, opened just a crack, allowed a draft to move the plastic draperies that hung over the glass. The movement created the semblance of someone walking slowly, legs lightly brushing together. I felt relieved and silly at the same time. It was years before I told anyone about my scary fantasy.

I don't remember much about the rest of the week's events, except that my grandfather's condition improved enough to allow him to move into his daughter's home. Grandpa lived just a short time before another stroke took his life. I've always been grateful that my dad was allowed to see his father that one last time, and I was happy to have had at least one grandfather who was a wonderful grandpa.

Local authorities had to be called to restrain Homer. His fear that he would have to be hospitalized was justified. He was admitted to the state mental hospital in Farmington, Missouri, some distance from his home. Diagnosed as being paranoid schizophrenic, he was hospitalized for several months.

The drive back home to Dixon seemed longer than the trip to Missouri. The autumn landscapes were beautiful, but no one seemed in the mood to enjoy them. Mom and Dad were quiet, lost in their own private thoughts, although they shouldered both tragic situations together.

I couldn't wait to get back to school and see my new friends. Dixon suddenly seemed like home to me, although only a few weeks had passed since we'd left Redbud Grove. I wished that the car could sprout wings and transport us to Dixon in minutes, instead of hours. I wanted to forget all about the last few days. Truth be known, I wanted to forget about my crazy uncle; and I did, for a while.

The first snowfall in Dixon that November was as beautiful as I had anticipated. There had been a few overnight dustings that couldn't be measured. They didn't really count as a snowfall, but one morning we woke to a fairyland of white that was breathtaking.

A soft, translucent glow from my bedroom window woke me early that morning. The face of the round, white alarm clock beside my bed, which always clanged at six-thirty, said five-fifty. I stayed under my covers for a few minutes, moving nothing but my eyes. Beneath the cozy layer of quilts, I turned toward the window. My view of the snow-covered mountainside brought me upright.

I threw aside the covers and ran to the window. The sight was spectacular! I danced up and down on the uncarpeted wood floor. It felt icy to my bare feet. My dad always stoked the basement furnace with coal every morning, but he wasn't up yet. I hopped from one foot to the other while I gazed at the winter wonderland just outside my house. Huge, fluffy snowflakes looked like feathers falling straight down from the sky. No hint of wind interfered with the cascade of what looked like a wall of white lace.

I shoved my feet into house slippers and quietly went downstairs. I grabbed my dad's heavy blue-plaid coat from the standing rack near the back door, and I hurried outside to get a better view of the transformed world of pristine white. An extension of the veranda-type roof that covered the front and one side of the house, also shielded the back porch; so I was protected from the heavily falling snow.

I drew a deep breath. Even with the hint of coal dust, which was always present in the air, I recognized the same, sweet scent of snow that I had loved during the winters back in Redbud Grove. Every object and building was softly rounded by the several inches of snow that covered everything in sight. It looked every bit like a fairyland.

"Sissy, what are you doing?" My mother stuck her head out the door. She looked at me as if she thought I was crazy.

"Oh, Mom, it's *beautiful* out here! Have you ever seen anything so gorgeous? I don't think we ever got this much snow at one time in Redbud Grove." I followed her back inside and hung Dad's coat on the rack. The aroma of coffee filled the kitchen, and I could hear the percolator as it bubbled happily on the range. My mother took bacon and eggs from the refrigerator and began to prepare Dad's breakfast. The furnace had kicked on. Warm air moved through the room, and I was cozy in my flannel pajamas.

I sat at the kitchen table and watched my mother go through the same motions she did every morning. Nothing changed except her choice of breakfast meats: bacon, sausage, or ham. Sometimes she made pancakes on the weekends. I wondered if she ever became bored with the same routine every day.

"Hey, look at the early bird." My dad, shaved and fully dressed, entered the kitchen. "What're you doing up so early?" he asked me. On school days, Dad was always gone before I arose.

"The snow woke me up," I grinned at him.

"Did the flakes fall too hard?" he countered. He roughed up my hair as he passed behind me. He poured a cup of coffee for himself, his one contribution to the preparation of his breakfast. I watched him lace the coffee with heavy cream and a good-sized teaspoon of sugar. He sat down beside me and smiled at me over the rim of his cup.

"Would you like to walk to school in this snow? I don't think your mom can get the car back up the driveway, if she takes you kids today," he told me.

"Dad! We never will get to school if we walk! There must be a foot of snow on the ground already!" I protested. I loved the beautiful landscape, but I had no desire to walk a mile in snow that was over my boot-tops.

We needn't have worried. Karen called to tell us that school had been cancelled for the day, so I waved good-bye to Dad and went back upstairs and crawled under the covers on my bed. They still retained a modicum of warmth; and in no time I fell into that blissful, trance-like state between sleep and dreaming.

The snowfall dwindled to nothing. By the following morning, the state road crews had magically cleared the snow, leaving high mounds along the winding streets. Mom drove all three of us to school, dropping off my little sister, Beth, first, then Bill, at junior high, before stopping in front of the big brick high school.

"There's chorus practice after school, Mom. We won't get out until five o'clock. Can you pick me up, or should I get a ride with someone else?"

"I'll be here, Sissy," Mom told me. She didn't like for me to ride with anyone else, especially a teenager.

"Okay. 'Bye, Mom."

"Study hard." I rolled my eyes, and Mom grinned at me, which was our standard routine every time she dropped me off at school. She tooted the car horn twice, another routine, and pulled away from the curb, while I hurried up the double landing of concrete steps.

Karen Courtney waved to me from her table in the cafeteria at lunchtime. By the time I arrived with my tray, Judy Duval and Beverly Bodine had joined her. I had just bitten into my ham salad sandwich, when Jerry Davis and Jimmy Duval, Judy's cousin, took the two remaining chairs at the table. All of us were in the choral group, and we had become good friends.

Suddenly Jerry leaned close to Jimmy and whispered something that caused Jimmy to choke. Jerry dissolved into giggles.

"What!" Karen demanded. "What's so funny!?" Jerry's blue eyes sparkled with glee. His voice, which had not completely finished changing, broke with his laughter. We had no clue what was so hilarious, but we couldn't help laughing with him.

"Ok, Jimmy, now what's so funny?" Judy asked. Jimmy looked at Jerry, who held up his right hand and indicated a measurement with his thumb and right forefinger, a space of about one inch. Jimmy's face turned red, and the two boys became nearly hysterical with laughter.

Jerry and I hadn't spent much time together since we had recognized each other at Karen's house last summer. Still, knowing that someone halfway familiar was walking along the same corridors I walked felt good. Jerry was always laughing, or flashing his brilliant smile, which emphasized the deep dimple in his cheek. It was easy to see why he had so many friends.

"I've got to get to class," I said. I picked up my books and the tray, and turned away from the table. "See you at practice." I looked over my shoulder and caught Jerry making that same measurement sign with his fingers. Jimmy nodded and held his hand up the same way. I shrugged and walked away.

I had barely left the cafeteria when Karen called to me.

"Sissy, wait!" I stopped and waited for her.

"What is it?" I asked.

"Jimmy told me what they were laughing about," Karen replied. Her eyes dropped to my chest. "You need to make an adjustment."

"What kind of adjustment?"

"Sissy, just go to the restroom and adjust your straps. You're, uh, kind of, uh, uneven. Come on, let's go to the restroom at the end of this hall." Still confused, I went with Karen to the restroom. I looked at myself in the mirror above a sink.

Good grief! She was right. One side of my chest was about an inch higher than the other. How embarrassing! How humiliating! It *would* have to be Jerry who noticed before anyone else! Well, he was a *boy*; so of course he would have noticed before any of my girl friends! I had just been thinking such kind thoughts about him. If I didn't kill him the next time I saw him, he would be very lucky.

I adjusted the offending strap beneath my red sweater, retied the silky white neck scarf, which was just like the scarves all the girls were wearing these days, and hurried off to Freshman Health, my first afternoon class. Still smarting from Jerry's keen eye for detail, I tended to hold my stack of books close to my chest until I reached the classroom.

Lillie Faye Snodgrass was in this class. A victim of alphabetical order, Lillie Faye sat in the back of the room. I glanced at her, just as she looked up and saw me. We stared at each other for a moment, and I saw something I had not noticed about her. She looked very sad. I smiled at her, unintentionally. It just kind of happened. Lillie Faye blinked a couple of times, and then she tentatively smiled at me. She was almost pretty.

I loved the choral department at school. The teacher, Mrs. Grimes, was an attractive woman, perhaps forty-five years old, with dark hair and blue eyes. A gifted musician, Mrs. Grimes knew exactly what she wanted from the chorus of seventy-five voices; and she knew how to get it.

I had never sung the kind of music she chose for the Christmas concert. The cantata was a compilation of secular and Christian Christmas music, and it was the most beautiful arrangement I had ever heard. Tears formed in my eyes as we sang "What Child is This?" The old Christmas carol, set to the words of the haunting melody, "Greensleeves," sent chills down my back. I was so impressed with myself when I actually learned the Latin words to "Oh Come, All Ye Faithful." I looked forward to every practice session.

The Christmas concert was spectacular. The Dixon High School band assembled in the gymnasium, making a huge half circle that filled the middle of the polished floor. The choral department waited in the hall while the band performed. I couldn't believe that the full, rich sound I heard was actually coming from a high school band. Redbud Grove had nothing like this! Leroy Anderson's delightful "Sleigh Ride" filled the auditorium, and the horse's neigh at the end of the piece made us laugh.

Dressed in black robes with white satin bibs, we took our places on the semi-circle of risers, next to the concert band. Mrs. Grimes held up her arms, and the pianist began the introduction. The sound that emanated from our group sent chills atop chills from my head to my feet, and I felt that I was part of something truly wonderful. At that moment, I had no regrets about coming to Dixon, West Virginia.

Following the concert, school was dismissed. On my way out of the building, I found myself walking beside Lillie Faye Snodgrass. She stared straight ahead.

"Hi," I said. She barely turned toward me.

"Hi."

"Did you like the concert?"

"It was okay. I didn't like Suzy Kirk's vulgar dance, but the rest was good." I had to think about that for a moment. Suzy Kirk was a senior, and she had been studying ballet for years, according to Karen. Suzy had danced, beautifully, to the music of "Dance of the Sugarplum Fairy" from <u>The Nutcracker Suite</u>. Suzy was dark-skinned, and her hair and eyes were equally dark, which presented a striking contrast to the white tutu and white ballet slippers she had worn.

"Why do you think Suzy's dance was vulgar?" I asked. "I thought it was beautiful."

Lillie Faye snorted with disgust.

"*All* dancing is sinful," she stated, "and the way she pranced around in that skimpy, awful costume was wicked. It makes boys lust after her." I couldn't believe what I had just heard.

"Lillie Faye, ballet has been around for centuries; and it's an art. People study and practice for years before they can dance like Suzy, and…"

"I don't care what they call it, it's still *sinful*," she replied. I had had enough of this conversation.

"There's my mom. Have a merry Christmas," I told her; and I escaped. I looked back from the safety of our car. I saw Lillie Faye join a tall, heavy man, who wore a long, black overcoat. I couldn't see him very well, but I could tell that his hair was coarse and black, and that he looked as if he had never smiled in his life. If that man were Lillie Faye's father, there was no wonder she looked so unhappy—and was so judgmental. I would have to think some more about Lillie Faye Snodgrass.

Christmas at our house that year could have been a model for Norman Rockwell. There was a fire in the brick fireplace. The tallest Christmas tree we ever had twinkled in front of the wide, living room window. At eight years old, my sister, Beth, no longer believed in Santa Claus. While it was sad that she had left the jolly old fellow behind, it was a relief not to have to keep up the pretense.

We opened packages early on Christmas morning, as we had always done. We ooh-ed and ah-ed over every gift. My mother had always saved wrapping paper, a holdover from the days when she had to do so. She could not bring herself to crumple and throw away the lovely papers and bows, so she spent a lot of time smoothing and rolling them around cardboard spindles.

We ate ourselves into a stupor, beginning with a special breakfast that included homemade cinnamon rolls. We skipped lunch, but nibbled on Mom's homemade cookies and candies until dinnertime, at four o'clock. The feast she spread upon the long dining room table, bought from a second-hand store in Charleston, was probably obscene. We could easily have fed the whole block. In addition to the traditional turkey and dressing, with the usual trimmings, Mom made other family favorites, many from recipes given to her by Grandma Chinn.

After the meal, we each found our favorite spot in the living room. Dad, from his reigning position, reclined upon the couch, ostensibly to watch the football game. We'd hardly settled in before the telephone rang. Bill grabbed it.

"Mom, can I go sledding with Joey Black?" Bill asked. He stood with the receiver in his hand, pleading more with his eyes than his words.

"Who else is going?"

"Just Joey and his big brother, Adam." Bill shifted from one foot to the other.

"Where are they going?" Dad asked. Bill spoke into the phone, then listened.

"Up on the ridge above the junior high school," Bill told Dad. Dad looked at Mom.

"Don't be sledding behind cars, Bill," Dad told him. "You can sled down the hills, but you *do not ride behind a car.*"

"Okay, Dad." Bill turned back to the phone. "I can go, Joey. What time? Okay, I'll meet you at the school. 'Bye." Bill ran from the living room, but a moment later his head appeared around the corner. "Dad, can you take me to the school?"

Dad sighed, heaved himself up from the couch, and patted his belly.

"Sure thing," he said. "I need the exercise."

"Do you really think that driving the car down the road a few blocks will work off all that dinner?" Mom asked.

"Yep. When I get back, I'll be ready for another piece of pumpkin pie. Oh, and don't forget to add the whipped cream." Dad grinned at Mom, who just shook her head.

About an hour after Dad returned, the phone rang again. No one moved to answer it, until the fifth ring coaxed Beth away from the dollhouse she had received for Christmas.

"Daddy, it's for you," she said, "from someone at a hospital."

Mom and Dad both rushed to the phone.

"This is Will Bannister." Dad listened for several minutes, without saying anything; and then he cleared his throat. "Is he conscious?" Mom moaned and clung to Dad's arm. "We'll be right there." Dad hung up the phone and put his arms around Mom.

"We've got to go now, Jackie. Buddy's been hurt, and they don't know how bad it is. Girls, get your coats." On the day we moved from Illinois to West Virginia, my brother had declared that he would no longer answer to "Buddy," his nickname. This was the first time Dad had reverted to the old name.

The winding streets had been cleared of new snow, but there were snow-packed, slippery patches that made driving hazardous. It seemed to take forever to get to the hospital. I stayed with Beth, while a nurse took Mom and Dad to the emergency room, where my brother lay injured.

"Is Buddy, going to die?" my little sister asked. Like the rest of us when under stress, Beth reverted to nicknames. I put my arm around her and rested my cheek on top of her head. She had voiced my family's fear.

Wish I May, Wish I Might...

"Nah," I answered. "He's too tough to die. He probably just got a little banged up. I bet he ran his sled into a tree. You know, sometimes he's not very smart." Beth giggled.

"You mean like the time his face got all black from the firecracker gunpowder?"

"Yeah, like that. He was lucky he didn't blow up the whole house that day. He'll be fine, Beth." I wished that I felt as sure as I sounded.

Mom and Dad were with my brother for a long time. When they came down the corridor toward us, Mom was wiping her eyes. Dad had his arm around her.

"What happened?" I asked. "Is he okay?"

Mom smiled through her tears.

"His right leg is broken, just below the knee. He has a big knot above his right eye, but he's going to be all right," she said. Dad looked grim.

"The last thing I told him was not to sled behind a car. The stupid kid didn't listen! He and Joey were on the same sled, tied to the back bumper of Adam's car; and the car skidded. Both boys were thrown off, and Bill was flung against a rock retaining wall. He's lucky he wasn't killed! Stupid, ignorant kid!"

"Shhh, lower your voice, Will. Be grateful that he *wasn't* killed," Mom told him. Dad looked down at her. There were tears in his eyes.

"I *am* grateful," he said. "I'm just so *mad* at him right now."

"Can he come home?" I asked. Mom shook her head.

"No, his leg will have to be in traction. They'll keep him here for a few days, anyway. Dad is going to take you girls home, but I'm going to stay with Bud—Bill, until they get him a bed. Then Dad will come get me."

"Okay."

"Don't worry about your brother. He really is going to be fine. Sissy, you and Beth could play one of the new games you got for Christmas, maybe <u>Sorry</u> or <u>Monopoly</u>." Mom gave both of us a hug, and Dad ushered us back to the car.

"What a way to end Christmas Day," Dad muttered as he started the car. None of us spoke during the drive back home. When we pulled up the driveway, the house looked beautiful to me. We had left lights on. Mounds of snow in the front yard reflected soft colors from the Christmas tree lights that blinked so invitingly from the living room window.

I played <u>Sorry</u> with Beth, but we both found it difficult to keep our minds on the game. Beth finally curled up on the couch and went to sleep, while I watched television until Mom and Dad came home. After

I went to bed, I thought about the cold, early spring night, just two years before, when I had broken my ankle. I think I began to get a glimmer of the fear and worry I had put my parents through that day. It would be so nice if we could foresee some of the consequences of our actions before we acted.

Since I was nearly fifteen, I was allowed to visit Bill in his hospital room. Mom stayed in the waiting room with Beth, who was not old enough to visit patients. Bill would have to remain in traction for two weeks before a heavier cast would be applied to his leg. He grieved most about wasting his Christmas vacation time in a hospital.

"I don't *want* to play Monopoly," Bill complained. "I can't reach the board, and I can't sit up enough to put it on my lap." So I placed the game on the window ledge and sat down in the chair beside his bed, determined to be pleasant. We were both startled when the door opened. A tall, heavy man with coarse, black hair entered Bill's room.

"Hello, Young Man." The stranger's voice was loud, hearty, and heavily Appalachian accented. I had become accustomed to hearing the soft West Virginia dialect, and could sometimes hear it in my own voice; but this man's speech was not the same. "I'm Brother Dewey Snodgrass, and I come t' see how y'all're doin' and t'have a word a'prayer with y'all. I visit all the sick an' afflicted in this h'yer hospital." My heart dropped. He was Lillie Faye's father, the man who had written the letter of complaint about my poem!

Without further ado, the man began to pray. He prayed and he prayed. He touched upon all of Bill's sins, even those committed before the boy was born, proceeding through his sinful years as a baby and child, up to the present day of his wicked, lustful adolescence. He told God he knew that Bill had brought down divine wrath upon himself, and that the boy would have to repent before God would ever see fit to heal the boy's stripes of transgression.

The longer Lillie Faye's father prayed, the louder he became. I peeked at his face. I was appalled to see white flecks of saliva in the corners of his mouth. I glanced at Bill. His eyes were wide, and he looked scared to death. Carefully, I slid my hand to the nurse's call button. I pressed it, hard.

Within seconds the door opened. A tall, white-clad nurse came bustling into the room and caught the preacher mid-tirade. Her lips tightened.

"I'm sorry, Sir; but you'll have to leave this patient's room now. He needs rest and quiet."

The man seemed startled. Appearing wild-eyed and disoriented, he stared around the room. He took a deep breath, drew himself to his full height, which seemed very tall, and then peered down at Bill.

"I will continue to pray, Son, that y'all will see the error of y'all's wickedness. Whut's y'all's name?"

"His name is Bill," I interjected, before my brother could reply. "Bill B-b-brady." Bill stared at me. Neither of us could believe that I had taken Joe Bob Brady's name.

"Sir, you'll have to leave!" The nurse meant business. Dewey Snodgrass strode from the room. "I'm sorry, Bill," she said. She efficiently fluffed his pillow and smoothed the sheet. "I suppose the man means well, but he harasses a lot of patients here. He's a self-proclaimed chaplain, and we've had a lot of complaints about him. I'll try to keep him out of your room." She smiled and left the room.

"How come you gave me Joe Bob's name?" Bill demanded.

"Because I didn't want him to know our real name," I replied. "He wrote that letter about my poem, and I don't want him to know who I am."

I had told Bill about the complaint and being called into Mr. Sheffield's office, but I hadn't told my mother. I preferred to keep her peacefully unaware of the whole incident. I didn't think that she would make much of a fuss; but I liked to keep my life as uncomplicated as possible, although it sometimes seemed that I went out of my way to *make* it complicated.

The days and weeks after Christmas passed quickly for me, but I don't think that my brother had the same perspective. It was February before the cast was removed from his leg, and he walked with a limp for some time. When new leaves appeared on the trees that covered the mountains, all traces of Bill's limp had disappeared. He had made a complete recovery from the accident.

Something happened between Mom and Dad. I think that I was aware of an undercurrent before I noticed the actual rift. It suddenly dawned upon me that my brother and sister and I were the only ones contributing to the conversations at the evening meals. Not only were they not talking to each other, our parents didn't look at each other, either.

Beth and Bill seemed not to notice, so I said nothing; but I watched, very closely. Divorce was unusual in those days. No more than a handful of the students in Dixon High had parents who were divorced. Come to think of it, murder was more common than divorce. When I learned the reason for the conflict in our house, I was relieved and disturbed at the same time.

"Kids, we're going to have company for awhile," my mother announced. She looked at Dad, who gazed steadily at her. "You remember that Uncle Homer was put in the mental hospital back in Missouri?" We nodded. "Well, the doctors think that he's ready to be released. He needs a place to stay and someone who will assume responsibility for him." Mom took a deep breath. "They have asked me, us, your daddy and me, to do that." The Bannister kitchen became very quiet.

"You mean he's going to stay *here, in this house*?" I asked.

"Yes, Sissy," my mother answered.

"But, Mom..."

"There are no 'buts,' Sissy," my dad interrupted me. "Your mom and I have discussed this. I'm not really happy about it, but we've agreed to let Homer stay here for a few weeks, until he's used to being on his own again." A warning flashed from Dad's eyes. It was obvious that Dad was uneasy about my uncle coming to live with us, but he was supporting Mom, presenting a united front.

"Daddy, will he try to kill us?" Beth asked. The thought was in my head, too. From the expression on Bill's face, he had the same fears.

"No, Beth. Uncle Homer takes medicines that stop him from having thoughts like that. His mind got sick, just like a body can get sick. He can't help it, any more than Bill could help his broken leg." Dad grinned. "Well, that might be a bad example. Bill's carelessness caused his leg to get broken, but Homer didn't cause his mind to get sick. It just happened."

There was no more discussion about the decision. In preparation for our guest, Beth's clothes and some of her treasured belongings were transferred to my room. My poor little sister was so afraid. While we arranged her clothes in my closet, I talked to her.

"You don't have to be afraid of Uncle Homer, Beth. He stayed with us before, when you were only three. Maybe he'll teach you how to play checkers, like he taught me."

"Was he scary?" Beth asked.

"Nope, not a bit," I told her. "He was quiet, but nice. Everything will be fine. Besides, Dad wouldn't let anyone harm us. He wouldn't let even the hint of harm come to us, now would he?" Beth shook her head. She cast her big blue eyes up at me.

"Sissy, can I have the wall side?" I laughed.

"Sure."

Wish I May, Wish I Might...

The first few days were awkward for everyone, except Uncle Homer. He spoke to each of us, politely enough, and then he retreated to Beth's room, where he spent most of his time. Homer had gained some weight, and the skin on his face looked healthy, not dark red. He truly was a handsome man.

At the supper table, Homer followed the conversation with his eyes, seldom speaking. He seemed to be interested. We tried to lure him into the repartee on occasion, but he answered questions in one of two words: yes or no, until an evening when he surprised us.

"Dad, did you play mumbly-peg when you were a kid?" Bill asked. Dad nodded.

"Yes, I did; and I was pretty good at it. Are you betting?" Dad asked. Bill's face flushed.

"Not much," he replied. "Only pennies."

"I played that," Homer volunteered. We were so shocked that we all just stared at him, but he didn't seem to mind. "My dad gave me a pocketknife when I was ten, and I used to beat the other boys." I knew that the dad to whom he referred was Uncle Oscar, Aunt Rosa's husband, who had died when Homer was about fourteen. Homer, like all his siblings, had no relationship with his biological father, Arthur Loring.

"Did you bet, Homer?" Dad asked, as if conversing with him at the table was the normal thing. A half-grin twisted Homer's mouth.

"No. I never had any money. We just counted points."

Days turned into weeks, then months; and winter came to an end. We had fallen into a routine that seemed to work, but a subtle change in Homer's attitude toward my mother began to be disturbing. He had never warmed to her, and most of the time he ignored her. One night after supper, Mom told Homer that she would be doing laundry the next day. She asked if he had anything he wanted washed.

"I'll do it myself!" Homer shouted. "You don't know how to do it! You never could do anything right!" It seemed that everything came to a halt, even our breathing. On his way to the living room, my dad returned to the kitchen.

"Homer, you don't talk to Jackie like that. She's done everything in her power to make you comfortable here." Dad stood right in front of his brother-in-law, steely eyes fixed upon Homer's black ones. Even a crazy man could recognize the seriousness of my father's intent.

"I'd as soon do my own wash." Homer looked at the floor.

"Fine," my dad said. "Jackie, let him wash his own clothes." Mom did just that, even down to letting Homer hang his wet clothes on the line in the back yard.

There were other indications that all was not well with Uncle Homer. Several times I saw him pull a window shade aside, just an inch or two, and peer out the tiny peephole he had created. In his room, he often stood for long periods at the window, shades pulled all the way past the sills. At timed intervals he pulled aside the shade a crack and stared through the opening.

"I don't think he's taking his medicines," Mom told Dad. "He's agitated and more paranoid, not like he was when he first came here. I think we need help." Mom spoke quietly into the telephone. Only I heard her. Bill and Beth sat at the kitchen table, heads buried in homework.

I raised my head from the history book in my lap. My eyes met my mother's while she listened to Dad's reply. Her concern was no surprise to me.

"I'll call them," she said. "Hurry home." Mom carefully replaced the receiver. "Sissy, I think that we're going to have to send your uncle back to the hospital. Someone will probably have to escort him, I imagine by bus, back to Farmington. I think that one of my uncles will come for him."

I let out a long breath, unaware that I had been holding it in for so long. Sadness for my uncle filled me, but it would be nice to have our household back the way it was—safe and not filled with tension. My hope was that it would happen without another confrontation.

One of my mother's cousins came for Homer. Russell Loring was several years older than Mom, nearly old enough to be Homer's father. There was a calm, reassuring aura about Russell, something that touched all of us, even Homer.

"Homer, I've come to take you back home, back to Missouri," Russell announced. "Would you like to go home?" Tears formed in Homer's black eyes, and he nodded. I think that there were tears all around. Even my dad blinked hard.

Very early the next morning, Russell and Homer stowed into the car's trunk what few possessions Homer had brought with him. As they started down the driveway, Russell waved; but my Uncle Homer did not look back. It was a beautiful, early spring day; and I felt as if my family had been granted a reprieve. It was as if we collectively breathed a sigh of gratitude.

By the time Homer left, I had acquired several friends, largely due to Karen Courtney's including me in just about all her social activities. After school was dismissed that summer, Karen and I spent a lot of time together. We both collected forty-five rpm records, and we exchanged the little black disks so many times we forgot who owned what.

We loved Elvis Presley. I had told Karen about my daring ride with Victor Delacorte the previous spring. Not only had I heard Elvis for the first time, belting out "Mystery Train" on the car radio, I had received my first kiss. I found it gratifying that Karen's big brown eyes grew bigger when I gave details of that momentous evening.

Karen Courtney's seventeen-year-old sister, Nancy, had a driver's license. Nancy was nice enough to take her sister and friends to various destinations: Saturday movie matinees, the skating rink, shopping at the Diamond's Department Store in Charleston, and sometimes just cruising.

My mother wasn't crazy about the latter, so I carefully maintained her state of blissful ignorance about those evenings. I didn't exactly *lie*, I just didn't fully disclose. One might think that I would have learned from past experience. I guess it just takes some of us longer to learn from our mistakes.

One of our favorite haunts was a little drive-in restaurant called Dooby's Place. For less than fifty cents, we could get a hamburger, with all the trimmings, and a big Coca-Cola. On warm summer evenings, several cars filled with teenagers parked along three sides of the little building. It was a noisy, happy place; and we gathered there every chance we could find.

I don't remember who suggested that we go to a revival meeting way up in the hills. A poster, announcing the date and hour, had been tacked to a wall of Dooby's Place. I think it may have started as a joke until someone dared someone. Before we fully examined what we were doing, three carloads of us were on our way out of Dixon and into the boondock regions of Appalachia.

"Where is this church?" I asked Karen.

"Oh, it's way off the main roads, way back in the hills. My dad drove us by there one time, just to show us where the snake-handlers went to church." My blood literally chilled.

"*The what*?!" I demanded.

"Snake-handlers." Karen sounded very matter-of-fact. "You know, people who hold snakes to prove that they're holy. If a handler is bitten by a snake, it means their faith isn't strong enough, or they've sinned or something."

"What happens to them if they do get bitten?" I asked.

Karen shrugged. "I guess they die."

"I don't think I want to do this," I whispered to Karen. "Do we have to go inside?"

"Oh, come on, Sissy. It's your chance to see why Lillie Faye is like she is."

"*We're going to Lillie Faye's church*?" My voice squeaked. I had visions of Lillie Faye's father, holding a writhing serpent, bearing down upon me to prove how wicked I was. It seemed that others felt as I did, and were not comfortable with this excursion. Majority ruled, and the caravan continued.

We turned onto a graveled, winding road, that was barely wide enough for two cars to pass each other. Tall, sheltering pines grew thickly along both sides of the road. Although darkness had not yet fallen, Nancy had to turn on the headlights.

Small dwellings, most made of rough-hewn boards and covered with tin roofs, could be seen here and there, nearly hidden behind the pines. Long, narrow dirt lanes wound upwards through the piney woods, as Karen called the heavy forest. Occasionally we could see the soft glow of a kerosene lamp, shining through a distant window. We drove for what seemed like a long time before Nancy slowed the car.

"Here's the turnoff," she said.

A crude sign pointed toward another dirt lane, showing the way to The Everlastin Covenint of Prayer. I did a double take at the spelling of the words on the sign. When Nancy turned onto the narrow, rocky path and began to drive into the oppressive darkness of the woods, I began to do some praying of my own.

We knew we were getting close to the church, although we could not yet see it. Several old cars and pick-up trucks lined the lane, and we could hear music before we drew near the wood-framed building. It was larger than I expected, unpainted, with a small bell tower atop the peaked, tin-covered roof. The windows were open; and loud, lively music filled the air. It sounded good.

We exited the cars and stood in a group outside the church doors. Now that we were here, many seemed hesitant to make the decision to go inside. Jerry Davis had ridden in another car, along with five other boys. He didn't seem the least bit hesitant. He grinned at me and jerked his head slightly toward the building.

Wish I May, Wish I Might...

"Let's go see what's happenin' in there," he said; and he led the way. I had forgiven him his less-than-kind measurement assessment, but I wasn't going to be the first to follow him. Jerry shamed the other boys into joining him, while we girls reluctantly brought up the rear.

A single door opened inward. We filed in as one body and sat in the very back. Instead of pews, there were splintery wood benches. Members of the congregation gave us curious glances; some smiled at us, and some frowned.

Right away I noticed that all the women and girls wore long-skirted dresses, with long sleeves and high necks. Some of the girls in our group were wearing cotton skirts and sleeveless blouses, but most of us wore pedal pushers or jeans. We hadn't considered a dress code.

The older women wore their hair pulled straight back from their faces, either in tight buns at the back of their necks, or in a coronet of braids. Some of the younger girls let their hair fall down their backs, catching it away from their faces with plain barrettes or bobby pins. The boys and men wore overalls or jeans, and looked much like all the other men in the area. Only the women looked as if they had come from two or three generations back.

Lillie Faye and several other people, all playing musical instruments, sat on the raised platform. Lillie Faye obviously knew how to play the accordion she held. She pulled the bellows back and forth with a smooth energy that spoke of years of practice.

Three other women played accordions; a man played a fiddle; two played banjoes; three played guitars of various sizes. A very large woman played a piano so briskly that the heavy instrument vibrated on the floor. They played three selections, one after the other, before Dewey Snodgrass joined them on the platform.

I had nervously looked around the church for any sign of snakes, but I saw nothing to indicate the presence of serpents. As long as I could hide behind the people in front of me, thereby avoiding eye contact with the preacher, I was relatively comfortable.

The ranting sermon wound down to a close. I took a deep breath, grateful that our visit of curiosity was about to end. I waited for a final amen. Instead of a benediction, Dewey Snodgrass quoted some scripture:

" *'And these signs shall follow those who believe: In my name shall they cast out demons; they shall speak with new tongues; They shall take up serpents....'* " Now that got my attention. The orchestra struck up a different tune, one I had not yet heard.

At the piano, the large woman beat the keys at a frenzied pace. Her heavy breasts swung with her exertion. Sam McGraw, one of Jerry's friends, made a rude comment. I couldn't hear what he said, but a couple of the boys giggled nervously. The music and singing were so loud I don't think anyone outside our group heard them.

Two men picked up a large pine box, from where it stood against a wall, and placed it upon a stand directly in front of the platform. Each man lifted an end of the cover and plunged their hands into the box. Anxiety made my heart pound. They could be reaching for only one thing, or *several* things!

Moans and prayers erupted from the congregation. Had I not been seated in the middle of the bench, I would have bolted from the building. I was thinking that there was no safety in numbers.

"Wow! Look at that!" Jerry's loud whisper sounded more excited than scared. The two men held the snakes high above their heads. It was evident that the writhing creatures were rattlesnakes. The preacher encouraged members of the congregation to "take up the serpents, and prove your faith," and many went forth to do as he bid them.

One woman began to shake, trembling as if she had no bones. She held out her arms, allowing someone to place a huge rattler across her extended palms. Her eyes rolled back, and her body continued to shake in a convulsive frenzy. The music increased in tempo. All around the church, men and women carried snakes of all sizes. Some of the serpents lay limp in the hands that carried them, but most writhed and twisted, seeming to struggle to be free. I knew how they felt! I wanted out!

"Look out, Girls," Jerry whispered. "Someone dropped their snake on the floor!" That did it. We cleared that bench as one body, pushing and shoving and trying to be the first one out the door. We had a major pile-up in the opening, and none of us was able to exit, until someone gave enough ground to let one person through. The screen door didn't close until we were all out of the building.

There had been no break in the music. None of the congregation inside seemed to notice that the last two pews in their church had suddenly cleared. Jerry laughed all the way to the cars.

"What's so funny?" I demanded.

"Aw, Sissy, I was only kidding around. There wasn't a snake loose in there." He chuckled again, and I hit him. "Ow-w-w! Sissy, that wasn't very nice!"

"I hope it hurt," I told him. "Don't you ever do that again!"

The farther down the mountain we drove, the braver we became. By the time we entered the city limits of Dixon, the humor of our experience had taken on gigantic proportions, while our cowardice diminished by the same degree.

I didn't tell my mother that we went to the snake handlers' church. I was pretty certain what her reaction would be. I did ask for her opinion of the religion.

"I don't know, Sissy," she said. "There was a small group of snake-handlers in the Ozarks, when I was a girl; but I never saw any of it."

"Why do they do it?" I asked. Mom shrugged.

"I guess they think they have to," she said. "Probably most of them grew up with it, and they think it's the only right way." Mom grinned. "Except for the snakes, they probably aren't too different from any church. I think that every denomination takes a few scriptures that seem to prove their various points. Then they set out to disprove everyone who disagrees with them."

"Is that why you don't like to go to church?" I pursued. Although Mom and Dad always sent us to Sunday school, they seldom ever attended, themselves. Mom thought about my question for a moment.

"Maybe," she said, "but I've always tried not to throw the baby out with the bath water."

"Huh?"

Mom laughed. "Sissy, don't you have something to do?" She turned back to the sewing machine, where she had been working before I had interrupted her. *So much for this discussion on religion*, I thought.

Now I had one more thing to store away and think about later, although I thought I knew what she meant. It seemed that she was telling me not to throw away something good, just because something less desirable might be a part of it. I sighed. Sometimes my head felt full of more things I didn't understand, than those I did.

I didn't see Lillie Faye again until school started in the fall. As luck would have it, we shared a sophomore English class. She caught up with me in the hall one day, much as she had the first time she confronted me.

"I saw you with your friends at our church last summer." Without preamble, she attacked. "I know why you came. You came to make fun of us, to make fun of me!"

"No, Lillie Faye, I didn't make fun of you. I only went because the whole group decided to go. I didn't...."

"I saw those boys laughing!" she said. "You think my dad is crazy! You think we're all crazy because we don't live like you!" I started to protest, but Lillie Faye wouldn't hear me. "But what if we're right and you're wrong? What if..."

"What if *you* are wrong, Lillie Faye?" I asked. "What if it doesn't matter how we dress, or what music we like, or if we like to dance? What if it's more important how we treat each other, than how we look? Don't you ever wonder about that?"

Tears formed in Lillie Faye's eyes, but they didn't fall. She blinked hard and kept them contained. We stared into each other's eyes for a long moment, and I saw something that surprised me. I saw longing. "Of course, I wonder," she whispered. In a face that should have been pretty, I saw longing and defeat. She turned away.

"Lillie Faye, wait," I said. She stopped. I reached out and touched her arm. She flinched, but didn't pull away. "I really didn't go up there to make fun of you. I promise, I didn't." She examined my face, and I saw a lessening of the tenseness in her body. Slowly, she nodded.

"I believe you," she said. I drew a deep breath. Almost unbidden, words came from my mouth that surprised me as much as they did Lillie Faye.

"Would you like to come to my house sometime?" A blank look of disbelief preceded a lovely smile on her face.

"Do you mean it?" she asked. What could I do, but nod? "I don't know...I don't know if my dad would let me come...but I'll find out. When?" Eagerness was in her voice, and I had to come up with a time.

"Uh, this Saturday afternoon?" I suggested. I wanted to retract the words before they completely left my mouth.

"We don't have a phone, but I'll let you know tomorrow."

"Ok," I said, and made a hasty retreat. I don't know how long she stood in the corridor, looking after me.

On the way home, I told Karen about my impulsive invitation to Lillie Faye. Karen stared at me as if I had lost my mind. I thought she was probably right.

"Why did you do a stupid thing like that?" she demanded. I shrugged.

"It seemed like the right thing to do at the time." I sounded like a wimp, even to my own ears. "If she comes, will you slide down the slope and help me?" Karen had to think about that for a bit.

"If I do, you'll owe me."

"Whatever you want," I promised. Karen slanted that look at me that always suggested how unbelievably naïve I remained.

"Even your new Elvis forty-five record?" I stopped on the sidewalk. Karen grinned. "I don't have to come," she added. My shoulders slumped in defeat.

"Okay. You can have my new Elvis." Actually, I thought I got the better deal.

The next day, Lillie Faye met me at the door of Miss Wilson's sophomore English class. I don't know how she convinced her father, but Lillie Faye had been granted permission to come to my house on Saturday afternoon. The girl seemed thrilled to death.

"My dad is taking my mom to get groceries and other stuff in town, and he said that he would take me to your house, but that I can only stay until they finish up what they have to do, so it won't be for very long...." Lillie Faye stopped to take a breath.

"Okay," I said. "What would you like to do on Saturday?" She looked blank.

"Do?"

"Yeah. Do you like to listen to music? Karen Courtney and I exchange Elvis records and..."

"Do you really listen to that disciple of the devil? Don't you know that his music is evil?" Lillie Faye seemed genuinely appalled.

"Actually, Lillie Faye, his music sounds a lot like the music you played in your church." I don't know why I said that. I guess the devil made me do it. "Anyway, you don't have to listen to it, if you don't want to. It was just a suggestion."

"Okay. I'm sorry. We can listen to anything you want." Hmmm. *An apology from Lillie Faye.* Maybe there was hope that a real, live, bona fide teenager existed somewhere inside her; but I wasn't looking forward to Saturday. I gave her directions to my house and scurried into the classroom. *What had I been thinking? The obvious answer was that I had not been thinking at all.*

I prepared my mother for our visitor. My brother and sister, who had made dozens of friends and enjoyed a healthy social life, were both gone for the afternoon. I whined to Mom that I wished I could un-invite Lillie Faye.

"Sissy, shame on you. You asked the girl to come here, to our home; and you're going to be nice and friendly while she's here. It sounds to me like she doesn't have many friends." Just the snake-handlers, I thought to myself.

When the old pick-up truck groaned up our steep driveway, I pasted a smile on my face and went to greet Lillie Faye. She climbed down from the passenger side, where she had been sitting next to her mother.

The little woman looked even smaller beside Lillie Faye's father. She didn't speak or look at me.

"We'll be back in 'bout a hour, mebbe a little more," Mr. Snodgrass said. "Y'all be good, now." He turned the truck around in the graveled space Dad had prepared for that purpose. It was too dangerous to back onto the street below.

"Hi," I said to Lillie Faye, who seemed unsure what was expected of her. "Come on in. Karen might come down and join us for awhile." The girl stepped onto the porch and followed me inside the house. "Mom, Lillie Faye is here," I called.

My mother came into the living room. For our guest's benefit, she had changed from her Bermuda shorts into a skirt and blouse. Changing my clothes hadn't occurred to me. I still wore jeans and a tee shirt.

"I'm glad you could come, Lillie Faye." Mom smiled warmly at the girl.

"You can just call me Lillie." She looked around the living room. "Your house is so nice," she said. The girl was actually pretty when she smiled.

After the first few minutes, Lillie Faye seemed to loosen up dramatically. Karen joined us, and we went upstairs to my room. Lillie didn't object when Karen put a stack of forty-fives on the record player. I noticed that she tapped her foot and even swayed a little to the beat of some of the rock and roll numbers.

"Lillie, have you ever worn make-up?" Karen asked. Lillie Faye's mouth dropped open, and her eyes grew bigger. She shook her head. "Would you let me put some on you, just for fun?" I held my breath, expecting a tirade on the sins of worldly practices.

"Well, my daddy wouldn't like it at all," she said.

"That's okay," Karen told her. "We'll wash it all off before he comes back." I stared at Karen. It would never have entered my mind to suggest that Lillie Faye Snodgrass wear make-up! "Sissy, put all your stuff on the dresser and we'll have a make-up party."

We pushed Lillie Faye onto the vanity bench, and Karen went to work on her. The first thing she did was to take the ugly pins out of Lillie's hair and brush the long length of it to one side, creating a soft, loose pageboy. Lillie stared at her image in the mirror. She held her breath as Karen applied a little color to Lillie's lips, and then brushed a tiny amount from the same tube onto her cheeks. We weren't allowed to use rouge. We improvised with the lipstick, blending it out to a soft, even color.

Wish I May, Wish I Might...

The effect was amazing, and Lillie Faye seemed transfixed. Her eyes were locked upon the mirror, and the image of the pretty girl who stared back at her.

"Now," Karen said. "Let's dance." She pulled Lillie Faye up from the bench and twirled her around. Lillie had to twirl, or she would have fallen.

"I can't!" Lillie said, but she kept moving. In no time, she was dancing as if she had done it all her life. Of course, the people in her church had done a dance of sorts. I'm not sure if it was because of the musical beat, or because they were trying to keep the snakes from striking them.

We collapsed onto my bed, all three of us laughing and breathless.

"Do you ever wear shorts or jeans?" Karen asked Lillie. No longer shocked at Karen's questions, Lillie shook her head.

"No. My dad doesn't approve of women and girls wearing anything but dresses, sometimes a blouse and skirt, if the skirt isn't too tight or too short."

"Don't you ever want to dress like the rest of us?" I asked.

"I could never wear pullover sweaters like you do," she told me. "My dad says that they are sinful."

"Is that what you meant that day in the hall?" I pressed. Lillie blushed.

"Sissy, I'm sorry about that; and I'm sorry that I complained about the poem. I didn't mean to get you in trouble. Sometimes, I just want to be like everyone else; but I'm so afraid of going to hell. My dad says that all teenagers that dress like you girls do, and listen to rock-and-roll music, and dance, and date and all that are going to hell!"

"I don't believe that, Lillie Faye!" Karen retorted. "I don't believe that for a minute! I think your dad is just mixed up!"

"If your dad thinks I'm such a bad person, why did he let you come to my house?" I asked her. Lillie Faye put her hands over her face for a moment, before she answered. Her voice was not much above a whisper.

"I promised him that I would ask you to come back to our church. He saw all of you last summer. He recognized you, Sissy. I'm supposed to be witnessing to you." Lillie laughed. "And just look at me! If my dad saw me looking like this, he would kill me."

"Lillie, your dad is here," Mom called from the bottom of the stairs. He was early!

"Okay, Mom. Tell them we'll be down in just a minute!" Lillie seemed to turn to stone. "Come on, Lillie, we've got to wash your face!

Hurry! Karen, put her hair back like it was! Hurry!" By the time we got Lillie back to normal, she had a healthy blush on her cheeks; but no trace of the makeup remained.

Lillie stopped us at the bottom of the stairs. She put one hand on Karen's shoulder, and the other, on mine. "I've had a really good time," she said. "Thank you. Thank you for being so nice to me." We walked her to the porch and watched her climb into the truck. She waved, and we waved back.

"Well, whattaya know about that!" Karen muttered. "She liked it. You know, she's not half-bad, Sissy. I kinda like her." I nodded.

"Yeah." I said.

Lillie was not at school on Monday morning. All kinds of rumors abounded, but one thing was certain. While conducting the usual Sunday evening service at the Everlastin Covenint Church, Brother Dewey Snodgrass had been bitten by a five-foot-long rattlesnake. We heard that he'd survived two other such venomous bites; but this time, he did not.

Their doctrine prevented the believers from seeking medical attention. Four days after he was bitten, Lillie's father died. Her family had no telephone, so I couldn't offer my condolences to Lillie. A week passed before she came back to school.

When Lillie did return, she seemed very subdued. She avoided me for several days. I finally caught up with her one day, as she hurried out of the building after school.

"Lillie, I'm so sorry about your dad...." Lillie Faye held up her hand.

"You don't have to pretend, Sissy. I know how you and Karen and all the kids felt about my dad, how you feel about all of us. It's my fault, you know. I let you and Karen sway me away from the true way, and God took my dad to punish me. Well, the law says I have to go to school here until I'm sixteen; but I don't have to be a part of all your worldly ways. You don't have to speak to me or pretend to like me. Just leave me alone." Lillie looked directly into my eyes. I had never seen such a cold, relentless fire.

Thereafter, Lillie Faye Snodgrass and two or three other girls from her church remained totally aloof from the rest of the student body. I did as she asked. I left her alone.

In fact, I left her so completely alone that I didn't notice when she dropped out of school. As she had promised, Lillie Faye's last day of school was the day before she became sixteen. Someone mentioned it, in passing. I didn't give it another thought.

A few years later, the hills and surrounding countryside all the way past Charleston, trembled with the preaching and denunciation of the new leader of Dewey Snodgrass's church. A young woman, filled with passion and dedication and a self-proclaimed baptism of fire, swept through the community. She left a wake of terrified, consecrated zealots to go forth and do likewise.

She had taken the name, Sister Lillie, Daughter of the Divine Covenant. Over the years, her followers numbered in the thousands. With the hundreds of thousands of dollars her converts provided, she built her own tabernacle on the site of the original small church, where her father had ministered until his death.

The spring of Beth's high school graduation, I came home to attend the ceremony. While glancing through the local paper, I noticed a box advertisement that announced the dates and times of Sister Lillie's crusade. For no reason other than curiosity, I decided to see for myself how my old classmate drew in so many followers.

The "cathedral" was spacious, simple in design, built upon the baseball diamond concept. The stage formed a small peninsula, a runway that extended into the center, cutting through the first four rows of theater seats. From there, the seats fanned outward into a huge circle that accommodated at least a thousand people, perhaps more.

Instead of a homespun band, the platform held a grand piano and a large, three-tiered organ, complete with gold pipes. A tall, well-dressed man led the music. The sound he extracted from the congregation was tremendous, while the pianist and organist supplied superb accompaniment.

Nervously, I examined every niche and corner for any sign of snakes. I saw none. I had looked away from the platform only momentarily. When I swung my eyes forward, Lillie Faye stood in the center of the stage, looking upward, her arms held high in supplication. I don't know how she had appeared so suddenly.

No longer dowdy and shy, Lillie Faye was dressed in a full length, diaphanous, white gown, belted with a silver rope. Her waist length hair fell from a center part into a straight, shiny brown cascade down her back. She was beautiful. Fascinated, I watched her performance, convinced that it was, indeed, a performance.

At one point during her diatribe, she ordered that the house lights come up, which they did immediately. Seated in the tenth row, center-left aisle, my view of Lillie Faye was excellent. I stared as she turned to one side and raised her arm in an imperious gesture. She moved in a slow half-circle, finger pointed accusingly at the audience, from one side to the other. Her eyes focused upon me, her finger pointed at me, and I saw recognition register upon her face.

Lillie Faye's eyes widened, and then narrowed. For just a moment, I thought that I detected pleasure on her face. The thought was fleeting. Lillie Faye began to beckon. She said nothing, just stood beckoning for long moments, her flashing blue eyes locked upon mine. When she spoke, her words seemed directed only to me. My hands gripped the arms of the theater seat so tightly that my fingernails turned white. It took the strong force of my own will not be drawn into the chasm of mindless response to her siren call. She slowly turned away from me, allowing her eyes to maintain contact with mine as she moved her body. I slipped from my seat and made a hasty exit.

Whether upon her own or with the help of others, Lillie Faye had acquired the ability to use her voice to great effect. She spoke without notes, without apparent cues of any kind. She took her listeners to the depths of despair at their failure to live by her edicts, and then transported them to the heights of her own brand of glory, all with her mesmerizing voice. There was not a snake in sight, but Sister Lillie didn't manipulate serpents. She manipulated souls.

Sister Lillie scared me to death.

During that same week, my mother was notified that her brother, Homer, had been readmitted to a hospital for the mentally ill. Mom seemed sad, but the responsibility for his condition and his treatment was no longer hers.

"Poor boy," she said. "It's just not fair that he inherited such a thing. I'm sure that his mother had the same condition. No sane person would treat children like she treated us. At least Homer had a good home when he was a child."

When my grandfather Loring died, at the age of ninety-five, I attended the funeral, mostly because my mother was not able to do so. I went out of respect for the position he held, not for the man that he was. Somehow, Homer was able to come to his biological father's funeral.

His appearance was so changed that I didn't recognize him. The tall, handsome young man that I remembered had become a heavy, stolid man with graying hair. He must have weighed well over three hundred pounds, and his speech was so slow and slurred that I had to really listen to follow his words. Even his eyelids closed slowly.

Wish I May, Wish I Might...

Over the course of the next thirty years, I received occasional notes and letters from Uncle Homer. Sometimes they came from his uncle's house; at other times a hospital's return address was on the envelope. The childlike scrawl was always printed in upper case letters, one page on both sides of the paper, and the contents were always the same. He was so heavily medicated that his writing was slurred.

Each letter inquired for my health, asked about my family, about my brother and sister and their families. He closed with a plea for me to write to him, which I always did...one letter in reply to his, until the next one. The last time I wrote to him, I sent pictures of my whole family. I attached little yellow Post-It notes to the backs, telling him a little about each person.

Some years later I received a call from my mother, asking me to please go see Homer. He was very ill, possibly terminally so. At that time, I lived within a few hours driving distance of the hospital; so the very next day I went to see Uncle Homer.

I arrived at the hospital at noon. The nurse at the station outside Homer's room seemed thrilled when I asked for him. "Oh, how nice!" she exclaimed. "He hasn't had a visitor, and he's so very ill." She took me to the room. "Mr. Loring, you have a visitor!"

Again, shock was my uppermost emotion at Homer's appearance. Only when he raised his black eyes to look at me did I recognize him. His thick hair was totally white, as was his skin. Much of the excess weight had disappeared, and his proportions were more nearly normal.

He sat in a chair, obviously for lunch, which sat on a tray in front of him. White cloths bound both his hands to the arms of the chair, whether to keep him upright, or to restrain him, I never learned. I touched his shoulder.

"Hi, Homer. I'm Sissy, your niece." I pasted a big smile upon my face. I watched the information travel slowly through his mind, and then he nodded.

"You are? Jackie's girl? Sit down," he said, and I recognized the same slurred, drugged voice. A nurses' aid patiently loaded what looked like baby food into a spoon and offered it to Homer. Obediently, he opened his mouth, took in the food and swallowed. Between bites he asked questions, much like those in his letters, about my family. His eyes traveled hungrily over my face, almost as if he were trying to memorize it.

For an hour, I visited with him. His hands never stopped twisting against the bonds that held him to the chair. My heart hurt for him.

Homer was sixty-nine years old, and he had never had a life, a lover, a family of his own, or freedom. Mindful of tiring him, I rose.

"Do you have to go?" he asked. I nodded.

"I don't want to make you too tired," I said.

"Will you write to me?" I nodded again.

"I'll write a long letter to you tomorrow," I promised. "I'll send you some more pictures." I leaned down and looked into his eyes. "You take care of yourself and get better, so that I can come back again." For the first time in both our lives, I kissed his forehead. We maintained eye contact until I was out of the room.

"Will you come back?" the nurse asked. I didn't hesitate.

"Yes, I will," I told her. "Except for a handful of half-nieces and nephews, none of whom live nearby, most of his relatives are gone. Can you tell me his prognosis? What's wrong with him?"

"Mostly kidney failure. He's been on such high dosages of meds and drugs all his life, and he's developed diabetes. Today is the best day he's had since he was admitted six days ago. No one thought that he would survive when he was brought in."

"Would you please call me if there's a change, or when he's discharged?" I asked. I hastily wrote down my name and telephone number.

"Oh, I would be happy to!" the nurse replied. "We're so glad that you came to see him."

Ooh, I thought. *More guilt, my very favorite thing.* After I got home, I made phone calls to my mother and my siblings, encouraging them to write to Homer. He was on my mind all that evening and long after I went to bed.

Sometime after midnight, the bedside phone rang. I hate late-night calls. They never bring good news. It was the hospital in Sikeston, Missouri, where my uncle Homer was a patient.

"Ma'am, I'm so sorry to call this late; but you did ask us to let you know should there be a change...Homer Loring passed away a few minutes ago." Something turned over inside my chest.

"I thought that he was better," I murmured

"He rallied yesterday just before you arrived. Maybe I shouldn't say this, but it almost seems as if he were waiting for someone to tell him good-bye. He was so pleased that you had come."

Tears sprang to my eyes. At least once in Homer's life I had been there for him, me, Sissy Bannister, the niece he had taught to play checkers. Perhaps a little of the guilt could be assuaged.

Wish I May, Wish I Might...

A few days later I received a packet in the mail. I opened it to discover the few letters and pictures that I had sent to Homer over the years. They made a pitifully small stack. He had saved everything I ever sent to him. I had grown up with so much, not materially, but in family and relationships and friends, very few of which had been granted to Homer Loring.

I thought about all the crazy people I had known during my life. There were many, all in varying types and conditions of instability. I am one of them. We all have foibles and quirks of some kind, something abnormal and different from the rest.

There are so many shades and colors of crazy. There's the red of rage, the black of depression, the purple of delusions of grandeur, the yellow of mania, the kaleidoscope of schizophrenia, the blue of melancholy.

I think my shade lies somewhere between purple and blue.

Amethyst, perhaps.

#

Summer's Child

Six-and-one-half years difference in age seemed like a large gap between my little sister and me. The older I grew, the larger seemed the gulf that separated us. Where once we had played "house" together, I being the mother and she the child, I could no longer be bothered with such a childish pastime. I'm sure that there were times when my self-centeredness hurt her feelings.

There was one thing my sister and I had in common that first year in Dixon. We missed the women who had filled the role of grandmother to each of us: Mrs. Lula for Beth, Mrs. East for me. I think that we both hoped to find other women to fill that void. I was fortunate to find a woman who did, at least for a while.

In most instances, it takes a long time, sometimes years, to develop deep relationships. On the other hand, a chance meeting can become a serendipitous event, stamped upon one's psyche with the force and sizzle of a branding iron. Within that moment, a sense of knowing, of recognition can bind two people together in a bond as thick as blood. Such was my first meeting with Willow Thornhill...

Our first spring in Dixon was glorious. Just as the hillsides began to show a slight tint of the softest green buds, white and pink dogwood trees blossomed in a rivalry of color and splendor. Leaves were in such a delicate state that the forms of trunks and tree limbs could be clearly seen upon the slopes, creating terraces of magnificent contrasts in color and texture. I gloried in it.

I tried to capture some of the magical scenery with my watercolors, but I failed beyond redemption. I had not yet learned how to make the colors run where I wanted them to run, and stop them from running where they shouldn't. Those paintings looked like blurred images of bad abstract concepts. Mr. Boudreaux had his work cut out for him if he were going to teach me how to use watercolors.

In spite of Karen's warnings about the art teacher, I found him to be a good instructor. Soft-spoken, given to wry smiles instead of laughter, he seemed to enjoy working with his students. I saw him angry only once, and that was with just cause.

Greg Boudreaux stood no more than three or four inches taller than I. Most of the senior boys in Dixon High were taller and heavier than he was. Thick, black hair grew over his collar, more as if he had forgotten to get a haircut than by design. Occasionally, he remembered; and the haircut was cause for teasing, which he endured with good humor.

A thin, neat mustache grew above Mr. Boudreaux's upper lip. I called it a Clark Gable mustache. There was a bit of similarity in their looks, but the art teacher had no hint of the ruggedness of the actor. Mr. Boudreaux was a pared-down, refined version, with high cheekbones, olive skin and sensitive features. His age could have been anywhere from thirty to forty years. To me, he was already old.

Brows the color of his hair framed dark brown eyes that could look at a student's effort and know immediately whether it should be saved or deserved instant destruction. He withheld neither praise nor criticism, and he was fair. I liked him.

During the first few weeks of class, I watched Mr. Boudreaux closely, looking for any sign that he was what Karen had called "queer." The concept was foreign to me, so I wasn't sure what I expected to see. The day came when I discovered that the man definitely liked girls, and I discarded Karen's notion about Mr. Boudreaux's sexual preferences.

Miss Seabrook stopped by the art classroom one morning during our session. She knocked delicately upon the door before she opened it. In an equally delicate voice, she requested permission to enter. Permission was, of course, granted.

Anna Seabrook's first year of teaching high school Home Economics corresponded with my freshman year. Tall, slender, blond and single, she created a stir among the older male student body. I suspect that she stirred a good bit of the male teachers' body, as well. Young, exuberant and beautiful as she was, how could they have resisted her?

"I'm *so* sorry for interrupting, Mr. Boudreaux," she said. "I need some posters made to use in my classroom, and I know that *no one* is more qualified to design them than *you*. Do you think that you could work me in?"

The ten boys in the class, six freshman and four sophomores, openly stared at Miss Seabrook. The expressions of teen-age longing on their faces reminded me of the way my brother looked at pictures of radio transistors and speakers in the Sears catalogue. The glazed look on our teacher's face wasn't much different.

Mr. Boudreaux jumped to his feet so quickly that he overturned an old coffee can full of sharpened sketching pencils and charcoal. Flustered, he tried to stop them from rolling off his desk; and he succeeded in scattering them in every direction. Mr. Boudreaux finally gave up. He hurried to the door, where Miss Seabrook stood in innocent, sensuous splendor. A hint of color touched his cheeks. Mr. Boudreaux was blushing!

"You're wrong about Mr. Boudreaux, Karen." Karen and I left school at different times that evening. I called her the minute I walked inside my house, not wanting to wait one minute to share my discovery. "He's not queer."

"How do you know?" Karen demanded. I told her what I had seen and how Mr. Boudreaux had reacted to Miss Seabrook.

"I bet he asks her out," I said. "I bet they fall in love and get married and have lots of little Boudreaux babies." I couldn't help giggling at the prospect.

"Like-fish-in-a-pickle-dish!" she retorted. Original, clever repartee was not our forte.

"Sissy, what in the world are you saying?" My mother stood transfixed in the hall between the living room and dining room. Her look of angry disbelief told me that I was in trouble, and I had no clue how to extricate myself from it. I wasn't about to get into that "queer" business with her. Some things simply could not be discussed with a mother. Besides, she probably didn't know any more about it than I did.

"Oh, nothing, Mom. Karen and I were just joking around." I beat a record-time retreat to my room.

Art class became my favorite class that spring of my freshman year. When Mr. Boudreaux announced that our next medium would be oil paint, I was thrilled. My fifth grade art teacher, Miss Welp, had taken our class on a field trip to the Art Museum in Champaign, Illinois. I had not forgotten the beautiful oil paintings that hung on the gallery walls.

At that age, I used crayons to color my drawings, some of which were quite good, in retrospect. Pencil drawing was something that came easily to me. I liked the vivid colors of chalk, but the dust could be messy. I longed for tubes of oil paint and thick canvasses. However, they were too expensive; so I tried my hand at painting with the simple little watercolor patches in the Prang box. My efforts were not memorable.

"The set of paints that you find on your tables today will have to last through all your studies and two paintings," Mr. Boudreaux announced. "If you run out, you'll have to buy your own replacement tubes. You'll notice that the titanium white is much larger than the rest. That's because we use it to lighten and highlight the other colors."

Mr. Boudreaux continued his discourse on oil paints and pigments, but I scarcely looked up. I caressed the smooth tubes, longing to squeeze out little piles of color onto a palette, as I had seen artists do in pictures and movies. Small mixing cups, a variety of brushes, and a palette knife completed the materials.

"I have some paintings to show you," Mr. Boudreaux said. From the storage closet he brought five canvasses, all different sizes. The first one he held up made me gasp, and other soft murmurs of appreciation filled the room.

Unframed, the painting measured perhaps three by four feet. It held a magnificent reproduction of a West Virginia mountainside in springtime. Blooming dogwood trees, in shades of pink and white, boasted petals that looked velvety soft. The hillside glowed with soft colors of budding leaves, allowing the forms of tree trunks to show. Below the slope, a wide panorama of soft, layered vistas stretched to infinity; and a lone eagle soared above the horizon.

The other canvasses were equally beautiful, and all contained a backdrop or foreground of the mountains in different seasons. In one of the smaller paintings, a little black dog sat transfixed, his eyes set upon a squirrel that teased from its high perch upon the trunk of a tall pine tree. The subjects were so realistically painted that I could almost see the quiver in the dog's body and the cocky twitch of the squirrel's tail. The same little dog watched a butterfly soar just out of reach in another landscape.

"Come closer and really look at these paintings," Mr. Boudreaux told us. "There are no better works anywhere in the state, perhaps in the whole country." He pointed out the play of shadow, how the artist had used perspective to instill depth and movement, and how there could be no light without darkness.

"Who painted these?" I asked. I had looked for a signature, but I found none.

"A local artist," Mr. Boudreaux answered. "If you look very closely, you can find the artist's initials located somewhere in each painting." I concentrated upon the largest canvas; and I finally found the initials, worked into the bark of one of the dogwoods: w-t, in lower case letters. How bizarre, I thought. If I were able to paint like that, I would put my name on the canvas in big, bold letters that no one could miss.

Mr. Boudreaux explained that a brush, held correctly, becomes an extension of the painter's hand. He demonstrated how to mix oil colors, how not to over-mix, which usually led to something that resembled mud. In his dexterous hand, the palette knife moved through the paint like a spatula through warm butter.

I was amazed at some of my own first attempts on canvas. For me, using oils was as different from using watercolor, as ballet was from field hockey. Occasionally, a totally unexpected combination appeared in the colors, or in the shadows. I learned to incorporate those beneficial accidents into the paintings. Oils quickly became my favorite artistic medium. Their smooth consistency remains moist and malleable, making it easier to incorporate changes in a painting over a longer period of time.

One day we heard Mr. Boudreaux's angry voice long before we approached the classroom. We stood outside the open door for several minutes before we cautiously sidled into the room, collectively trying to leave one leg in the corridor. Mr. Boudreaux paced back and forth before one of w-t's paintings, which was propped upon his desk.

Someone had vandalized the painting of the little black dog peering up at the squirrel against the lovely backdrop of a verdant hillside. Either in ignorance of the painting's value or with deliberate malice, the perpetrator had painted a graphic obscene connection between the animals, destroying the innocent woodland scene.

"Sit down!" We sat, afraid to move, afraid to breathe. "Who did this?" A boy snickered, a sound that quickly disappeared when the teacher turned on the one who dared. "Do you think that this is funny?" he demanded. A deep red flush colored Mr. Boudreaux's cheeks, and his dark eyes flashed dangerously.

"No, Sir."

"Do any of you know who did this?" We all shook our heads. I tentatively raised my hand. He nodded at me.

"Mr. Boudreaux, can you fix it? I mean, can you remove the red paint without hurting the picture?" He gazed at me for several seconds before he answered. He took deep breaths, obviously fighting to regain his composure.

"I probably can," he replied. Gradually, his normal color returned; and sanity replaced the rage in his black eyes. "If any of you knows who's responsible for this, tell me anonymously, either by phone or note." He shook his head. "Ignorance is tolerable, just barely; but malice and stupidity are inexcusable."

I never learned the identity of the culprit. I don't know whether Mr. Boudreaux ever discovered who had damaged the painting. What I did know was that I never wanted to be the object of his rage, for it was a wondrous phenomenon of nature, much like a Midwest tornado, something to be avoided.

Many of Dixon's winding roads and paved streets ran between steep slopes, without the safety and convenience of sidewalks. Where sidewalks appeared, they were narrow, providing space for single-file pedestrians. Speed limit signs were posted, but many drivers ignored them. In some areas, pedestrians and animals walked at their peril.

On one of the rare afternoons that I walked home from school alone, I heard a soft whining close to the sidewalk. The sound came from a brushy slope to my right, not quite head-high. I stopped and listened. I heard the whining again, and I knew the sound of pain. Carefully, I started up the slope, pushing aside the rhododendron and azalea bushes that flourished there. Lying on its side, a small black dog, a Schnauzer, raised its head and looked at me.

"Oh, you poor little thing," I murmured. One hind leg was obviously broken, and there was a bloody cut along the dog's side. Carefully, I crawled up the slope. "Where do you live, Baby? Oh-h-h-h-h-h, I know that hurts. Sh-h-h." I don't remember exactly what I said to the dog after that, but I kept murmuring softly, until I was close enough to touch it. Soulful dark eyes searched my face as I moved closer.

Still crooning what I hoped were reassuring sounds, I extended my hand toward the little animal. A tiny pink tongue licked my hand, and the stump of a tail wagged briefly. The effort resulted in a pain-filled whine. I gently caressed the fuzzy face before I scooted down the slope.

As quickly as I could, I ran up the cindery driveway of the nearest house nestled into the hillside, just above the street A decrepit pick-up truck stood inside the open garage, which was located on the lower level of the small house. I knocked sharply upon the door, three steps up from the garage floor. When no one came immediately, I banged with my open palm.

"What?" Impatience filled the voice of the woman who pulled open the door.

"A little dog has been hit by a car and it's really hurt. Is it--?" Before I could complete the sentence, the woman pushed the screened door. I had to move quickly, to avoid being shoved down the stairs.

"Where is she?" a deep, throaty voice demanded. We both ran down the driveway, and I pointed to the spot where I had left the wounded dog. "Ah-h-h-h, Sophie," the woman sighed. She knelt beside her pet, moving careful hands along the little body.

"Go back to the garage," she commanded. "Behind the half-wall there, you'll find canvases. Bring me a big stretched one. Well, don't just stand there! Go!" I went. Propped against the wall were canvases of all sizes. I grabbed the largest one and hurried back down the cindery driveway.

"Scoot it beneath her when I lift her," the woman ordered. As gently as if she were moving the most precious thing in the world, she scooped the little animal into her arms, lifting her just enough to allow me to maneuver the canvas. "There now, Sophie-girl," she crooned. "You're all right." The woman looked at me. "You take that end." She nodded her head toward me, and together we carried Sophie up the driveway and into the house.

The door opened into a square, compact kitchen. Wood cabinets lined one wall, and a long table stood in the center of the room. A number of glass jars on the table contained up-ended paintbrushes. Tubes of paint, a table easel, a wood palette and rags covered most of the table's surface. The woman shoved everything to one end, clearing enough space for the injured dog.

Mesmerized, I watched while she examined her pet. It was my first opportunity to focus on the woman. Tall and extremely thin, she looked as if a strong wind could carry her on currents, like a blown-about feather. Long, thick, salt-and-pepper-gray hair, leaning heavily toward salt, was caught at her neck with a piece of cloth.

I guessed her age to be somewhere around sixty-five, but she might have been younger or older. Skin as wrinkled and dark as tanned leather covered her high cheekbones. I couldn't tell if the color resulted from suntans or if her skin were naturally brown. Vertical lines formed along narrow upper and lower lips, but her teeth were beautiful. Deeply set eyes, the color of star-onyx, concentrated upon the job her sinewy hands attended.

"Don't just stand there gawking at me, Girl; bring me that slat on the counter." I jumped when she spoke, and I hurried to do her bidding. I heard a small snap. Sophie yelped. "There, there now, Sophie. We'll get a splint on this little leg, and you'll be just as good as new." I felt a little queasy. I had never before heard a bone snapped into place.

"Who are you?" The woman's voice was husky, throaty; and it spoke of thousands, perhaps tens of thousands, of inhaled cigarettes. The one I had interrupted still smoldered in the ashtray on the table. Mid-movement, she reached for it and drew deeply on what was left before she ground the butt against the glass.

"Sissy Bannister," I answered. "I was on my way home from school when I heard your dog whine."

"Do you live far from here?"

"No, it's only a few blocks, on Symington." I glanced around the room, while she broke the slat and tied the makeshift splint with pieces of soft rags, torn from one of the pile on the table. I ambled around the table, slowly maneuvering until I stood before the small canvas that rested upon the easel. "Oh-h-h-h." I couldn't stop the gasp of appreciation.

"You like paintings, do you?" she asked. I could only nod. "Would you like to have that one?"

"Huh?" I sounded dense to my own ears. "Oh, yes, Ma'am! I mean, sure! I mean, really?" A raspy laugh greeted my less-than-brilliant response.

"I was just finishing it when you banged on my door. The paint needs to dry, so you'll have to leave it here for a few days. I'm grateful to you for telling me about Sophie."

"You're welcome," I told her. "Ma'am?"

"Yes?"

"What's your name?"

She lifted her black eyes to mine. Our gaze held for several seconds before she spoke. "Willow Thornhill. I'm pleased to meet you." Willow Thornhill held out a brown hand, and I offered her mine. Her grasp was firm and brief, and I could feel the bones beneath the skin. She nodded her head, as if pleased. "Is your mother expecting you to be home at a certain time? I don't mean to kick you out, but I don't want you to be in trouble."

"Yes, Ma'am. My mom has probably already called my friend, Karen."

I briefly caressed Sophie's soft hair and headed for the door.

"You can come by any time," Willow Thornhill told me.

I grinned to myself the rest of the way home. *Willow Thornhill,* I thought. I knew exactly who she was. I had seen the tiny initials, the artist's signature, all but hidden upon a leaf in the painting: w-t. I had found the painter of West Virginia's beautiful hills and mountains, the creator of all those wonderful paintings stored in Mr. Boudreaux's classroom. I felt as if I had discovered a national treasure, which wasn't far from the truth.

"Mom, you should see Willow Thornhill's paintings." From the time I arrived at my house, until I helped set the table for supper, I talked non-stop about the unique woman, the little silvery-black Schnauzer, and the paintings that filled her kitchen. "I can't believe I've actually met a real *artist*!"

"Can I go with you to see the dog?" Beth asked. I had to think about that. I instinctively knew that I had just met someone who was going to be very important to me, and I hesitated to share.

"Why don't you wait a while, Beth?" Mom suggested. "Sissy just met the lady." Silently, I blessed my mother.

Jealously, I guarded my discovery. I told no one about the artist, but I thoroughly examined the paintings in Mr. Boudreaux's classroom. Obviously, the little dog in the landscapes was Sophie, Willow Thornhill's pet. Closer examination revealed dates, tucked into the painting in the same manner as the artist's initials.

"They really are nice, aren't they?" I hadn't heard the teacher approach. I turned toward him, and we nearly bumped noses. He laughed. The scent of peppermint lingered pleasantly on his breath. "I didn't mean to startle you," he said. He pointed to a patch of mist in the painting, where it swirled at the base of a mountain. "I've never been able to duplicate that effect, but I keep trying. This artist can make you practically feel the mist."

"Where did you get these paintings?" I asked.

"I bought them at art shows, but not all at once. I bought one the first year I taught here; and I try to buy one whenever I find them. I can't always afford them." Mr. Boudreaux picked up a canvas and gazed at it with appreciation. "I keep thinking that one day I'll run into the painter. I've never met him."

I smiled. I felt a peculiar closeness to Mr. Boudreaux, almost a kinship of sorts. I opened my mouth to tell him that I had met that artist, who was not a "him." He turned back to his desk, and the moment passed. It probably wouldn't have made a difference, had I told him at that moment. It's just something I've wondered about, now and then.

The first time I went back to Willow's house was a Saturday afternoon. I had finished my weekend chores, and I had permission to visit a friend. Although I had told my mother about meeting Willow Thornhill, I hadn't told her about the painting that was to be mine. It was a treasure I wanted to, figuratively, hug to my chest in secret, like knowing that I was going to receive a longed-for Christmas gift.

Sophie barked in welcome, an excited little "wo-wo-wo" when I entered the open garage. Even with the splint on her leg, she did a bit of a dance, a sure sign that you can't keep a good dog down. I heard a husky cough from the back of the garage.

"Well, come on back here." I followed her voice and the trail of cigarette smoke. Willow had amassed a stack of stretched canvasses. She extracted a black tack from her mouth and hammered it onto the stretcher she held. "There. That's the lot of them." Willow sounded tired.

She placed her hands in the small of her back and leaned backward. She grimaced momentarily, before she smiled at me. Unbound, her mass of graying hair fell around her face and onto her shoulders, softening the sharp angles of her face.

A black tunic, trimmed in what looked like Indian beading, fell loosely below her hips. A long, tiered skirt, made of the same black fabric, fell just short of her moccasins. I'm sure that I stared. The only things missing to complete the scenario were a wig-wam and a campfire.

"What's the matter? Have you never seen an Indian before, or just not a Cherokee?" Her husky voice sounded gruff, but her black eyes were twinkling.

"Neither," I replied. Willow laughed. She indicated the stack of canvasses. "Grab as many as you can carry," she told me. Together we carried them into her house, where she instructed me just how and where she wanted them stored. Sophie tagged along, taking the three steps one at a time.

The following few weeks were some of the most interesting of my life. After school dismissed for the summer, I had more time to spend at Willow's studio, which was her whole house. She told me many things about her life, including her heritage, which was only partially Cherokee Indian. Her grandmother had been a North Carolina Cherokee; but according to Willow's own description, her itinerate Irish grandfather had been nothing but a drifting scalawag. Apparently, the only decent thing he ever did was to marry Willow's grandmother.

While I watched Willow paint, she told me stories, some of which had been handed down to her through generations of women. After a time, she put a canvas and palette in front of me and told me to paint what I saw in my head. I had to think about that for more than a minute. It seemed that my head was mostly empty.

One day, as I listened to a story about a long trek that took the tribe along the Great River, I started to paint. While she spoke, I could smell the river, could see the currents that carried massive logs and forest debris, and could hear the rush of the mighty waters. I was transported.

"Where is that?" Willow demanded. Startled, I lifted my brush from the canvas.

"I-it's-it's—the river in Redbud Grove." It was. Without consciously deciding to paint it, I had captured the Embarras River at flood stage in early spring. Somehow, I had created shimmering reflections of the fully blossomed redbud trees.

At least a half-mile of the purple-pink trees line the bank of the river, and tourists come to photograph the spectacular scene in Redbud Grove every spring. When the blooms fall, the ground beneath the trees looks as if a thick, pink carpet has been spread there. Tears formed in my eyes, totally unexpected, embarrassing tears. The reflections on the canvas seemed to move through my distorted vision.

"Look." Willow ignored my tears. She scraped her palette knife through white paint. With a few deft strokes, she created ripples on the river in just the right places. Her touch completed the painting, and I knew that I would always remember the moment of fulfillment. Together, we had created a thing of beauty. "Don't do anything else to it," Willow commanded. "You can fuss a painting to death."

By the time school was out, I had a solid A in Mr. Boudreaux's art class. I didn't tell him that the improvement to my paintings that he found so astounding came from Willow's instruction, not from his teaching or from my own ability. He did seem rather pleased with himself.

During that summer, I made at least one visit a week to Willow's house. Karen and I spent a lot of time together, as well as with our group of friends; but I didn't tell her about my new friend. I simply didn't want to share Willow Thornhill with anyone.

Every time Sophie heard my steps crunch upon the driveway, she began to bark a greeting. As her leg healed and her mobility returned, the little Schnauzer danced around my feet. She wasn't satisfied until I picked her up and let her wash my face with her pink tongue. Sophie was a sweet dog, playful and responsive to those she loved.

One day Willow didn't feel like painting. The cough, which was her constant companion, seemed worse. She poured coffee into big mugs and laced one with a heavy dose of cream and a spoonful of sugar, which she gave to me.

"Come in here." Willow led me into the small living room, and through a short hall. She opened a door to a back room. It was the first time I had been anywhere but inside the kitchen. My eyes widened at the panorama before me.

Paintings covered all four walls, leaving no space unadorned. I had never before seen such things, unimaginable things. Unlike her peaceful landscapes, her soaring vistas and life-like animals, these canvases were filled with vivid colors. Close-up portraits of faces twisted in pain hung beside paintings of magnificent, copper-skinned figures in various poses. Some of the pictures were filled with bloody, tortured bodies, and knife wielding figures inflicting unspeakable atrocities on men, women, and children.

Willow coughed, a harsh, rolling sound that seemed to come from deep inside her chest. I turned to her, startled at the magnitude of the spasm. She held up one hand and shook her head. Her long mass of hair flew around her face. Willow held a handkerchief to her mouth for a moment, before she quickly shoved it into the pocket of the long, colorful skirt she wore. A small stream of coffee spilled over the edge of the cup, held in her other hand.

"I'm all right," Willow said. "I do that occasionally—nothing to worry about." She sat in one of the two easy chairs and indicated that I should take the other one. "What do you think?" she asked.

"I don't know." I couldn't stay seated. "Who are these people? Why have you painted such—such..."

"What's the matter, Little White Girl? Can't you take it? Is it too real for you? Doesn't this look like the "cowboy and Indian" movies you see?" Willow's questions taunted me, and her tone held impatience. "Do you like only pretty pictures, with nice little animals and sweet flowers?"

Stricken, I turned to Willow Thornhill. I couldn't stop the tears that spilled from my eyes and trickled slowly down my cheeks. Her face was the same, lined, pleasant face that I had grown to love. No bitterness showed there.

"Sit down, Sissy." Willow's voice became gentle. "I want you to see, really see, who I am, what I am." Her black eyes moved over my face. I sat down beside her, and she reached out to take my hand. She squeezed my fingers before she let go. She lifted the mug and took a long swallow of the black coffee.

"I told you that my grandmother was a Cherokee. Most of the subjects of these paintings are from stories she told me, some of her life, some that were told to her by her mother and grandmother, some that were passed down from others." Willow indicated a particularly vicious scene.

In it, a once handsome Indian strained against the ropes that held him to a tree. His face, contorted in agony, emitted a perpetual, silent scream. Another warrior, obviously from a different tribe, held a bloody knife in one hand. In his other hand, he grasped a length of intestine from the gaping wound in the bound man's abdomen. The picture made me nauseous, and I turned from it.

"Look at it." I shook my head. "Sissy, look at it. I want you to see, to know where and what I come from, and who my people are. Look." I swallowed hard and glanced at the painting.

"The man tied to the tree is my great-great-grandfather," Willow told me. I think that my mouth dropped open. "The other warrior is a Choctaw brave, one of the most cruel and brutal of that particular tribe."

"Why is he doing that to another Indian?" I asked. Willow smiled.

"They were enemies. That was nearly two hundred years ago, Sissy. White men were spreading over the country by then, but they weren't the only enemy of the Indians. Many different tribes were at war with each other, but my great-great-grandfather had something this brave wanted."

"What?" I asked.

"My great-great-grandmother. Look at the background of the painting, Sissy. What do you see?" I forced myself to look past the terrible foreground. Kneeling beside a small body was a woman, and behind her stood a child. The woman's hands, held out in supplication, hovered over a tiny, bloody form on the grass. Her features were not discernable, but a mother's suffering was apparent.

"The baby on the ground was the woman's son. The child standing behind her became my great-grandmother. The Choctaw allowed the girl to live, but he clubbed the baby boy to death." Willow sounded so detached. I shuddered at the unspeakable cruelty. Willow swept her arm in a wide circle, taking in the entire room.

"This is a history of my people, the Cherokee part of me," she said.

A disturbing thought struck me. "Willow, do you have children?" I asked. For a long moment, she didn't answer.

"Somewhere, I have a daughter."

"Was her dad an Indian?" I asked.

"No. He was a married white man who took a thirteen-year-old girl he lusted after, but that wasn't enough. He took her baby, too."

Willow pointed to a painting. I looked at the sad-faced figure of a very young girl. A black shawl covered her head and fell in soft folds across her shoulders. In profile, she stood gazing at the backs of a departing couple. Barely visible, a baby's head peeked over the woman's shoulder.

"Who are they?" I asked. Willow rose and moved toward the painting.

With a finger, she touched the face of the young girl. "This was me, a long, long time ago." Her finger moved across the canvas until it came to rest upon the baby's head.

"I called her 'Summer.' He changed her name to Marie: Marie Delaine." Another coughing spasm shook Willow. She covered her mouth with the handkerchief; and when she took it away, I saw the blood. "You stay here," Willow commanded. "I'll be right back. Study the paintings."

Sophie followed her mistress, whining and disturbed. I did as Willow told me, hoping that she was going to be all right. Half-heartedly, I began a tour of the makeshift gallery. It was an amazing display. Not all of the paintings were filled with horror. Some showed peaceful campfires on starlit nights; children in buckskin, playing with pebbles; women creating beautiful beadwork on chamois garments; a golden-skinned young man embracing his lovely sweetheart.

The room held a spectacular panorama of an era long-gone. Willow had put the lives and souls of her ancestors, as well as her own heartache, on canvas. It would be some time before all the ramifications of what she had told me would become clear to me. Still, I was old enough to understand how and when she had a child, at a time she was barely more than a child, herself.

One of the paintings seemed strangely out of place. The subject was a lodge, built of logs, nestled among tall pine trees. Light spilled from the lower windows, creating rectangular pools of light upon the veranda. What looked like comfortable chairs stood along the wall, seeming to wait for guests. Dusk hovered beyond the trees, just short of full-fledged darkness. What should have seemed lonely had the appearance of a haven. I couldn't make a connection to the other paintings.

When Willow returned to the room, she acted as if nothing unusual had happened. She held a glass of water, and her face was pale; but she made no reference to the frightening coughing spasm. She pointed to the picture of the lodge.

"That's my home," she said. "Rather, it's one of my homes."

"Huh?" Stupid, yes; but my reply was the only single word that could get past the flood of questions I wanted to ask. "I thought that this house is your home."

"This is just a place to paint," Willow told me. "I have several little houses like this, scattered across several states."

"Where's this place?" I pointed to the lodge. Willow touched the porch in the painting.

"This is Eagle's Landing," she said. "It's in the mountains of North Carolina, my favorite, I think. I spend more time there, between painting sessions, than in any other place." She cocked her head and narrowed her eyes at the picture. "My house in Northern California, along the coast, is my second choice; but this hillside in North Carolina was my home when I was a child. Buying it brought a special satisfaction to me."

I was having a hard time comprehending all that Willow had just confided to me. The woman I thought was simply a local painter was much, much more. "Why?" I asked. "I mean, why do you live different lives?"

Willow smiled. "Because I can," she said. "People are intrigued with anonymity. If those who bought and loved my paintings knew that I was just some half-breed Cherokee woman, they would lose interest. There are many descendants of the Cherokee nation scattered from here, throughout the Carolinas and Tennessee; so I don't especially stand out."

"Then people around here really don't know who you are?" I asked.

"No. Only you; and you, of course, will tell no one, Little-White-Girl." Willow smiled at me, looking into my eyes for so long that I felt as if she could read my very soul. I knew that I would not betray the confidence and trust she had bestowed upon me.

Summer days blended into each other so easily that they appeared seamless, day turning into night, night turning into day. I went swimming with Karen and our friends two or three times a week, and we spent at least part of nearly every day together. My first full summer in Dixon was a happy one. The only flaw in it was my concern for Willow Thornhill.

Willow's cough grew worse, but she seemed unconcerned. Sometimes, just breathing was a struggle for her. When I voiced my concern, she waved her hand in dismissal.

"I'm fine," she insisted.

"Willow, I saw the blood on your handkerchief," I said.

"It was nothing, Sissy. I may have a little cold or something. Don't worry about it. I'm just not as young as I used to be."

Every time I went to her house, Willow insisted that I paint, even when she left her brush untouched. Her black eyes burned with intensity while she instructed me. Unsatisfied with mediocrity, she often made me wipe out what I had painted. Willow rarely praised, but her tiny half-smile let me know when she was pleased with my efforts.

School started in September. I felt secure in my friendships, and perhaps just a little cocky on the first day of my sophomore year. In this case, familiarity didn't breed contempt; it bred confidence. I shared some classes with Karen, with Jerry Davis and with Beverly Bodine. New friendships sprouted, as spontaneous as Midwestern mushrooms on an early spring day.

Apparently, new friendships had developed for some of the faculty, as well. The student body was abuzz with the news that Mr. Boudreaux and Miss Seabrook were dating. It was impossible not to notice the new, brisk jauntiness in Mr. Boudreaux's step, and impossible to ignore the even more pronounced bounce in Miss Seabrook's bosom.

"I *told* you he isn't queer!" I whispered to Karen. She stuck out her tongue at me.

Anticipation filled me at the prospect of showing off my newly acquired artistic skills to Mr. Boudreaux. Willow had taught me the secret of creating the mist that the art teacher admired. I couldn't wait to demonstrate my prowess. Second year art class made geometry almost bearable.

As I approached Willow's house one Saturday afternoon in late September, I heard Sophie barking long before I reached the door. I knocked, and Sophie nearly knocked me down when I pushed open the door.

"Sophie, you come back here!" I called. The little dog ignored me. She ran to the boundary fence, where she squatted for the longest time, before she came bounding back to me. She ran inside, barking and looking back to see if I followed, which I did. Sophie led me to the back room, the one that held the dozens of paintings.

"Willow!" I cried. The woman lay on the floor. Her eyes were closed, and I thought that she was dead. The front of her blouse was covered with blood; and a small pool had formed beside her head, where it had rolled from her mouth. Sophie whined pitifully.

I ran to the kitchen and dialed the telephone operator for help. She assured me that she would send an ambulance. I wet a towel and hurried back to Willow. When I touched her face with the cold cloth, she opened her eyes.

"Don't move, Willow. Help is coming," I told her. I wiped the blood from her face, thankful that the bleeding had stopped. Willow made no effort to rise. She watched me, staring directly into my eyes.

"Key," she whispered. I leaned closer.

"What key?" I asked.

"To this room." Willow's whisper was so faint that I brushed my hair back and placed my ear close to her mouth. When I raised my head, she looked toward the door, then back at me. I followed her gaze, and I saw a key hanging beside the doorframe. I pointed to it.

"That key?" Willow closed her black eyes in affirmation.

"Lock...room...after...." I nodded my head.

"I'll lock it, Willow. What should I do with the key?"

"Keep..."

"Okay. I'll keep it for you until you want it back," I promised. Willow smiled faintly and closed her eyes.

Sophie was distraught when the ambulance attendants entered the house. I had to grab and hold her to keep her from nipping at the heels of the men who placed Willow on a stretcher. The men told me where they were taking Willow, and within moments the screaming ambulance raced along the winding streets. There was nothing left for me to do but lock the gallery room, lock the house, and take Sophie home with me. She led easily on the leash.

"Sissy, what are we going to do with a dog?" My mother, hands on her hips, looked as aghast as she sounded. No dog had been in our house since we'd lost our little white "Pup" in Redbud Grove; and we had not replaced the misnamed cat, Juliet. It wasn't for lack of soliciting on Beth's part. She loved animals almost as much as she loved chocolate.

"Mommy, we have to keep her!" Beth declared. I held the leash in my hand, but I had already released Sophie. As if recognizing a kindred spirit, Sophie leapt into Beth's lap, where she wriggled in puppy ecstasy.

"Well, Mom, I couldn't just *leave* her," I said. "She's housebroken and she isn't any trouble. Willow lets her stay inside all the time." My voice and eyes pleaded with my mother to understand.

"Your dad is going to have a *fit*! You *know* he won't let the dog stay inside."

"He will, if you say it's okay," Beth said. "I'll take care of her, all by myself." I looked at my little sister, and I knew that Dad was already defeated. When Beth turned her big, pleading blue eyes upon him, he was a goner.

As it turned out, Beth didn't have to do much begging. Sophie won Dad over with one soulful look and one little, extended paw, something I had not seen her do. By nightfall, Sophie was well established in the Bannister house.

My mother drove me to the hospital that night. I didn't know what to expect, and I wasn't completely certain that I would be allowed to see Willow. The receptionist told us the room number, reminding us that visiting hours would be over at eight o'clock. Our footsteps rang loudly on the checkerboard tiles to the elevator.

Butterflies did a jitterbug inside my stomach as we approached Willow's room. That afternoon, her skin had taken on an ashen gray color; and I was afraid that she would die. I expected to see her in even worse condition, but shock at her appearance left me nearly speechless.

"Well, don't just stand there, Sissy. Come on in." Willow's husky voice sounded close to its usual strength. Her wonderful hair floated around her head. She ran both hands through it and twisted it into a knot. "I don't suppose you have a rubber band or a scarf, do you?"

"I think I do," Mom replied. I should have known that she had all necessary odds and ends within the confines of her bag. Magically, she produced the band and extended it to Willow. The women clasped hands. "I'm so glad to meet you, but I'm sorry that it's here." Willow laughed, a small sound that ended with a cough.

"Thanks to our Sissy, I'm much better," Willow said. She pointed to the tubes running into her arms. "It seems that I'm running a bit low on blood. This is the second pint since they brought me here, and they tell me I'll need another. Do you happen to have a cigarette in that bag?"

"No, I don't smoke. I don't think they'll let you smoke in here," Mom said, "at least as long as you're on oxygen." I had seen the tubes connected to her nose, and I could see that they came from a large tank, beside the bed.

"This is just a nuisance," Willow explained.

"How long do you have to stay here?" I asked.

"The shortest time possible," Willow replied. "As soon as they finish running the plasma, I'm going home." She did. Two days later, Willow Thornhill left the hospital.

Beth cried when I put the leash on Sophie. "Why can't she stay here for a few days? Doesn't Mrs. Thornhill need to rest and get better?"

"You can come with me, Beth. It's not a long way, and you can lead Sophie, if you want." Beth thought about that for a moment, dried her tears, and nodded her head.

"Okay."

Willow met us at the door. I don't know who was the most ecstatic with the reunion, Willow or Sophie. I think that the love between the two made it easier for Beth to return the little dog to her owner.

Weak and a bit wobbly, Willow obviously needed rest. I don't know what prodded me to follow through with the notion that had flitted through my head for several weeks. It just kind of popped out of my mouth.

"Willow, would you like to meet my art teacher, Mr. Boudreaux? He has several of your paintings, and I know that he would like to meet you." Willow's eyes narrowed while she gazed at me through the smoke of her cigarette.

"Is he worth my time?" she asked.

"I think so," I replied. "He loves your paintings." Willow grinned.

"Then he must be all right. Anyone who likes my work must have great taste." Willow laughed at herself. I put my hand on my little sister's shoulder and guided her to the door. "Sissy, wait. Where's the key?" I knew which key she meant. I withdrew the gallery room key from the pocket of my jeans and gave it to her. Beth watched the transaction, and her big blue eyes grew larger. "Thanks, Sissy. Tell your teacher to come by next Saturday; and you come, too." I nodded, hesitated, but then turned to go. "What is it, Sissy?"

"Willow, I know that you're sick. What's wrong with you?"

Willow took a long drag from her cigarette and blew an equally long stream of smoke into the air. She frowned. Her mouth turned down wryly, mockingly.

"They tell me that I have lung cancer," she said. "I've known for a long time, so there's no point making a big fuss about it. They also tell me that I should give up smoking, but it's too late to make a difference. Besides, giving it up now would hurt me worse than the cancer." Willow chuckled, which brought on a slight cough.

"Don't worry about it, Little-White-Girl. I still have some good days left. I think that some of the old tribes had the right idea about dealing with illness and old age. When the old people got sick and couldn't care for themselves, they just disappeared into the wilderness and let nature take its course."

On the way home, Beth was very quiet for a long time. I suppose that neither of us felt like talking. We had started up our driveway before she spoke.

"Why did Mrs. Thornhill call you 'Little-White-Girl'?" I shrugged.

"I don't know, Beth...maybe because she's part Cherokee Indian. She called me that one day, and she's done it ever since. I think it's kind of like a nickname or something."

"Oh," Beth said. "I guess it means she likes you." My little sister was sometimes wise beyond her years. "What about the key?" She was also very persistent.

"I was keeping it for her until she got out of the hospital." Evasion and truth can be two sides of the same coin. I suspect that the same theory could be applied for evasion and deception.

The following Monday, I waited until everyone else had left the classroom before I approached Mr. Boudreaux. His was my last morning class, so I had plenty of time to speak to him during the lunch hour.

"Yes, Sissy?" He looked up from his desk when I paused in front of it.

"Mr. Boudreaux, do you know the name of the artist who did your paintings?"

"No, I don't. I'm not sure why, but it seems to be some kind of mystery in the community. I know that he's a resident and that his initials are W.T. Other than that...." He shrugged. I nearly trembled with what I had to tell him.

"Would you like to meet the artist?"

"Of course, I would. I just don't know how to go about it."

"I can introduce you," I told him. That got his attention.

"You can what?"

"I can introduce you to the artist, Willow Thornhill. It's a woman, not a man." Mr. Boudreaux laughed.

"Sissy, I think you're pulling my leg."

"No, really, Mr. Boudreaux, Willow told me to ask you to come to her house next Saturday afternoon." Mr. Boudreaux leaned back in his chair, formed a pyramid with his long fingers and stared at me. I could see the speculation in his dark eyes. He thought that I couldn't be serious, but the possibility that I was telling him the truth intrigued him.

"How did you meet this lady?"

Briefly, I told him about the previous spring day when I had discovered the injured Sophie and about the friendship that resulted from that moment. I told him how Willow had taught me and why my work had improved so much. When I described the way Willow painted the misty landscapes, Mr. Boudreaux was convinced. He agreed to meet me at Willow's house the next Saturday afternoon.

Watching the relationship unfold between Willow Thornhill and Greg Boudreaux was similar to witnessing the laying on of color across a canvas. Much as charcoal sketches form the structure of a painting, their first meeting established the outline of a beautiful work of art. All I had to do was stand back and watch.

"How long have you been painting?" Greg asked.

"All my life," Willow replied. "When I was a child, my grandmother taught me how to make paint from berries and plants and tree bark, just like her mother had taught her. We painted on pieces of wood, animal hides, even rocks. It wasn't a far leap to oils, but finding money to buy them was a long journey."

Amazed at the loquacious Willow, I lapped up every word. She had talked freely to me, especially since the first day I saw her hidden paintings; but she had never spoken with such fervor and detail. It was a beautiful thing to behold. She even forgot to smoke the smoldering cigarette that was permanently fixed between her fingers.

Willow's strength seemed to increase measurably every time she met with Mr. Boudreaux. Although I wasn't present every weekend, I felt honored to be allowed into the inner sanctum of their flowering friendship. Intrigued as I was with them, I still thrived on football games, friends and Saturday night movies.

The weather grew colder as November settled upon the mountains. Willow's cough became more pronounced, and her complexion acquired a translucence that seemed out of place on her dark skin. When I asked about her health, Willow just waved her hand, as though brushing aside a pesky gnat.

"I'm as all right as I'm going to be, Little-White-Girl. Don't fret." All I could do was follow her wishes.

Willow had told Mr. Boudreaux many stories about her ancestors, but I hadn't heard her speak to him about her personal life. When she began to ask questions concerning his life, my teacher seemed eager to share his history. I learned more about him than I could have imagined. As he spoke of his parents, his sister and his home, I began to see him as a person, not just a teacher.

"My father claims to be a New Orleans Creole, but I suspect that there's more Cajun in his background than he wants to admit," Mr.

Boudreaux laughed. "Personally, I enjoyed playing with my Cajun friends more than anyone else, when given the opportunity. My mother wasn't as strict about that as my father was. She's always been more accepting and less prejudiced."

"Is your mother a native of Louisiana?"

"No. She's originally from North Carolina. Her parents sent her to Tulane University, and that's where she and my father met. Mother was one of the few women to attend college back then. My grandfather insisted that she go, but I'm not sure that she really wanted it."

"That seems strange," Willow mused. "I think that very few men encouraged their daughters to go away to school, especially that many years ago." Mr. Boudreaux laughed.

"My grandfather was an unusual man," he said.

"Did your grandparents have other children?"

"No, they didn't. Evidently my mother was the delight of his life, but I always had the feeling that my grandmother wasn't quite so indulgent. My paternal grandmother was very loving, but Grandmother Delaine was distant, even cold, at times. My sister, Laura, was named for her; but that didn't seem to please my grandmother at all."

Willow became very still. She leaned against the back of her kitchen chair. "Sissy, bring me a glass of water," she commanded. I hurried to do her bidding. Willow cleared her throat, drank long from the glass, cleared her throat again. "What is your grandfather's name?" she asked.

"Eduard Delaine," Mr. Boudreaux replied. "He came from a family of big plantation owners. I'm not proud of the heritage, but I understand that his father owned slaves in North Carolina, before the War Between the States."

"Is your grandfather still living?"

"No. He died several years ago, and my grandmother died a short time after he did."

"Your mother's name?" Willow's voice was so husky that I was afraid she might have another coughing spasm.

"Marie. Marie Delaine Boudreaux."

"Willow...." I said.

"Sissy, there are some envelopes on the counter that should be mailed. Please drop them into the box on the corner on your way home."

"But...." I protested.

"Go now, please, Little-White-Girl." There was no affection in the title. The look Willow Thornhill directed at me held nothing but implacable black eyes. I patted Sophie's head and moved toward the kitchen door.

"'Bye, Mr. Boudreaux," I mumbled.

"I'll see you Monday, Sissy." He looked bewildered.

All the way home, I struggled with a tangle of emotions. I couldn't believe what I had just witnessed. The drama was better than a story, a book, even a *Technicolor movie*! I didn't want to be left out of the climax of the whole thing! Wow! How often is anyone privileged to be part of such an unfolding? Certainly not many fifteen-year-old girls! I couldn't wait until Monday to find out what Willow had told my teacher. I didn't see how Mr. Boudreaux could be anything but Willow Thornhill's grandson. It was just too good to be true!

"What's the matter with you, Sissy? You're as fidgety as a first-grader," Karen told me. She was right. We sat at one of the long tables in the cafeteria, where many students gathered before school on cold days. I was hoping to catch a glimpse of Mr. Boudreaux; but it was nearly time for the first bell, and he was not in sight.

"Nothing's wrong," I replied. "I guess I'm nervous about mid-terms." Well, I might have been, a little. It was all I could do to get through Spanish II and European History classes that morning, both of which required concentration. When the history session was over, my feet fairly flew along the corridors to Mr. Boudreaux's classroom.

He looked up and smiled at me. I smiled back, intently studying his face, looking for any sign that he had learned of his ancestry. There was nothing. He opened class as usual. Deflated, I sat down. At the end of the class, I approached his desk.

"Mr. Boudreaux, was Willow feeling okay when you left her Saturday?"

"She seemed to be a little tired, but I think she was all right," he replied. "I didn't stay much longer than you did. Is there someone to look after her, to run errands for her and see that she gets groceries?"

I hadn't thought about that. "I'll find out," I told him.

"Mom, can we drive by Willow Thornhill's house on the way home?" That was my greeting to my mother when she picked me up at school that afternoon. A light dusting of snow had fallen during the day, not enough to make the streets slick, but a portent of things to come. The thought of Willow without food or medicine disturbed me, and I voiced my fears to my mom.

"Sure, we can," she said. "I'd better just drop you off there, and pick you up after I get Bill and Beth." I always loved my mom, but sometimes I really liked her.

I knocked on the back door of Willow's little house and walked in, just like I always did. I knelt to welcome Sophie, who greeted me with wet puppy kisses and Schnauzer antics, barking and laughing in her own way. When I stood up, I stared in dismay at the cardboard crates and packages that lined the kitchen walls.

"Willow?" I called. A muffled replay came from the interior of the house. I followed the sound and found Willow in the gallery room, surrounded by more large packages. Many of the paintings had been removed from the walls. It became obvious to me that they were encased in the heavy crating. "Willow, what are you doing?"

"Well, Little-White-Girl, what does it look like I'm doing?" Willow's voice was strained and sounded weak, even breathless. "I'm packing up these canvasses."

"Why?" I asked. Willow sat upon the straight-backed chair in the center of the room.

"It's time to go back to California," she told me. "It's getting cold here, and I want to be near the ocean before the heavy snow falls." She pointed to an open crate. "Hold the top of this down while I tape it." I did as she told me, fear making my fingers fumble.

"When are you leaving?" I asked, and it was impossible to stop the tears in my eyes from spilling onto my face. I blinked really hard.

"Within a few days," she replied. She kept taping.

"Willow, did you tell Mr. Boudreaux....?"

"Sissy, I'm sure that you have some romantic notion about a big family reunion or some such nonsense; but it's not going to happen. It's too late." I couldn't believe what she was saying. "It's not fair to your teacher, to Greg." When she said his name, there was a quiver in her voice.

"But, Willow, he's your grandson, your daughter's son! He's *Summer's* child! He thinks you're wonderful, the most wonderful painter in the world! He talks about your work in the classroom all the time!"

"I'm sure that's true, Little-White-Girl; but how wonderful do you think he'd feel to discover that his grandmother is a quarter Cherokee, that his mother...?" Willow stopped.

"Oh, Willow! You could meet your daughter! Wouldn't that be wonderful?"

"Stop!" I had never before heard such anguish in a human voice. "Stop." I think that the whisper was worse. I dropped to my knees beside Willow's chair. Sobs shook her wasted frame, but only for a moment.

"Willow, I'm sorry. I didn't mean to make you cry," I apologized through my own tears.

"Don't be foolish, Little-White-Girl," Willow said. Magically, she was in complete control again. "You don't have the power to make me cry. It was simply a moment of weakness. It won't happen again." She sighed. "I'm just very tired."

I recognized the sound of our car's horn, and I knew that my mother had come for me. I ran through the house and stuck my head out the back door. "I'll be right out, Mom! I've got to get my coat." I ran back to Willow, who was standing next to the crated painting.

"When are you going to leave?" I demanded. "You won't go before I can see you again, will you?"

Willow Thornhill smiled at me. The fine bone structure of her face was apparent beneath her dark skin, and an other-worldly something glowed in her black, black eyes. I knew that she loved me.

"Sissy, Sissy," she whispered. "Don't worry so. You'll see me again, perhaps in the colors of a sunrise, or in the star-lit blackness of a winter night. Now you go on home with your mother. I'm fine." Willow raised her arms, pulled me to her, and hugged me, gently, as if I were the fragile one. When my arms went around her, I could feel her bones beneath her clothing. I was afraid to hug her tightly, afraid that she would break. She whispered in my ear. I couldn't understand the Cherokee words, but I knew that they meant something special.

My mother honked the horn again. I turned at the door of the gallery room, turned for one more look at my friend. Sophie sat at Willow's feet. She looked from me to the face of her mistress, but made no effort to come to me. I raised my hand in a brief wave.

"'Bye, Willow."

"Good-bye, Little-White-Girl."

I had no opportunity to go by Willow's house until the following Saturday. I had tried to call, but the operator had stated that the phone had been disconnected. I surmised that Willow was making preparations to leave, as she had told me she would.

There was no sound of Sophie when I opened the back door. The kitchen counter was cleared of supplies, and the table was bare. I knew before I entered the room that Willow was gone. The furniture was still in place. The only things missing were the painting supplies, Sophie, and the essence of Willow.

I walked through all the rooms of the little house, saving the gallery for last. I knew that it would be empty; and it was, except for the two chairs in the middle of the room. I picked up the envelope that lay on one chair, knowing that it was for me before I saw my name. I opened it and read the brief message:

Sissy,

In the bedroom closet, you will find a painting. It's yours to do with as you choose: sell it or keep it, as you wish. I won't be returning to Dixon or to Eagle's Landing. I have deeded that property to Gregory Boudreaux. All the other paintings that were in this room have been delivered to his home here in Dixon. I asked you once if he were worthy of my time, and you told me that he was. I believed you, and you were right. Now I'm counting on you to prove that you are worthy of my trust. I believe that you are.

Some of the old ways are still the best ways, Little-White-Girl. There is no Willow Thornhill, only the initials: w-t. I took the name because I liked it. In other galleries throughout the world, there are paintings with other initials: b-w and k-m and s-d, for example. You don't need to know the names they supposedly represented, and you couldn't pronounce my real name. Don't even think of trying to discover who I am. You can't do it. Only a handful of people know, and they don't dare tell anyone, for many reasons.

Knowing you has been a pleasure. You have a talent, not a great one, but adequate; and painting should bring you a lot of satisfaction. Through you, I've learned that Summer has a good life, and that Summer's child is a fine man, who shares my love of painting.

The world is waiting for you.

Make good choices, Little White-Girl.

Willow

I folded the note and returned it to the envelope. I knew that I would never see Willow Thornhill, or whatever her real name was, again. Like her people in the old days, Willow had decided to disappear into the wilderness.

In a near dream-like state, I searched for the bedroom closet and opened the door. As promised, a crated canvas stood against the wall. I lifted the package and placed it upon the bed, which was still covered by a faded hand-made quilt. Carefully, I opened the crate and pulled out the painting.

It wasn't what I expected to see. I smiled at the peaceful image of Eagle's Landing, relieved that Willow hadn't left one of the sad, terrifying paintings of her heritage. A one-line note was tucked inside the frame:

For the days when you need a restful retreat.

Mr. Boudreaux finished the school term, but he resigned at the end of the year. Evidently, Miss Seabrook wasn't the love of his life. When Mr. Boudreaux moved to North Carolina, Miss Seabrook wasn't with him. She stayed at Dixon High as the home economics teacher. Mr. Boudreaux's mysterious inheritance, windfall, or whatever people chose to call it, remained just that: a mystery.

Several times, Mr. Boudreaux asked me why Willow Thornhill had all those wonderful paintings delivered to him and then just disappeared. I always shrugged my shoulders. I knew why Willow had done it; but I didn't understand it.

The painting of Eagle's Landing was not the only legacy I received from Willow. About six months after Willow left Dixon, we received a notice that a package would be delivered to our house at a specific time. Receipt of the package would require a signature.

The time of delivery was four o'clock on an early May afternoon, just about the time my sister, brother and I would be coming home from school. Since I had turned sixteen in February, we reasoned that I could surely sign for a package. As it turned out, all three of us were at the house when the package arrived; but none of us was prepared for the contents.

"Sophie! It's Sophie!" Beth squealed. An excited bark from the slated wood crate confirmed my sister's words.

"I think she knows you," the deliveryman laughed. He carried the crate to the backyard, where he opened it and freed the little Schnauzer. She ran to Beth, then Bill, then me. Sophie repeated the cycle several times between short periods of nervous squatting. Tears ran down Beth's happy face. It was a bit like watching a rainbow beyond raindrops.

Dad made the obligatory grumbles about having a housedog, but it didn't take him long to put up a fence around the back yard. During the next few years, he spent many evenings in front of the television, watching his baseball games, with Sophie curled upon his lap. The little lady captured all our hearts, and she seemed happy.

However, there were times that Sophie paced the house, nosing and looking into every corner. From there, she whined at the back door.

When we let her out, she walked around the confines of the fence, softly whining occasionally. After a while, she asked to come back inside.

I don't know how long it takes dogs to forget former owners, but I've formed an opinion about Sophie's memory. I believe that she never forgot Willow. Although she grew to love us, and she had many good, happy years with us, I'm convinced that she grieved for the woman who loved her first.

Mr. Boudreaux turned Eagle's Landing into one of the finest art galleries in the country. The paintings that Willow had kept secret for so many years drew collectors and admirers from around the world. American Indian artists were prominently featured in the gallery, with a heavy leaning toward the Cherokee of North Carolina.

With no knowledge of his heritage, Gregory Boudreaux honored his mother and his lineage in a way that I'm certain Willow would have found pleasing. Perhaps she lived long enough to be aware of it. I hope so.

It was years before I understood Willow's reasons, but I finally did comprehend. Undeclared love can be the strongest, most unselfish of emotions, especially when declaration could cause pain to the one so loved. Perhaps, sometimes, old ways *can* be the best ways...

I hope they were for Willow.

#

Feuds

"Sissy, don't look now; but I think you have an admirer...*I said don't look!*"

"Don't look where?" I demanded. Karen and I shared a concrete bench beneath an oak tree on campus. It was early May of our sophomore year. Several dogwood trees grew on the campus, and the sweet aroma of lingering blossoms teased us with their fragrance. Birdsong filled the air, and bees buzzed around the blooms.

"He's leaning against a tree over there." Karen nodded her head slightly, indicating an area behind and to the right of me.

"Who is it?" I asked. Karen chuckled.

"Jack McCoy. Do you know him?" I shook my head.

"I've seen him around, but not close-up. It would be hard to miss the jock of the school, with all those girls around him."

"Yeah, I suppose."

"Is he as cute close-up as he is from a distance?" I asked.

"Drop-dead-gorgeous."

"And he's looking at *me*?" *Well, now. This sounded interesting.* "What's he doing?"

"Nothing. He just walked away with Dick Powers." Karen sounded disappointed.

"Are you sure he wasn't looking at you?" I asked. Karen twisted her mouth.

"I'm sure. I've been drooling over him since I was in the sixth grade and he was in the eighth. He's always looking for a new girl. I guess he just discovered *you*."

"Who is he?" I asked. "I know he's Jack McCoy, but where does he live and what's he like? What kind of person is he?"

Karen leaned against the tree and pulled her feet onto the bench. She wrapped her arms around her knees.

"I've heard that he's a distant relative of the feuding McCoys," she said.

After studying <u>Romeo and Juliet</u> in Miss Porter's English Literature class, I had remembered a movie I had seen when I was ten or eleven years old. The theme of the Shakespeare play and the movie, Rosanna McCoy, were the same. It was the story of the feud between the Hatfields and the McCoys, two mountain families who had hated each other for years. They spent most of the on-screen time killing each other. In spite of the bloodshed, I had thought it was one of the most romantic movies I had ever seen. A girl from one family fell in love with a boy from the other, and there was lots of kissing involved. I had liked the kissing parts.

"Oh, yeah, the McCoy movie was shown here, too. There was some controversy—even made the local newspapers. It's a true story. The Hatfields lived on this side of the river, and most of the McCoys lived across the river, in Kentucky."

"You mean all that feuding stuff is true? It really happened?" I demanded.

"Cross my heart."

"Are they still doing it? I mean, killing each other?"

"No, I don't think so. I've heard that the two families have some kind of reunion now and then. I've also heard that some of the younger ones have tried to get the feud started again, but nothing much comes of it." Karen looked at me for a moment, and that speculative glint was in her eyes again. "Can you keep a secret? I mean, *really keep it*?"

"Sure. I guess." I shrugged.

"I've heard that some of the Hatfields have a still up in the mountains." Karen's voice was little more than a whisper.

"What's a 'still'?" I asked. Karen grimaced.

"I forgot," she said, "you being a Yankee and all." She grinned. "Okay, okay, you're just a Midwesterner. Anyway, a still is where they make moonshine whiskey. My dad buys moonshine from some of the hill people, but I'm not supposed to know about it. I heard him tell one of his friends that it's better stuff than he can buy at the liquor store."

I didn't know what to say. I knew that some of my uncles drank whiskey. Before my favorite uncle had been converted and become a Baptist preacher, he had been intoxicated a lot, probably as much or more than he had been sober. My dad still had an occasional beer with

Wish I May, Wish I Might...

his new buddies after work, just as he had done back in Redbud Grove; but he had never been a whiskey drinker.

"What about Jack McCoy?" I asked. "You said you thought that he was related to the feuding McCoys?"

"I'm not sure, Sissy. There's talk that they're from the same people, but Jack doesn't live way back in the hills."

"Where does he live?" I pushed.

"On Razorback Ridge, where those great big houses are, the ones that look down on Dixon," she said. "Jack's dad owns a concrete mixing plant outside of town, closer to the river. Two of Jack's uncles are partners with Mr. McCoy; and they all live high on the same ridge."

"Oh, you mean those *mansions*, where one of the houses has a round turret-like thing?"

Karen nodded. "That's where Jack lives. His daddy started building that house just before World War II started. My dad said that they had to stop working on it during the war, because of a shortage of building materials. I *love* that house! I've always called it 'the castle.' I wish I could see the inside of it."

Time would tell whether or not Jack McCoy could be interested in me, a lowly sophomore; but if that proved to be true, I might gain admittance to the "castle." I hadn't seen him up close and personal yet, so I didn't know if I would agree with Karen's description of Jack as dropdead gorgeous. Speculation about his house wasn't even plausible.

As it turned out, I had to agree with Karen. Jackson "Jack" McCoy was the most incredibly handsome boy I had seen in all my sixteen years. Victor Delacourt's dark, brooding good looks were challenged by Jack's, even smitten as I had been with Victor.

I first saw Jack, close-up, on the school baseball diamond during one of Dixon High's spring practice sessions. He was at bat, just as Karen and I climbed into the bleachers behind the home plate screen. We joined the other students who stayed after school to watch the first practices. If a tall, muscular body were a part of the criteria for gorgeous, the boy certainly qualified. Jack was tall, but not lanky, like many teenage boys. He looked solid and coordinated.

Cra-a-a-a-ck!

Jack didn't have to run. The ball soared into the air and out of the field. Jack trotted around the bases, his long legs moving gracefully along the white base line. He stepped on home plate and looked at us. He smiled, took off his cap and made a small bow before he picked up his bat.

I'm reasonably certain that my mouth dropped open in awe at the sight of his handsome face. Jack McCoy's hair was platinum-streaked blond, and he was one of the few boys in the school who didn't have a crew cut. His hair was dazzling in the sunlight. Across the fifteen or twenty feet that separated us, I could see his incredible, light brown eyes, which sparkled dangerously against the golden, tanned skin of his face. It was rare to see such eyes on someone with blond hair.

All his features fit together just right—nothing too big, or too small, or too *anything*! How could one boy be so perfect? He was even more handsome than Jeff Franklin, the auburn-haired young man who had betrayed the Amish girl, Rebecca, back in Redbud Grove.

I decided that there had to be something wrong with Jack. Maybe he kicked small animals. Maybe he was disrespectful to his mother. Maybe he had bad breath.

"Didn't I tell you?" Karen demanded. "Jack is drop-dead gorgeous, just like I said." I nodded.

"Yeah, he's kinda cute."

Karen stared at me, and snorted.

"Cute? You think he's *cute*? Come on, Sissy. You can't tell me there was anyone back in your Redbud Grove that was as good-looking as that boy right there!" Karen gestured toward Jack, who was on his way to the dugout.

"We-e-l-l-l," I hedged, "well, maybe not quite; but there were some great-looking guys." I watched Jack join his teammates on the bench. "How come he dates so many girls? Did they all dump him, or did he do the dumping?"

"Sarah Young told me that they went out twice, she let him kiss her, and he never called or asked her out again."

"What about the other girls? How many has he dated?" I asked.

"Oh, I don't know." Karen sounded exasperated. "He's probably dated a dozen girls this last year. Now he's started on the sophomore and junior girls. I guess he's lost interest in the seniors, at least the ones he dated. I don't think any girl he asked ever turned him down."

"Hm-m-m, maybe that's the problem," I mused. "Maybe they've all been too easy to get." I made up my mind that, should Jack McCoy ever ask me out, I would tell him "no," at least the first few times. Of course, that was a moot point, because he probably wouldn't ask me.

My mother had told me that I could single date after I turned sixteen, which I had the past February. Unfortunately, no one had asked me since my birthday. Karen and I and our group of friends socialized as a whole, both boys and girls. We had a great time together. I didn't look forward to the day when couples would pair off and break up our happy little bunch.

"Oh, look, Sissy! Coach Harrison is throwing another fit! Look at that!" Karen pointed toward the dugout, where the coach was, indeed, unleashing his wrath upon an unfortunate boy. Coach Bob Harrison, a short, stocky, middle-aged ex-jock, coached baseball every spring; but his love was football. Coaching baseball was just something he had to do to fulfill his contract. He also taught Drivers Training during second semester, when no team sports demanded his presence. Basketball wasn't in his job description.

I detested the man. My secret name for him was Bubba, simply because it fit him. Dad had insisted that I take the driver training course in order to get my license, and I could hardly wait to walk out of Coach Bubba's classroom for the last time.

The coach's tirade finally ended, and he walked away from the dugout. Had he witnessed the gesture directed his way from the boy he had just verbally abused, Coach Bubba would probably have done bodily harm to him. Some of the boy's teammates slapped his back in agreement with the gesture.

"Did you see that?" Karen asked. She was delighted.

"Yes, I saw it. It's a good thing the coach didn't. Are you ready to go? I have a lot of homework, and I need to go home. Do you want to come down to my house and study?"

"Yeah, sure; but aren't you going to wait and see if Jack comes back?"

"No, I'm not," I answered. "I'm not waiting around for *any* boy! Let's go." I skipped down the bleachers. Karen followed, grumbling all the way.

The following Friday evening, Jack McCoy called my house. Beth answered the phone. "Sissy, it's for you! It's a boy!" she yelled.

Needless to say, she hadn't covered the mouthpiece. I sprang from my chair at the kitchen table, where we were still having supper, and lurched into the living room. The only phone in our house rested upon a small end table beside the sofa. I grabbed the receiver from Beth, hoping to forestall further embarrassing audible comment from her. I covered the mouthpiece with my hand.

"For goodness' sake, Beth! Did you have to yell?" I whispered angrily. My little sister shrugged, grinned broadly, and ran back to the kitchen. I counted to ten. "Hello," I said, sending dulcet tones across the telephone wires.

"Hi, Sissy. This is Jack McCoy." I blinked—more than once. My first thought was that Jerry Davis was trying to play a trick on me. "Hello, Sissy? Are you there?" No, it wasn't Jerry's voice. My second thought was that Karen Courtney was going to have a fit when I told her about the call.

"Yes, uh, I'm here." How could I talk to someone who had never spoken to me?

"Oh, well, I know we don't really know each other; but I've seen you around school. You were at baseball practice with Karen the other day." Pause.

"Yes." I was really on a roll. I had said a total of half a dozen words already—all equally intelligent.

"Would you like to go to a show tomorrow night? With me?" Confidence oozed from Jack McCoy's words, like honey squeezed from the comb. I counted to five this time.

"I'm sorry, Jack. I already have plans." Inwardly, I groaned. I must be crazy! I had turned sixteen in February, and here it was early May; and I had not had a real date yet! And Jackson McCoy had just asked me to go to the movie with him! *Hard to get! Be hard to get!* I told myself. There was utter silence on the other end of the phone.

"Oh." Jack sounded as if he couldn't believe his ears. "Is it something you can get out of?" he asked. I grinned, hoping that he couldn't hear the smile in my voice.

"No, I'm sorry, it isn't." I was so proud of myself.

"Well, how about next Friday night?" he pressed. I nearly jumped up and down.

"I can't," I answered. "My brother's junior high graduation is that night." The regret in my voice was real.

"Oh, yeah, that's right. I have a cousin graduating that night, too. Maybe I'll see you there."

"Sure," I replied.

"Well, anyway, I'll see you at school."

"Okay."

"Bye, Sissy."

"Bye." I hung up the phone and squealed all the way into the kitchen. Mom and Dad stared at me as if I had lost my mind. I danced around the table once before I sat down to dessert.

"Anybody we know?" Dad asked. His voice had that wry, just-short-of-sarcastic tone he loved to use.

"Jack McCoy! Mom, Jack McCoy asked me to go to the show with him tomorrow night, and I turned him down! I turned Jackson McCoy down!"

"Are we supposed to understand why?" Mom asked.

"Because I'm going out with the gang! Isn't that great?"

"What'd I miss?" Dad asked Mom, who shrugged her shoulders. "Is that the boy who's pitching all those no-hitter games?" I should have guessed that Dad would know about the winning high school baseball team.

After Dad had come home from the war in Europe, he had listened to ball games on the radio every night. The sports caster voices of Harry Carrey and later, Jack Buck, on KMOX, St. Louis, had provided my lullabies, play-by-play. Now they continued to be our houseguests, via television, because Dad wouldn't miss a televised or radio broadcast of a Cardinal baseball game. He often turned down the volume on the television and listened to the radio announcers.

"Yes, Jack's the pitcher for the Dixon Wildcats."

"I heard someone at the foundry say that scouts came to watch him play last year, when he was just a junior. Maybe I'll go to some of his games. Why don't you get me a schedule, Sissy?"

I rolled my eyes in exasperation.

"Sure, Dad."

"How come you don't want to go out with him? Not that I'm in a hurry for you to be running around with older boys." Dad grinned. "A baseball player must be a nice boy."

"Oh, really?" Mom purred. "*You* played baseball when you were a teenager, Will." They exchanged a look. Dad's face turned a bit pink, and he cleared his throat.

"Would you kids like to go to the drive-in tonight?" he asked.

Neat save, Dad, I thought. *Subtle, too.*

"Can we go see that scary one?" Beth asked.

"You'll have nightmares again," Mom warned her.

"No, I won't! Anyway, if I do, I'll just get in bed with Sissy."

"Joey asked me to go to the skating rink," Bill said. At fourteen, my brother's voice had changed; and for the first time in our lives, he was a fraction taller than I. It was a little disconcerting.

"I'll pass," I said. "Karen's coming down, and we're going to study for semesters."

"How come?" Mom asked. "You have several days before finals."

87

"Yeah, but she needs help with English; and I need her help in algebra. We'll probably go to the drive-in tomorrow night, anyway." We did.

One car filled with boys and the other with girls parked in the back row of the Dixon drive-in theater. The first feature, "The Creature From the Black Lagoon", had all of us screaming with laughter. The second one, "Invasion of the Body Snatchers," was a bit scary, even for me. Jerry and Jimmy, who had gone to the concession stand for popcorn, slipped silently back to the car that held us five girls. Simultaneously, the boys reached inside the car, one on either side, yelled and grabbed the nearest girl. They screamed, which scared the rest of us; and we all screamed in tandem.

"Sh-h-h-h-h-h!" Hisses came from cars on both sides and in front of us. Someone must have complained about the noise, because it wasn't long before a security person, armed with a long flashlight, asked us, none too politely, to vacate the premises. It was years before I learned how the movie ended.

On Monday morning I took the necessary books from my locker and slammed the door. In a hurry, as usual, I quickly turned and ran right into the solid body of Jack McCoy. "Well, hello," he said. He carried no books, so he steadied me with both hands. Even as flustered as I was, I recognized caresses on my shoulders. I wondered who had told him where to find me.

He flashed a brilliant smile, and I realized that anyone who knew him would have told him anything he wanted to know. At eighteen, Jack stood at least eight inches taller than I, and was probably still growing. I considered myself tall at five-feet-six, but looking up at him made me feel much shorter, even downright petite.

"Hi," I replied.

"I'm Jack," he said.

"I know. I'm Sissy."

"I know." We both laughed. Surprisingly, it was the easiest thing in the world to be talking to Jack McCoy.

"Would you like to go to Dooby's with me for a Coke after school?" he asked.

"Don't you have ball practice?"

"No, we have a home game at seven. I won't have to report in at the field until six-thirty. Meet me out front after school. I have my own car."

"Okay." I agreed. So much for being hard to get. I couldn't wait to tell Karen that I wouldn't be walking home with her that afternoon.

Somehow, I got through my classes all day without fidgeting; but as soon as the last bell rang, I ran to the restroom. I put on fresh lipstick and recombed my long ponytail, turning and twisting before the inadequate mirror. I wanted to look my best.

The last school bus drove away from the curb as I left the building. Several parent-driven cars pulled in front of the school, waiting to pick up sons and daughters. I spoke to several classmates while I waited, hoping that I didn't look as nervous as I felt. I didn't know what kind of car Jack drove.

The insistent honking of a car's horn drew my attention. Parked far down the line of waiting vehicles was a long, yellow convertible; and sitting behind the wheel was Jack McCoy. My heart beat with excitement as I walked, with what I hoped was nonchalance, to the car. Jack reached across the seat and pushed the door open for me. I slid onto the leather upholstery, feeling the strangest urge to pinch myself, just to be certain I wasn't dreaming.

At Dooby's, many of Jack's friends, all seniors, gathered around the car. I knew most of them only by name. Polite to the core, Jack introduced me. The girls were less than friendly, but I overlooked their covert hostility. They stood beside the convertible, while *I* sat upon a cool leather seat next to Jack McCoy. I could afford to be generous.

It was one of the best half-hours I had ever known, one of those rare, golden pieces of time when nothing could be more perfect. An aura of timelessness surrounded us; and the ordinary sounds of laughter, of ice clinking in the Coke glasses, even the loud throb of Buddy Holley's voice on the radio, singing "...all my hugs and all my kissin, you don't know what you've been a-missin, oh boy....", seemed encased in crystal, shimmering with light.

It was at that moment that I began to fall in love with Jack McCoy, at least what I thought was love. Being the object of envy could have been a factor. Sitting beside the most desirable boy in school was a powerful aphrodisiac. He had it all: movie star looks, a killer car and girls at his disposal. I couldn't believe that Jack had developed an interest in me, but there I sat, right beside him, at his invitation.

Although we hadn't actually dated, Jack began to call me nearly every night after supper. Due to the location of the phone in our house, having a private conversation with him was difficult. Four pairs of ears frequently tuned, with equal attention, to the television and my dialogue. After ten or fifteen minutes, Dad could be depended upon to utter the same words.

"Time to hang up, Sissy. Someone else may be trying to call."

Jack's persistence was amazing, considering that he knew I wasn't allowed to date, even on the weekends, until finals were over. While his grades were as beautiful as his face, apparently without much effort, I had to work for my A average. The strong muscles in my left arm were the direct result of carrying a heavy stack of books home from school every night.

Baseball practice could have become an after-school Mecca for me, but the music department's spring concert practices were held at the same time. Mrs. Grimes felt that the musical arts department was just as important as the sports events. Coach Harrison disagreed. Jack wasn't part of the choral group, but three of the baseball team members were, which led to a mighty battle of wills between the two department heads.

"Bunch a'sissies," Coach muttered, when the three boys missed a ball practice. "If you're gonna' play ball, then *play ball*! Leave that high-brow stuff for the pansies!" I knew this, only because the boys told me.

In the late afternoon of the concert's final practice, the rivalry between Mrs. Grimes and Coach Harrison escalated into outright war. The chorus was halfway into a medley of beautiful show tunes, "A Tribute to Romberg," when the auditorium door flew open. The coach, deadly purpose on his face, came striding militantly down the center aisle.

"Davis, Carter, and Mitchell!" he yelled. "Report to the ball diamond, *now*!"

Mrs. Grimes lowered her arms, and the accompanist stopped playing. "Stay precisely where you are, Boys." Mrs. Grimes didn't raise her voice. She turned slowly and faced the belligerent, stocky coach, looking down upon him from her elevated position on the stage. Coach Harrison stood with his legs planted slightly apart, his fists on his hips, and a sneer on his face.

"May I help you, Mr. Harrison?"

"Yes, Ma'am, you can! Send them three boys on down here. I need 'em at the ball field. We have a big game here tomorrow night with South Charleston, and they're supposed to be at practice." Coach impatiently looked at his watch.

"I'm sorry, Mr. Harrison. I need *those* three boys at this final practice for the spring concert. They're part of an ensemble, and their presence is vital." I don't think the coach caught Mrs. Grimes' subtle correction of his grammar.

"Ma'am, you can get other little boys to sing your pretty songs; but I want Jerry Davis, Wes Carter, and Donnie Mitchell down here! RIGHT NOW!" Coach pointed to the floor in front of his feet.

I caught Jerry's eye. His lips twitched, but he couldn't hide the half-grin. His eyes twinkled with a devilish sparkle that showed how much he enjoyed being a third of the tug-of-war object between the two teachers. I couldn't read Wes and Donnie, but I think they were less inclined to laugh. Mrs. Grimes glanced at her watch.

"I will dismiss the boys in forty-five minutes. Then they may go to ball practice, or wherever they choose," she said. She nodded to the pianist, who immediately started playing at the beginning of the number that Coach Harrison had interrupted. Mrs. Grimes raised her arms; and on the downbeat, the chorus filled the auditorium with Romberg's best.

"DAVIS! CARTER! MITCHELL!" Coach roared. We kept our eyes on the director and continued to sing. After pacing back and forth three steps in each direction, the coach turned and strode angrily up the aisle, slammed the door open, and then slammed it shut. A small, pleased smile barely lifted the corners of Mrs. Grimes' lips. There was an added exuberance to our voices that was not lost on our director.

"I don't know why the coach raised such a ruckus," Jerry told Karen and me after the practice. We discussed the confrontation as we walked with the three boys to the ball field. "Donnie's a senior, and he's a great short stop; but Wes and I are only sophomores, and Coach rarely uses us. I think it was just a power play." He laughed. "Mrs. Grimes didn't give an inch, did she?"

Karen and I joined friends on the bleachers and watched the final minutes of practice. Jack stood on the pitcher's mound, striking out teammate after teammate. Should a batter actually hit a pitch, it was a pop-up, easily caught. Jack's wind-up was like ballet, slow and graceful; but his pitch was so fast that the ball was a blur.

When the practice was over, Coach Harrison berated the three chorus members. Everyone could hear his harangue. In no uncertain terms, he expressed exactly what he thought of the music department, of any boy who wasted time with it, and specifically, what he thought of Mrs. Grimes, quote: "I don't care what she pretends to teach here, as long as she leaves my boys alone! No one on my teams has time to waste on chorus-y music stuff, that high screechy noise that woman calls music! I wouldn't give two cents for all that crap, or for her either! She's a senseless waste of taxpayer's money!"

"Wow!" Karen's voice was low, but her dynamics were loud. "Can he get away with that? What if someone tells Mrs. Grimes what Coach said?"

Someone did.

We never learned who was responsible for the anonymous note Mrs. Grimes found on her desk. It told in detail what Coach Harrison had said. No one took responsibility, but everyone in chorus knew about it. Mrs. Grimes interviewed Jerry, Wes, and Donnie. Not one of them would admit to hearing what the coach said.

The concert was wonderful, as all of Mrs. Grimes' presentations were. We girls looked as bewitching as teenage girls can in pastel gowns of blue, pink, yellow, green and white; and the boys were grand in their dark trousers and white shirts. Mrs. Grimes could be described only as elegant in her long, black gown, which revealed, we thought, a surprisingly well-preserved figure.

Charlotte Grimes was forty-nine years old and had been a widow for four years. Returning home from his job at the sprawling chemical plant beside the Kanawha River in Charleston, Tom Grimes' car had skidded on a curve, plummeted through a guardrail and tumbled end-over-end into a gorge. The winding roads could be treacherous in rain, snow, or sleet. Many accidents occurred on them, several of which were fatal.

The Grimes' only son, a teacher in a southern California elementary school, had come home for the funeral; but he left Dixon the following day. Charlotte Grimes was a competent, independent woman who had managed well on her own. She had earned the respect of the community and of the teaching staff, except for Coach Harrison.

The night of the concert, Mrs. Grimes seemed stately, poised, and completely unperturbed by the coach's derogatory remarks about her. She stood taller, somehow. If anything, she was even more dignified.

A few days later, the school was abuzz with speculation. Someone had let the air out of all four of the coach's car tires. Mrs. Grimes would have been first choice as the perpetrator, except for her dignity and the fact that she was a woman. What did women know about tires in those days?

"Coach says that someone from South Charleston probably flattened his tires; at least, that's what he told us." Jerry said. "We beat them pretty bad, you know." Jerry was crowing, just a little. He had hit an unlikely grand slam in the last of the ninth, winning the game. He was awfully close to being unbearable with his victory. Coach Harrison was probably right about a disgruntled fan doing the damage to his car.

Wish I May, Wish I Might...

The last day of my sophomore year arrived, and I was halfway through high school. It didn't seem possible. I wrote a long letter to Sharon Bennett, back in Redbud Grove, describing the concert and giving her a word picture of Jack McCoy, down to the last detail. I hoped that she was green with envy, but she probably wasn't. I had already received her six-page letter, in which she had given me a similar description of her new boyfriend, someone from Tuscola, a small town north of Redbud Grove.

The first Saturday of summer vacation, Jack McCoy and I went on our first real date. I bought a light blue, sleeveless blouse and matching full skirt, complete with blue-ribbon-trimmed can-can petticoat, just for the evening. My outfit was the trendiest thing in fashion that spring of nineteen fifty-six.

My hair fell well below my shoulders and formed loose waves around my face. Mom no longer fussed about the length of it. I don't know if she became used to it or just gave up. As I combed my hair that evening, I stared at my reflection in the mirror, remembering the night I had secretly met Victor Delacourt. I applied a light touch of a soft rose lipstick, recalling the bright red one I had borrowed from Sharon that night. What a stupid kid I had been! What a lot I had learned in two short years.

My image in the mirror was a bit thinner, and I was proud of my smaller waist. My friends and I strived to attain perfect thirty-six, twenty-four, thirty-six figures, as professed by many of the movie stars of the day. I had the thirty-sixes down. That twenty-four continued to elude me, but I was fairly pleased with my twenty-six inch waist. I slipped my feet into blue ballerina slippers, twirled once to see my skirt billow gracefully, and ran downstairs to wait for my handsome date.

Jack took me to a movie at one of the local theaters. He held my hand during the show, an indication that we were on a "real date." Two years after my experience with Victor, I was still a little nervous; and on the way to Dooby's, after the movie, I maintained a safe distance between Jack and me. I didn't want to give him the wrong impression.

My curfew was eleven o'clock, so there was plenty of time for a burger with the crowd at Dooby's. We laughed and fast-danced to the jukebox; and I had a wonderful time. At twenty to eleven, Jack took my arm and escorted me to the convertible—actually *escorted* me! On the way home, I sat a little closer to him, not touching, but closer.

Jack walked me to the front door. Uneasy and clumsy, I didn't know how to bid him a gracious goodnight. Would he expect a kiss? Would I let him, if he did? If he did, should I kiss him back?

"I had a really great time," I said.

"So did I," Jack whispered. He leaned toward me so quickly that I barely had time to turn my head enough to evade a full-out kiss. I hadn't planned the evasion. It was just instinct. His lips brushed my cheek, not quite touching the corner of my mouth. "Good night," he said. His soft chuckle sounded pleased, not upset at all.

I hurried inside and closed the door. I had actually had a real first date, survived it, liked it, and hadn't made a complete fool of myself. I was ready for the second one.

Two days later, someone painted the name of Mrs. Grimes on a big billboard, right across the semi-bare bottom of a child. Several residents reported the incident to City Hall, and the offending graffiti was promptly removed. While most people thought that the culprits were teen-agers, my friends and I weren't so sure.

"I betcha Coach Harrison did it," Wes Carter told us. "Now he thinks that Mrs. Grimes let the air out of his tires. He's always saying something about her at practice."

"I don't think she would have done that," I offered.

"I don't know, Sissy," Karen said. "Coach said some pretty mean things about her. She's been taking care of her own car for a long time. I bet she knows all about tires."

"Oh well, there's nothing we can do about it. Let's go swimming!" With only a little persuasion, Karen's sister, Nancy, allowed all of us to pile into her car, where we packed together like melted Milk Duds in a box. We had gathered at the Courtney house for the afternoon, and from there we headed straight for the swimming pool.

The pool was full of people. All ages and sizes splashed from one end to the other. Even the baby pool was crowded. Karen, Rowena, Beverly and I maneuvered through moving bodies to the deep-water barrier, where we managed to find space at the holding ledge on one side.

This was the first summer my mother had allowed her children access to the public swimming pool. Her fear of polio had abated a little, and she wanted us to learn how to swim. Much to her chagrin, my brother already knew how. He had learned a few years previously, while visiting our cousins in Southern Illinois. After a couple of the older ones threw him into the pond several times, he had to swim or drown. He swam. I didn't yet have it mastered; but I could, at least, float.

"What're *they* doing here?"

"No way!"

"I may have to go to school with them, but I'm not gonna stay in the same pool with them!"

Murmurs and complaints, some whispered, most not, filled the air; and several people climbed onto the concrete that surrounded the pool. It didn't take long to discern the reason. Six young black boys, all between the ages of eleven and thirteen, from the looks of them, came through the shower room door and headed for the pool. They jumped into the cool water and began to play, splashing and diving and doing summersaults.

"Let's get out," Karen said. She started to pull herself out of the water.

"No." My three friends looked at me. "No, I'm not getting out."

"Are you crazy? We can't stay in the water with them! They've never been allowed in here before this summer, and I'm not staying!"

"Karen, they're just kids having a good time; and they're no different from you or me."

"Listen!" Karen was angry. "You may be from the North, and things might be different up there; but we have our own way of doing things. You live *here* now! The government may have desegregated our schools and our pools and everything else, but I don't have to swim with those—those...."

"Don't you dare say it!" I interrupted her. "No, it's not much different back in Redbud Grove; but my mother has never allowed us to use that word! I hate it! Get out of the pool, if you have to; but I'm going to stay right here! The rest of you can go, too; I don't care! I'll walk home, if you don't want to wait!"

Karen and I glared at each other. She shifted her eyes to Bev and Rowena, who looked from each other, back to me.

"I guess I'll stay with Sissy." Rowena's soft green eyes met Karen's brown ones.

"Me, too." Bev said.

After several silent moments, Karen sullenly dropped back into the water. She muttered under her breath, but she stayed in the pool. My eyes searched for the three boys of our group, and found them, all three swimming and yelling and having a great time. They didn't care who came into the pool.

Karen was cool to me for the rest of the day, even after we went back to her house. She barely answered me when I told her good-bye. I left her alone for two or three days, hoping that she would cool off; and she did.

When Karen was speaking to me again, I told her about the busload of colored people who had been stranded in the park in Redbud Grove, and how upset some of the residents had been. I told her everything about that day, except for Lucinda. I never talked to anyone about what had happened to Lucinda.

"Well, the same thing would have happened here," Karen told me. "Wait a minute. No, it couldn't have, because the coloreds have always lived here. They just never went to school with us before last year."

"Where did they go to school?" I asked.

"They've always had their own schools."

"Were they as nice as ours?" It was funny how quickly I had come to think of Dixon High as "my" school.

Karen had the grace to look embarrassed. "No, they weren't," she admitted. "Can't we talk about something else, like, maybe Jack? When are you going out with him again?"

I sighed. The serious conversation had just reached a brick wall with Karen.

"When he asks me, I suppose. Maybe."

Someone threw a brick through Coach Harrison's back door window. There were no witnesses, but two boys told the coach that they had seen a green Buick speed down the street behind his house immediately after the incident. Coach Harrison was livid. Everyone knew that Mrs. Charlotte Grimes drove a green Buick.

School had been dismissed less than two weeks, and the town had a full-fledged feud between two teachers on its hands. Coach Harrison made an official complaint, which had to be investigated by the police. Karen's mother worked at the county courthouse, and she kept us abreast of each new development.

"The police went to Mrs. Grimes' house to question her," Mrs. Courtney told Karen and me. "There was no real evidence. Mrs. Grimes told them that she absolutely did not throw a brick through Harrison's back door window. She told them that she would have aimed for his head, had she thrown one. The officers really got a charge out of that!" Mrs. Courtney laughed. "They couldn't arrest her just because she drives a green Buick." With wry smiles of anticipation, the residents of Dixon waited to see what would happen next. Unfortunately, we didn't have to wait very long. The feud became very ugly.

Charlotte Grimes lived in a brick house on a hillside that was dotted with upper-middle-class dwellings. Her husband's life insurance and her own teacher's salary allowed her to live comfortably in the home where she had reared her only child. Karen pointed out the house to me one day as we walked to Rowena's. We thought that we were too old to ride bicycles, and no one was available to drive us. It was a long walk along the hilly streets. Sidewalks had not yet been constructed along many of the thoroughfares, but traffic in the residential areas wasn't often hazardous.

The landscaped hillside garden in front of Mrs. Grimes' house was a showcase. Her love of gardening and flowers was apparent in the beautiful display of annuals, perennials and flowering trees. A stone fountain stood in the center of a flagstone-paved area that had been leveled to provide a delightful oasis, complete with a small wrought iron bench. In the form of a child tipping a watering can, from which water poured into a basin, the fountain was a landmark in the neighborhood.

Mrs. Grimes' house was closer to the street than ours, which put the fountain just about head-high to passers-by. It was a lovely thing, and Karen and I stopped to admire the craftsmanship of the sculpture. The trickling water splashed softly into the basin. Whimsically, I thought that the happy sound was what put the smile on the fountain girl's face.

"Good afternoon." Mrs. Grimes stepped from the walkout basement garage and waved to us. "Isn't she lovely? My husband gave the fountain to me for our twenty-fifth wedding anniversary."

"It's really nice," I said. Nice. What an innocuous word! "I mean, it's beautiful," I amended. "Where did she come from?"

"Somewhere in Charleston." Mrs. Grimes followed a flagstone path that meandered down her hillside garden. She pointed out several unusual plants to us, calling their horticultural names with ease. Her pride and love for her home and handiwork shown in the smile on her face and the sparkle in her eyes.

Karen and I never failed to stop and admire the garden on our jaunts to Rowena's house. It was a perfect place to rest and catch our breath along the steep hillside journey. I looked forward to the break.

The wanton destruction of the fountain and the beautiful plantings in Charlotte Grimes' garden made the front page of the Dixon Chronicle. Two pictures of the smashed sculpture, torn-out plantings and the overturned bench accompanied the newspaper's account of the vandalism. None of her neighbors had heard anything unusual the night of the attack against the teacher's property.

Coach Harrison became an immediate suspect. The Dixon police department no longer considered the feud between the two teachers as harmless. It had become a serious matter. They took the coach to the police station for questioning, where he was adamant that he was not guilty of the terrible destruction to Mrs. Grimes' property.

"Do you think that Coach Harrison would do something like that?" I asked Jack. We sat together in the swing glider my dad had built the previous summer. Jack's arm rested lightly along the back of the swing, barely touching my shoulders. With one foot, he moved the swing. The air movement created by the gentle sway felt good to my skin. The summer night air was warm, almost sultry.

"I don't know," Jack replied. "I suppose it's possible; but I think he's more likely to take a direct approach. I think he'd just go smash the fountain while Mrs. Grimes was watching, instead of sneaking around in the dark." Jack's hand lightly cupped my shoulder. "What about Mrs. Grimes? Do you think she tossed the brick through his window?"

"No, I don't," I answered. "I think that she would never do any of those things." Jack drew me infinitesimally closer to his side. I let him.

"Well, then, we agree." Jack's face seemed much closer.

"I guess we do."

"Sissy."

"What."

"Sissy?"

"Hum-m-m?"

"What'cha doin'?" My sister bounced through the back door. In the next second she had plopped onto the glider seat opposite Jack and me. I sat up straighter, and Jack pulled slightly away from me.

"Not much, Beth," Jack answered lightly. "What are you doing tonight?" He sounded much more patient than I felt.

"Well, I was gonna go to my friend's house for a sleep-over; but she got sick, so I hafta stay home. Sissy, would you and Jack like to play a game? Daddy said to come ask you." Jack removed his arm from the back of the swing.

"I thought I might take Sissy to get some ice cream," he said.

"I'll go ask," I told him.

I went into the house, where I found my dad stretched upon the sofa, watching a baseball game. The Cardinals weren't playing, so Dad's eyes were deceptively half-closed. He didn't care who was playing, as long as he could watch a ballgame.

"Dad, Jack wants to take me to get some ice cream. Can I go?" It was a long moment before my dad answered. My mother watched us from her easy chair.

"If you'll bring me back some strawberry ice cream," Dad said. I was trapped. It wouldn't take long to eat ice cream at Dooby's, and we would have to hurry home before Dad's ice cream melted.

"Okay," I answered. "We won't be long."

"I like my ice cream hard." He knew that I knew what he meant. There would be no long way home that evening. At any rate, Jack and I had a respite from my little sister's chaperone duty.

Jack drove along the streets faster than usual. The wind in my hair felt like freedom, wonderful and wild. I sat closer to Jack than I had previously, not quite touching, but almost. A different feeling was between us that night, a current of an unknown something, perhaps anticipation, but I wasn't sure of what.

"Do you really want ice cream?" Jack asked. I hesitated.

"No." My answer was a near whisper.

The car accelerated, and it seemed that we were flying. Jack didn't drive far. Within a few minutes, he stopped the car near a small clearing. We were completely surrounded by tall pines. He reached for me and I went into his arms as easily as if I had been there many times. His lips were full and warm and sweet. I knew that I would always remember that moment, no matter what, for as long as I lived.

We didn't talk. We had only minutes, and we communicated without words. I sighed, completely happy just to be with Jack McCoy. Jack seemed as happy to be with me. The five minutes we spent there in each other's arms were better than hours with my friends. I didn't understand how it could be, but it was.

"We've got to go," Jack said. Reluctantly, he withdrew his arms; and I moved back to the center of the passenger's side. I couldn't help but compare how wonderful I felt with Jack to how scared, albeit thrilled, I had been that one evening with Victor Delacourt. Growing up was an amazing thing.

We bought a pint of strawberry ice cream for my dad, and Jack drove as fast as he dared back to my house. The frost on the carton had not even begun to melt. Dad grinned at me when we took it inside. I grabbed a spoon from the kitchen and handed both items to him.

"Is it hard enough, Dad?" I asked. I watched while he opened the folding sections of the carton and dipped the spoon into the solid brick.

"Just right," he murmured around the mouthful of cold ice cream. "You must have hurried."

"Yes, Sir," Jack replied. He slanted his beautiful, light brown eyes toward me. "I did."

Mrs. Grimes and Coach Harrison filed lawsuits against each other. The senseless destruction of her prized garden and fountain finally got through the music teacher's dignified exterior. The football coach vehemently denied responsibility and accused his accuser of damaging his car and his house. Mrs. Courtney told us that the city police chief was at wit's end. He couldn't decide whether neither or both were lying, so he washed his hands of both of them. The only other recourse was lawsuits.

People took predictable sides. The sports-minded aficionados, mostly men, sided with Coach Harrison. The rest of those who cared sided with Charlotte Grimes. I had reached the point of not caring. I was bored with all of it.

Both cases were thrown out of court. It seemed that life would return to normal for both of the litigants. No untoward events occurred, nothing in either camp was vandalized, and I continued to dream about Jack McCoy.

Then one night, the guilty party was caught red-handed, so to speak. Unsure just whom to believe, the police chief had staked out both premises, without telling either party. Both teachers were chagrined and relieved to discover that neither of them was responsible for the terrible, destructive events that had happened.

The police caught Tony Fields, a disgruntled ex-high school baseball player, on Coach Harrison's front porch, a can of red enamel paint in one hand and a big brush in the other. He wouldn't say what he had planned to paint upon the Coach's house.

His friend, Marty Higgins, the lookout, had run; and he was caught trying to flee up the hill behind Coach's house. It's really difficult to run uphill. They were the same two boys who had reported seeing the green Buick, the night the window was broken in the Coach's house.

Both boys were arrested, and they confessed to all the vandalism. At first it had just been a prank, they said. Then the boys had decided to see how far they could take it, how far each teacher could be pushed before they did something really dramatic, like attack or kill each other. Those boys were real sweethearts.

For a long time after that, I thought about feuds. I wondered if all feuds started over something trivial. One evening I asked Jack about the Hatfield/McCoy feud.

"What started it?" I asked. "Was it a misunderstanding or did someone else start it, something like Coach and Mrs. Grimes?"

"I'm not sure," Jack replied. "I've heard several stories. There's one about a stolen pig, or a killed pig. One side said it was theirs, and the other said it wasn't or something. And then there was a fight over some ground or a riverbank or some stupid thing. I don't really know and I don't care. We're so distantly related that is doesn't matter to me."

He placed his hands on each side of my face. "I'd rather think about you." He kissed me, softly, gently, as if I were made of porcelain. Distracted from the intriguing Hatfield/McCoy saga, I concentrated upon the present: being sixteen and the girlfriend of the most popular boy in school

Still, I couldn't get the senseless feuds off my mind. The potential of bodily harm to the two teachers scared me. It troubled me. I found myself wondering why people let themselves get so caught up in a thing that they were ready to kill over it, whether it was a piece of sculpture, money, a relationship, or a piece of land. Such conflicts had to begin with a small thing.

Cocooned within my state of blissful ignorance, I was unaware that a big feud had already begun in a little area of South Asia. The far-off country, of which I had not yet heard, whose name I did not yet know, would affect my life forever.

It was called Viet Nam.

#

Sally's Mountain

My mother was a natural-born nurse. She was in her element when one of her children was sick. I used her nurse syndrome to great advantage many times; and I'm sure that my brother and sister did, also. To my credit, however, I abused her concern only during the years we lived in Redbud Grove. After we moved to West Virginia, I was much too involved with friends and high school activities to malinger.

There were a few snowy mornings when I was tempted to plead feigned illness, to enjoy an extra hour or two beneath warm covers, and to experience the pampering my mother so loved to lavish on her ailing offspring. As I grew older, I resisted the temptation. I hated to miss a day at Dixon High.

My brother, Bill, was the least likely to take advantage of Mom's soft heart. However, on several occasions, I winked at my little sister, Beth, becoming a co-conspirator in her manufactured bellyaches. I understood her too well.

My mother had not attended high school. She had been a good student; and her teacher had pleaded with my grandfather to allow his daughter to further her education. Grandpa Loring wouldn't allow it. He saw no need for any of his children to waste more time in school.

Without telling us, Mom enrolled in a class in Dixon, passed it with the highest grades in the group, and received her high school equivalency diploma. Mom was an avid, eclectic reader. Medical journals, as well as novels and biographies, were a part of the stack of reading material she regularly checked from the library. None of us considered her choices unusual. We were so proud of her. In honor of her achievement, Dad took us to dinner at the nicest restaurant in Dixon; and that's where Mom dropped her bombshell.

"I'm going to nursing school."

Four pairs of eyes fixed upon my mother's face. I stared at her in stunned disbelief. None of my friends had a mother who was going to school! Besides, mothers didn't do that! They stayed at home and were just— *mothers*.

"You're what?" Dad asked. He looked at her with something akin to horror.

"I'm going to nursing school," Mom repeated. She continued to eat as if she had not just declared that she was going to turn our world upside down. "I can take classes three days a week, with an occasional evening course thrown in. I can have a practical nurse license in eighteen months."

"But what about taking care of the house..."

"Mom, what about me...."

"Who's going to drive me to football practice and...."

We all began to talk at once. Mom just kept eating. While we stuttered and moaned in exasperation, she quietly finished a serving of her favorite dessert, southern pecan pie. One by one, we became silent, at which point, Mom looked up, smiled sweetly and said, "I'm sure we'll manage just fine." She beckoned to the waitress. "Could I please have more coffee?"

Our life changed.

My sophomore year came to a close just as my mother began summer school. I had passed driver's training, and I had a brand new driver's license. I had envisioned long, sunny days in the company of my friends, much as I had spent the previous summer. I had entertained the fantasy that I would actually be able to drive my friends to the movies, but that was not to be.

Mom wouldn't allow me go steady with Jack McCoy, but at least I could out with him occasionally, interspersed with group dates. It was better than not being able to date at all. That's what I told myself, anyway.

On the days Mom went to school, it was my responsibility to stay with Beth and to prepare the evening meals. My dad and my brother and sister were not pleased with my culinary efforts, but Mom praised every meal I made. We had macaroni and cheese often.

After a few weeks, we fell into a relatively comfortable pattern. Dad stopped complaining so much about Mom's being gone for occasional night classes. We could all see that Mom was happier and that she was doing something she really loved.

The first day she spent training in Dixon Memorial Hospital surpassed her expectations, and she came home ecstatic. She had found her niche, her calling, her heart's greatest dream. I was only a tad jealous.

One evening, Mom was late coming home. Dad ate his supper, but he kept turning to look at the clock on the kitchen wall. I could tell that he was worried. When the lights of Mom's car finally came up the hill, Dad hurried out to meet her. I had already cleared the table and put the food in the oven to keep warm for her. The kitchen door opened.

"Hi, Mom. Want me to dish up something for you?" I asked. "Mom! What happened?!" My mother's stark white uniform was spattered with blood, and big stains made horrible blotches on the front of her skirt. She leaned on Dad, who supported her with one arm around her shoulders. We were all talking at once, asking questions, scared, not sure whose blood we saw.

"I'm okay," Mom said; but she didn't look okay. Her pale skin and trembling hands were not reassuring. "No, really, Kids, I'm not hurt. The blood isn't mine." Well, that was a relief!

"Whose blood is it?" Beth demanded.

"Yeah, did somebody die?" Bill sounded more excited than concerned.

"Yes, Bill, somebody died," Mom replied. She sounded very weary. "Just let me sit down." Dad pulled a chair out from the table, and I quickly prepared a dinner plate for her.

Beth filled a glass with ice, and Bill poured tea into it. Mom raised the glass to her mouth; but her hand was shaking so badly, Dad had to steady the glass for her. She looked at the food on her plate.

"I'm sorry, Sissy; I can't eat now. I've got to get out of these clothes." Dad hovered, ready to support Mom should she need it. They went into their bedroom. I heard bath water running, so I cleared the table again.

"Wow," Bill said. "I wonder what happened?"

"Yeah," Beth answered. "Maybe there was a car wreck, or something like that."

"Mom will tell us what happened when she feels better," I told them. Dad came into the kitchen.

"Your mom will be out in a little while," he said. "She needs to get cleaned up, and then she'll feel like eating." I thought that Dad looked a little pale, too. Like us, he had thought that the blood on Mom's clothes was hers.

When she came back into the kitchen, Mom did look better. She wore her favorite robe of scruffy, faded pink chenille, and matching faded scuffs. My mother grew up during the lean, needy years of The Great Depression; and she simply couldn't throw away anything that had an ounce of use left in it.

Mom cut up worn-out towels into smaller squares and sewed several layers together, making thick potholders, which she called the every day holders. She kept her nice, store-bought holders to use when we had company. Thrift was ingrained, but she had her pride.

"Sissy, I don't want much to eat. I think I'll just have a sandwich and this tea," Mom told me.

"I'll make it, Mom. You sit down and rest." I was surprised when she did as I suggested. That wasn't at all like my mother.

"What happened, Mommy?" Beth asked.

"Yeah, who died?" Bill's voice held an undercurrent of excitement. Mom took a long drink from her glass and looked at Dad.

"Will, I don't think I'll ever get used to some of these people."

"What people, Honey?" Dad asked.

"The hill people, those who live far back in the mountains. It's almost like they're from another country, or a different century."

"What happened tonight, Jackie?"

Mom's lower lip trembled slightly before she answered. "I saw a man shoot and kill his brother." I felt the same shock that registered on the faces of the rest of my family.

We sat, spellbound, as Mom began to talk. We didn't move until she had finished telling us about the people who came from high in the mountains above Dixon. They had brought their own brand of justice into the hospital, and it was certain that none of us would ever forget them.

Still a trainee, most of my mother's hours at the hospital were spent accompanying nurses, watching and learning from them, often completing records and filling out forms. That's how she came to witness the Kendall drama. Much of what she learned about the family came from overhearing their conversation in the hospital. The rest she picked up from the medical staff. The incident gave all of us a new perspective on the mountain folk above Dixon...

Avery Kendall owned two thousand mountain acres of the most luxurious, virgin timber in Kanawha County, West Virginia. The ground had been passed to him from his father, and from father to son for generations before them. Upon the death of a father, ownership was conveyed to the firstborn Kendall male child, without exception. That's the way it had been done since the first Kendall this side of the Atlantic Ocean laid claim to the mountainside.

Fortunately, each Kendall had fathered at least one son. The dilemma of having only a daughter as an heir had never been a factor. A woman in charge of Kendall ground would have been unthinkable. Given the proclivity to large families among the Kendalls, it seemed unlikely that such a thing would ever come to pass.

High in the Appalachians, remote from the evolutionary process of civilization, life for the Kendall clan and the rest of the far-flung hill people continued much as it had for two hundred years. They kept to themselves. By various, effective means, they discouraged outsiders from venturing onto their land.

An occasional United States Revenue representative, looking for illegal whiskey distilleries, trespassed onto Kendall property. A couple of them disappeared completely, leaving no trace of car, footprints, hide nor hair. After that, the government, wisely, left that particular hillside alone for many years.

Over a twenty-year span of childbearing, Lorna Kendall presented her husband with two sons and six daughters: Jacob, Jude, Jewel, Garnet, Opal, Pearl, Ruby, and Sapphira. Although she owned no jewelry, Lorna Kendall had a penchant for sparkling things. She named her daughters accordingly. Avery named his sons.

The only reading materials in the Kendall home were a Bible, read only by Lorna, and a Sears Roebuck catalogue, both of which were the source of names for the Kendall children. Old issues of the catalogue were taken to the three-hole outhouse, where they furnished reading material, as well as sheets of toilet paper. Nothing was wasted in the Kendall household.

By hill standards, the Kendall house was large. It nestled among tall pines at the edge of a mountain meadow, several ridges beyond the forested, rocky slopes that rose above Dixon. Built of pine logs harvested from the hillside, the house consisted of one all-purpose room across the front that served as gathering room and kitchen. Three bedrooms, of equal dimensions, opened onto the main room, squaring the back of the house with the front.

The house was built on a downward slope. A high porch, supported by four-feet-high pine logs, spanned the front. Three blue-tick hounds resided beneath the porch. It provided a cool place for them in the summer and a warm one in the winter.

Hand-hewn wood shingles, replaced as needed, roofed the entire structure. A thin column of smoke rose continuously from the chimney, for the stone fireplace, which was the only source of heat, was also used for cooking. Stained with the smoke of thousands of fires, the fireplace remained a thing of beauty, made of colorful stones that had been gathered and mortared by Avery's grandfather.

A few of the mountain men had purchased wood-burning cook stoves for their women, but not Avery Kendall. Avery clung to the old ways, walking the paths that had been set for him by his father, and by four generations before him. That led to a conflict. Avery's elder son, Jacob, most often called Jake, was more of an independent, forward thinker. He longed to add a touch of modern convenience to their lives.

"Pa, I don't see why we cain't have us a truck." It was not the first time Jacob had brought up the subject.

"'Cause I ain't havin' one a'them noisy things on my hill, is why." Avery never raised his voice to his children. There was no need. His word was law, had always been law, and would continue to be the only law observed in his household.

At the age of forty-seven, Avery Kendall was a strong, wiry, lean man, with well-defined muscles in his long arms and legs. He stood just short of six feet tall. His hair was coal-black, without a trace of silver in the collar-length strands. Avery sported a full, lush mustache; but the rest of his face was clean-shaven and smooth, unlike his younger brothers, who grew heavy beards.

Eyes as black as his hair peered at his world, passing judgment upon people and circumstances with a steady, unperturbed gaze. If he were proud of the physical resemblance his eldest child bore to him, Avery gave no indication. People often made the observation that Avery "shure had left his mark on that boy, Jake."

"But, Pa..."

"That's the end of it."

"But, Pa, it'd be easier to git supplies up from the valley, and we would'n hafta hitch up the mules ever' time Ma needed somethin'. It'd be a lot easier on them mules, and they'd be fresher fer loggin'."

"Jacob."

At twenty-five, Jacob Kendall carried the same weight and height as his father. For the space of five seconds, Jacob held his father's stare before dropping his eyes to his own hands, clenched tightly upon his thighs. Jacob had not yet reached the point of openly defying Avery

Kendall. Appeased, Avery's tone became conciliatory, or as near to it as was possible for him to reach.

"It's gittin' on near supper time, Jake."

"I'll be eatin' over at Mandy's." The younger man rose from the cane-bottomed chair and pushed the seat under the table. He strode toward the front door, took his wide-brimmed black felt hat from a wall peg, and quietly let himself out of the house. In a short time, the sound of hoof beats could be heard heading down the slope.

Avery's wife, Lorna, didn't look up from the fireplace, where she was carefully transferring the bubbling contents of a black iron kettle into a large stoneware pot. She never interfered with the actions or conversations between the men in her family, not even her sons. Her task had been to give birth to them, rear them through childhood, and then take her hands off completely.

"Ruby, Sapphira, put the tins on the table. Supper's ready." While the two younger girls placed four metal plates and four knives and forks on the long plank table, their mother dumped steaming cornbread from a cast iron Dutch oven onto a large platter. Avery remained at the head of the table, where he had been seated during his conversation with Jacob.

"Where's Jude?" he asked.

"He's sparkin' the Cutter gal over on Bear Ridge," Lorna answered. Neither of them looked at the other. "Said he'd be back 'fore late."

"Huh." Avery grunted and proceeded to eat the savory stew his wife placed before him, scooping up succulent pieces of squirrel and vegetables that had simmered on the hearth all day. "Looks like one a them boys'd pick a gal and marry up with her, 'stead a-chasin' all over the hills after ever' little skirt they see. We need some more boys to git started loggin'. Don't know why you could'na dropped more boys, 'stead'a them useless girls."

"Pa, Garnet and Pearl is gonna' have babies. Maybe they'll git boys," ten-year-old Ruby offered.

"Wouldn't matter none if they did," Avery answered. "They ain't Kendalls."

"Ruby, Sapphira, finish up, now," their mother ordered. Her lips had tightened at the mention of her two older daughters, but she offered no comments. Outwardly, she ignored the implied reproach from her husband. She knew, had always known, how disappointed he was in the number of sons she had borne him.

Jewel and Opal both married before they reached their fifteenth birthdays. They had married brothers, sons of Avery's moonshine competitor, Abe Ridley, who lived two ridges away. Not given to displays of emotion, Avery had not reacted to the insult outwardly.

After the girls eloped with the Ridley brothers, Avery simply never mentioned their names. He forbade his wife to talk to them should they come back home for a visit, which they never did. It was as if the girls had never been born. Going to the Ridley's was out of the question, so Lorna Kendall privately mourned the loss of her daughters.

Garnet and Pearl also married very young, and their choices of husbands proved only a tiny bit more acceptable to Avery Kendall. At least their mates were not in direct competition with him. Garnet's husband, Cory Adams, hired out to any logger who would use him; and occasionally Avery took him on. Cory was a convenience when Jacob or Jude were gallivanting across the state line into Kentucky, or skirt-chasing on a far-off ridge.

Lannie Cox, Pearl's mate, was a musician. He could play a fiddle sweeter than any birdsong heard in the mountains. His haunting music seemed to charm the wind into soft, accompanying breezes that wafted the melodies across the hills and glens.

In the hills, making music didn't pay much; but Lannie was also skilled in turning bird's-eye maple and tiger maple into beautiful musical instruments: dulcimers, fiddles, and autoharps, all of which brought him a fair price at the shops in Dixon and Charleston. Of Avery's four sons-in-law, Lannie was the one he least respected, and the one least likely to ever need a handout from Avery. That galled Avery.

Grandchildren were considered a blessing; but Avery Kendall wanted grandsons from his sons, especially from Jacob, his first borne, an assurance that his name would be carried into perpetuity. Sons from Jude would be acceptable. None of the other offspring mattered as much.

Evidently, Jacob couldn't or wouldn't make up his mind to settle on one woman. It was beginning to look as if Avery, himself, would have to take a hand in choosing a young wife for Jacob, preferably one with hips made for bearing many sons. If the boy didn't pick a wife soon, one would be found for him.

Avery sopped up the last bit of stew with a piece of cornbread and washed it down with a long swallow of his best moonshine. A deep, rolling belch announced that he was finished with his supper. He pushed away from the table and went outside, leaving his women to clean up after him.

Avery settled into his own personal, handcrafted rocking chair, where it sat in its customary place upon the front porch. He looked across the clearing that sloped gently downward. Trees like those upon the surrounding hillsides once covered the clearing. They had been chopped down and used to build the cabin that had belonged to his father and his grandfather. Only traces of a few stumps remained. Soft indentations in the ground showed where other trees had stood.

Evening settled softly upon the mountain. Ghostly mists rose from the forest floor, heralding the approach of night. In the twilight stillness, a doe with two fawns appeared, stepping cautiously from the shelter of the tall pines, into the edge of the clearing. Either unaware or unconcerned with the presence of the man on the porch, she grazed peacefully, often raising her head to watch the cavorting fawns.

Moving nothing but his eyes, Avery watched the deer until darkness fell completely upon his domain. Soft light from a kerosene lamp cast golden highlights upon the porch's wide, pine planks. Gentle night sounds rose as the night deepened. Crickets, tree frogs and the haunting call of an owl lingered in the damp, mountain air. Peace reigned in Avery Kendall's domain.

Unexpectedly and unannounced, Jude Kendall brought home a bride, a seventeen-year-old girl named Sally Cutter. The couple arrived at the Kendall cabin early one Saturday afternoon. Jude had been keeping company with the girl, but he hadn't mentioned to his folks that he intended to marry her.

"Ma, Pa, Sally and me got married this mornin'. We'll be stayin' here till I can put us up a cabin." There was no doubt in Jude's mind that his parents would be pleased with his decision. He was correct.

A smile of delight lit up Lorna Kendall's work-worn face. There would be another female presence in her house, a young girl to fill up some of the empty space in Lorna's heart, left by her four absent daughters.

Avery looked up from the ax head he held on his lap. He let it rest atop the whetstone he was using to sharpen it. His black eyes took in the young couple, where they sat atop the wagon seat. Two matched mules pulled the wagon, the whole rig obviously owned by Sally's father. Jude's mule was tethered behind the wagon.

"We'll unload Sally's things and take her pa's wagon back in a day er' two," Jude continued. He jumped from the wagon and turned to assist his new bride to the ground. Sally smiled down at her handsome husband, her blue eyes bright and her cheeks pink with happiness. She wore a dress of rosebud-sprigged white cotton, which she had made. It was a lot shorter than met Avery's approval, but it was in keeping with the fashion dictates of the summer of nineteen fifty-five.

Sally's blond hair tumbled around her shoulders in bouncy curls. There was an impish, confidant air about her that set Avery's teeth on edge. Silently, he calculated how long it would take to set her right, to mold her into an appropriate wife for a Kendall man. He figured that it wouldn't take long. Hard work could take the feistiness out of any little female. At least the girl looked strong and healthy and capable of producing sons for Jude.

"You kin have off til come Monday mornin'," Avery said, and pointed his finger at his son. "We'll start early t'fill that order from Pemberton's down in Dixon. See to it." Avery went back to sharpening his ax head.

Lorna fussed and bustled around the cabin the rest of the afternoon. She had plenty of beds, but she fretted over how to distribute sleeping quarters. She considered moving Jacob's bed to the front room, allowing Jude and Sally to move into Jacob's room. Upon further pondering, she changed her mind. It would be easier and probably much less disruptive to move two cots for the two little girls into the front room. So that's what Lorna did, leaving Jacob's room undisturbed. It seemed unfitting to move the older son out of his room.

Lorna supervised the unpacking of Sally's dowry. A leather-bound trunk, Sally's hope chest, contained the following items: four handmade quilts; two sets of hand-hemmed bed linens, which included embroidered pillowcases; a dozen dish towels, made of bleached feed sacks; two feather pillows, encased in blue and white striped ticking; a rolling pin, made of maple; a few towels and wash cloths; a set of ruby red dishes, service for four, which her mother had collected as bonus pieces inside containers of oatmeal; a blue enamel percolator, given to her by her grandmother; and a few pieces of cast iron cookware. Sally could hardly wait to start using her housekeeping wares in her own home.

Summer passed uneventfully, but an undercurrent of unrest seeped into the Kendall household. More and more, Avery had to depend upon Jude as his right hand man, instead of Jacob. Many nights Jacob didn't come home. When he did return from his overnight excursions, he was quiet, just short of surly, to everyone except his father.

Avery Kendall would not tolerate disrespect from anyone, especially his children. He might overlook a bit of sowing wild oats in a young man, much as he would nod at the antics of a young bull; but there was a line. Jacob knew exactly where his father's line lay.

Totally captivated with her young husband, Sally, blissfully unaware, lavished care and devotion upon Jude. She found excuses to touch him at every opportunity. She patted his back when she sat at the table beside him. She touched his hair when she walked behind him, blushing with delight when Jude returned her caresses.

"Girl, cain't you keep yer hands off the boy while we eat?" Avery demanded at supper one night. Stricken, Sally dropped her hand into her lap, embarrassed that she had been caught patting her husband's leg. Jude merely laughed, but Jacob's smoldering black eyes stared at Sally for a long, assessing moment.

Jacob felt hard, unrelenting anger that Jude had married before him and was on the way to establishing a family. He could see that their father was depending more and more upon Jude. An ugly, bitter knot of envy formed within Jacob's chest; but the thing that rankled inside him the most was his growing desire for his brother's wife.

During the warm summer nights, Sally had become a near obsession to Jacob Kendall. He could hear her and his brother in the room next to his. Many evenings he slipped quietly from the house to escape the sounds and murmurs of their closeness. Unlike the times he went seeking comfort from hopeful mountain girls, Jake walked the slopes on those warm nights, restless and troubled.

He didn't pretend to himself that he was in love with his brother's wife. Jake didn't hold much to the notion of love. He simply wanted Sally, with a passion he couldn't deny; and that made him angrier with Sally than with himself.

After a time, he began to tell himself that Sally knew how he felt, and that she went out of her way to taunt him. At the supper table, Jake often cast veiled glances at her, noting the way the lamplight created golden highlights in her wavy, blond hair. Sometimes his throat tightened at the sound of her laughter, at the way she caught her lower lip between her white teeth in concentration. It was easier to blame that beautiful, soft-skinned, firm-fleshed girl than to believe that she was ignorant, even innocent of the havoc her nearness created inside him.

A good distance away, high above the Kendall cabin, Avery and Jude began to clear a spot for the newlyweds' home. Jacob managed to keep himself busy elsewhere, either at the still or at the logging site further down the mountain. By using a winch and rope and a pair of mules, Jacob was able to load smaller pine logs onto a long wagon.

Working alone made the work go more slowly, and it took Jacob down the mountain to Dixon more often than his father liked. It couldn't be helped if they were to get the cabin finished by winter. Both

Avery and Jacob wanted Jude and Sally gone from the house, but for different reasons.

It was Avery's hope that more privacy would result in a quicker crop of sons, although he was pretty certain that another Kendall was already on the way. He had developed an eye for ascertaining signs of pregnancy, whether in horses, dogs, or women. Avery hoped that seeing Jude's woman in the family way might prod Jacob into settling down and getting some sons of his own. The boy had to beget at least one son to get the mountain.

Avery had noted and understood the searching glances that his older son cast toward Jude's wife. Not much escaped his sharp, coal-black eyes. Getting the young couple into their own cabin would be good for everyone, especially Jake.

August drew to a close, and the summer heat became oppressive and humid. As a rule, cool breezes moved through the tall pines, creating giant, fragrant fans that kept the mountains comfortable, while valley people sweltered in the humidity. However, there was no respite from the heat in the hills that summer. Tempers grew hot and short.

Avery pulled Jacob away from logging the pines to help build Jude's cabin. That didn't assuage the resentment that continued to grow within Jacob's heart. It was more like pouring gasoline onto a raging fire.

"Jude can build his own cabin," Jake muttered; but he still worked the crosscut saw with his brother. The walls went up quickly, and the day came when the last hand-hewn shingle was nailed into place. Avery surveyed the handiwork of Kendall men, and he knew a fierce pride in his sons, a pride that he would never allow himself to express.

"Jake, go down and bring up the other team. While we're here, we'll cut out some logs fer yore next load," Avery ordered. Without a word, Jake did as he was told.

Following a long afternoon of helping Lorna cold-pack sweet corn from the sloping garden, Sally filled a small handled basket with a snack for the men. She hadn't seen Jude since before dawn that morning, and she longed just to look at him. Eagerly, she started the long trek up the winding path to the cabin that would be her home.

When the heat had turned so oppressive, Sally had stopped wearing the near-mandatory slip beneath her clothes. No self-respecting girl would appear in public without a slip, but Sally felt comfortable and modest in the solitude of the mountain. Her father-in-law had not commented on her attire, so it seemed that she hadn't broken some unwritten dress code.

There was a sense of freedom in the way her skirt swirled around her legs. The movement of the thin fabric created a modicum of breeze. She could almost make herself believe that a bit of air stirred among the trees. Sally blew wisps of hair from her face. She unbuttoned the first four buttons of her dress and shook the collar. It didn't help much.

Sally looked straight up at the sky, a narrow strip between the towering pines. She searched the sizzling band of blue, looking for the tiniest hint of a cloud, but there was none. She experienced a momentary feeling of vertigo.

"Oh...," she breathed softly. She stopped and bowed her head for a few moments to regain her balance. The dizziness passed; and when she looked up, she stood no more than two feet away from Jacob.

Sally stared at her brother-in-law. She had never before been so close to him. He seemed to tower over her, standing as he was on the higher slope of the path. Something in Jake's face sent a chill over her body, and she shivered, in spite of the heat. Sally's breath caught in her throat, and she knew a moment of pure, unadulterated fear.

Jacob didn't consciously move a muscle as he gazed down at his brother's wife, but his jaw tightened. It was as if his mind had conjured up the very image that burned inside his head. He could see tiny beads of sweat on her upper lip and the dewy trickle that ran down her throat and disappeared into the pink bodice of her dress. Hungrily, his eyes sought every shadow.

Jacob had removed his shirt. Like Sally, he looked for relief from the heat. The blue chambray garment hung from the wide-blade ax that he carried across his right shoulder. The left suspender held up his dark work trousers, leaving the right side dangling. He stood perfectly still. The purpose of his trip down the mountain flew out of his mind at the appearance of this radiant girl.

Unable to look away, Sally couldn't move. The strength and darkness of Jake's mood held her captive, as surely as if he had bound her with rope. She noted the black hair that grew thickly across his chest, and the sinewy muscles in his long arms, like, yet unlike, his brother. He had never been friendly to her, and they had not carried on a conversation; but she had never been afraid of Jake, until now. Sally cleared her throat.

"You scared me," she said. A nervous half-laugh escaped her lips.

"Did I?"

"I didn't think I'd see anybody...." Sally's free hand strayed to her open bodice. Her fingers trembled too badly to close even one button. Jake's eyes followed her movements, then flashed upward to her face.

"I'm takin' a bite up t'y'all," Sally explained. She held up the basket. Jacob remained silent. "Well, I guess I'll be gittin' on." Sally took a tentative step, than another; but Jacob didn't move. "There's plenty in the basket, if you'd like somethin'," she continued.

Sally edged around him on the path, careful not to let her pink cotton skirt brush against him. She moved slowly, nearly holding her breath, as wary of him as she would be of a rattlesnake. Jake turned with her.

"I'd like somethin'," Jake muttered.

With his left hand, he grasped her upper arm and spun her around. Eye to eye with Jacob on the slope, she could feel his warm breath on her face. Too startled to speak at first, she could only gasp. Jake's hand closed tightly around her arm.

"Yer hurtin' me, Jake! Let go!"

Jacob tossed the wide ax he'd held with his right hand. With a heavy thud, half of the razor-sharp blade buried itself into the ground, leaving the other half exposed. A shaft of sunlight struck the metal and sent dazzling rays into the dark, pine forest. Sally closed her eyes against the sudden blinding brightness.

In an instant, Jacob's arms encircled Sally's body. He drew her against him and covered her mouth with his, grinding and hurtful, seeming more bent upon causing her pain than in taking his pleasure. The basket fell from Sally's hand; and the contents scattered upon the slope, where they bounced and rolled out of sight.

Desperately, Sally tore her mouth away from Jacob's punishing touch. She pushed against his chest with her free arm, striking wildly at his face, before he captured and pinned both arms to her sides. A low growl came from Jacob's throat.

"I see you," Jacob muttered against her cheek. "I see you flittin' round me like a moth at a lantern. I know what yer doin', an' I know what you want. Jude ain't doin' right by you, is he? He ain't givin' you what you need." His mouth closed on the soft skin at the base of her throat.

"Stop it, Jake! Let me go! Jude! Jude, help me!" Sally's voice rang against the hills, and she drew breath to call again. Jacob pressed one hand against her mouth.

"Hush! Hush, now! I ain't fixin' t'hurt you!" Jacob leaned forward and the momentum of his body took Sally to the ground. The girl struggled with all her strength, fighting and flailing; but she was no match for the wiry mountain man. Jacob breathed hard, more from excitement than from his efforts to subdue the young woman who fought to be free of him. He laughed.

"Like a wildcat, ain't you...a hot, sweet wildcat. You know what you been doin' t'me. I *know* you do! You been teasin' me and movin' in front a'the fire, just so's I could see you through that thin dress. You call t'me with yer eyes, all blue and bright. Now I'm here. I'm here...."

"No, Jake! It ain't true! I didn't! Jake, *don't!*"

"Hush, Girl...." Intent upon the woman beneath him, Jake didn't see the shadow that fell across the path.

"Jacob."

The voice was quiet, deadly. Jacob froze.

"Jacob, git up."

Silently, Jacob rose and faced the stony visage of his father.

"Sally, git up an' fix yerself. Git on down t'the cabin."

Sobbing softly, the bedraggled girl buttoned her dress and shook broken bits of dried grass from the skirt. She wiped her mouth. The gesture wasn't lost upon Jacob.

"Tell Ma you tripped an' fell." Without a word, Sally did as she was told. Avery Kendall fixed his cold, black eyes upon his elder son. He spat upon the ground. "I come after you t'tell you not to fetch t'other team. Changed m'mind." He spat again. "You ain't no better'n a houn' dog. You ain't as *good* as ole Blue, cuz that ole dog won't take a bitch when it ain't willin'."

"Pa, I..."

"Hush. You ain't got nuthin' t'say I wanna hear. You git on down the hill an' git yer stuff out'a my cabin. I cain't stomick a man that'd force his brother's wife. I don't want you 'round no more."

"But, Pa...."

Avery turned his back upon his son and started back up the mountain. Jacob followed his father. He grabbed the older man's arm, trying to stop him, trying to think of something to say that would change his father's mind. Jacob knew that the course of his life hung in the balance of the next few minutes. He had to convince his father that he would not have committed the ugly act that only moments before had been his single-minded intention.

Avery pulled away with such force that he lost his balance. Before Jacob could stop him, Avery fell and rolled down the steep slope, coming to rest, belly down, upon the exposed half of the embedded wide-axe blade.

"Pa! No, Pa!" Jacob ran to his father and gently turned him onto his back. Blood poured from the deep slash in Avery Kendall's abdomen.

"I think you've kilt me, Jake," Avery groaned. Frantically, Jacob pressed his shirt against the injury, desperately trying to stop the blood that poured from the gaping wound.

"Ma'll know how to fix it, Pa! Hold on, now!" Jacob Kendall picked up his father and hurried as quickly down the hill as he could go, toward home.

Lorna Kendall asked no questions. She took one look at her blood-soaked husband and set to work. She made a thick, heavy pad of clean rags and pressed it tightly against his abdomen. Within seconds the pad was red with Avery's blood. She worked for several minutes, before she turned to her son.

"I cain't stop it, Jake. We got to take him down t'Dixon. Hitch the team, an' do it quick!" As Jacob lifted their father into the wagon, Jude arrived, wondering why Avery and his brother had not returned to the building site. Lorna gave instructions. "Jude, you and Sally drive the team. Jake and me'll hold yer Pa. Ruby, you and Sapphira sit agin' the front, an' stay outa the way. Move them guns over t'the side." The younger girls carefully scooted the two loaded shotguns to the side of the wagon. It took a long time to get to Dixon.

"We should'a got a truck, Pa! We need a truck!" Jacob shouted at Avery, but Avery didn't respond. Lorna kept exchanging blood-soaked rags for clean ones, keeping as much pressure on the wound as she dared. When they arrived at Dixon Memorial Hospital, white-coated emergency staff rushed Avery inside.

Avery's wife and children were ushered into a waiting area, where they huddled together in a quiet little knot. Sally clung to Jude. Jacob, whose face seemed set in stone, remained in the hall. Hands clenched at his sides, he stared at the closed emergency room doors. The shirt he had thrown on at the cabin, hung open, stained with his father's blood.

Jake looked at his bloody palms. He wiped them on the legs of his pants, but the blood had dried and would not come off his hands. A woman dressed in white with a striped apron that covered her uniform, approached him. She extended a wet towel to Jake, who gratefully used it.

"Is there anything else I can do for you?" she asked, when Jacob returned the bloody towel to her.

"No, Ma'am." Jake turned away from the emergency room doors and joined his family. Sally didn't look at him.

"How'd he come t'fall on that axe?" Jude asked.

"He tripped an' lost his balance," Jacob replied. He would say nothing else. After what seemed like hours, but was less than one, a white-coated doctor approached the Kendalls.

"Mrs. Kendall, we've done all we can do for your husband. I'm afraid he just lost too much blood. I'll take you to his room. He's conscious, but I don't think he has much time. I'm very sorry." Stoically, the family followed the doctor.

Strong, indomitable Avery Kendall, motionless upon the hospital bed, looked very small and very white. His dark hair fell across his forehead, framing a face that was as pale as the sheet. His family gathered around him, no one speaking. After a bit, Avery opened his eyes. His took slow, shallow breaths; and he seemed disoriented for a moment. Slowly his eyes focused, recognition apparent as he looked at each face.

"Got a thing t'say." Avery's weak voice held the same resolve that had filled his life. "Jude, you take the place. Don't go sellin' the pines t'no timber companies. Keep it. Parcel it. Give it t'yer boy when he comes. He's already on the way." Wide-eyed, Jude looked at his young wife, who blushed and nodded, wondering how Jude's pa could know a thing like that.

"Pa, you cain't..." Jacob's voice broke.

"I can, an' I have." Avery whispered. "Jude, take care a'yer ma, case no one else wants 'er. Jake, you can have the still, but that's all. Hear me, Jude. Jake don't get nuthin' else...not nuthin'..." Avery's eyes focused once more on Jacob, his first-born child and son. "You should'na touched yer brother's wife, Jake...yer like a dog, a no-good-fur-nothin' dog...."

They were Avery Kendall's last words.

Jacob turned away and left the room, his steps quick and purposeful. Stunned silence hung in the air. There was no weeping. Jude stood transfixed, staring at the still face of his father. Slowly, he turned to Sally, the question in his dark eyes; and he saw the answer in her tear-filled blue ones.

A rage such as Jude had never experienced coursed through his body. He shook with the force of it. His chest felt as if it would explode with his fury. He grasped Sally's upper arms, unaware that his fingers dug into the bruises left by his brother's hands.

"When?! When did he touch you?!"

"Today!" Sally sobbed. "Today, on the trail! I was comin' to you, and he..." A growl of rage erupted from Jude, the quiet boy, the gentle son, the boy-child who was always kind to his mother.

"I'm fixin' t'kill 'im!" Jude ran from the room after his brother, but Jacob had already disappeared down the corridor. Jude brushed past the doctor and attending nurses and trainee.

"Jude, wait! Jacob's yer kin! Jude!" Lorna called after her son. All she wanted to do was take Avery back to the mountains for burial, and now her sons were hell-bent upon killing each other.

A flurry of activity erupted at the far end of the corridor. People scurried in every direction, ducking into open doors and dropping behind desks. Jacob Kendall, fierce, determined, mountain man, loaded double-barreled shotgun against his shoulder, strode toward his kin. Purpose set his face like granite.

Jude, enraged as he was, recognized that he was no match for the heavy weapon his brother carried. He pushed open the nearest door, rushed inside, and wedged a chair against the doorknob. The ground floor window was his only route of escape, a thin one, at best.

A shotgun blast splintered the door and reverberated throughout the room. The woman in the hospital bed screamed hysterically. She cowered beneath the sheet, screaming for help. Jude managed to open the window, but there hadn't been enough time for him to climb through it. He turned to face his brother, and he recognized the face of death.

"That mountain is *mine*!" Jacob said.

"Jake, no!" Lorna screamed. "Jude's yer brother!"

"I ain't got no brother." Jacob's voice sounded exactly like his dead father's, soft, steady, and deadly. "That mountain is mine, and I mean t'keep it. They was *both* supposed t'be mine and I aim t'keep what's mine."

"Jake!" Desperately, Lorna Kendall pulled at Jacob's arm.

"You cain't never take it back, Jake," Jude told his brother. "You cain't undo it, once it's done..."

Jude stood beside the window, knowing what his brother was about to do. Had Jude reached the shotgun first, he would have done the same thing. The knowledge was on both their faces, determination on one, resignation on the other. In a final, desperate move, Jude lunged toward Jacob.

The second shotgun blast drove Jude Kendall into the wall, where he slid slowly to the floor. He looked up at the man who had been his big brother, his leader, his protector, his idol, and was now his executioner. Even as the light faded from his black, Kendall eyes, Jude whispered to his brother.

"She'll...never be...yers...Jake...."

"Oh, Jackie, Honey, you could have been hurt, or killed!"

Dad put his arms around Mom and drew her close to him. We all had tears running down our faces, as Mom's story came to an end.

"How'd you get all that blood on you?" Bill asked.

"After Jake Kendall shot his brother, he just calmly walked out of the room, looked at me, and left the hospital. He looked me right in the eye. I thought that he was going to kill me, too; but he just looked at me and kept walking.

"He went down the hall and out the door. We all hurried to the poor boy's side and tried to help him, but it was too late. With a shotgun fired at that range, he didn't have a chance. I don't understand how a man could do that! How could he just shoot his brother and calmly walk away? Someone said that it was over timber on a hillside!"

None of us slept much that night. I heard my parents' murmuring voices long after the rest of us went to bed. I couldn't fathom how anyone could kill his brother. I didn't like my brother sometimes, and there were times he didn't like me; but we would never *hurt* each other! The love between us was always there, even when we were fighting over some stupid thing.

The next day, news of the murder was plastered across the front page of the daily paper. Graphic photographs of Jude's body and of the family appeared on Charleston's television news broadcasts for several days. Extended family members came down from the hills to assist Lorna in returning what was left of her family back home.

Avery's three brothers, all heavily bearded and stern faced, escorted the bodies of their older brother and nephew back up the mountain. People gathered along the highway and secondary roads to catch a glimpse of the procession, which was made up of a mule-drawn wagon and Kendall men on horseback. Even the spectators were silent.

Jacob Kendall disappeared. For months, he successfully eluded capture by the dozens of law enforcement officers and patrolmen who searched for him. Numerous rumors abounded. Some said that Jacob had gone to the mountains in Kentucky, where he had courted, not with marriage in mind, several young girls. Others said that Jacob had been seen as far away as Arkansas, in the Ozarks. Still others reported hearing that Jake was hiding in the hills high above Knoxville, Tennessee.

Lorna Kendall never again left the mountain. Unable to grieve for Avery, she mourned the loss of her younger son, Jude. Torn between grief and anger at Jake, Lorna surrendered what little authority she held to her daughter-in-law, the lovely, pregnant young Sally.

On a cold, rainy night the following March, Kanawha County deputies captured Jacob Kendall. No one knew whether luck or a tip from a disgruntled moonshine competitor sent the law to the finished cabin of Jude and Sally Kendall, where Jake was found, sound asleep. Even the toughest man must rest.

Jacob put up no struggle. The half-dozen shotguns aimed at his body formed a mighty deterrent to resisting arrest. The way down the mountain led past the log house that had always been Jake's home. Stoically, he kept his head from turning toward the glow of kerosene lamps that cast wavering reflections upon the wet porch.

From inside the house came the distinct, plaintive cry of a newborn baby, announcing that Jude's son had arrived upon the mountain. Jacob Kendall stopped mid-stride. Beneath the heavy growth of beard, which had appeared upon his face during his exile, muscles tightened in his clenched jaw. He didn't move until the barrel of a shotgun prodded him, but he never glanced toward the cabin.

None of the deputies could explain exactly how Jacob managed to escape. The most plausible explanation seemed to be that Jake had suddenly bent his knees, causing the two men behind him to stumble. They, in turn, fell into the other four men, creating a domino effect. When they finally stopped rolling down the dark, slippery slope, Jacob Kendall could not be found. Embarrassing as it was, no one could pinpoint the whereabouts of the most wanted man in Kanawha County.

What transpired later that year could only be described as just....

As a result of Avery Kendall's death, Lorna's married daughters returned to visit with their mother. The tragedy took a huge toll on the older woman. She died shortly after the birth of her only grandson, called Jude, for his father. Sally mourned the loss of her mother-in-law, for Lorna had been good to her.

Sally Kendall took control of her household. She struck a deal with her two brothers-in-law, who agreed to work the timber for a share of the proceeds. She grew physically strong from gardening and working long hours to keep her two young sisters-in-law fed and clothed. The only times she rested during the day was when she nursed her baby boy, and at night, when she fell into bed.

By September, she was confident that she would be able to hold what was left of the Kendall family together. Her child was a constant source of delight; and he was the image of Jude, the young husband she had adored. She rarely allowed tears to overtake her. She was afraid that they would weaken her, and she had to stay strong and resolute.

There had been no reported sightings of Jacob Kendall. Most people seemed to think that he had left West Virginia for good, but Sally didn't believe that theory. In her heart, she knew that Jake would come back. A Kendall wouldn't walk away from the mountain, not even if it killed him.

Late one October night, Sally opened her eyes, instantly awake. She listened, but there were no sounds from the baby or from the girls in their rooms. Hot coals sizzled in the fireplace, flickering into occasional flames that sent gently moving shadows upon the living room walls. The soft light flowed through her open bedroom door; and it should have been reassuring in the cool, dark night.

Sally could hear nothing to disquiet her, but her skin crawled. Her breath quickened. She lay very still and forced herself to breathe quietly. Her right hand closed slowly upon the loaded shotgun that was her constant bed companion.

"What took you so long?" she whispered. From the darkest shadows in the room, she sensed movement. Sally didn't have to see his face to know that it was Jake.

"You knowed I'd come fer you, all the time." Jake's voice was barely more than a whisper, but Sally heard the steely purpose in it. "This mountain is mine, and yore part of it. It's took me some time t'figure it all out, but now I know. Jude got t'you first, but you was meant t'be mine. You was *always* meant t'be mine. I'll raise that there boy as mine, and I mean t'claim you, too. Here. Now. So be still, Woman. I don't want t'hurt you, but I will...."

Sally didn't move. She watched the shadowy figure of Jacob Kendall remove his coat. She remained still when he approached her bed. She didn't move when she heard the rustle of fabric. It wasn't until he bent over her that she raised the shotgun.

"No, Jake. This mountain ain't yours. It's mine." The blast threw Jacob Kendall against the wall, where he slid and crumpled in much the same manner as his brother had fallen. "And Jude's," Sally whispered.

Once again, the Kendalls were nine-day wonders in the news. No charges were filed against Sally. The county sheriff came close to saying that she deserved a medal for saving the county the cost of a trial.

My mother felt about Sally much the same way as the authorities, that the young woman's actions were justified. I think that most of the women in Dixon concurred. I'm not sure that all the men did.

Eventually, my mother was able to sleep through the night without terrifying dreams. She said that the hardest part to forget was the lack of remorse on Jacob Kendall's face, and the expression of triumph in his eyes, as he'd walked past her. That, and his statement of ownership: "That mountain is *mine!*"

Jacob Kendall was right about owning the mountain. A portion of it would always be his, an area two feet wide by two feet long, six feet deep.

He was buried in it.

Sally Kendall grew stronger and more confident. With a determination born of pride and duty, she learned how to deal with timber buyers and lumber men. Before she reached the age of thirty, she had earned the respect of the industry. She managed the Kendall forested hillsides with a skill that neighbors admired and eventually emulated.

Sally withdrew from the Kendall moonshine stills. She turned over the operation to Avery's brothers, and she took no profits from the sales. Within a few years, revenuers infiltrated the customer base. They destroyed the whole Kendall moonshine operation, causing many broken hearts in Dixon and the surrounding countryside. Kendall cousins occasionally tried to re-establish a still, but without much success.

Sally never remarried. Many young and older men alike came courting, but not one could fill the empty place in her heart left by Jude Kendall. Sally had idolized him in life. She worshiped him in death.

Young Jude grew strong and tall. Mountain folk declared that he was the spittin' image of his father, but Jude showed no interest in assuming the role of Kendall patriarch. He loved school and pursued education with a thirst that amazed his teachers. Sally indulged her son's every wish for books, for maps and magazines, and eventually, for college. While Sally became the head of the first feminine Kendall line, Jude became the first Kendall scholar.

Through the years, several novels by Jude Kendall reached the bestseller list; but one book became the favorite of his readers. More biographical than fiction, the book set the town of Dixon a-twitter with renewed gossip and interest in the Kendall scandal of nineteen fifty-six. The title was a simple one:

<u>Sally's Mountain.</u>

#

Diane

My sister had a lot of friends. Little girls could be found at our house on any Saturday or Sunday, and often overnight. Mom allowed slumber parties in the summertime, but only on nights that she didn't have to work at the hospital. Sleepovers were not entrusted to my dad and me, for which my father and I were grateful.

One of Beth's friends lived three blocks up the hill from us. He and Beth were the same age, and they shared many of the same likes and dislikes. While Beth had a group of girls that were her best friends, and Robbie had his own group of buddies, the two children occasionally spent a summer afternoon together playing Monopoly or Sorry.

Sometimes the competition grew fierce at the kitchen table, where the game boards were laid. Robbie had an advantage over Beth, one that she never seemed able to recognize. Beth played games with a formidable determination to win, which often clouded her judgment. Robbie, on the other hand, stayed calm and objective, planning his strategy and winning more times than he lost.

Robbie Anderson was a handsome child, an indication that he was going to be a very handsome man. His friendly blue eyes sparkled with mischief, but there was a shy sweetness about him that kept that mischief in check. Light brown hair waved slightly above his forehead, and a small dusting of freckles bridged his nose. At ten, his teeth showed no gaps or unevenness, promising years of a dazzling smile.

Dad teased Beth about her "boyfriend," which always set her off. "Daddy, Robbie is my friend!" Beth's indignant reply was delivered with flashing eyes and militant stance.

"Well, he's a boy; and he's your friend," Dad explained. "Doesn't that make him a boyfriend?" At that point, Beth shook her head, rolled her eyes and walked away in disgust.

It wasn't long before my parents and Robbie's family turned a nodding acquaintance into a friendship. While my brother and I had other interests that summer, the Andersons and my parents often took Robbie and Beth on Sunday afternoon outings. They visited and toured much of the spectacular countryside around Dixon and Charleston; and Hawk's Nest State Park was a favorite attraction of theirs.

Like my parents, the Andersons loved to play cards. As summer closed and the nights grew cool, they set up a weekly card game on Saturday nights, alternating houses. The smell of popcorn and cider on autumn evenings added a warm, spicy aroma to the house, enhancing cutthroat games of Pinochle and Canasta, played at the kitchen table.

Most Saturday nights, I worked at the A&W, went out with my friends, or had a date with Jack McCoy. On rare, occasional weekends that I didn't go out, I enjoyed listening to the sounds of friendly warfare from the kitchen. It was good to hear my mom and dad enjoying evenings with their friends. I couldn't recall a time when they'd been happier.

Walter and Diane Anderson were easy to like. While Walter possessed a quiet, dry wit, Diane was vivacious; and her spontaneous laughter was contagious. It was simply impossible not to respond to the sound of her mirth.

Of medium height, Walter's warm brown eyes crinkled at the corners when he smiled, an indication that he smiled often. Initially, he appeared to be shy; but the more time we spent with him, the more we appreciated his quiet, often droll humor. His witty philosophy sometimes sent my dad into helpless laughter, something we didn't often hear.

Diane Anderson's slim figure looked great in everything she wore. Nearly as tall as her husband, the two of them turned heads at ballgames or PTA meetings. The quiet dignity of Walter was a perfect foil for the sparkling personality of his wife.

Medium length, warm blond hair, worn in the manner of the movie stars I had admired when I was younger, turned into a smooth pageboy that brushed her shoulders. Lively blue eyes and a wide, generous mouth lent character to her face. Diane's skin glowed, like only classically beautiful Norwegian skin can do.

While neither of the two were openly demonstrative, it was obvious that the Andersons adored each other. Something about the way they exchanged glances, as though they were silently communicating, spoke as much or more than words would have. I wondered if I would ever experience that kind of love.

One Saturday night Diane looked especially pretty. She had swept her hair into a smooth chignon, a style I had never been able to master. On my way to an evening with friends at Karen's house, I stopped in the kitchen to get a drink. I told Diane how much I admired her hair-styling skill.

"Oh, Honey, there's nothing to it," Diane replied. "Come by my house sometime, and I'll show you how."

"Really?"

"Sure," she said. "Don't let Gerta scare you. She's big, but she's gentle; and she loves children."

"Who's Gerta?" I asked.

"Gerta is Diane's German Shepherd," Walter said. He looked up at me. "She's a *German* German Shepherd. She doesn't respond to English, only German."

"I'm teaching her English commands, though. I imported her for breeding," Diane explained. "We aren't set up for it yet, but my dream is to place as many German shepherds as possible. I love them." Intrigued, I would have enjoyed learning more about her obvious passion for the animals. Perhaps it was the result of watching all the Rin-Tin-Tin movies, but I had always been fascinated with the idea of owning a German shepherd.

When I opened the kitchen door, Sophie slipped into the room. As excited as only a Schnauzer can get, she ran around the kitchen table, greeting every person with an excited "Woof!" Dad told her to go to her bed, and Sophie obediently scurried to the folded quilt beside the kitchen door. Diane laughed.

"Sophie could walk under Gerta without touching the shepherd's belly," she said. Diane smiled at me. "I would love for you to come to my house, Sissy. You could meet Gerta, and I'll show you how to fix your hair. Maybe I'll even tell you a story or two."

"Okay." I grinned and waved at the foursome. On my way up the slope, I thought that Diane could probably tell some interesting stories. There was something about her that caught my interest, but little did I know just how fascinating her tales would be.

It wasn't long before I took Diane at her word. On the next Saturday afternoon that I had charge of Beth, I called Diane. Beth would much rather play with Robbie than spend the day with me, and I would rather visit with his mother. Learning how to create a new hairdo would be a bonus. No special occasion called for an elaborate hairstyle; but before one did, I wanted to know how I would look in a sophisticated upsweep.

"Sure, Honey. Come on over," Diane told me.

"What about your dog?" I asked. "Is she friendly?"

"She's very friendly, and she loves kids," Diane told me. "Don't worry about Gerta."

Beth chattered all the way to the Andersons' house, which was no more than three winding blocks. It seemed longer, since the way was so steep. From Diane's small front yard, she could see a tiny portion of our red roof, a switchback or two below.

As we walked, I let my eyes wander across the magnificent autumn colors spread across the wooded mountainsides. It was our third year in Dixon, and I loved it more with every passing season. Not even the smell of coal in the crisp, crackling air could diminish the beauty. While I often thought about Redbud Grove, I no longer felt the pang of loneliness that I had experienced when we first came to Dixon.

"Beth, do you miss your friends in Redbud Grove?" I asked.

"Sometimes," she answered. "Sometimes I can't remember faces. Do you remember my friend, Valerie?" I recalled the little girl with short, straight blond hair, a pixie-shaped face and big blue eyes. I nodded.

"Well, when I think about her, I can hear her giggles in my head; but I can't see her face," Beth told me. I looked down at my little sister. I knew exactly what she meant. Whoever said that thing about absence making the heart grow fonder didn't know much about reality.

"Look! There's Gerta!" Beth pointed, and she walked faster. Behind a chain-linked fence, a huge black and tan German shepherd ran back and forth, barking with excitement. I'd never had occasion to walk up this street, so I had never seen the Anderson's house or Gerta.

Diane hadn't exaggerated when she'd described her dog. A tall fence surrounded the Anderson property; and the beautiful, dark-faced shepherd patrolled the boundaries. She greeted Beth with happy whines. The front door of the house opened, and Robbie bounded across the small porch and into the yard.

"Hi, Beth! Hurry! There's a cowboy movie on TV!" Robbie motioned for Beth to follow, and she did. Gerta turned to me. Uncertain, I stopped. Her tail still wagged, but her grinning muzzle showed wicked-looking white teeth.

"Come on up, Sissy," Diane called from the porch. "Gerta, come." Diane hadn't raised her voice, but the beautiful dog turned and trotted to her mistress. "She wouldn't hurt you unless you posed a threat to me or Robbie," Diane continued. "Let her smell you, and next time she'll know who you are."

I did as Diane told me. Gerta's head reached my hip; and she weighed probably seventy-five or eighty pounds, possibly more. The beautiful animal sniffed my feet, and progressed upward. I extended my hand, palm down, and let her take in as much scent as she wanted. Apparently satisfied that I wasn't a potential enemy, she licked my hand. Gerta had accepted me.

"Come in, Sissy. I'm glad you called. Do you drink coffee? I just made a fresh pot, and I made a new recipe called 'blond brownies.' Have you or your mother tried it yet?" Diane led me through the living room, where Robbie and Beth already lay upon the floor in front of the television set. I followed Diane into the cozy kitchen, where the mouth-watering aromas of coffee and brownies mingled.

It was a wonderful room. A round table stood in the middle of the floor, which was covered with shiny linoleum in shades of rust, red, green and cream. White bead-board cabinets, topped with red countertops, lined one wall. Four white graduated canisters, with red apples painted on them, set the theme for the kitchen.

Throughout the room, the red apple motif peeked from enough places to create a bright, friendly, happy place. I felt comfortable and welcome. Diane's smiling face could not have been more gracious. I sat down at the table, where she indicated.

"Do you want cream and sugar in your coffee?" she asked. I nodded. Coffee had not yet become a daily thing for me, but I enjoyed a cup on cool days. We sat at Diane's kitchen table, where we ate more brownies and drank more coffee than we should have. It was the beginning of a friendship that was as warm as that glorious, autumn afternoon.

As we talked, I forgot all about hairstyles. Curious about Diane and her family, I asked a lot of questions. It was as if I had said the magic word, an "open sesame," for the most incredible tale came pouring from Diane's tongue. She told me about her childhood, about her meeting with the young soldier who would become her husband, about the fascinating, sometimes horrendous, events that had taken place in her life. I sat, mesmerized, as she spoke. Diane's many stories linger in my memory, but no other had the same impact upon me as the one she told that first day; and this is how I remember it....

The farmhouse looked like others in the rural community. Two-storied, the structure's front door and two windows were shaded by a porch that stretched from corner to corner. A tall catalpa tree stood at the edge of the yard. Various other species of trees surrounded the house, casting shadows and shade at all times of the day. At first glance, the place seemed neat and orderly. Further examination showed a lack of warmth, a touch of austerity, bordering on coldness.

Due to the years of the Great Depression, not many rural communities looked prosperous; but many yards held colorful pots of flowers or cheery blooming borders of some kind. In the rural area outside Madison, Wisconsin, the Langston house was the exception. Stark white paint covered the clapboards, and the grass was neatly cut. The windows sparkled, accented by black usable shutters; but the place bore no evidence of anything but utilitarian care.

"Diane, you come straight home from school. There's work to do." Fifteen-year-old Diane Cross closed the front door behind her and hurried down the porch steps. The strident voice of her aunt rang in her ears, the same words that followed her out the door every school morning.

Diane looked up at the soft blue sky of spring. With every step that led her farther away from the house, her sense of freedom deepened. She knew that it was only for the day, but she appreciated every moment. The mile walk to the hard road was no hardship; it was a respite.

Diane walked briskly. The stack of books fit nicely in the crook of her left arm. They were not a burden to her. She had dubbed them "the weight of knowledge." Gratitude for the opportunity to go to high school vied with homesickness for her mother and two older brothers. She thought about them with longing and sorrow every day.

Early morning sun cast beams of light upon the new green of leaves and struck scattered glints like diamonds across dewy, rolling pastures. Holstein dairy cattle grazed inside the fences that lined both sides of the dirt road. The cows on the left side belonged to Hugh Langston, the husband of her aunt, Bertha Langston.

Although Diane called him "Uncle Hugh," she felt no family connection to the man in whose house she lived. From the day of her arrival, eight months previously, Uncle Hugh had let her know exactly how unwelcome she was. That very day he had told her that her continued presence in his house depended upon how well she did her assigned chores. There were many.

Diane stayed out of his sight as much as possible. She didn't like him. Tucked into a specially fashioned tab on each pair of his overalls, Hugh Langston carried a blacksnake whip. He never left the house without it. During the time Diane had been a part of the household, she had witnessed Hugh's skill with the whip. He could knock a squirrel out of a tree and decapitate a rabbit on the run, as well as a snake as it slithered through the grass. Diane had a healthy respect for his skill with that whip.

By the time she arrived at the two-lane highway, it was seven-thirty. She had been up since four-thirty, mandatory in the Langston household. She had helped her aunt with the milk separator, a hand-turned machine that drew the heavy cream from the milk that was brought into the house in heavy five-gallon buckets. Some of the cream was set aside to make butter, but most of it was poured into tall metal cans and sold to creameries. Diane had begun to detest the smell of warm milk.

Every morning Diane helped her aunt prepare breakfast for Uncle Hugh and his son, Milton, both of whom expected the meal to be on the table and ready to eat when they came into the kitchen from the dairy barn. It always was.

The heavy meal of ham, sausage and gravy or bacon, eggs, oatmeal and fresh biscuits was served no later than six o'clock every morning. Only once had Diane made the mistake of allowing the home cured bacon to become too brown. Uncle Hugh hadn't said a word. He had merely tossed the offending piece onto his plate, shoved it away and left the table. Milton, a tall, hulking man of twenty-three, had done the same. Life was hard at the Langston house, but not unbearable.

Diane leaned against a fence post and watched the few cars that passed along the highway. In the spring of nineteen forty-three, few vehicles traversed the rural areas outside the cities. Those that did usually transported young soldiers, newly introduced to war, to and from train stations. Madison, Wisconsin, was a fair-sized city, the hub of the outlying countryside; but it was not a metropolis like Milwaukee or Chicago.

Diane stepped forward as a car approached from the crossroad on the other side of the pavement. She ran across the highway and climbed into the nineteen thirty-eight Ford, driven by Estelle Parkinson, who drove her two daughters to school in Madison every day.

"Hi, Diane." When the door closed behind her, Diane felt as if she had entered another world, one where a mother talked to her daughters and their friends as if they truly mattered.

"Hi, Sue. Hi, Betty." Like Diane, the teenaged girls wore dresses made from floral feed sacks. Not many farm families had money to spend on store-bought clothes. Diane sighed and leaned against the velvety mohair upholstery. For a few hours she could pretend that, like the Parkinson girls, she belonged to a complete family.

"Diane! Hurry up with that strainer!" As quickly as she could, Diane finished drying the heavy metal milk strainer. She hurried to the screened-in back porch where her aunt waited with the pails of evening milk. Supper simmered on the wood stove. It wouldn't be long before the two men would come in from the barn, ready to drop into their chairs and eat.

Wondering how her aunt had managed without her, Diane ran back into the kitchen to dish up the hot food onto plates as soon as she heard the men open the back door. No words were exchanged between them and her aunt. Diane knew there would be no greeting for her, either. She had learned that conversation seldom took place in the Langston house.

Quietly, she placed the brimming large pottery plates upon the square table. Its shiny, dark green surface gleamed in the light from the single overhead fixture. Like indoor plumbing, electricity was a luxury in most rural areas. Diane had considered electric lights a miracle, but a bathroom was beyond the scope of her imagination. A hand pump at the kitchen sick and a small, enclosed area on the back porch provided sponge-bathing facilities. A reservoir built into the iron stovetop supplied hot water.

A marvelous cook, Aunt Bertha seemed to enjoy teaching Diane her craft; and the girl had developed a liking for it. Over the weeks and months, Aunt Bertha had relegated much of the cooking to Diane, who was an apt student. Sometimes, Diane caught a likeness to her mother in her aunt, but it was fleeting and only physical.

By eight o'clock each evening, the kitchen chores were completed; and Diane was allowed to retire to her bedroom, one of three large rooms upstairs. Her aunt and uncle shared the one bedroom downstairs. The routine never varied. She finished her homework and went downstairs to wash. Out of courtesy, she still bade her relatives, where they sat in designated chairs in the living room, a brief "good night," no longer expecting a reply.

Hard work was a tremendous inducement to slumber. Every night Diane went to sleep within minutes of snuggling beneath the covers. She seldom heard the heavy footsteps of Milton on the stairs. Most nights, Diane closed her door; but in the hot summer evenings, she sometimes left it open, to facilitate any breeze that might filter through her window. Not once on those nights did she hear Milton hesitate at her door, where he stood with his head bowed, listening to her breathe.

Sundays provided the only break in the weekly routine. There was never a respite from the twice-daily milking; that was as certain as sunrise and sunset. As soon as Sunday breakfast was finished and the kitchen restored, Milton drove his mother and Diane to the little Methodist church three miles down the dirt road, in the opposite direction of the highway.

Milton never went inside the church. His father didn't hold with church, but the man had never tried to stop his wife's attendance. He seemed totally indifferent. When Bertha had first married Hugh Langston, she had encouraged him to go with her. Not only did he refuse to go, he would not allow his twelve-year-old son to go, either. Diane welcomed the opportunity to escape the dairy farm.

Sunday lunches were the only cold meal of the week, either leftovers from Saturday or a cold roast, prepared the previous day. During the winter months, Diane had retired to her room on Sunday afternoons; but this glorious spring day beckoned to her. Sunday afternoons belonged to Diane.

"Aunt Bertha, is it okay if I go for a walk to the creek behind the far pasture? I promise I'll be back in time to help with the milk."

"Why do you want to go there?" Bertha frowned.

"I thought I'd take a book and read for awhile, but I'll probably just walk. I'd like to follow the creek," Diane said.

"Look out for the dogs." Milton didn't raise his head from the newspaper in his hands.

"What dogs?" Diane's eyebrows rose of their own accord.

"The Steinbergs on the next farm have three or four German shepherds. They're not friendly. You'd best stay away from them."

Diane shivered. She liked dogs, but she had no desire to confront a pack of what she knew as German police dogs. "Do they come on your property?" she asked.

"I've seen them roaming along the fences in the woods," Milton told her. He raised his head and looked directly at her, something he didn't often do. Diane stared at her step-cousin.

Tall and stolid, Milton Langston looked nothing like his father, who was tall and very lean. Diane had decided that he must favor his deceased mother. Sandy brown hair, thick and straight, seemed to have a mind of its own. It grew collar length or longer, until he decided to trim it himself. Milton's light blue eyes fixed upon Diane, whose darker blue gaze stared back at him. She examined his face, thinking that the freckles across his nose made him look a little younger than his twenty-three years.

Milton's upper arms, hard and muscled from years of strenuous work, strained the sleeves of his chambray shirts. The half-moon shaped scar on his left cheek, the result of a cow kick when he was a child, lent a rakish air to his otherwise pure farm-boy countenance. Unfortunately, the injury had not only scarred Milton's face. It had also damaged his eye, which made him 4-F and kept him from being drafted into the army.

"Just watch out for the dogs," he repeated. A slight flush crept upward from his neck, and he dropped his eyes to the newspaper.

"I will," Diane promised.

"You be back here by five," her aunt instructed.

"How will I know when it's five?"

"Watch the sun. Shadows get long at four." There was no room for discussion after Hugh's edict. Diane nodded and quickly left the room before any one decided that she couldn't go to the woods. Winter had been long and hard for her, and she wanted the freedom of fresh air. Should she want or need to, the liberty to cry would be hers.

Diane made a quick pass through the kitchen and grabbed a biscuit and a piece of cold meat from the platter on the table. She wrapped it in a small piece of feed sack toweling and stuffed it into the pocket of her skirt, although the Langstons didn't hold with eating between meals.

The Langston farm stretched three-quarters of a mile behind the buildings, and ran a half-mile of frontage along the dirt road. A distance behind the house stood the dairy barn and a separate, smaller barn that housed a team of black plough horses. Most of the acreage was fenced for pasture, while the remainder of the rolling fields was planted in grain for the animals. Twenty-five Holstein cows and one bull comprised the dairy herd, not a big operation, but sufficient to provide the Langstons with an adequate living. Hugh and Milton had to work steadily to keep it running smoothly.

Diane followed the lane behind the barns. It provided access to all the fields, all the way to the strip of woods at the far side of the property. She made certain that a fence stayed between her and the pasture where the huge bull grazed. On more than one occasion she had witnessed the massive creature snort and paw the earth. One time she had seen Milton barely clear a fence in front of the charging bull.

The sun felt good on Diane's back. The shrill cry of a hawk filled the air. Diane looked up, shading her eyes with her hand. Puffy white clouds floated across a glorious blue sky, and the air smelled of new grass and sprouting buds, of life. She walked swiftly, hoping to spend as much time as possible along the creek that separated the farm from the adjoining property.

In a short time, Diane reached the woods. New, soft green leaves provided a dappled canopy above the rocky creek. She found a long flat rock that jutted over the water and sat down. She swung her legs over the edge of the smooth surface, but the rock was high enough that her feet stayed dry. She placed her book beside her. The woods were too beautiful to waste upon a story.

The quiet sounds of rippling water and happy birds drifted across Diane's young spirit like floating dandelion down on a current of spring air. She closed her eyes and thought about her mother. It would soon be a year since acute appendicitis had taken the life of the young woman, only days before her thirty-fifth birthday. Diane's father had been gone for months before, ostensibly to look for work out west; but he had not returned.

Diane wondered how her two brothers were coping with their new lives. Each had gone to different relatives, miles apart. The only other option had been an orphanage for the three children. Sometimes Diane thought that an orphanage might have been better. At least they would have been together.

She sighed and opened her eyes. "Well, hello," she said. "Where did you come from?" Perched upon the rock, not six feet from her, was a black and tan German shepherd puppy. He cocked his head and wagged his tail. Diane extended her hand. "I won't hurt you. Are you friendly?" The tail wagged faster.

The puppy rose to his big feet and came to her. She touched his head, and suddenly he was in her lap, licking her face. Diane laughed, something she didn't often do on the farm. The dog wriggled in her lap and whined in puppy ecstasy when she rubbed his belly. From the corner of her eye, Diane caught movement at the same time she heard a low, menacing growl. She froze.

With a happy yip, the puppy leapt from Diane's lap and bounced across the rock to the huge animal that had appeared from nowhere. Diane didn't move a muscle. She couldn't have moved, had she so wished. The shepherd's teeth bared in a warning snarl. Unperturbed, the puppy frolicked around his mother. For what seemed like an eternity, Diane remained still, willing the dog to go away.

She was surprised when the animal sat down and started to lick the puppy. Slowly, Diane shifted to look fully at the pair. The mother lifted her head and looked at Diane, but the snarl did not reappear. Even more slowly, Diane retrieved the snack from her pocket. She crumbled the meat and bread in her hand, and inch-by-inch she stretched her arm along the rock. The big dog's ears pricked upward, but she made no move toward Diane.

The food trickled from Diane's fingers. She pulled her hand back and clasped her fingers together in her lap. She decided that one of two things would happen: the dogs would consider the food as a friendly gesture, or they would eat it and her, too. Immediately, the puppy sniffed and found the food, wolfing it down without a thought of sharing with his mother. The larger dog watched from where she sat. When the puppy approached Diane, the mother stood, but didn't growl.

Diane allowed the pup to lick her fingers, but she made no effort to touch him. With a motherly "woof" and a long look at Diane, the big dog led away her offspring. At the edge of the woods, she looked back at the girl. Diane wasn't certain, but she thought that the bigger dog wagged her tail, just a little.

From that moment, Diane determined to win acceptance and friendship from the mother German shepherd. During the weeks of summer, she escaped to the woods every Sunday afternoon that she could; and she managed to take scraps of food each time. After a few weeks, she found both animals waiting for her upon the rock.

"Hi, Bobo. Hi, Missy." Diane had no idea what names were attached to the dogs, so she assigned her own. To the pup, she gave the nickname of her younger brother, Robert. Missy was the name Diane longed most to hear, the name her mother had called her. It seemed to fit.

Bobo came bounding. Missy stood up, and her tail definitely wagged a greeting. Both dogs eagerly took the scraps that Diane scattered upon the rock. She withheld a morsel until they were finished. Slowly, she extended her open hand to Missy, who gingerly took the food from Diane's hand. She touched the shoulder and then the head of the huge animal. She held her breath, afraid that Missy would reject her; but the dog seemed not to resent Diane's touch.

"You are so beautiful, Missy," she murmured. Missy sat down, and Diane was certain that the splendid dog smiled at her. It was the happiest day Diane had experienced on the farm.

In July, Diane's sixteenth birthday fell upon a Saturday. She had made no mention of the date, certain that it would make no difference to her relatives. When Aunt Bertha brought a white layer cake to the supper table that night, Diane didn't know what to say.

"I remember when you were born," the woman said.

"This is for me?" Diane asked. Her aunt nodded.

"Happy birthday."

Diane rose and went to Aunt Bertha. She threw her arms around the woman's neck. It was the first time she could remember actually touching her aunt. A flush rose in Bertha's weathered cheeks, and she seemed embarrassed.

"Sit down and eat," Hugh ordered. "There's no need to make a fuss."

"Uh, happy birthday," muttered Milton.

"Thank you! Thank all of you, so much! Mom always made cakes for our birthdays, but I didn't expect..." Sudden tears choked her voice. She stopped trying to talk and took a bite of the cake. Like everything else her aunt made, the cake was delicious.

Sometime in the night, Diane woke to the sound of far-off thunder. Muggy, heavy air seemed oppressive in her upper floor bedroom. She threw a shirt over the cotton slip that was her nightwear and tiptoed downstairs for a glass of water. The voices of her aunt and uncle could be heard through their open bedroom door, and Diane walked softly, not wanting to draw attention to her presence.

"The girl's old enough," Hugh said. "It's time that she stops this school foolishness and settles down. Milton will make a good man for her."

"I don't think she'll go along with it," said Bertha. "He's too old for her."

"He's just right. I don't see anyone else coming to court her. I've already told Milton, and he's agreeable. They can get married this fall, give her time to get used to the idea. I've wasted enough money on that girl."

Diane held her breath. They were talking about *her*! *Her and Milton*! Carefully, she retraced her steps back to her room. She closed the door, not caring that she shut off the faint draft from the window. What could she do? The thought of marrying Milton made her nauseous. *She didn't want to marry anybody*! She wanted to finish high school and go to teacher's college.

Thunder followed a sharp streak of lightning. Heavy rain began to fall. It sounded as if it would beat through the roof above Diane's head. She sat on the floor beside the open window and let the rain blow upon her burning skin. She didn't know what she was going to do, but she knew that she would never marry Milton Langston.

The days that followed seemed to fly. Diane said nothing of what she had overheard, and she avoided looking at Milton. She was afraid that she would see the truth of Hugh's words in his son's eyes. To avoid church on Sunday, she pleaded a headache. She retreated to her room as soon as the pickup truck carried away Milton and Aunt Bertha.

The room measured six paces one way and ten the other. Diane counted them as she paced back and forth, knowing that she had to find a way to escape from her relative's house. She took her small suitcase from beneath the bed and quietly folded into it as many of her clothes as possible. Several things she left in the tiny closet, just in case someone should look. Her schoolbooks were too heavy and bulky to carry, so she would have to leave them. Satisfied with her choices, she shoved the case under the bed.

With new eyes, Diane watched the three people who had been her rescuers. Nothing seemed different, but she had come to consider them potential jailors. Milton, as quiet as ever, never quite met her eyes. Aunt Bertha, quick to find work for Diane's hands, suddenly allowed the girl an hour or so of free time two or three days a week.

It was Hugh who began to change. His tone softened when he spoke to Diane, and once he tried to smile at her. Diane thought that the effort nearly cracked the skin of his face. She was certain that he would approach her any day with the news of her impending engagement to his son.

Diane watched for an opportunity to transfer her suitcase to a safe place outdoors. It came sooner than she expected. On a hot early August morning, she knew that the time had come. The men worked in the farthest field, moving and stacking the big rocks and stones that worked their way to the surface every year. Aunt Bertha, her long white apron hiked up to form a basket, gathered vegetables from the garden, while Diane prepared the noon meal.

Quickly, while a cast iron pot of stew simmered upon the stove, Diane gathered the suitcase and as many of her other belongings as she could carry. She hurried down the stairs and went quietly out the front door. Her heart raced and her breath quickened as she hid her things beneath the low-growing branches of a bushy, prickly cedar tree in the front yard. She ran back inside the house, barely able to take up a nonchalant stance in front of the stove before her aunt came into the kitchen.

"It's unmercifully hot," Aunt Bertha said. Diane hoped that her flushed cheeks would be attributed to the heat. She watched her aunt empty the contents of her apron into the big rectangular sink. The woman pumped cold water onto them, rinsing the dark soil from the fresh produce. The bright colors of tomatoes, onions, cucumbers, carrots and sprigs of herbs mingled against the white-fronted sink. The sight made Diane sad. *I could have been happy here*, she thought.

"Diane, I have something to tell you." Diane forced herself to place her fork beside her plate. She looked up at Hugh, amazed that he continued to eat as if he were not about to destroy her world. "You won't be going back to school next month. It's a waste of time and money. Since you have no place to go, you can marry Milton and live here, just like you are now." He forked more sliced tomatoes to his plate, then pointed the fork toward Milton.

"He'll make a good husband. You couldn't find a better one. The two of you can make a family here, and you can take care of me and Bertha, when the time comes." Hugh stared at Diane. "Well? Do you have anything to say?"

Diane swallowed, hard. "I, uh, uh, don't know what to say."

"Milton, do you want to marry this girl?" Hugh demanded of his son. Milton glanced at Diane, back to his dad, and nodded. Nausea swept over Diane at the thought.

"Then that's settled," Hugh declared. Bertha said nothing.

"I'll have to think about it," Diane stated. Hugh glared at her.

"You think about it real hard, Girl. Two days. You think for two days."

The next morning, Diane completed her chores without speaking to her aunt. Her mind raced, mapping out escape routes and plotting time frames. She could feel Bertha's eyes upon her.

"It won't be so bad. Milton is a gentle boy, for all his size." Bertha's words startled Diane. For a moment, the sympathy she heard in them was nearly her undoing.

"Aunt Bertha, I..." Diane stopped. The moment passed, for the closed-off veil had already dropped into place on the older woman's face. There would be no support from that quarter. She was surprised when Bertha continued.

"When you're finished with the breakfast dishes, you rest awhile. Go to the creek or to your room. I'll make dinner. You need to settle your mind." Diane nodded. "Your mama would like it if you had a home, Diane; and this is all you've got."

Diane washed the dishes and emptied the dishwater at the edge of the garden, the custom of the day, so as not to waste a drop. She returned the white enameled pan to the pantry and hurried through the kitchen door. She wanted to see the shepherds one last time, and this would probably be her only opportunity. Her mind was set upon leaving that very night, just as soon as the others were asleep.

In the horse barn lot, Hugh bent over the hoof of a big, black draft horse. Diane saw him straighten and watch her as she ran along the lane, but she didn't acknowledge him. Let him think what he might, she had permission to leave the house, even if it was the middle of the day. She ran all the way, not stopping until she was beneath the shade of the tall trees. She reached the rock and dropped onto the hard, craggy surface.

The dogs were not there. It was too early in the day. Diane hadn't expected them to be waiting for her, but she had hoped. Breathless from her run, she drew in gulps of air, which became sudden, uncontrollable sobs. She cried from loneliness, fear and despair. Running away was the only solution she could find, but she had no destination.

A soft whine close to her ear brought a smile to Diane's tear-streaked face. She raised her head and looked into the eyes of Missy, who had become her friend. The big dog licked Diane's cheek. She could swear that the dog understood her misery. Diane put her arms around the thick neck and buried her face in the furry shoulder of the lone female creature that returned her affection. Bobo was nowhere in sight.

They sat together for several minutes, the girl and the dog. Gratitude for the dog's friendship filled Diane's heart. She was unprepared for the low growl that rumbled against her cheek. Missy rose to her haunches. Diane followed the dog's gaze. About fifty feet away, whip in hand, stood Hugh Langston.

"What are you doing with that dog?" he demanded. "Get away from it! You don't have the sense of a goose!" Hugh advanced toward them. Missy bared her teeth and moved between Diane and the angry man. The hair on the dog's neck stood up. The growl deepened in her throat as she rose to her full height.

"She won't hurt me, Uncle Hugh! She's my friend."

"I said to get away!" His voice was the catalyst that set in motion the course of events that caused Diane to have nightmares for years. With the speed and force of a rocket, Missy launched herself from the rock toward Hugh. While the dog was in midair, the heavy blacksnake whip wrapped itself around her throat, cutting off the vicious, chill-raising growl. She dropped to the ground, where she writhed and struggled to breathe. The more she fought, the tighter became the whip. Braced against a tree, Hugh Langston wrapped the whip around the trunk; and the beautiful dog was finally still.

"No!" Diane ran to the dog. "No! No! No!" She screamed repeatedly, but she knew that the animal was dead. She tore at the whip that was deeply imbedded. It had cut through the furry pelt and hide, all the way into the flesh. "Why? She wouldn't have hurt me! Why?"

Hugh came toward her, winding the whip as he walked. He uncoiled it from the dead dog and wiped the blood on the grass. "Because she came at me," he said. Diane flew at him. Grief and rage overcame her fear of the man, and the bottled-up resentment toward him and the way he treated his family lent momentum to her feet. Undaunted, Hugh held out the heavy handle of the whip, pushing it against Diane's chest. The force of it nearly knocked the wind from her.

"Nothing comes at me and lives, not while I've got this whip in my hand. You'd best remember that. Get back to the house. You've got work to do."

Diane looked back at the dog where she lay so still upon the grass. "I can't leave her like this," she sobbed.

"I'll put her on the other side of the creek, where she belongs. Damned dogs. All they're good for is chasing cows. Get on back to the house, like I said." With the whip handle, he nudged Diane. She stepped back and watched while Hugh grasped Missy's two front feet and began to drag her across the ground. Nauseous, she turned toward the house. Not thirty feet away, hidden in a clump of brush, was Bobo.

Terrified that Hugh would spot him, Diane ran away from the creek as fast as she could. Bobo was old enough to survive on his own, but Diane's heart broke for him. She knew how it felt to lose a mother.

That night, when Diane came downstairs to bathe, she quietly put together a small packet of food left over from supper. She had been unable to eat, but she knew that she would require some sustenance at some point after she left the farm. Uncertain whether someone might look in on her, Diane undressed and crawled into bed at her usual time. Darkness was long in coming.

Wisconsin's summer light doesn't wane until after nine o'clock. Diane forced herself to remain quietly in bed for at least another hour, afraid that someone would hear her if she even turned beneath the sheet. She actually semi-dozed, until the soft sound of her bedroom door opening woke her. She lay very still. She forced her breaths to come slowly; and after a few moments, she opened her eyes just a slit. The figure in the doorway, hand on the knob, was Hugh Langston. Diane scarcely breathed until he closed the door and went down the stairs.

For another hour, Diane remained in the bed before she decided to leave. She gathered up the same clothes she had worn that day, picked up her shoes and made her way from the room, inch by inch. She stopped to listen after every step, terrified that someone would hear her. Not until she was behind the big cedar tree did she put on her clothes and shoes. She grasped the handle of her small case; and without looking back, she ran along the dirt road, toward the highway and freedom.

A half-mile or so away from the house, Diane stopped to catch her breath. In the starlit night, sounds of cicadas and frogs mingled with the occasional barking of a farm dog. In the far distance, the plaintive, lonesome wail of a freight train could be heard. Diane wasn't afraid of the night, but the rustling in roadside brush startled her.

"Bobo!" It was a toss-up as to which of the young creatures was happiest to see the other. With a happy woof, the German shepherd pup ran to Diane. She scooped him into her arms. "Are you following me? You miss your mother, don't you? I miss mine, too." She placed him back on the road and picked up the case. "I've got to go, Bobo. You go back home now."

The dog would not leave her. After several attempts to make him go back, Diane gave up and kept walking. At the highway, she tried once more; but Bobo was determined to stay with her. The two of them, side by side, began the long trek toward Madison, one of them afraid of what was ahead, the other, not caring.

Three hours they walked, without a single vehicle passing them from either direction. The early morning sky began to lighten. Several miles remained between them and Madison, and Diane was very tired. She took the packet of food and sat down upon the case. Eagerly, Bobo sat on the ground beside her, wagging his tail at each portion she gave him.

The lights of a car approached, headed toward Madison. Diane averted her head, afraid that the driver might be a neighbor who could recognize her. She held tightly to Bobo, uncertain what he might do. The car slowed and stopped just ahead of her. Her heartbeat quickened when the driver's side opened and a man climbed from the car. "Miss, are you all right?" The masculine voice held concern. "Do you need a ride into Madison?" Against the distant, faint glow of morning, Diane could see only a silhouette. As he drew closer, the light tan of his khaki army uniform was a comforting sight.

"Yes," said Diane. "Yes, I do need a ride; but I have a puppy with me."

"That's fine," the man told her. "I like dogs." He lifted Diane's suitcase and put it in the back seat of the very old car. "You can both ride in front with me. Come on." Without a qualm or hesitation, Diane picked up her dog and climbed into the car.

"Thank you so much," she said.

"You're welcome. My name is Walter Anderson, but you can call me Walt. Everyone does." He started the car, and they bounced onto the pavement. Above the noise of the engine, Walt Anderson continued to talk. "I'm on a thirty-day furlough...got into Chicago yesterday; and my buddy loaned me his car to drive to Madison. My folks live there. What's your name?"

"Diane Cross. This is Bobo."

"Hello, Diane Cross. Hello, Bobo."

All the way into Madison, Diane listened to the soothing sound of a friendly voice. As it grew lighter, she liked what she saw of her chauffeur. His face was smooth and tanned, and he had warm brown eyes. She found herself telling him about her mother, about her life and loneliness in the home of her aunt, and about Hugh's plans for her.

Without asking where she wanted to go, Walt Anderson took Diane and her dog to his mother's house, where she was welcomed as an honored guest, and where she felt safe and secure for the first time since the death of her mother. For Diane, falling in love with the young soldier was as easy and natural as breathing. As for Bobo, he lived in perpetual puppy heaven....

"So that's how you met your husband? How romantic!" I exclaimed. "When did you get married? Where did he go when his furlough was over? What happened to Bobo?" Diane laughed.

"Honey, we don't have time today for me to tell you," she said. "Do you want more coffee or would you like to get started on your hair?"

"My hair," I told her. "Diane?"

"Yes?"

"How old were you when you got married?"

"Seventeen, the year after Walt picked me up on the highway," she said.

"Diane, how did you know he was the right one?"

"Oh, Honey. I just knew. That's something no one else can decide for you. You know it in your heart."

"Were you ever sorry that you married so young?" I asked.

"Sissy, it was the best thing I ever did in my whole life. I wouldn't trade places with anyone else in the country, in the world, in the whole universe!" Diane lifted my heavy hair and began to work her magic.

"Not even for Elvis?" I teased.

"Honey, when you've got the best, you're not tempted by the rest." She nodded with confidence. "And that, Dear Girl, is a fact."

I believed her.

#

Chains

From our very first date, Jack McCoy and I drifted into going steady. My mother wasn't happy about it, and my dad was only a bit more accepting of the budding relationship between Jack and me. I know that he was influenced by Jack's baseball skills. Dad never missed an occasion to engage Jack in conversation about statistics, batting averages, home runs, RBIs, player trades and outstanding plays.

At sixteen-and-a-half, I thought that I should be granted more freedom; and there had been a slight loosening of the stringent rules. I think that was also the result of my dad's fascination with Jack's athletic prowess. He was convinced that a baseball player had to be one of the good guys. My curfew was extended from eleven o'clock on Saturday nights, to eleven-thirty, which didn't allow for much time between the end of a movie, a snack, and the ride home.

When I announced that Jack and I planned to double date with another couple, I was allowed an extra half-hour, till midnight; but Dad preferred that I be dropped off at my house first. Most nights, Jack and I respected Dad's wishes. There were a few evenings, when the movie let out early, or the other couple wanted to be alone, that Jack took me home last. I always explained the reasons to Mom or Dad, whoever was still awake when I got home.

On those nights, that lovely yellow convertible seemed to find its own way to the clearing where Jack had first kissed me. I enjoyed those short times with Jack, and it really was only moments that we spent there. He was always sweet and gentle, even restrained; and I never felt threatened. I couldn't imagine that he would ever do anything to upset or offend me. I thought that he was just about perfect.

One hot August evening, following a movie, Jack and I sat in his convertible outside my house. A soft breeze moved through the pines, filling the starlit night with their pungent scent. Jack's arm fit loosely around my shoulders. It was one of those magical evenings, when everything seemed right.

"My mother wants you to come to our house for dinner next Monday," Jack told me.

"Why?" I asked. "Does your mother feed all your girlfriends?"

Jack laughed. "She knows all the girls I've gone to school with, since kindergarten. I've told her about you, and she'd like to meet you."

"Don't you mean she wants to look me over?"

"Will you come?" Jack blew softly against my temple, stirring my hair.

"Do I have to dress up?"

"Why don't you wear that pretty, pink lacey dress, the one with the straight skirt? You wore it to Butch's wedding," Jack suggested. I turned my face up to look at him, to see if he were serious, or just teasing me. That pink dress was the only near-formal garment I owned. I had bought it to wear to a wedding, happy that it had been marked down to half price, which had also thrilled my mom.

The bride was the daughter of one of the foundry's employees, and my dad's family had been invited to the wedding. Mom made quite a fuss over it, since it was the first wedding to which we had been invited in Dixon.

The event had occurred shortly after Jack and I met. The only reason Jack had seen that dress was that he knew the groom, who had invited Jack to the wedding. I had been surprised to see him there.

"Wait a minute, Jack. Is this dinner one of those formal things, where the guys wear ties and the women drip diamonds, like in the movies?"

Jack laughed at me.

"No, Silly. I just thought you looked pretty in that pink dress."

I knew that Jack was manipulating me, and I didn't like it. I knew it deep inside, where we sometimes don't like to look too closely, because we might not like what we see. That contrary thing that lived in my psyche reared its obstinate head.

"Why can't I just wear a skirt and blouse or jeans? You know, like we wear everywhere else? Is your mother throwing a party?"

"No, Sissy, just dinner. No one will be there except my mother and dad and you. My sister, Deanna, is visiting some cousins across the river." Jack took my hand in his and laced our fingers together. He leaned forward and kissed me, once, twice. "Please?" he whispered. "Wear the pink dress?" He kissed me again.

How was I supposed to deny him when he wheedled like that? I knew that I was going to wear that dress, even while I resented the knowledge. Although Jack and I had been officially dating all summer, he had never taken me to his house. Karen had asked me repeatedly why I didn't just tell Jack that I wanted to see the place.

"I would!" she had declared. "I've known him since first grade, but I've never been to his house. He's had lots of parties up there, too. I was never one of the lucky ones that got invited." I hadn't known how to reply to that. Here I was, still a bit of the new kid in town, with an invitation to the Camelot of Dixon. I was sure that Karen was going to be jealous, but I couldn't deny being curious about Jack's house.

What would it hurt to give in on the dress? Besides, there was only one week left before Jack had to leave for college. While I was a little sad that he was going away, I was also excited about my own approaching school year. I was going to be a junior in high school, and I could hardly wait.

When Monday evening arrived, my pink dress and I appeared downstairs. My mother's eyebrows peaked; but she made no comment. When Jack and his navy dinner jacket walked into the living room, Mom's brows rose higher. It was very hot, without a vestige of cooling breezes, and much too hot to wear a dinner jacket.

"You look nice, Jack," she said.

"Thanks, Mrs. Bannister." Jack turned to me. "Sissy, are you ready? You look really pretty, except—I was hoping you'd wear your hair down."

I could feel my face begin to warm, but not from the heat. I had pulled my hair into a curly ponytail, the only plausible way to wear it on such a hot night. Due to the oppressive humidity, little damp tendrils were already beginning to curl on my neck and around my face. I was looking forward to the drive in Jack's convertible.

"It's too hot to wear my hair down, Jack," I said. "I'd look like a drowned rat, with my hair in sweaty strings all through supper, excuse me, I mean *dinner*." The evening had barely started, and I was already on the defensive.

"We have air conditioning." Jack's words hung in the hot room, and no one said a word for what seemed like ages. I shrugged.

"Well, Jack, it's ponytail or nothing," I told him. Jack laughed.

"Ponytail, it is," he said. "You look pretty, no matter how you wear it."

I think there was a compliment in there, but the words didn't bear too great a scrutiny at that moment. I was hot and disgruntled.

The McCoy house perched high upon a hillside, overlooking the city of Dixon. The winding, paved driveway boasted six—I counted them—switchbacks, before it widened onto what looked like a small parking lot. I honestly tried not to gawk, but I don't think that I succeeded. Tall pines lined the terraced boundaries of the property, seeming to form a barrier from the rest of the mountain. Beautifully groomed flowerbeds, filled with every conceivable annual and perennial, flowed among the pines and along the front of the house.

I had never before seen such a house. Tall pillars supported a roof-covered drive-through in front of the house, and that's where Jack stopped the convertible. Years later I learned that the covered "porch" was called a *porte cochere*.

The main body of the house was built of what looked like flagstone: big pieces of rock in various muted shades of brown, cream, tan, gray, blue and rose. Light from inside the house cast a colorful glow through the mullioned stained-glass windows. At one corner of the house, a magnificent, rounded turret rose from ground level, all the way past the second floor, peaking at the roof of the third story. The turret was built of old, faded brick, which had acquired a rosy, antiqued hue. Tall, narrow windows indicated each floor of the turret.

The house reminded me of my fairytale fantasies. I wanted nothing more than to stand quietly and absorb details of the manor and grounds, but Jack opened the heavy, wrought-iron-banded oak door. He escorted me inside, placing one hand at my back.

My first impression was that the walls were lined with gold, which I quickly realized was golden oak paneling. A crystal chandelier, sparkling like diamonds, dangled from the ceiling of the round second-story-high foyer. As Jack ushered me along, I caught a brief glimpse of gold-framed portraits upon the circular walls.

Our steps echoed upon the black and white marble squares, until we descended four wide, parquet steps onto a wide expanse of parquet floors. Extending immediately to the right and to the left were curving staircases that climbed upward to meet and form a bridge above the center of the spacious room.

Hallways extended at both ends of the bridge, leading to what I assumed would be many bedrooms. At the far side of the room, a massive stone fireplace rose above the bridge and disappeared into the second floor ceiling. The raised stone hearth stood a good three feet above the floor; and the firebox was wide and deep. It reminded me of scenes from movies about kings and castles.

Seated on a pale green brocade sofa, placed at a right angle to the fireplace, was Jack's mother, Cynthia McCoy. I had seen her picture on the society pages of <u>The Chronicle</u> many times. Jack's father, John McCoy, lowered the newspaper he was reading and rose immediately from the dark green winged-back chair. He folded the paper, and placed it upon the cushion.

"Mother, Dad, this is Sissy Bannister. Sissy, I'd like you to meet my parents." Jack sounded so formal. I had been less than formal when I introduced Jack to my parents.

Jack hadn't exactly lied to me. Neither he nor his father wore ties, but they both wore dinner jackets; and Mrs. McCoy could be described only as regal. My half-price pink dress might have appeared a tiny bit above gauche, next to her sleek, light blue sheath. Her only jewelry, besides her sparkling wedding and engagement rings, consisted of a beautiful gold and sapphire brooch, with matching earrings.

"How lovely that you could join us, Sissy," Mrs. McCoy said to me. Her soft, gentle voice held the most refined southern accent I had ever heard.

"Welcome, Sissy. We've been hearing a lot about you, Young Lady." Mr. McCoy sounded like other Dixon men. His inflection was less precise than his wife's, and his voice seemed warm and hearty.

"Thank you," I replied. "It's nice to meet you."

Dinner wasn't served in the dining room, for which I was very grateful. I caught a glimpse of that spacious chamber as Jack escorted me to a smaller, though lovely, six-sided nook, with windows that overlooked beautiful, sloping flower gardens. The backdrop of a tall, pine-covered mountainside provided a picturesque setting.

A buffet, set in silver containers and crystal serving dishes, was arranged on a mahogany sideboard. I relaxed a little. I had almost expected dinner to be served by uniformed servants.

"Jack tells us that you previously lived in Illinois," Mrs. McCoy said.

"Yes, in Redbud Grove."

"Where is that, in relation to Chicago?" Mr. McCoy asked.

"I'm not sure," I replied. "It's about thirty miles from Champaign-Urbana."

"Oh, then we know the general vicinity," Mrs. McCoy continued. "Our Jack will be attending The University of Illinois in a short time, won't you, Jack?" She smiled sweetly at her son. Jack looked at me.

"Yes, Mother, I will; and I'm going to miss my family and friends, very much."

"Oh, Darling, you'll be so busy with classes and parties and your fraternity that you'll hardly give us a second thought." Jack's mother dismissed his remark with a wave of her hand. I felt as if she had dismissed me, too.

The meal consisted of baked chicken, numerous fresh vegetables and salads. A tall glass bowl held a beautiful strawberry trifle. It nestled within another glass container, which was filled with ice. One look at Mrs. McCoy's smooth, manicured, stain-free hands told me that she had not prepared the food.

I couldn't eat much. I felt as if I were being examined beneath a microscope. Somehow, I managed to swallow at least a bite or two of everything on my plate.

I wasn't surprised when Jack's mother picked up a small, crystal bell and shook it discreetly. From nowhere, a young, uniformed woman appeared and began to quietly clear away our dishes. She refilled our water glasses and disappeared, without once looking at any one at the table.

"Let me get you some dessert," Mr. McCoy offered.

"Thank you." I watched him dip a generous serving of the strawberry trifle. A large, diamond and onyx signet ring on his right hand caught the light and reflected prisms upon the silver serving dishes. I thought about my dad's hands, how it was practically impossible for him to scrub away every vestige of the black molding sand from his fingernails and cuticles. He was a hands-on supervisor. When Mr. McCoy spoke to me, I thought for a moment that he had read my mind.

"I understand that your father works at the foundry," he said.

"Yes, he's a supervisor there."

"What does your mother do? Is she involved in any local civic endeavors?" Jack's mother questioned. I looked at the woman. I took in her expensive clothes, her perfect hair, and her perfect fingernails. I thought of my mother, who seldom bought a new dress, who had never had a manicure, who cut her own hair, and who still had sixteen months of training before she would be a licensed practical nurse.

"No," I answered. "My mother has no time for charity work. She works as a student nurse at the hospital, which is part of her nurses training. The rest of the time, she takes care of our family."

"Oh, my," Mrs. McCoy quietly exclaimed. "I hope she wasn't at the hospital during that unfortunate episode a few months ago."

Unfortunate episode? A man killed his brother, and she considered it an unfortunate episode?

"Actually, after Jake Kendall killed his brother, he walked right past my mother. She was one of those who helped try to save Jude Kendall's life."

"Oh, dear." Mrs. McCoy seemed at a loss for words. Mr. McCoy cleared his throat.

"How fortunate that your mother wasn't hurt, Sissy. Would you care for anything else from the buffet?" he asked.

"No, thank you," I replied. "I've had enough." I looked at Jack.

"Mother, if you will excuse us, I'd like to show Sissy the grounds." He pushed his chair back and pulled mine out for me.

"Of course, Dear. Sissy, I'm so happy that you came for dinner this evening."

"Thank you, Mrs. McCoy. Everything was very good." Mr. McCoy stood and extended his hand. His clasp was firm.

"Thank you for coming, Sissy. Enjoy the gardens. See you later, Jack."

As we left the room, I heard Jack's father murmur, "Cynthia, make me a martini, very dry. No, make a pitcher of them."

Jack escorted me through a rear hallway and onto a bluestone terrace that flanked the back of the mansion. Various pieces of wicker furniture and lounge chairs formed conversation areas along the length of it. A twenty-feet wide concrete stairway curved downward from the terrace. Walkways led in various directions from the stairs, flowing into the floral gardens. A majestic fountain, visible from all angles, rose from the center of the formal gardens.

It was all so beautiful, and Jack proudly pointed out areas of special interest: a bronze unicorn; a lacy, wrought iron bench large enough to hold four people; small, playful statuary of children and animals; enough unique, lovely things to fill many gardens. I hadn't been aware of the gradual climb until we reached the tall pines that formed a boundary around the gardens. We sat upon a stone bench, facing back toward the way we had come.

"Oh, Jack."

"Nice, isn't it?" he said.

"Oh, it's beautiful!" From where we sat, we were eye-level with the second story of the house, clearly visible across the expanse of the magnificent gardens. I had never before seen anything like the color and design that seemed to flow downward from our feet to the terrace.

"One day it will be mine," Jack said. He stood, put his hands in his pockets and surveyed his potential kingdom. Whereas I admired the beauty of the place, Jack saw something else.

"What about your sister?" I asked. "Wouldn't you share this place?"

A frown flitted across Jack's perfect forehead. "Deanna will be well taken care of; but as the only son, this estate will be mine." I looked up at his face, amazed at the expression I saw there. He was only eighteen years old, but I caught a sense of the man that Jack would be. I felt a sudden chill.

"I should be getting home, Jack," I told him. The spontaneous smile that lit his handsome face erased all trace of what I thought I had seen. I blinked. Perhaps I had misread him.

Jack chattered all the way back down the mountain and into town. I couldn't think of much to say. I listened to him go on about how much his parents liked me, and that he knew that I had made a good impression on them. I wryly wondered if he had considered the impression they might have made upon me.

"I'm glad you wanted to leave early," Jack told me. "We can take a drive and then go to the pine grove for awhile." There was confidence in his voice.

"No, not tonight, Jack. I really want to go home."

"Why?" He sounded so surprised.

"Because I just do."

"But, Sissy, I only have a couple of days left."

"I know; but I want to go home, Jack."

He hardly spoke to me from then until he drove up our driveway. He would have walked me to the door, but I stopped him.

"I'll talk to you tomorrow," I said. I hurried to the porch and waved to him from the doorway. Jack stood half in, half out of the car. He looked confused. That was okay. I was confused, too.

"Hi, Honey," Mom called from the living room. "You're home earlier than I thought you would be." I joined her and my dad, who looked up from the ballgame on television. Bill sprawled sideways in the overstuffed chair, his long, lanky legs dangling over the arms. Beth lay on her stomach, face propped with her hands, watching the ballgame.

"Where's Jack?" Bill asked.

"He went home. He has a lot to do."

"When does he leave?"

"Thursday. Well, I'm going up to change out of this dress."

"Did you have a good time at Jack's house? What's it like?" Mom was curious.

"It's a big house, Mom, way too big. Jack's mom and dad were very nice, and supper was nice, too. We had chicken. Well, I'm going up to change." I fled from the well-meant inquisition.

I didn't know what I was feeling. I really liked Jack, and I enjoyed being with him. He was a brilliant student, handsome as a movie star, sought after at school by both boys and girls; and he cared about me. Of that, I was certain.

Jack could have gone to college on a full athletic scholarship, but there was no financial need. He said that he didn't want to close the doors on other options. With his outstanding scholastic record, the university was glad to get him.

Now the time had dwindled down to just two more nights before his departure, and I wasn't sure how I felt. I took off the pink dress and placed it on a hanger. It had lost its appeal to me.

I slipped into cotton pajamas and crawled onto my bed. My room was hot, even with the window wide open. I positioned the small rotating fan, a prized possession from my attic room in Redbud Grove, so that it brought in the sweet, pine-scented air.

It was still early. The round alarm clock on my desk showed just short of nine o'clock. I turned on the little AM-FM radio, which was always set to a popular music station. The sweet harmony of the Everly Brothers flowed through the room: *I bless the day I found you, I want to stay around you, now and forever, let it be me....*

For no apparent reason, tears began to flow down my face; and before I knew it, I was in the throes of full-blown sobs. I muffled them in a pillow, and curled my body around another one. I don't know how long I cried. When I finally stopped, I was exhausted. The fan cooled the room, and I drifted off to sleep.

When I woke the next morning, the sun was higher in the sky than when I usually arose. I wandered downstairs, still in my pajamas. Mom had already left for work. Beth was in bed, and Bill was gone. There was a note from Mom on the kitchen table, instructing me to watch Beth, to make hamburgers for supper with the meat in the refrigerator, and to remind Bill to mow the lawn.

The phone rang, and I jumped.

"Hello?"

"Sissy? Are you okay?" The concern and hurt in Jack's voice touched me. "Did I do something to upset you?"

"No, Jack. I guess I was just tired last night. In fact, I just got up."

"Oh, good." The relief in his voice touched me. "I've got to go to Charleston with my parents today, and from there they want me to go with them across the river to pick up Deanna and see some relatives, before I leave for college. It'll be late when we get back. I just want to make sure that you're saving tomorrow night for me, Sissy. It's my last chance to see you for months."

I didn't even hesitate. "Sure, Jack. I'll be waiting for you tomorrow night."

"Sissy?" There was a long pause. "Sissy, I'll see you tomorrow."

Jack took me to a new restaurant for supper the next evening. We were the youngest people in the dimly lit dining room. It felt strange to me. Jack was quiet, even preoccupied. He sat close to me in the high-backed booth, closer than he usually did.

When the waiter asked if we wanted dessert, Jack answered for both of us, something he never had done. "No," he said, "just the check." He ushered me out of the restaurant and into the car, still without speaking.

From the corner of my eye, I watched Jack as he drove. He seemed tense, not like the confident, easy-going boy I knew. He drove straight to the pine grove, the quiet place that we had begun to call "our spot."

I was going to miss Jack. We had been dating for three months. At first, I had been more curious than interested. I had found it flattering that the most popular, most handsome senior boy at Dixon High was interested in me. It may have been my "hands-off" policy that had challenged him originally, but now I was sure that he really cared about me.

"Sissy, you won't date other guys after I leave for college, will you?" I wanted to say that I would *never* date another boy, but a contrary little quirk inside me made me hesitate just a bit too long for Jack's liking. "You *are* going to date, aren't you?!"

"Wel-l-l-l," I said. "You don't expect me to believe that you're not going to look at other girls, do you? You'll be out there at the University of Illinois, with all those college girls; and I *know* you'll ask some pretty blond, brunette, or redhead to go out with you. So why shouldn't I date, too?" I think that, at first, I was merely teasing Jack; but after I had said the words, I heard the ring of probability in them.

The memory of Jeff Franklin's handsome face flashed before me. Back in Redbud Grove, Jeff had declared undying love for Rebecca, the Amish girl, before he'd gone away to school. By Thanksgiving, he'd already found a new girlfriend; and he'd brought her home to meet his parents at Christmas! I had only been twelve years old at the time, but

I'd never forgotten my disappointment in Jeff Franklin. I had vowed to myself that what had happened to Rebecca would *never* happen to me!

Jack hit the steering wheel with both hands.

"No, I won't! And I don't want you going out with other boys!" Jack had never before raised his voice to me. "Don't you know that I love you, Sissy?!" I stared at him in stunned disbelief. Love? Did he say *love*? We were too young to say words like that to each other. I didn't know how to answer him. "Well? I just told you that I love you! Aren't you going to say something?"

"Jack, I'm only sixteen. I'm going to be a junior in high school."

"And I'm only eighteen, but I know that I love you!" Jack certainly sounded sure of his feelings. He took a deep breath. "Okay," he said, "maybe I'm rushing things a little. Okay. Okay." He leaned against the seat and pulled me into his arms. He pressed his lips against my temple, and then rested his chin atop my head.

I relaxed against his chest. This was the Jack I knew, the Jack who made me feel safe, the Jack who wasn't a threat to me.

"Sissy, will you wear this?"

"What?"

"My class ring." Jack slipped the big, heavy ring off his finger and held it out to me. "I know it's too big, but I'll get a gold chain; and you can wear it around your neck. Would you?"

I looked at the ring, where it rested on the palm of his hand. I had thought about this moment. Receiving a boy's class ring was something that all high school girls anticipated. It looked so big, and I could almost feel the weight of it on a chain, pulling at my neck, pulling me down. *What was wrong with me?*

"Oh, Jack, I don't know." I thought of my mother. "I'm not sure my mom would let me wear it, even if I took it."

"Well, you can take it and keep it in your room or somewhere. I just want to know that you have it and that you'll think of me when you see it."

I looked into Jack's face. His beautiful brown eyes were imploring, wistful and sad. How could I *not* accept his ring? *This was Jack McCoy, and he was asking me to take his ring*!

"Okay," I sighed, "but I can't promise that I'll wear it."

"That's fine, Sweetheart. Just keep it until I can replace it with something better." His tone had gone from wistful to smug. Misgivings stirred in my heart; and a thought, unbidden, came to me. *Jack McCoy was used to having his way and getting what he wanted.* As much as I liked him and enjoyed being with him, I felt a spark of relief that he was going away to college; and the next moment I felt guilty for the thought.

With gentle fingers, Jack tipped my head up; and he kissed me. It was nice; but, for me, something was missing. I pulled away from him and looked at the clock on the dash.

"We'd better go, Jack. It's getting late."

"Okay. Just sit close to me."

I nestled into his side and placed my head on his shoulder. He steered the car with his left hand and rested his right arm around my shoulders until we drove up our driveway. Jack came to the door with me, where he pulled me tightly against him and wrapped his arms completely around my body. He had never held me like that before.

"Jack, don't," I murmured. Instantly, he loosened his grip and gave me breathing room. "Good night," I told him.

"Sissy!" His voice was a whisper, but an intense one. He leaned forward and kissed me again, but with a passion he had always held in check. I responded, but only briefly, before I pulled away completely. "I'll write to you every week, Sissy; and I'll call on weekends. I'll miss you, Sissy."

"I'll miss you, too, Jack," I whispered.

"I'll call you tomorrow morning, just before I leave. Okay?"

"Sure." I quickly kissed his cheek. "Good night, Jack." I slipped inside, where I leaned against the front door and listened to Jack's steps as he walked to his car. I stayed there until the sound of the engine had completely faded away. My feelings were all over the place: guilt, sadness, mixed with a sense of loss that vied with a feeling of relief.

Suddenly, a strong wave of homesickness for Redbud Grove washed over me. The pang was actually physical, causing a painful surge of longing throughout my body. I wanted to walk upstairs and find myself in my old attic room, with the window that looked upon the eastern night sky. I wanted to wish upon the same star I had wished upon the first summer I had slept in that room. I wanted to feel the sprinkle of raindrops that sometimes had spattered through the screened window and cooled my skin on a hot summer night. I wanted to look out and see Julie Kitchen, pushing her wood cart past our house.

"Be sure to lock the door, Sissy," Mom's quiet voice filtered into the front hall. She was letting me know that she knew what time it was, which appeared to be some minutes past my curfew.

"Okay, Mom. Good night."

"Sissy, is everything all right?"

"Sure, Mom. See you in the morning."

I took a deep breath, locked the front door behind me, and started up the stairs. The lump in my throat was so big that tears couldn't get around it. I don't know what it was that made me so sad; but I knew one thing was certain. At that moment, what I wanted most was to be a child again. It was the first time I had experienced that longing.

It wouldn't be the last.

When school started, I was ready for it. I was sixteen, a junior, I had my driver's license, and I didn't have to answer to a boyfriend. I took a part-time job as a carhop at the A&W drive-in. Funds were not as tight as they had been before we came to Dixon, but I wanted to earn my own money. Most of what little salary my mother made at the hospital went to pay back the money she had borrowed for her tuition. She always managed to save enough to give us spending money; but I wanted to feel that I could, at least, buy my own records and lipstick. I promised Mom that I would keep my grades up, so she agreed that I could work a few hours a week.

Unfortunately, those few hours bit into my social life. When I was free, Karen wasn't. Karen Courtney had begun to date Matt Smith, a tall, lean, rugged-looking boy who had been out of high school for a year. I didn't know him, but Karen seemed to think he was wonderful. Matt worked at a local garage/gas station six days a week. Every Saturday night he took Karen out somewhere. Karen raved about him nearly every minute she wasn't in class.

"Oh, Sissy, Matt is so *sweet* to me! Do you know what he said last Saturday?" The question was rhetorical. "He told me that my eyes sparkled like stars in a night sky. Isn't that the most romantic thing?" Another rhetorical question. "And look." Karen pulled up the chain that she wore around her neck. She dangled the heavy class ring upon it. "It's too big for my finger, even with lots of yarn wrapped around it; so I just wear it here, close to my heart."

I blinked once, twice. It took that long to decide whether or not she were serious. She was. I swallowed the snide remark that wanted to burst forth from my tight lips.

"Yeah, that's nice, Karen. Are you going to the football game this Friday night? It's a home game. We play South Charleston, and I don't have to work." I was excited about the first game of the season, but not just because of the intense rivalry between the towns.

Coach Harrison always put on a show, striding up and down the lines, yelling at the officials, shouting in the faces of the boys on his squad. It was worth the price of admission just to watch him. He seemed oblivious to the fact that he consistently made a fool of himself.

"Wel-l-l-l, I don't know. Matt doesn't like for me to go anywhere without him, but I'll talk to him and see if he cares. He has to work tonight. The night shift guy got fired, and they're short-handed."

"Karen, are you telling me that you have to ask your boyfriend's permission to go to a football game with your friends?"

"Not exactly ask permission, Sissy," Karen said. "He just likes to know where I am and who I'm with." She actually sounded as if she were flattered.

"That's the way my dad is about me," I told her, "and my little sister," I added. Karen blushed.

"Well, isn't Jack like that with you?" she demanded.

"Jack and I don't have the same kind of relationship that you and Matt do," I said. "He's probably already looking around at the girls on campus." Was that just a hint of wistfulness I heard in my voice? "Although he *did* give me his ring," I couldn't help adding. The first letter that Jack had sent to me was inside a small package, along with a fine, gold chain and instructions to thread it through the ring and wear it around my neck, just as Karen wore Matt's ring. I had left the chain inside the box; and I had placed the ring there, too.

"Why aren't you wearing it?" Karen asked.

"Because I don't want to. It's too heavy, and it weighs me down." Karen looked at me as if I had suddenly taken complete leave of my senses, never to regain them.

"Don't you like Jack any more?" Karen asked.

"Of course, I like him! It's just that—I don't want to talk about this. Are you coming to the game with me, or not?" Karen hesitated for the space of five or ten seconds.

"Sure," she said. "It'd be fun to go to the game together. Why don't we see if some more of the gang will go with us?"

To our surprise and delight, we found that several of our friends planned to attend the game. Karen, Beverly, Rowena, and Judy met me at the ticket booth. We found seats in the bleachers; and it wasn't long before Jimmy, Jerry, Donnie, Wes, and Gary joined us.

It was early in the season, and the sun was still above the horizon when the game started. Once the glowing red orb touched the tops of the mountains, however, twilight was immediate, followed quickly by deepening dusk and darkness. It was a little too warm for football, but the evening was wonderful for gathering with friends.

Wish I May, Wish I Might...

Floodlights illuminated the football field, and there was an air of anticipation as we yelled with the cheerleaders. It felt so good to laugh and joke with my friends. I experienced a twinge of guilt about Jack McCoy, but only a tiny one. As much as I liked Jack, I was totally caught up in a world without him, a world filled with fun, friends and freedom.

The Dixon Wildcats were not playing well. Tom Vickers, the senior quarterback, fumbled every catch; and Coach Harrison was livid. By the end of the third quarter, the score was about as lopsided as it could get: thirty-six to nothing; and we had the nothing.

"Look at that!" Jerry pointed to the coach, who had grabbed Tom Vickers's jersey and was pulling the boy off the field. They were about the same height, but Coach Harrison outweighed the boy by a good fifty pounds. We couldn't distinguish his words. The coach's face was vivid red. His eyes were filled with a murderous rage, and his facial muscles contorted with anger.

Boos and hisses rose from the fans in the bleachers, but the coach continued berating his quarterback, all the way to the sidelines. He looked down the line, picked another player, and sent him into the game. Tom followed the coach, obviously trying, unsuccessfully, to talk to him. Tom took off his helmet and tossed it toward the team bench on the sideline. It bounced and struck Coach Harrison on the back of both legs.

As ferocious as a rabid dog, Coach Harrison turned and backhanded Tom Vickers across the face. Tom staggered and stumbled over a teammate's feet, which careened him onto the bench, lined with padded football players. They broke his fall before he rolled to the ground.

All sound in the field dwindled to startled gasps, followed by stunned silence. It was only then that Coach Woodrow "Woody" Harrison lost the manic look of fury that had contorted his features. He rushed to Tom's side and extended his hand to help the boy stand. Tom ignored the coach.

Leaping agilely to his feet, Tom picked up his helmet. Without a backward glance, he jogged along the sidelines and off the field. As one, all the boys along the field followed him. Within moments, the whole Dixon High School football team, the Wildcats, cleared the field.

Pandemonium erupted in the bleachers. Fans went wild, cheering and applauding, stamping their feet upon the bleachers, whistling, creating a stupendous show of support for the boys' actions. Someone threw a soda bottle at the coach, but missed him. Other bottles followed suit.

Appearing bewildered, Coach Harrison ducked and ran toward the middle of the field. South Charleston's team headed for the locker rooms, and the officials gathered around the coach. They escorted him from the field to his car, which caused additional cheering from the home fans.

"I never *did* like that man!" Beverly said. Her dark brown eyes sparkled like coal.

"I didn't, either!"

"Me, neither!"

"I think he's always been crazy!"

"Me, too!"

We slowly made our way through the crowd. Laughter, anger, dismay, derision, every emotion imaginable was apparent in the remarks and bits of dialogue we heard on the way to the parking lot. I didn't envy Coach Harrison.

"Maybe the school board will finally fire that old tyrant and hire a good coach!"

"None of the boys like him! They just put up with him, 'cause they wanta play ball!"

"Now, Harvey, you know he had a winning baseball season."

"Well, yeah, but only 'cause a' that McCoy kid!"

My heart lurched.

That McCoy kid.

For the first time since Jack left, over a week ago, I felt a pang of longing for him. I didn't *want* to miss him! This called for immediate action.

"Hey, let's go somewhere," I said.

"Dooby's."

"Dog 'n Suds."

"A & W."

"What'll we do? Flip a coin?"

"No," said Karen. "Let's go to my house! We haven't had a party for a long time!" So we piled into cars and headed up the winding streets to the Courtney house. On the way, we stopped at a grocery store and shared the cost of chips and sodas. Nobody had much money, but by pooling our resources we managed to finance plenty of snacks and drinks for everyone.

On Friday nights Karen's parents always went out, so we had the Courtney house to ourselves. We were good kids. Not one of us would have damaged anything in Karen's house, or in any other home. None of us smoked; and, as far as I knew, none of us drank, not at that time, anyway.

Karen's dad kept a supply of liquor in a cabinet, which was always locked. The more I knew about Mr. Courtney, the more sure I was that he kept it locked to insure that no one stole his moonshine, not necessarily because he was worried about his daughters.

Karen fingered the chain around her neck all night, swinging Matt's class ring back and forth. I wanted to snatch it from her and toss it down the nearest hill. Watching that ring dangle from the chain made me think of Jack's ring, resting in that box. I didn't *want* to think about it. As much as I liked Jack, I didn't want to be bound to him by a ring on a chain.

In spite of my ambiguous feelings, I enjoyed the party. We played records, laughed, danced, ate mounds of potato chips, drank gallons of soda, and had a wonderful time. I'm glad we did. It was the last gathering that all ten of us would attend together. Life for one of us was about to take an unexpected turn, a bend in the road that had no detours and no way back.

It was bound with invisible chains.

Eternal chains.

Heroes

My dad never talked to us about THE WAR. I had learned what little I knew about it from old black and white newsreels, which were shown at the Ritz Theater, back in Redbud Grove. Every movie was preceded by a newsreel, which we endured, knowing that a cartoon would follow. I grew up thinking that the war had been fought and won in black and white. I never saw colored prints or colored newsreels.

My mother kept many photograph albums. One of them held only pictures of my dad, from rare, faded prints as a child, to many snapshots of him in uniform. Rows of colorful medals adorned his uniform jacket. As the war progressed, so did the number of his medals.

Dad was most proud of the many sharpshooter medals. Long before he was drafted, my dad was a crack shot with a rifle. My mother often told stories about Dad's hunting skills that kept meat on their table when they were first married. I grew up with stories of his prowess.

As one story goes, when I was a baby, they were reduced to a meal of gathered field greens one spring day. They had no money, and Dad had one shell for his rifle. He went squirrel hunting, hoping to bring back meat for his nursing wife. Mom could still tear up when she told how my dad came home with not one, but two squirrels, killed with one shot.

"I'm just glad he doesn't have a Purple Heart," was Mom's standard reply when Dad's medals were mentioned. A small wood chest with a metal hasp held his medals, along with a pocket-sized, steel-covered New Testament, and three bracelets. Gold-tone buttons, some covered with crossed rifles, red and blue ration tokens, and war ration books completed the collection of war mementoes.

The testament was always carried in the breast pocket of a soldier's uniform, over the heart. We had heard stories of bullets being deflected from the metal cover of the book, thus saving the soldiers' lives. The bracelets were made from the aluminum of airplanes that had been downed over Italy, where Dad had spent most of his time in Europe.

One of the bracelets had two entwined hearts atop it, and inside the hearts were the words: To my darling wife, with love, Will. On the outer sides, Italy and 1945 were engraved. Two smaller identical bracelets had two hearts engraved on them. One read: To Sissy from Daddy, Italy, 1945; and the other, To Buddy from Daddy, Italy, 1945. Dad had sent them to us months before he returned home, and they were our prized possessions.

As I grew older and tried to question him about his experiences, Dad never answered me. He wouldn't even look at me. It seemed that he simply shut down at those times. Eventually, I stopped asking.

Two of my dad's brother's, one older and one younger, also survived World War II. Uncle Jim, Dad's next-older brother, had spent most of his time in the South Seas and Japan. Uncle Sonny, the younger one, had been sent to the front lines in Europe.

At the age of eighteen, Uncle Sonny had been wounded during the Battle of the Bulge. Shrapnel hit his ankle, which led to gangrene; and his foot was amputated. The infection had already spread upward, and eventually his leg was removed at the knee. Unfortunately, that didn't stop the gangrene. The final amputation left the eighteen-year-old boy with nothing but a stump, barely long enough to fit into the prosthesis, which the government provided for him.

My Uncle Sonny spent the next few years drinking heavily. He and his young bride had married before he went overseas. After he returned, they had two children right away, a boy and a girl. Shortly after the little boy was born, my dad had moved us to Redbud Grove; so we rarely saw Uncle Sonny's family.

Through letters from relatives, we learned that my uncle had been converted to Christianity and had become a Baptist preacher. All of us found that hard to believe, but it proved to be true. My paternal grandmother had been a God-fearing, church-going Baptist, who took her children with her to church every Sunday. She died at the age of forty-five, when my dad was fourteen, leaving five children at home. With her death, the church going ceased. Thereafter, the children who were left in that home were without benefit of clergy.

One beautiful day in October of nineteen fifty-six, my junior year, we received a letter from Uncle Sonny. He was going to hold a revival in a town not far from Dixon, and he wanted to spend a night or two at our house. We were thrilled! Any time a relative from far away could visit was a time of happiness for us. It happened so rarely.

Even though my mother was a trainee at Dixon Memorial Hospital, she still managed to oversee preparations for our guest. Mom had three older brothers, but she said that Uncle Sonny was like a younger brother to her. She had known him all his life.

"Your Uncle Sonny always thought that you were the prettiest little thing," Mom told me; and she was off and running with the same stories she had told me since I was very small. I could repeat them with her, word for word.

"When you had just started to walk, Sonny stayed at our house quite often. One morning, while he was still in bed, you toddled to his bedside and kissed him and patted him, until he woke up and paid attention to you. He was about fifteen then. When he got up, he discovered that you had peed all over his pants, which he had left beside the bed." Mom laughed, remembering. "They were the only clothes he had!"

Mom decided that Beth's room was more practical for my uncle, since it was on the ground floor. Although he could navigate stairs with his artificial leg, and never expected nor asked for favors, it just made sense for him to stay downstairs. Beth could share my room for a couple nights. We would both cope the best that we could. I'm not sure which one of us had the greater hardship!

"Hi, Hon!" I ran into my uncle's outstretched arms. His hugs felt so warm and loving and secure. My dad was not a hugger, but his brother was. Beth received her hug, but my brother held out his hand. Uncle Sonny grasped it, gave it a good shake, and then pulled Bill into his arms and hugged him, too. Bill might be fourteen; but to our uncle, Bill was still a kid.

Uncle Sonny, whose real name was Leslie, was taller than my dad. While Dad had the Bannister blue-gray eyes, my uncle's eyes were dark brown, like their mother's. My uncle was thirty years old that summer, tanned and handsome and healthy-looking. My dad's slender five-feet-ten-inch frame seemed much smaller next to his younger brother's six-feet-two, two hundred pound stance.

One thing was certain: the three of us shared the same crooked smile, even to the down-turned left corners of our mouths. That caused a warm sense of kinship inside me. I had always been able to recognize my dad in my features, and seeing some of the same traits in my uncle made me feel good.

"This country is really pretty," Uncle Sonny said. Before we went into the house, we took him on a short tour of the back yard, where my mother had cultivated a vegetable garden, now brown from the frosts. A few hardy zinnias surrounded the garden plot, but most of the plants had died. Mounds of blazing gold, bronze and purple chrysanthemums formed a vibrant, colorful border along the back of the house.

Uncle Sonny looked upward, toward the tops of the surrounding hills and soft, multicolored peaks. He smiled. I was proud of our home in the hills.

"It has the same colors of the Ozarks in the fall," he said, "just taller. Say, Billy-Boy, bet I can beat you in a race up that hill, even with just one leg!" And then he laughed. If my brother hated anything, it was being called "Billy-Boy." Only Dad's brothers called him that, and only Uncle Sonny could get away with it. I loved my uncle's laughter. It was spontaneous and long, causing his brown eyes to nearly disappear into the crinkles of mirth that had formed around them.

At supper that night, he told us about his children. There were now six of them, and eventually there would be nine. Someone had once made a crude, tasteless remark about his ability to produce so many children, a remarkable feat, since he had only one leg.

"Just think what I could have accomplished with two," my uncle had retorted.

Long after the rest of us went to bed, I could hear the voices of my dad and my uncle downstairs. I heard occasional words; and I realized that they were discussing the war, something I had never heard my dad do. Curious, I carefully ascertained that Beth was asleep. I crawled from the bed and tiptoed to the top of the stairs. I sat down on the third step from the top, close enough to hear, but hidden in the shadows.

I hadn't eavesdropped on my parents since we left Redbud Grove. Actually, their nightly conversations back then had filtered through the vent, into my attic bedroom. Anything I had learned from those chats was purely accidental, well, mostly. This foray was intentional, bent upon gaining some insight into my dad's war experiences.

The nightly sounds of crickets and cicadas could be heard through the open windows. It was a comforting, eternal serenade that echoed from the pine-covered, sweet-scented hillsides. The essence of autumn filled the air: that poignant smell of decaying gardens, along with the hint of smoke from piles of raked, burning leaves. The seasonal aroma almost covered the aura of coal dust from the mines, a lingering thing that never quite went away.

"...couldn't believe all those kids lined up along the streets." I caught the last part of my Dad's sentence. "There was one little boy, about five, Sissy's age at the time, that pulled on my pants leg. He wanted to sell his sister. 'Hey, G.I.! You come home me! Fifteen minutes! Sister for choc'lat! Clean girl! Sister for choc'lat!' Sonny, that kid's family was starving!" I had never before heard such anguish in my father's voice.

"What'd you do?" my uncle asked.

"I grabbed what I could from my rations and tossed it to him. We were on the march, and I couldn't stop. He caught it; and then I heard him going to the men behind me, saying the same words to them. I don't think the kid knew the meaning of the words. He was like a parrot, repeating what he'd been told to say."

"How far were you behind the front lines?"

Dad was silent for a long moment before he answered.

"Probably three or four days, a week at the most."

I felt a chill at his words. I had just learned more about my dad's days in the army than I had known during all the years since his discharge. I hadn't dreamed that he had been so close to the front lines.

"We'd been in Sicily for a few days. Then they shipped us to the mainland of Italy; and we moved from the coast, north. I don't remember how long we were there before we moved out; but all along the way there were bombed-out houses and people trying to survive the best way they could.

"There were little kids digging in piles of garbage, looking for scraps of food, just something to eat. Poor, filthy, starving little kids, no bigger than Buddy and Sissy back home."

"Yeah, we saw a lot of that in Belgium, too." The tone of my uncle's voice said more than his words. "When we were advancing, we passed through towns and villages where people were still burying their dead and looking for more bodies in all that rubble from the bombs. I won't ever forget the screams and the wails when they found more dead relatives in that mess.

"It was so cold. Just about all of us got frostbite or frozen toes and fingers. At least we had food."

"Were you scared, Sonny? I mean, when you got close to the front, were you afraid? You were just an eighteen-year-old kid!"

"I was so scared, my teeth chattered," my uncle almost laughed; but it might have been closer to a sob. "The sounds of the machine guns, the tanks, the grenades, the mortar shells...after a while, I stopped hearing individual sounds. It was more like a constant whine and shelling. I remember thinking that it must be like the hell Mommy used to tell us about. Remember?"

"I remember." I barely heard Dad's reply. The two men I loved most in the world were silent for several minutes.

"But you must have been just as scared as I was, Will. You had two little kids back home, and Jackie, all depending on you."

"I couldn't let myself think about them during the day, but at night I couldn't help it. Sometimes I cried at night, Sonny. I cried because I just knew that I'd never make it back to see them; and they'd grow up without me, without a daddy."

I put my knuckles in my mouth to stop the sobs that threatened to give me away, but I couldn't stop the tears. The picture of my daddy, crying at the edge of the frontlines was unbearable; but it was already branded into my heart and mind.

"Will, I really prayed when I saw my buddies fall all around me. We were so close our arms touched; and then they'd be gone, maybe with no face left, or arms shot off, or guts hanging out. Will, you know what I prayed for?"

Dad must have just shaken his head.

"I prayed that there would be enough of me left to send home, so I could be buried with my kin. I never thought that I would survive that awful, hellish inferno." He cleared his throat. "You know, I didn't even feel the shrapnel that hit my ankle. We were stumbling over the bodies of our own men, trying to gain some ground.

"I fell into a foxhole and collapsed there for I-don't-know-how-long, with my eyes shut, trying to get enough courage to climb out of that hole. I was hoping that the battle would just be over. When I finally climbed out, my foot wouldn't hold me. I fell on top of other bodies, some still alive, most dead. A medic finally decided that I was a live one, and I was sent to a hospital tent and then transferred out. The rest, as they say, is history."

"Do you ever dream about it?" Dad asked.

"Oh, yeah. I dream about it a lot, but not as much as I used to. Will, you know I stayed drunk for three or four years after I got home. I think maybe I drank to blot out the sounds in my head, and the pictures behind my eyes." Uncle Sonny laughed. "That was really stupid. I was carrying them with me every step I took. The liquor blurred it some, but nothing ever took away the pain." I heard the sound of his knuckles rap upon his wooden leg. "It's impossible to forget this; but after I stopped drinking, the dreams stopped coming so often. Maybe the booze fed the nightmares."

Dad cleared his throat, tried to speak, and cleared his throat again.

"I'm glad you made it home, Sonny." Dad's voice broke.

"Me, too, Will. Me, too. I'm glad the war ended before you reached the front. One of Mommy's boys crippled is enough! Well, now. Why don't you show me where you want this one-legged preacher boy to sleep!"

I heard the rustle of movement, and I knew that they had stood.

"Sonny?" Dad hesitated.

"Yeah, Will. I love you, too. You know, Will, I think that a lot of Mommy's prayers have been answered. Remember how she used to pray out loud for all of us? And by name? She called out the names of all nine of us! I was only eight when she died, but I still remember hearing her pray." He laughed. "Used to embarrass me to death."

There was the sound of two men embracing, slapping each other on the back, followed by coughs and clearing of throats.

"Your room is on the other side of the bathroom, right through there. Do you need anything?"

"Nope. See you in the morning. G'night, Will."

"'Night, Sonny."

There was the sound of my uncle's uneven gait as he walked down the hardwood-floored hall, and then the soft click of Beth's bedroom door. I sat on the step, hiding my face in my lap. I hoped to stifle the sobs that threatened to pour from me, at least long enough for my dad to get into his bedroom.

"Sissy?"

I lifted my head. Dad stood at the bottom of the stairs. I didn't think he could see me in the shadows, and I was sure that I had made no sound. I looked down at my dad. From the light in the living room, I could see the tracks of tears still on his face. It broke my heart. I jumped to my feet and ran quickly down the stairs, barely touching the individual steps.

I threw myself into the strong arms that had lifted me high when I was little, arms that had curled round me when he read to me from books he didn't like to read, arms with hands that had spanked me when I needed it, and arms that now cradled and rocked me while I shed tears for the anguish he had known. I finally understood why he never spoke to us of those horrible war years. He was sparing us.

"Daddy, I'm so sorry," I whispered. "I'm so sorry."

"Sh-h-h-h, Sissy," he murmured. "It's all right now. All that is over. It's behind us." He kissed my forehead and turned me toward the stairs.

"You get to bed. Everything is all right. We're together, and we're all right."

"I love you, Daddy." I couldn't remember ever saying the words. My dad cleared his throat again.

"Goodnight, Sissy." Although he didn't say it, I knew that he loved me, too.

Dad seemed quieter for several days after Uncle Sonny left. In the evenings, he watched every televised baseball game the Cardinals played. When television reception was bad, he listened to games on the radio. Mom put in some night shifts at the hospital, filling in for vacationing nurses. Some nights I sat up late with Dad, just to keep him company after Bill and Beth went to bed.

We didn't talk much those evenings. I usually had a sketchpad in my lap, and Dad often watched television from a prone position on the couch. Occasionaly Jack McCoy called me. Dad no longer seemed to mind how long we talked on the phone. Mom had finally installed an extra-long cord, which allowed us to carry the phone into the dining room for more privacy.

One night, after talking to Jack for a few minutes, I re-entered the living room to find my dad intently watching the screen. He sat upright, one hand gently caressing Sophie, who sat as close to him as she could. For a man who didn't like house dogs, Dad gave a good impression of someone who was crazy about our little, adopted Schnauzer.

"What are you watching?" I asked.

"Sh-h."

I sat down in the rocking chair to watch. It was a re-broadcast of the Nazi war crimes trials, held in Nuremberg, Germany. Mesmerized, I watched the testimony and then the graphic, horrible scenes from the death camps and concentration camps, filmed both by the Nazis and by the liberating troops at the end of the war.

With my hands in my lap, I stared at the screen, unaware that tears were running down my face. I gasped at the sight of thousands of dead bodies of men, women, and children, mountains of them, naked, wasted, twisted into grotesque forms. Horrified, I stared at the piles of gold teeth fillings, gold watches, eyeglasses, wedding rings and other jewelry, at the high stacks of clothing and shoes and handbags. All those things had been taken from the prisoners, mostly Jewish citizens of Europe.

"Oh, Daddy!" I whispered.

"Just watch, Sissy. Watch and remember what you're seeing."

I didn't want to see any more, but I couldn't tear my eyes from the screen. When it was finally over, I felt cold. I couldn't comprehend the extent of evil that human beings could perpetrate against fellow human beings. I felt sick, physically and emotionally. I slowly turned to look at my dad.

"You saw this, didn't you?"

When Dad answered, his voice was very soft. "Of course I did."

"You were there. That's why you didn't come home as soon as the war was over. I remember. You didn't come home until the next summer, just before Bethy was born. You were part of the clean-up crew!" I could hear myself babbling. The longer I talked, the higher pitched my voice became.

"I remember the day you came home! There was a big hole in the screen door of the little apartment and you stuck your head inside the hole and said hello and I looked up from where Buddy and I were playing on the floor and then I ran and threw my arms around your neck and you were laughing and you told me to unlock the door and you had your uniform on and your big soldier's hat and you kept saying Sissy unlock the door so I can come in but I wouldn't let go because I was afraid that you would go away again and never come back so I just held on...." I stopped and drew in a deep, cleansing breath.

My father and I sat in the living room of our house in Dixon, West Virginia, ten years after the event. There was a new understanding between us. I had discovered my dad's horrible memories of the war, and he had discovered his daughter's fear of losing her father. We stared at each other, Bannister eyes to Bannister eyes, for a long moment. Dad smiled.

"How about some ice cream?" he asked.

"Race you to the icebox!" I answered, and I bolted for the kitchen. I was aware that I had reverted to old phrases twice: I had called my brother "Buddy" and the refrigerator "icebox." It didn't matter. My brother didn't hear me, and my dad didn't care.

It was one of the sweetest nights of my life.

That autumn, a new program was introduced at school. I'm not sure what or who was responsible for influencing him; but Mr. Sheffield, the principal, was receptive to a student council request that students be allowed to hold "sock hops" in the cafeteria and nearby corridor after school each afternoon. Larry Mathews, president of the student council, chose the music and appointed students to play the records on a portable phonograph.

Larry, one of the most popular boys in the school, was a compact, well-put-together athlete, who played football and was a member of various school clubs and organizations. His status was earned, for he was one of the most pleasant, friendly boys I had ever known. It was largely due to his leadership that the sock-hops were such a success.

Various teachers were enlisted as chaperones. They wandered along the sides of the corridors, watching with practiced eyes to see that couples didn't dance too closely to each other. Most of the music selections took care of that problem.

The rock-and-roll favorites of the day, sung by Elvis Presley, Jerry Lee Lewis, The Big Bopper, Bill Haley and The Comets, and Buddy Holley rang through the cafeteria. Very few slow ballads were played at the sock hops.

I rarely stayed after school for the dances. Most of those who did were couples, and they never danced with anyone else. Since I wasn't dating at all, it was embarrassing to stand around and watch others having a good time. Evidently, everyone thought of me as "Jack McCoy's girlfriend." Not one boy had asked me for a date since school started.

While I didn't really want a "boyfriend," going to a movie with someone or just hanging out with a friend at Dooby's would have been nice. I think that's what I missed most. I might have been tempted to date another boy, had one been courageous enough to ask.

Confusion reigned inside my head. Letters, one or two a week, came from Jack. They were filled with information about his schedules, his classes, his teachers, people he had met, books he thought I should read. Every letter ended the same way: "I miss you, Sissy. Promise that you aren't going out with other boys! I'll be home as soon as I can. Love, Jack."

I saved Jack's letters. Some silly, fantasy-based side of me found it romantic to keep them, tied with a pink ribbon, in my souvenir/treasure drawer. Sometimes I rummaged through that drawer, taking out items and looking at them, remembering occasions and people they brought to mind.

Among the growing stash was the framed photograph of the couple that Julie Kitchen had told me were her parents; autograph books filled with the signatures, notes and rhymes of my Redbud Grove friends; programs from school plays and Christmas events and concerts; my eighth grade diploma; buckeyes from the trees in Redbud Grove; school scrapbooks; library reading circle awards; and numerous things that held importance only to me.

My letters to Jack were not as long as his letters to me. There were only so many ways to describe my days at school, my trips with my friends to Dooby's, and ballgames. Then one day that changed, and I had enough exciting data to fill a lot of pages.

Racial desegregation was officially abolished by the United States Federal Government in nineteen fifty-four, the year we moved to Dixon, West Virginia. Until that time, small outlying schools sent their black eighth grade graduates to the Dixon High School for Colored Students. It was housed in an old, brick building, once used by the white junior high school student body of Dixon, who were now ensconced inside the old high school for whites.

The newly built high school had held classes for three years prior to our relocation to Dixon, and new policies were being observed inside the walls. Many black students were enrolled at Dixon High. The student body seemed peaceful enough. A few shoving matches occurred in the corridors. Aside from that, I had heard nothing about any real confrontations during my freshman and sophomore years.

I caught snatches of conversations among disgruntled students sometimes, as I went from class to class. However, I wasn't aware of extreme hatred on either side of the segregation issue. I think that what I had witnessed was a classic case of "the tip of the iceberg."

During my junior year, Delia Brown's gym locker was three down from mine. Delia was a senior, a tall, slender, beautiful girl with ebony skin and long hair that formed shiny ringlets, without a hint of frizz. She was a precursor of Diana Ross, and heads turned when Delia Brown moved down a hall or entered a classroom. I was envious of her long, shapely legs. I told her so, which made Delia laugh.

"You don't have to worry, Sissy," she told me. "You're put together just fine." Along with the West Virginia drawl, which I had come to emulate, Delia's voice held a warm, husky, honey/South quality that was irresistible.

Following gym class one afternoon, Delia seemed subdued and unusually quiet. Her answers to my questions were monosyllabic. I kept pushing.

"Is something wrong?" I asked. Delia looked at me for a long moment before she answered.

"I've been banned from the sock-hops after school."

"Why?" I asked.

"They say that my dancing is vulgar."

I hadn't seen Delia dance, but I couldn't imagine that anything she did would be vulgar. She had too much class. I hadn't seen a lot of the world, or even of my own country, at that time. A lot of my opinions about a lot of things had been formed partially from movies I had seen and books I had read. I was already wise enough to recognize quality in people when I saw it, and Delia was "quality."

"Show me," I suggested. Delia looked at me as if I'd lost my mind, and then she smiled.

"Okay."

In the middle of the girls' locker room, filled with teenaged girls in various stages of dress and undress, Delia Brown began to softly sing the words to "That's All Right, Mama, Anything You Do." Dressed only in her white cotton bra and panties, Delia began to move. She gyrated and twirled and danced in her bare feet, moving to the beat she created with her own singing.

I started to clap my hands to the rhythm, and then more girls joined me. We formed a ring around Delia, clapping and dancing in spontaneous response to her exuberance and her graceful movements. The locker room reverberated as other voices took up the song, which bounced off the walls and added volume.

"What do you think you're doing?!"

We all stopped in mid-move. Miss Evers, the girl's P.E. instructor, shoved her way into our circle. Something about Miss Evers had always made me uncomfortable. Following every gym class, she sat at a small table in the locker room, checking to see that every girl took a shower, placing an X beside our names in her notebook as we complied. We were excused for one week each month, which was duly noted in her records.

I was always careful to tuck my towel completely around my body when I came out of the shower stalls, which didn't help much, considering that the stalls were not enclosed. Miss Evers, who was short, stocky, and very muscular, simply gave me the creeps. It was rumored that she was "butch," a phrase that I thought I knew the meaning of; but I wasn't entirely sure. Just to be on the safe side of uncertainty, I kept my towel tucked tightly.

"Dancing." Delia's statement of fact fell just short of flippant.

"Girls, get dressed. *Now!*" Miss Evers glared at Delia. "You get dressed and come into my office." She turned to me. "What're you looking at?" Miss Evers's cheeks were flushed, and a small vein pulsed in her neck. Her gray-streaked, light brown hair was cut very short, exposing her ears and forming short bangs across her forehead. It was bristly in the back, like a boy's.

"Nothing." Miss Evers glared at me for a moment, before she did a military about-face and stormed into her office, located in a corner of the locker room. "Absolutely nothing," I muttered to her retreating back. Delia laughed out loud.

"Hey, Sissy, that'll get you sent to Mr. Sheffield's office."

"It wouldn't be the first time," I retorted. I shrugged into my white blouse, a difficult task, since my skin was still damp. I stepped into a half-slip and then into my cotton skirt that had a white geometric design on a black background. White bobby socks and black and white saddle shoes completed my toilette. There was no real need to hurry. Gym was my last class of the day, and I didn't have to work at the A&W until the weekend.

"What'd I tell you?" Delia didn't sound surprised or upset, just resigned. "If any of you white girls danced like I did, no one would say a word."

"I don't know, Delia," I shook my head. "The only white person I've seen dance like that is Elvis, and you know what teachers and grown-ups think about him." I laughed. "Can't you just see my dad's face if he saw me dancing like you just did? To say nothing of my Mother's face! She would just die; no, she would kill *me*!"

Delia fastened a wide, gold elastic waist-cincher around her tiny middle and stepped into black penny loafers. She made a striking figure in her red blouse and full black skirt.

"Well, maybe I'll see you tomorrow; and maybe I won't," she said. She gathered her books from her locker and gave me a big grin. "They may not let me come back to school."

"That's silly, Delia. They won't expel you for dancing."

"It's been done for less," was her enigmatic reply.

Delia wasn't expelled, but she was suspended for a week. I couldn't believe it. No announcement was made, but word of her suspension spread throughout the school.

"Mom, there was no reason for them to do that to her," I complained at the supper table. "Delia is a really nice girl. It was partly my fault, because I asked her to show me how she danced. One of the teachers that chaperone the sock-hops told her she couldn't dance there anymore, and I wanted Delia to show me why."

"Did you explain that to Miss Evers?" Mom asked.

"No, she didn't give anyone a chance to say anything."

"Why don't you go to Mr. Sheffield and tell him it was all your fault?" my brother suggested. "Then he can expel you, too. It'd be cool, having a sister expelled from school." I just looked at him.

"Delia hasn't been expelled," I patiently explained to my brother, the comedian. "She's only suspended for a week. It's just not fair."

It's just not fair.

The words triggered memories of the busload of colored people from Alabama, who had been stranded in the park in Redbud Grove, people who had not been allowed to stay overnight in the town. My sense of justice had been mightily provoked back then, too. Living in a segregated town didn't lend much opportunity to take a stand.

"What are you going to do about it?" my dad asked. He took another piece of fried chicken from the platter, ladled more gravy onto his plate, and dipped the chicken into the gravy, a practice repeated by my brother. I had enjoyed eating Mom's fried chicken like that, too; but small waists don't remain small with fare like that. My chicken remained gravy-less.

"What *can* I do?" I asked him.

"Well, if you really feel responsible, maybe you *should* talk to the principal. Sometimes you have to pick your fights." I looked at my dad. I wanted to ask him if he had picked his fights, but I already knew the answer. He had been drafted during the war, so he had no choice in that particular fight; but knowing his temper, I suspected that he had picked many.

"Maybe I will," I said.

By morning, I had decided that I would go to Mr. Sheffield and explain what had happened in the locker room. My intentions were good, but I got lost in the shuffle of racial hatred. A spark of that hatred ignited a fire in the corridors before I ever reached the principal's office.

I didn't hear the remark that started the fight. Loud, angry voices suddenly filled the hall. There were tangled arms and legs and boys of all sizes and shades of black and white shoving and wrestling on the granite floor. I heard phrases that I had never heard before, from both races, phrases that I hoped never to hear again.

Some, I didn't know the meaning of; and some made me blush, because I did know. I hugged the walls, along with several dozen other girls of both races. At first, we tried to simply stay away from dangerously flailing arms and legs.

"You let go a'my brother, you honky white trash!" Priscilla Hayes, a small, thin freshman, leaped upon the back of Marty Cooper, who had straddled Louie Hayes, the tall, lanky brother of Priscilla. Louie was a junior, and Marty was a senior and a football player. He outweighed the Hayes boy by close to one hundred pounds.

Priscilla launched her body like a missile at Marty's head. She wrapped her arms around his throat and pulled back with all her strength. Try as he might, Marty could not dislodge the determined girl. She wrapped her legs around his back and locked her forearms beneath his chin. Marty had no option but to let go of Louie, who scrambled to his feet.

By that time, teachers had appeared upon the scene. The fortunate members of the melee who were close to exits made discreet, opportune retreats. Priscilla and Louis Hayes were not in that number. Neither was I.

When it finally became my turn to give an accounting to Mr. Sheffield, I was ready. I had, as my father said, picked my fight. I had made up my mind to tell Mr. Sheffield about Delia's unfair suspension.

"What did you see in the hall today, Sissy?" Mr. Sheffield looked at me over his glasses. His full lips pursed, and I wanted to grin at the image of a puckering fish that popped into my mind. Discretion flew to my rescue.

"I don't know what started the fight," I said. "I do know that Priscilla Hayes was only trying to get Marty Cooper off her brother. Marty had Louie on the floor and was beating him up."

"Who started the altercation?" Mr. Sheffield pressed.

"I don't know, Sir. It just suddenly happened. I didn't see who hit first."

"Very well, Sissy; that will be all." I had been dismissed.

"Mr. Sheffield?" He looked up at me.

"Yes?"

"Mr. Sheffield, I'd like to tell you what happened in the locker room with Delia Brown a few days ago."

"I already know what happened, Sissy. Miss Evers made a full report."

"Yes, Sir, I know; but I'd like to explain that it wasn't Delia's fault. It was mine."

"How could it possibly have been your fault, Sissy? Delia Brown was behaving in a most unseemly manner for a young girl, and we will not tolerate that kind of vulgarity." Mr. Sheffield's voice rose.

"But I asked her to show me how she danced, to show me why she was banned from the after-school dances. That's all she was doing. It's not fair that she was suspended, that she has to miss school just because she's colored!" There! I had said it! Mr. Sheffield stood up, but I was still a fraction taller than he.

"Sissy, the matter is closed. We treat all our students fairly here, and we are trying to make the best of an uncomfortable situation." A muscle twitched in Mr. Sheffield's cheek, and there was a dangerous glitter in his pale eyes. "You go to class, now." I stood up and turned away from his desk. "Sissy!" I looked over my shoulder at him. "I don't ever want to hear that you have instigated further incidents. Do you understand?"

"Yes, Sir, I understand." He indicated with his hand that I was dismissed.

On my way to class, I pondered over what I had just learned about the principal. He was a racial bigot of the worst kind, because he cloaked it behind his position. From my first encounter with him, I already considered him a hypocrite. I realized that he governed the students, over whom he had control, by a code of ethics different from his own.

I had been taught to respect positions of authority, to revere those who had charge over me. It was disillusioning to lose respect for two of those people in less than one week. It made me wonder how many others, how many of the men and women I had thought of as heroes, were much less than that.

Teachers were my heroes, people of knowledge to whom I deferred. School principals and superintendents were right up there with policemen and high-ranking officials. If they could not be trusted, who would be our role models, our heroes?

Even as the question formed in my head, I knew that there was one who would never let me down, no matter what happened, no matter what circumstances. Within my own little corner of the world lived my real, live, personal hero.

My dad.

Love and Other Insanities

My junior year at Dixon High continued on the same sweet, positive note as it began. The corridors seemed brighter. Familiar faces smiled at me, and hands waved in recognition. I felt secure in my position, just one grade away from the promised land of the superior senior. It was amazing how much difference two short years made. I was, no doubt, a bit smug in my role of near-upperclassman.

I had the best of all possible worlds: I could participate in as many extra-curricular activities as I could carry and attend as many football games, parties, and movies as my parents would allow. If people thought that I still had a boyfriend in college, it just upped my status...unless and until someone came along who piqued my interest.

It was easy to spot the freshman. Most of them were smaller than the other students; and they all wore the same disoriented, flustered expression that marked them as targets for light-hearted hazing. Well, maybe some of the hazing wasn't so light-hearted.

After the one racially oriented fracas in the corridor, tensions had lessened. There may have been other incidents outside the school, but I was never a witness to anything violent. For the moment, tolerance seemed to rule the day. It certainly made for a more pleasant atmosphere.

Rock and roll music didn't only "rock" the music world. It rocked everywhere: churches, schools, radio, television, records and homes. We had our favorite singers; but without question, the supreme rocker was Elvis Presley, who was just at the pinnacle of his beginning. He had not yet attained the heights that awaited him, but in the autumn of nineteen fifty-six, we knew that he had changed the face of music.

Karen Courtney and I still collected his records. We no longer traded, since neither of us wanted to give up a single black plastic disk.

Karen spent most of her free time with her boyfriend. Our long telephone conversations and walks together from school became occasional, instead of daily. I missed her; but I had formed new friendships, too. When Karen called one Friday evening to invite me up to her house, I was surprised. Her Fridays and Saturdays were reserved for her boyfriend.

"I want you to meet my cousin, Ginger Bellini. She's just moved here from California, and you've *got* to come on up!" Excitement filled Karen's voice, so I discarded my junior-year-dignity long enough to climb up the hill to her house.

When Karen and I had discussed our families, she had told me about her only cousin, Ginger. Karen hadn't believed me when I had told her I had nearly seventy first cousins, so I had started naming them. She had stopped me somewhere near thirty. Counting my parents' children, there were forty-five first cousins on my dad's side. On my mother's side, there were twenty-four. Seven of us had been born within the same eighteen months. A visit from any of them would have been nice; but I had a soft spot in my heart for my cousin, Ada, who was only three months older I.

"Come on in, Sissy. This is Ginger, my California cousin." Pride and a bit of awe shone on Karen's beaming face.

"Hi." I smiled at Ginger Bellini. The smile she returned was dazzling. The reddest lipstick on the planet framed the whitest teeth I'd ever seen.

"Hello." Ginger's sultry voice would have seemed more appropriate coming from a lounge singer. I wouldn't have been surprised if she had suddenly burst into a steamy rendition of "Stormy Weather" or "Blues in the Night." Everything about the girl seemed to smolder.

I finally understood what natural strawberry blonde hair was supposed to be—not yellow-blonde, not truly red, but a perfect blending of the two. Ginger's long locks, genuinely strawberry blonde, fell in soft, beguiling waves to her shoulders. Parted on the left side, a deep wave brushed the lashes of her left eye and flirted with her cheek before it curved along her neck.

October-blue-sky eyes, fringed with long lashes that were heavily coated with mascara, seemed friendly enough. Ginger's skin emanated California sun as surely as gardenias give off the scent of the South. I could practically inhale sun and surf from her body.

Ginger wore a sundress unlike any I had seen on the girls at Dixon High. Thin spaghetti straps held up the square, low-cut bodice, made of a gauzy, white fabric with small red polka dots on it. A full skirt accented Ginger's tiny waist. It was obvious that a strapless bra had to be holding up a perfectly proportioned bosom. Not wearing one was totally unacceptable in those days. Ginger tossed her hair.

"What do you do for fun here?" she asked. I looked at Karen, who stared at her cousin. Karen fingered the chain with her boyfriend's ring on it, which still hung around her neck.

"What do *you* like to do?" I countered. A throaty laugh preceded Ginger's answer.

"Probably nothing that's possible here," she said. "Our house isn't far from the beach. I spend a lot of time there with my friends, but I don't see a beach anywhere around here."

"There's a nice pool," Karen said. She sounded so eager to please her cousin.

"After swimming in the ocean, a pool is like a bathtub." I was surprised that the disdain in Ginger's voice didn't manifest itself in the form of a literal upturned nose.

"Gosh, if Dixon had known you were coming, I bet the mayor would have had a channel to the Atlantic dug for you." I couldn't help myself. I hated snobbery, and from what I'd heard from Ginger so far, she sounded like a genuine snob.

"That's really funny!" Ginger laughed, a belly laugh that crinkled her eyes and showed her marvelous teeth. Karen's glare at me became a nervous giggle. "I'm sorry, Sissy. I guess I sounded pretty nasty, huh? I really am sorry."

"That's okay," I shrugged. "I wasn't very nice, either. Welcome to Dixon."

"Thanks."

Karen beamed at both of us. "I knew that you would like each other," she said. Ginger and I glanced at each other and grinned. We both knew that it was too soon to tell.

"Where's your house?" I asked. Ginger looked at Karen.

"Ginger and Aunt Rosalie will be staying with us for awhile," Karen said. "They don't have a house yet."

"Oh. Well." That avenue of conversation didn't lead far. "Well," I repeated. "I'd better head home. It was nice to meet you, Ginger. See you later. 'Bye, Karen."

Ginger Bellini hit Dixon High School with the force of an Atlantic Ocean hurricane. Just about every boy in her wake was flattened and washed ashore, to lie at the feet of the golden California girl. Jerry Davis was no exception.

The Monday after I met her, Ginger walked into the cafeteria with Karen. They headed straight for our table, which included the usual group: Jerry, Gary, Wes, Jimmy, Karen, Beverly, Rowena, Judy and me. Since I had already been granted a look at Ginger, I observed the boys observe her.

Karen actually beamed as she presented the girl. "Hi, Guys. This is my cousin, Ginger Bellini. She's from California," she said, as if that fact alone were cause for celebration.

It was better than watching "The Three Stooges." The boys' common initial reaction was shock, followed by quick swallows, and then an automatic brush of a hand through the hair, a straightening in the chair, just a hint of inflating a masculine chest. I almost laughed aloud. Jerry recovered first.

"Hi, Ginger. I'm Jerry." He flashed her that killer grin, his blue eyes a-twinkle and dimples a-dimpling. Ginger tilted her head just a fraction and looked at Jerry through her heavy mascara. I could almost hear a collective groan of teenage desire from the four boys. I stared at Ginger, amazed at her blatantly flirtatious stance.

She had to be aware of the pheromones in her aura. Everyone else was. Ginger couldn't help it. At sixteen, she had the sex appeal of a younger, trimmer Marilyn Monroe. The proportions were the same. They just came in a smaller package. Ginger wore another skimpy topped sundress, but this one at least had wider shoulder straps. I know that Mr. Sheffield would not have allowed her to come to school in the dress she had worn the day I met her.

For her first day at school, Ginger wore a belted frock of blue the exact shade of her eyes. A hint of lace traced the low neckline, magnetically drawing the eye of any beholder. The soft fabric of the skirt fit smoothly down the length of her hips and thighs and fell into a flirty fullness at her knees, without benefit of ten layers of starched, scratchy can-can petticoats.

At that moment, I made the decision to drop full petticoats from my wardrobe as soon as possible. Watching Ginger, I was aware that all that can-can fabric simply camouflaged assets. Within a few weeks, most of the girls at Dixon High had stopped wearing them, too.

"Hi, Jerry. How are you?" Ohmigosh! Ginger actually fluttered her eyelashes.

"Good. I mean, I'm fine…uh, just great." He was so hooked. "Uh, what classes are you taking? I mean, what rooms are you in?"

"We don't know yet, Jerry," Karen said. "She just registered this morning, and they don't have her schedule yet. She's been going to class with me today."

"Oh." Jerry just sat there, grinning at Ginger, while Ginger grinned back at him! I couldn't believe it. Ginger was looking at Jerry with that same smitten, "You're wonderful!" expression. Just that quickly, Ginger and Jerry became an item.

When the after-school sock-hops began, the couple to watch was Ginger and Jerry. I don't know whether Jerry had always known how to dance like that, or if he was inspired to new heights by having Ginger as his partner. At any rate, Jerry was the envy of every senior boy in school.

Another new face at Dixon High created an equal amount of interest among the girls of all ages, including Miss Seabrook and three or four other single female teachers. The school board, voting seven to one, had finally ousted Coach Harrison. It was rumored that he resigned, which was probably true; but I don't think he was given a choice. After he had assaulted our own quarterback the previous fall, he had been relieved of all coaching duties. He had been allowed to finish the year as the Drivers Training instructor.

Coach Harrison's replacement was twenty-seven years old, unmarried, and looked like Charlton Heston. Lucas Esmond stood about five feet ten inches tall. The muscles in his chest and shoulders were well defined through his shirts, and his thighs looked as solid as the trunks of small trees. His dark brown eyes complemented his hair that was too red to be chestnut and too dark to be red. His wide mouth, with its full, provocative lower lip, smiled readily, to the delight of the titillated female student body and staff. I thought that he was handsome, all right; but he was a *teacher*, too old and too off limits...at least, for most of us.

"Don't you think he looks a lot like that actor, Charlton Heston?" Amanda Evans gushed after PE class. Conversation in the girls' locker room probably wasn't much different from the boys', but perhaps less graphic. Somehow, the opposite sex was discussed more than any other topic while we showered and dressed.

"Yeah, he really does."

"I think he's cuter."

"What's the matter with you? He's too old to be cute."

"Well, he's handsome."

"And sexy." There were hushed giggles at that remark. We weren't supposed to know what "sexy" was, much less say the word.

"Shhhh. Miss Evers will hear you."

"Do you suppose she thinks Coach Esmond is...you know, sexy?" The last word was whispered. Someone snorted in a very unladylike manner, and laughter filled the locker room.

"Time's running out, Girls!" Miss Evers called. We dressed quickly and continued our speculation in the corridor.

We learned that Mr. Esmond had coached at only one other high school, a small campus in Indiana. He had played college football. Although he was recruited, he went into teaching instead of professional football. During his second year of coaching, he had a champion football team. He took his team to the state playoffs every year he coached, winning three of those four years. It was rumored that Mr. Esmond wanted to stay with his Indiana team, but the Dixon school board had made him an offer he couldn't refuse.

Miss Seabrook, the home economics teacher, nearly beat the lashes off her eyelids every time she saw Mr. Esmond in the halls. It had been a year since the art teacher, Mr. Boudreaux, had left the campus; and single male teachers were hard to find in Dixon High. In fact, Mr. Esmond was the only one.

To our knowledge, Miss Seabrook dated no one else. By anyone's standards, the new coach would be just perfect for her. Miss Seabrook seemed to think so. Although Mr. Esmond was polite, even friendly to her, he didn't appear to be overwhelmed with her charms.

The year promised to be very interesting. We were barely through the first weeks of school, and the air seemed to vibrate with new people, new relationships and new tensions. I was eager to get up in the mornings, just to see what each day would hold.

"Sissy, guess what!" Karen came running through our kitchen door, without bothering to knock, a courtesy that she had never omitted. It wasn't late, but twilight was settling quickly on the east side of the mountains. I was surprised to see Karen. We had just finished a long conversation on the phone.

"What?" I asked. I sighed inwardly. No doubt, her boyfriend, Matt, had said something insanely romantic that just screamed to be repeated.

"Oh, Sissy, you couldn't guess in a thousand million years!" Karen was practically squealing.

"Well, *tell me*!"

"Sissy, oh, Sissy, you're just going to *die*!"

"For goodness sake, Karen, just tell me!"

Wish I May, Wish I Might...

"We're going to see Elvis!" she screamed. I stood there, looking at my friend. Her words made no sense whatsoever. I knew that the girl had completely lost her mind.

"Calm down, Karen," I soothed.

"Didn't you hear what I said? We're going to see Elvis, Sissy!"

"Who's going?" I decided to humor her.

"A bunch of us! You, me, Matt, Ginger, Jerry and whoever you want to ask, since Jack can't be here! Can you believe it? We're going to see Elvis!" One thing was certain: Karen believed what she was saying.

"Just where and when is this supposed to happen?" I asked. "Do you want a glass of tea?"

"No, no, I don't want tea! I want you to *listen* to me! Ginger's dad works for a ticket agency in California, and he sent six tickets to Ginger! He's coming to Charleston!"

"Ginger's dad is coming to Charleston?" I asked

"No, Sissy! Elvis is! *Elvis Presley is coming to Charleston*!" Karen finally had my full attention. A tingle started at the top of my head and rushed all the way to the soles of my feet. Could Karen possibly be telling the truth?

"When?" I was afraid to believe it.

"This month*! Sissy, in less than two weeks we're going to see Elvis! We've got tickets to see Elvis! Third row tickets, Sissy!*"

"He's going into the army," I reminded her.

"Not before his concert in Charleston!" Karen crowed.

"What's all the noise about?" My brother ambled into the kitchen. He waved a careless hand in Karen's direction. At fourteen, Bill was taller than I, something I still found hard to accept. His voice had changed. Sometimes, much to his embarrassment, it squeaked. He was a freshman in high school, another thing that seemed impossible. I had always fancied myself so much older, so much more advanced than my little brother. Apparently, many of my fancies were just that: fancies, not facts.

"Bill, we're going to see Elvis! Ginger's dad got us tickets!" Karen blurted. "Maybe you could go, too! Jack isn't here, and Sissy can't take another boy."

I wanted to kill her—right there—in my mother's kitchen. I was afraid to look at Bill. What if he thought that Karen meant it, that she had just invited him to go along? How could I possibly go to see Elvis, with my little brother as my date?

"Wow!" Bill said. I looked at him from the corner of my eye. My heart sank. Right of top of the most incredible news of my life came this cruel joke. My brother was as excited about the possibility of going to an Elvis concert as Karen and I were. Even I didn't have the heart to tell him he couldn't go with us. What was I thinking? Neither of us had permission to go at all yet.

"We'll have to ask Mom and Dad," I said. The unappealing prospects of the ride to Charleston took away some of my enthusiasm. Car seats were wide enough to carry six people comfortably; but when four of the passengers were two dating couples, it left the other two people in an undesirable position, especially a brother and sister. I was beginning to have a very bad feeling.

I needn't have worried. As it turned out, the concert was held on a Saturday night. The varsity team played on Fridays. Bill's freshman football team had to play on Saturdays, so he couldn't go to the concert. All I had to do was come up with another person, but who would go with me?

I didn't want to ask any of the boys in our gang. That would have been almost like taking a brother. The only other boy I thought I might like was David Trask, a senior who had transferred to Dixon from Savannah, Georgia. I knew how difficult it was to change schools. It must have been especially hard at the beginning of his senior year.

Another plus about David was his total ignorance about Jack McCoy. If I could convince the other four not to mention Jack, David and I could have a good time. I didn't consider that David would be a real "date." He just happened to be a good-looking boy who didn't have a steady girlfriend.

"Sure," David said, when I asked him. "I like Elvis. I'd love to go." David was as tall as Jack, but lean and lanky where Jack was muscle-y. Brown hair and kind, blue eyes made a nice combination. David had played varsity basketball in Savannah, and Coach Esmond had put him in the lineup for the Dixon team. I hoped he'd get to play.

When I told Karen that I had asked David Trask to go with us, I thought that she was going to have a heart attack. Her eyes grew big and round, and her mouth dropped open in a caricature of disbelief. She shook her head.

"You can't!" she exclaimed.
"I already did."
"No, Sissy, I mean you really can't!"
"Why not?"
"Because Jack's coming home!"

It was my turn to display that classic look of disbelief. I shook my head, as if to clear it. In his last letter, Jack had written nothing about coming home. It wasn't possible.

"No, he isn't."

"Yes, Sissy, he is! It's supposed to be a surprise. I called him a couple of days ago and told him about the concert, so he's coming home to go with us."

"When did you call?" I asked.

"The same day you said that your brother couldn't go. I just thought.... Sissy, don't you want to see Jack?" Now that was a good question. Did I? I didn't know. Such a tangle of emotions warred inside me, primarily, dismay at how I was going to explain to David Trask that I must rescind my invitation. That would undoubtedly take me off his list as a potential friend.

"Why did you *do* that without telling me?"

"I thought that it would be a good surprise." Karen's voice trembled. She was near tears. What was the matter with me? Of course, I wanted to see Jack. I would just have to explain the situation to David and hope that he wouldn't hate me.

"Okay, Karen. It's all right. When is Jack coming home?"

"He told me that he'd leave Urbana about mid-afternoon on Friday. He'll have to drive most of the night, and he'll be here early Saturday. He said that he wants us all to go in his convertible. Won't that be fun?" I was sure that the convertible would be a treat for Karen. Her boyfriend's souped-up nineteen forty-eight Ford was fast, but it wasn't very glamorous. I nodded. A sense of anticipation began to grow inside me. I convinced myself that Jack's coming home was a good thing, that I had missed him, and that I would be glad to see him.

"You have to pretend to be surprised," Karen told me. "Jack is going to pick up all of us at my house and then come for you. So you've *got* to act surprised!" I promised that I would.

David was gracious, even nonchalant, when I told him about the backfired surprise; but I saw the disappointment in his eyes before he shrugged. "Don't worry about it," he said. "It'll probably be so noisy, you won't even get to hear Elvis sing. See ya." He walked away and didn't look back at me. I couldn't blame him.

My parents obviously knew about Jack's plans. They both looked so coy and smug that I wanted to laugh at them. They managed to keep relatively straight faces the day of the concert, until we heard the car pull into the driveway. I grabbed a sweater and headed to the front door.

"Sissy, won't someone come to the door to get you?" Mom asked. Oh brother, I thought.

"No, Mom. Matt's driving, so I'll just run out to the car." I played the charade right down to the wire. I turned back to the door, and I stopped dead in my tracks. I didn't have to pretend to be shocked. The sight of Jack McCoy, so tall and blond and handsome, looking at me with absolute longing in his beautiful light brown eyes, momentarily took my breath.

"Hi, Sissy," he said. I couldn't move. Jack opened the screened door and came inside, smiling his gorgeous smile. It had been only a month since he'd left Dixon, but I had forgotten how devastatingly handsome he was. He came to me, wrapped his arms around me right there in front of my mom and dad, and kissed my forehead. "Surprise," he whispered softly.

"How—when—what--?" I stuttered. Jack laughed.

"I'll explain in the car," he said. "Good night, Mrs. Bannister, Mr. Bannister. It will be late when we get back, but I'll take good care of Sissy." I looked over my shoulder at my parents, both of whom were beaming.

"Have a good time. Be careful." They were practically in unison. Jack and I had scarcely cleared the front porch before he turned to me and pulled me into his arms. I was nowhere near ready for a kiss, but Jack wouldn't be denied. He raised his head, smiled into my eyes and kissed me again, briefly. "I've missed you," he said. I believed him.

"Hey, come on!" Matt called from the car. He and Karen were packed into one half of the back seat. Jerry and Ginger effectively covered the other half. I did a double take at Ginger's dress. I had thought that my sleeveless, white sundress with its square neck and belted waist was becoming; but Ginger's garment made me feel downright dowdy.

Fire engine red, her halter dress showed as much or more of Ginger's upper body than a bathing suit would have. Her hair fell onto her bare shoulders, and her baby-blue eyes sparkled behind her fringed, mascara-laden lashes. Ginger sat in the crook of Jerry's left arm, and Jerry looked as if he were in a heightened state of euphoria. Matt and Karen cuddled, equally engrossed with each other.

Jack backed the convertible down the driveway. After he entered the street and straightened the wheels, he patted the seat beside him. "Come sit close to me," he said. Nervous, excited, filled with anticipation for the concert, I obeyed. He felt warm, comfortable, and I relaxed against his side.

The wind in my hair, the familiar scent of pines, muted laughter from the back seat, the subtle scent of Jack's aftershave, all filled my senses with the joy of being young and alive. The winding way to Charleston seemed short. The sweet, early autumn evening stretched before us like a magic carpet, promising a ride of music, excitement, and romance.

The university grounds and surrounding blocks swarmed with people of all ages, but mostly teenagers. Every possible parking place was full, so we had to park several blocks away from the auditorium. Excitement filled the air, as electric as the guitars that were being tuned for the upcoming performance. City policemen and university security personnel maintained order the best they could.

When we finally reached our seats, I couldn't believe how close to the stage we were. The warm-up band, shiny in their black sequined jackets, were so near us that we could see the color of each musician's eyes. Only one stood in shadow, head a bit down, looking at his guitar while he played an intricate run.

Karen and I sat next to each other, flanked by Matt and Jack, while Jerry and Ginger had the aisle chairs. Karen touched my arm.

"Pinch me!" Karen shouted into my ear.

"Why?" I shouted back.

"Because I don't believe I'm really here!"

I laughed. The music and the fans were so loud that no one could hear me. Several girls had already left their seats. They danced with abandon to the beat of the rock and roll that reverberated throughout the large auditorium, a crowd of them right in front of the elevated stage. The music ended with three loud, prolonged bangs; and the audience went crazy.

"Ladie-e-e-e-e-e-e-s and Gentlemen!" The master of ceremonies, dressed in a marvelous tuxedo, grasped the microphone. He paused dramatically. "El-l-l-l-vi-s-s-s Pre-e-e-s-s-s-s-s-ley!" He stepped back. All of us rose to our feet. The band kicked off the introductory beats of "You Ain't Nothin' But a Hound Dog."

Elvis Presley erupted onto the stage. The energy he generated sizzled as shiny and electric as the silky black shirt he wore. He leaned into the microphone, and his voice filled the auditorium. He could be heard above the screams and squeals, and my shrieks were in the mix.

A large, flattop guitar, attached to a gold strap around his neck, seemed to become a part of his gyrating body. The band swung into the bridge between verses, and Elvis danced across the stage, arms extended, his left leg moving as if it were boneless.

Karen and I looked at each other, clasped hands, and jumped up and down with the rest of the crazy-in-love-with-Elvis crowd. It was pandemonium; it was madness; it was chaos; it was wonderful! Raw, sensual energy flowed from every cell in the young man's body. His dark hair crackled with it. His pout-y mouth and half-closed eyes radiated beams to his adoring fans, while the music throbbed and vibrated through every fiber of our bodies. It was a night I would never forget.

For close to thirty minutes, with scarcely a seam between them, Elvis Presley simply flowed from one song to the next. Scattered among the familiar ones, like "Heartbreak Hotel," "Don't Be Cruel," and "Blue Suede Shoes," were numbers he hadn't recorded.

"Thank you. Thank you very much." Gentle, gracious words of thanks were his first verbal communication with the audience. Soft chords from the guitar player behind Elvis sent a unified sigh from the throats of hundreds of teenaged girls. We knew what was coming.

"Love me tender, Love me sweet, Never let me go..." The sweet words of the ballad, coming from the throat of Elvis Presley, seemed to be directed straight at me. Every girl in that crowded auditorium thought the same thing. I didn't know or care what the boys were thinking. A collective sigh, followed by thunderous applause, filled the room when the song ended.

"Ladies, we have a young man up here that plays a mean guitar...and he's *single*! Show us how it's done, Vic!" Elvis stepped back, and a young man, also dressed in black, stepped forward. The man's guitar was a beautiful thing, red with lots of shiny chrome and white mother-of-pearl.

Spotlights played around the stage, occasionally highlighting the performer's hands, but never lingering upon his face. The song was unfamiliar. There were lots of minor chords, and the beat was infectious. It was music that demanded dancers, who soon filled the area in front of the stage, Jerry and Ginger among them.

It didn't take long for the light man to discover Ginger. A spotlight settled upon her and Jerry. Before the guitar man was finished, a space was cleared around them; and people stood back to watch the dazzling girl in the red dress and the boy with the contagious smile.

Jack stood behind me, his arms wrapped loosely around my waist. We swayed to the music, caught up with the beat, with the crowd, with celebrity. The music moved to a crescendo, climbed quickly up the chromatic musical scale to a deafening finale. Mesmerized, I watched the guitarist. He bent over the neck of his guitar in a low bow. His thick, dark hair grew a little bit longer than the other members of the band.

The spotlight rested fully upon him. I stared. My heart began to race, but I couldn't believe what my eyes were telling me. It couldn't possible be....

"Ladies and Gentlemen, Victor Delacourt! He wrote that little number! Take another bow, Vic!"

It was Victor*! My Victor*! The night I had first heard Elvis on Victor's car radio, he had told me that some day he would play with that new singer, Elvis Presley! I continued to stare while the crowd roared in appreciation. Unbelievable! How had Victor managed to get to Elvis?

I don't know what caught Victor's attention. It might have been that I was the only girl in the front rows who was standing perfectly still. It may have been that my staring caught his eye. All I know is that suddenly Victor Delacourt was looking right at me. No more than twenty-five or thirty feet separated us.

A slow smile twisted Victor's mouth. Oh, I remembered that mouth! Victor gave a small salute. I could read his lips. *Hi, Sissy Bannister,* they said. I smiled at him. *Hi, Victor Delacourt.* A huge grin showed his beautiful teeth, and the girls in the audience responded with more screams and squeals.

I don't remember who held the greater part of my attention for the rest of the evening. It was probably a toss-up. Yes, the thrill of being in the presence of Elvis Presley, the man who had changed the face of music, was tremendous. Yet, watching Victor Delacourt, the boy who had given me my first kiss, the boy who had awakened in me the knowledge of sensual power, carried its own magic.

When the concert ended, the musicians played long after Elvis left the stage. We didn't try to leave the building. The six of us, along with a few hundred of our newest friends, stayed to listen to the band. The curtains descended as the band continued to play, and then the music ended. In a perfect world, I would have rushed backstage to see Victor, to—to—I didn't know what. The crush of people was just too great, and I didn't know how Jack would react, should I attempt to see Victor.

"Hey, Sissy! Sissy Bannister!" My name reverberated from wall to wall.

"Who's calling you?" Jack asked.

"Well...." I started to explain.

"Sissy, who *is* that?!" Karen demanded.

"It's Victor Delacourt," I replied.

"The guitar player?" Disbelief filled Jack's voice. "How would he know your name?"

"I knew him in Redbud Grove," I answered. In unison, Ginger and Karen both began to ask questions.

"You knew *him*? How? When?"

"I told you about him, Karen. Remember?" Karen frowned in concentration, and then her eyes grew round.

"*That* Victor? The one...?"

"Yes."

"Let's go backstage! Sissy, you've got to see him! *He remembered you!*" Karen grabbed my hands. I looked at Jack. There was no smile on his face. Inexperienced as I was, I knew that a meeting between Jack and Victor Delacourt wouldn't be a good thing. The memory of my last encounter with Victor made my face warm. What if Victor mentioned something about the night he had driven me to a cornfield, about the moments we had spent there? I shook my head.

"No, Karen. Victor was just being nice. I was still in grade school when he was a senior, so I'm surprised that he even remembered my name. Let's just go."

"Good idea," Jack said. He put his arm around my shoulders, and the six of us joined the crowd that snail-walked to the outer doors. At the exit, I looked back. Standing between the curtains was Victor Delacourt, holding a microphone. I don't think that he could see me, but he sent a final message.

"Sis-s-s-s-s-y, where are you? Awwkkkk, pawwkkk, pawwkkk..." He delivered a perfect chicken squawk over the microphone and then disappeared behind the velvet curtains. I did an about face.

"What was that?" Ginger asked. I shrugged.

"You got me," I replied.

The drive back to Dixon was pleasant enough. Not much conversation came from the back seat, but I think that a lot of communication was taking place. I sat close to Jack while he told me about campus life. He didn't ask what had been going on with mine. He stressed that he never asked any of the college girls for a date, and he reiterated that he didn't want me to date other boys.

"Have you, Sissy? Have you dated anyone else?"

"No," I answered. "Jack, you've only been gone a month. Besides, everyone knows that I was dating you...." Jack squeezed my shoulder.

"I know," he said. He took his eyes from the road long enough to plant a quick kiss on my forehead. It was nice, and Jack generated warmth. The night air had turned chilly in the mountains. I shivered. "Are you cold?" Jack asked.

"A little." Jack pulled off the highway at the next crossroad and put up the top of the convertible. He was so thoughtful, and he did everything possible to make me happy. "Thank you," I said. He flashed his charming smile at me, drew me back against his side, and drove onto the highway. There was still no conversation from the back seat.

I dozed. I had always been a car-sleeper at night. Something about the drone of the engine was hypnotic, and it was getting late. I didn't wake until we arrived at Dooby's.

It was eleven-thirty, but a number of cars were still at the curb. Instead of ordering from the car, as we usually did, we went inside and ordered milkshakes. The six of us gathered around a table for four, but it wasn't long before we were joined by several of Jack's friends, all eager to question him about college life at the University of Illinois. Jack was in his element. Matt looked uncomfortable. Jerry looked bored.

Jerry went to the jukebox, inserted a dime, and came back for Ginger. They began to dance to the music we had just heard in concert. "Love Me Tender" throbbed throughout the little hamburger joint. Matt and Karen followed Jerry and Ginger, which left Jack and me at the table, in the company of Jack's friends. I sighed.

The milkshake made me drowsy. My eyes grew heavier with each sip. With the music came images of Elvis. The concert was already taking on the quality of a dream. I concentrated more on the music and less on the conversation at the table. I rested my head on one hand and closed my eyes. I drifted...

The music came from far away. It echoed hauntingly as I swayed to the sweet melody. I picked up the hem of my filmy white dress and danced, as weightless as gossamer, as graceful as softly falling snowflakes. A figure materialized in the hazy glow. He wore a silky black shirt that seemed to drip moonbeams and starlight.

I couldn't see his face, but the voice belonged to Elvis. He picked up the words of the song and sang them just to me. Slowly, we moved toward each other, drawing closer and closer, as though pulled together with the force of a magnet to metal.

He leaned toward me, and I raised my face to his, knowing that he was going to kiss me. I knew that he couldn't resist me, as I could not resist him. Starlight struck his face. I smiled. I knew that it was you, I said; but there were no words.

Of course, you knew, he said. His thoughts were open to me, as mine were to him. His lips touched mine. Hi, Victor Delacourt, I said. Hi, Sissy Bannister, he replied; and he repeated my name over and over – Sissy...Sissy...Sissy....

"Sissy! Sissy, wake up!"

I opened my eyes. My face rested on my arms, which were pillowing my head on the table in Dooby's. Laughter rang around me. I raised my head. Jack put his arms around my shoulders and helped me to stand.

"Wake up, Sleepyhead!"

"I was dreaming," I told him.

"About me, of course?" Jack's friends laughed.

"I don't remember." I smiled, blinked and shook my head, trying to clear away the image that lingered there. Why would I dream something so stupid, so completely out of the realm of possibility?

Really? Who would have thought it possible that Victor Delacourt would be playing in Elvis Presley's band? Who would have dreamed that you would ever see him again, or that he would recognize you when he did see you? Now my thoughts were talking to me!

"Where are Jerry and Ginger?" I asked. "And Karen and Matt?"

"They got a ride with Hank. Come on, Sissy." It was well after midnight. My curfew had been extended, but only enough to allow for the winding way home from Charleston. Jack opened the driver's side door, and I slid beneath the steering wheel. Jack followed.

"What time do you have to get home?" he whispered in my ear. I looked at the clock on the dashboard.

"In about twenty-five minutes."

"That doesn't give us much time," Jack complained. "I want to be alone with you."

"We're alone," I said. "We can sit in the car at my house until I have to go inside. Mom or Dad, maybe both, will be awake; but they won't mind, since you just got home."

Jack put his arms around me. He nuzzled my neck, my cheek, and finally kissed my mouth. "I guess I'll have to settle for that, at least for tonight," he said. His voice was petulant, like a disappointed child. "I wish we could have gone to the concert by ourselves. That would have been a lot more fun." Jack started the car.

The house was dark, but I knew that Mom left the kitchen light on above the sink. Only fifteen minutes remained before I had to be inside the front door. Jack gathered me close against his chest.

Wish I May, Wish I Might...

"Did you miss me?" he asked.

"Sure, I did." Well, I had, a little.

"Show me," he whispered. "Show me how much you missed me."

"Jack..."

Jack McCoy didn't want to talk. He kissed me with a hunger and intensity that he hadn't shown before, as if he had to make up for lost time. There was no place to breathe from one kiss to the next. His mouth was hard, not gentle and sweet, as I remembered.

"Jack, don't...." I said. He buried his face against my neck. His breath was hot and quick against my skin.

"Sissy, why won't you kiss me back? Like this, Sissy; kiss me like this!" Jack's ragged whisper was hot in my ear. His mouth slid against my cheek and locked onto my lips. I felt his teeth and his tongue, pushing and demanding, while he held my head with both hands. *This wasn't right.*

I grabbed his wrists with my hands and pulled my head away. "Jack, I don't like this! You've got to let me go inside now!" Jack rested his forehead against mine and held me like that while his breathing slowed. I didn't relax my hands on his wrists until he slowly brought his hands down.

"I love you so much, Sissy," he said. "Don't you love me, too? Don't you want to kiss me and hold me and let me touch you? Don't you know that's the way to show me you love me?"

"Not like that, Jack. I don't...."

"Okay, Sweetheart, okay. I missed you so much! I guess I got a little carried away. I'm sorry." Jack kissed the tip of my nose. "You go on in, and I'll call you before I leave tomorrow morning. Don't worry, Sissy. I won't rush you again. I love you."

"Good night, Jack." I scooted to the passenger door and hurried out of the car. I didn't know what to say to him. I fled to the safety of my parents' house. Although I was a little afraid of Jack when he was so intense, fear wasn't as much a factor as was dismay. I knew that I had to end my relationship with Jack McCoy. He wanted more than I was willing to give. *No one* was going to control my life like Jack obviously wanted to do.

I had made up my mind. The next letter Jack received from me would be the one that announced the end of our five-month-long relationship. I was too young to tie myself down to one boy anyway. I had dreams to dream and goals to strive for and attain before I settled on one person. Besides, Victor Delacourt still held a place in my young heart and memory. Not even the wealthy, handsome Jackson McCoy could dislodge that image. I didn't know whether any other boy ever could.

I wrote the letter. The reply surprised me:

"Don't worry, Sweetheart. I know that you're young. I also know that when the time is right, you'll give yourself to me. You and I are meant to be together, Sissy. I'll wait for as long as it takes. I love you. Jack"

I shrugged. If Jack wanted to believe that, it was okay with me. In the meantime, there were football games to attend and friends to see and honor rolls to attain. I felt as though I had been released from prison.

"I broke up with Jack, Mom," I announced. I don't know what I expected, but the relief on my mother's face convinced me that I had made a good choice. Dad, on the other hand, was sorry that I had let the best baseball player in Dixon's history get away.

The night that I saw Elvis Presley was memorable in many ways. Not only had I seen my music idol close up and personal, Victor Delacourt had let me know that he still remembered me. In addition to those two positive events, I had freed myself of the burden of a possessive boyfriend. It had been a red-letter night.

Several weeks later, Karen called me one evening "Sissy, can you come up? I need to talk to you." Karen had not even said hello when I answered the telephone.

"Sure. You mean now?"

"Yes."

"I'll be right there," I told her. I hung up the phone and shoved my arms into my jacket. It was November, and the nights grew dark early. "Dad, I'm going up to Karen's for a little while. Okay?" Dad grunted permission from the living room. Mom was filling in for a friend, again, at the hospital. Beth and I had finished washing the supper dishes.

"Better not stay long," Dad called.

"I won't." Sophie danced in little circles at my feet when I opened the kitchen door. She accompanied me up the slope, following the path worn by my feet and Karen's. The little dog whined in disappointment as I climbed the rock retaining wall. After I crossed the upper street, I could hear her barking at the back door, demanding that someone let her back into the house. I grinned, knowing that it would be my dad who opened the door for her.

Karen met me on their front porch. I barely had time to speak to her mother and her Aunt Rosalie before Karen took me to her room and closed the door.

"Where's Ginger?" I asked.

"With Jerry, of course," Karen replied. Her eyes were puffy. It was easy to see that she had been crying.

"What's wrong?" I asked.

"Everything," she said; and she started to cry again. I put my arms around her. Karen rested her head on my shoulder and sobbed, quietly, but desperately. "I don't know what to do! I've been so stupid!"

"About what? Tell me what's wrong."

Karen sat up and wiped her face with her hands. She grabbed a handful of tissues from the box on her bed, and I knew that she had been at the crying stage for some time.

"You can't tell anyone," she stated.

"Who would I tell?"

"Sissy, I—I think I'm going to have a baby."

I was stunned. I didn't know what to say. A baby!

"Oh, Karen," I whispered. "Are you sure?" She nodded her head.

"About three months, I think," she said. "I was pretty sure last month, but I kept hoping...." The enormity of what she had just told me was overwhelming.

"Karen, how did you...I mean, how could you, uh...uh...when did you and Matt, uh...?" I stammered to a halt, not knowing how to put into words what I wanted to ask.

"I know what you mean, Sissy. Didn't you and Jack ever...you know...get carried away?"

"No!"

"Not even a little?" Karen seemed surprised.

"No!" I shuddered.

"Didn't you ever want to...you know...go a little farther?"

"No!" I remembered the last time that I had been with Jack. "Well, I think *he* did; but I didn't! Karen, isn't that stuff supposed to wait until you get married?"

"Well, sure, I guess," Karen said, "but you don't really think that everybody waits, do you? I know for a fact that Martha Dooley and Susie Williams are...you know. And they aren't the only ones. I thought that you and Jack were probably... too."

I shook my head. I remembered the day in the park beside our house in Redbud Grove, when Lucinda Barnes had told me that I was "a baby" for being naïve about men/women relationships. Evidently, my thinking hadn't changed much on that topic. At the moment, considering Karen's situation, I much preferred my naivety to her experience. I wouldn't have traded places with her for the world.

"Have you been to the doctor?" I asked. Karen's attitude shifted back to being the scared girl that she was.

"No! I can't go to a doctor! He'd tell my mom!"

Something about that struck me as funny, and I started to grin. Then I had to giggle; and pretty soon, I was laughing.

"Sissy, it's not funny!" Karen was indignant, and I couldn't blame her.

"I'm sorry, Karen. It just sounds like you're more afraid that the doctor might tell on you than you are about the baby." Reluctantly, Karen grinned.

"I think I am," she admitted. "My mom is going to be so mad, and my dad...." Karen shook her head at the prospect.

"Have you told Matt?"

"Yes."

"What did he say?"

"He wants to run away and get married before we tell anyone. Sissy, you're the only one I've told, except Matt."

"Are you going to elope?" The idea of getting married at sixteen seemed awfully drastic, but so did being pregnant. I thought about the Amish girl, Rebecca, in Redbud Grove. At least Matt wanted to marry Karen. He wouldn't abandon her.

"I don't think I have a choice," Karen sighed. "I know that Matt loves me. He has a good job and he can support us. I just hate to have to drop out of school!" Tears flowed down her face again. "You know, my mom was only sixteen when she got married. She didn't even start high school. Her life turned out okay."

I looked down at my hands. From what I had seen of the relationship between Karen's parents, I wasn't convinced that Mrs. Courtney's life was so "okay." It seemed to me that Mr. Courtney cared more for his moonshine whiskey than he did his family. I hoped that Matt would treat Karen better than Mr. Courtney treated his wife. I cleared my throat.

"When are you going to get married?" I asked.

"Matt says that we should do it this week. We can get blood tests in Kentucky. I'll just have to say that I'm eighteen." Karen didn't sound like a happy bride-to-be. She sounded like the saddest person in the world.

The elopement of Matt Smith and Karen Courtney was the talk of the high school for several days. My mother was appalled. She cast questioning glances at me, when she thought I wasn't aware; but I knew what she was thinking. *If it could happen to Karen, it could happen to Sissy.* I'm sure that Mom was even more grateful that I had walked away from Jack.

My romance might have ended, but Jerry Davis and Ginger Bellini were inseparable. With Karen no longer in school, Ginger and I became closer. She and her mother still lived at the Courtney house, and occasionally I visited with Ginger there. That's how I learned what was really going on with Ginger's parents.

"Don't be fooled, Sissy," Ginger told me one evening. "My dad isn't going to join us, like my mom has told everyone. He was having an affair with his secretary, and my mom found out about it."

"Oh, Ginger, I'm sorry," I said. Ginger shrugged.

"Don't be. Several of my friends' parents are divorced, too."

"Are your parents getting one, a divorce, I mean?" She shrugged again.

"I don't know. I overhead Dad tell Mom that he didn't want a divorce. He wants to stay with Mom; but she's so mad I don't know if she'll ever go back to him. He keeps sending things to us, trying to buy us back, I suppose. But Mom's still awfully mad."

"Do you think you might go back to California?"

"Who knows? I'm beginning to like it here, but I wish we'd get our own house if we stay."

"Well, you have Karen's room to yourself now."

"Yeah." Ginger frowned.

"Have you seen Karen? Does she come home?" I asked. I had hoped that she would call me after she settled into Matt's apartment, but I had heard nothing from her.

"She and Matt came by to get Karen's clothes, but Uncle Dave wasn't very nice to them. Aunt Mary cried a lot."

"When you see her, would you tell her to call me sometime?"

"Sure." I suppose that Ginger relayed my message, but I didn't hear from Karen for a long time. I hoped that she was happy, that marriage was what she had dreamed it would be, and that she had a sweet, healthy baby. I couldn't imagine what it must be like to carry a new life inside my body.

I couldn't get the unhappy face of the Amish girl, Rebecca Yoder, out of my mind. What should have been such a happy, joyous thing had turned out to be life changing and traumatic for both of the young, pregnant girls.

More than ever, I was determined not to let it happen to me. I was learning that all actions have consequences, some more far-reaching and permanent than others. I was in no hurry to leave my youth behind. I was happy living with my mom and dad, my brother and sister, and Sophie. I didn't want the responsibility of adulthood. Not yet.

Not for a long, long time.

Broken Pieces

From the day I was born, my mother was over-protective with her children. Having her third child, a three-week-old baby boy, die in her arms magnified her fear. I could understand that. I'm sure that all parents, especially mothers, worry about their children, at least those mothers who are worthy of the title. As the firstborn, there were times when I felt smothered by my mother's fear. I thought that her anxiety bordered on paranoia.

In December of nineteen fifty-seven, I was two months from the age of eighteen and was a senior in high school. As such, I enjoyed a relative sense of freedom, because my mother focused less of her concern upon me. At that time, Bill was a football-playing sophomore. Mom considered him an untargeted male teenager, not as vulnerable as the Bannister daughters, especially my little sister.

Beth, who was only eleven, caught the full force of Mom's protective persuasion. Being the baby of the family may have given special privileges to Beth; but it also put her in the position of being the last little birdie in the nest. From my vantage point, I grinned and was happy that I had been the first fledgling; and my wings worked just fine.

One Thursday evening after supper was over and the kitchen put back in order, our family gathered in the living room, as we did most nights. No ballgames demanded attendance, no sports or music practices were scheduled, and Mom had worked the day shift at the hospital.

"Who wants popcorn?" Mom asked.

"Me!"

"I do!"

"Sure!"

"Great idea, Honey!"

"Who wants to make it?" was Mom's next question. There were no volunteers. With a sigh and a grin, Mom got up and went back to the kitchen. Feeling a little guilty, I followed. While Mom put a dollop of Crisco and a spoonful of butter into the big, heavy saucepan she used to pop corn, I took clean, used, cottage cheese cartons from a cabinet.

There were many of them. My mother never threw away anything that could be re-used. The right size for serving popcorn, a stack of the tall plastic containers stood in the bottom of a cabinet, right beside the neat pile of paper sacks and empty fruit jars.

Since Mom had become a nurse, she no longer had time to make a big garden and can fruits and vegetables, as she had done in Redbud Grove and the first year we lived in Dixon. She refused to dispose of the jars, saying that she might find time to garden again, someday. I didn't doubt that one bit.

We had just settled down with our popcorn when the telephone rang. Beth turned down the volume on the television while Dad answered. Bill groaned and looked at me with disgust.

"It'll be for you," he told me. "It always is."

"Shhhhh!" Dad commanded. "Go ahead, Tom. I couldn't hear you." Dad listened for several minutes. We all grew still as a look of disbelief turned to horror on his face. "Oh…my…God." Dad's monotone, hushed voice sent chills down my back. "And that's all they know?" he asked. He cleared his throat. "Okay. Okay, Tom. Thanks for calling. Is there anything we can do? Anything…?" Dad listened again. "Okay, Tom. Let us know if you hear anything else." Dad returned the receiver to the cradle.

"Will, what is it?" Mom's voice was filled with dread. Dad looked at her, and tears filled his eyes. He shook his head.

"There's been a…a…. How could anyone…?" Mom got up and went to Dad. She knelt on the floor beside him.

"What's happened, Honey?"

Dad wiped his eyes with his hands and cleared his throat again. He swallowed hard. His eyes fastened on Beth, and his lower lip trembled.

"Beth, come here, Honey." Dad patted the couch beside him. "Sit here." Beth obeyed. Dad put his arms around her and drew her close to his side. "I'm afraid there's some really bad news, Bethy. There's been a…a…something bad has happened to your friend, Connie Staunton."

"What, Daddy?" Tears had already formed in Beth's big, blue eyes. Dad touched her dark curls, and he kissed her forehead. "Honey, someone found her in a ravine behind Duggan's garage, about a mile out of town. I'm afraid Connie is dead, Sweetheart."

"Oh, no!" Mom cried. She put her arms around Beth and Dad. "Oh, no, no, no!" Bill and I remained still, too stunned to move. Connie Staunton was Beth's best friend. She lived two blocks down the hill, and the girls walked to and from school together. I couldn't comprehend that the sweet little girl would no longer giggle with Beth in the room down the hall.

"Dad, what happened to her? Was she hit by a car?" I asked. My voice trembled. Dad shook his head.

"I don't know the details, Sissy. We'll find out more later, okay?" There was something in his eyes, as if he were trying to stop me from asking more questions. I nodded, and he looked relieved.

It was a hard night. We tried to console Beth, but nothing helped much. Mom drew a hot bath and bathed Beth as she had not done for a long time. When they were finished, we gathered together in the living room, trying to gain comfort in closeness. A little later, we moved to the kitchen and sat around the table while Mom made hot chocolate. No one seemed to notice that the television's canned laughter continued quietly in the living room. I don't remember what programs were playing. I just recall the soft background hum.

Mom sat on Beth's bed, reluctant to leave until the child went to sleep. It was only after Dad looked in on her one more time that he gathered us into a small circle and relayed to us what Tom Foster had told him. It was beyond our scope of comprehension.

"Connie wasn't hit by a car," Dad said. "Someone killed her." Mom gasped. "Someone raped and killed that little girl and then dumped her body into the ravine, like unwanted garbage. Someone...." Dad put his hands over his face. I felt nauseous. Bill looked sick, too.

"Will...." Mom began.

"I'm sorry, Jackie. I know you'd rather I not tell all the details in front of the kids, but they need to *know*! They need to know that there are sick animals out there! They need to watch and help protect their little sister...." Dad broke down and cried. It was only the second time that I had seen my father cry.

We couldn't have avoided hearing the details. For the next several days, the murder of Connie Staunton was uppermost in the news media and in all conversations. Such an unspeakable thing hadn't happened in Dixon during anyone's memory. Unfortunately, Connie wasn't the only little victim.

We learned that within the past year, two other girls, both ten years old, had been murdered in Charleston. A nine-year-old girl from Huntington had disappeared, and another eleven-year-old girl's body had been found near Hawk's Nest. All had been bound with rope, raped and strangled.

Christmas, only three weeks away, was tarnished with fear. Kanawha County mothers and fathers were reluctant to let their daughters out of their sight, and the Bannister household was no exception. As a child of the target age, Beth had lost the last vestige of her freedom, at least until the murderer of little girls was found.

After two weeks with no further incidents, the panic abated somewhat, but not completely. Children were encouraged to walk in groups, to watch for each other and to report any strange cars or men in their neighborhoods. Parents began to breathe a little easier.

On the last day of school before Christmas vacation, Mom was called in to work the three-to-eleven shift. Colds and flu had taken a toll upon the hospital staff, as well as townspeople. My mother called the high school and left a message that Bill and I were to pick up Beth at her school. We were both irritated. It was a long walk from the high school to the grade school. Fortunately, we found a ride with a friend, Linda Graham, who drove her own car.

"It would be nice if one of the other mothers could drive Beth home," I grumbled.

"It's okay," Linda said. "I don't mind picking her up at all. I hope they find the creepy killer before he hurts anyone else. It's too bad all the little kids don't have rides home."

"I wish you could have a car," Bill told me. We batted the complaint ball back and forth all the way to Beth's school. High school dismissed later than elementary, so only a few children were still waiting in front of the school for parents to come for them. There was no sign of Beth.

We waited in Linda's car for Beth to come out of the building. After ten minutes, I went inside to look for her. She did have a tendency to dawdle, which only added to my irritation.

"Beth left some time ago," Mrs. Gordon told us.

"But she was supposed to wait for us," I said. "Our mother called and left a message for Beth to wait until we got here." The teacher looked through papers on her desk. She shook her head.

"There's no message for Beth," she said. I hurried back the way we'd come.

"She's gone home," I said.

Wish I May, Wish I Might...

"Mom and Dad are gonna kill us," Bill muttered. I thought that he was probably right.

"Let's hurry. I bet she's walking with some of her friends. Pokey as she is, we can probably catch her." Linda drove slowly along the first block, but there were no children in sight. She drove us the twelve blocks from the school to our house on Symington.

Light had begun to fade early that afternoon. There had been a light snow the first of December, but no more had fallen since then. When we exited Linda's car, heavy clouds, laden with un-fallen snow, hovered low on the mountains, creating a sense of impending doom. More than anything else in the world, I wanted my little sister to be inside that house.

"Thanks, Linda," I tossed over my shoulder. She waved, turned her car around, and drove down the hill.

"Beth? Beth, are you home?" I called, as soon as we opened the front door. There was no answer.

"Bethy? You'd better be here!" Bill yelled. Except for the excited barking of Sophie from her pen in the back yard, there was no sound.

"I'll start calling her friends," I told Bill. "You check with the neighbors. She's probably stopped somewhere along the way. She may have gone to Robbie Anderson's." For fifteen minutes, I called and talked to as many of Beth's friends as I could remember. One little girl had seen her walking with Tammy Brooks, who lived a short distance from the school, so I called Tammy's house.

"Yes, Beth walked with me to my turn-off. She said that she was going to run home, 'cause her mom didn't want her walking by herself. I think she was a little scared, 'cause she started to run real fast."

"Thanks, Tammy." Now I was terrified. The only thing left to do was call my mother at the hospital. After that, the sixth day before Christmas became a nightmare. Mom came home, and Dad arrived shortly after she did. It was nearly four o'clock, and Beth had left the school a little after two. We were crazy with fear.

"Sissy, all we asked you to do was *walk home with her!*" Dad yelled at me.

"Daddy, no one gave Beth the message!" I cried. "Bill and I got there, and we looked for her; *but no one told her we were coming!*" Dad walked back and forth across the living room floor, alternately brushing his hands through his hair and yelling at God.

"Will, Will, listen," Mom sobbed. "We need to go from house to house all along the way to school. Someone must have seen her!"

"We've got to call the police," Dad told her. "We need help." It seemed like a long time before the police car arrived, but it was probably no more than ten or fifteen minutes. After talking to Mom and Dad, one of the officers called for assistance.

"Mr. Bannister, we need you and your wife to stay here at the house, in case your little girl comes home or calls you."

"No, I want to go with you!" Dad argued.

"No, Sir, you stay here. We'll find your little girl."

The waiting was unbearable. Mom cried. Dad paced and alternately muttered and raged. Bill and I sat together on the couch, too scared to do anything. I stared at the unlit Christmas tree and thought about the night we had decorated it together. I looked at individual ornaments, recognizing the ones that had graced the first Christmas tree we ever had. I got up and plugged in the light cord. The tree burst into brilliance, sending reflections throughout the living room.

"Sissy, what are you doing?" Dad demanded.

"I want Beth to see the lights of the tree when she comes up the driveway," I told him. "There's no snow, but the lights still shine through the window; and she'll be able to see them...." I put my hands over my eyes and cried.

My mother came to me. She put her arms around me and pulled me close to her. She murmured reassuring words close to my ear, but I think that it was as much for her as it was for me. It was nearly five-thirty, and darkness had fallen in the mountains. I couldn't stand my own thoughts. When the telephone rang, all four of us momentarily froze before Dad grabbed it.

"Hello!" Dad shouted into the receiver. He listened for two seconds, looked up, and relayed the message. "They found her!" He listened some more. "Thank you! Oh, thank you so much!" He replaced the receiver and held out his arms to my mother. "She's okay, Jackie! They're going to bring her home!"

We cried, laughed, hugged, cried some more, and repeated the whole cycle until we saw the lights of the police car come up the driveway. Both policemen got out of the car and brought Beth into the house. She looked so scared.

"Elizabeth, where were you? Why didn't you wait for someone to get you at the school? Didn't we tell you not to walk by yourself? Didn't...?" One of the officers held up his hand.

"Mrs. Bannister, this little girl is some kind of a hero. Don't be too hard on her. We'll let her tell you where she's been and why." The man touched the brim of his hat and turned away. "You folks have a Merry Christmas," he said. The two men left.

Beth took off her coat and gloves. Nervously, she looked from Mom's face to Dad's. Dad got to her first. He picked Beth up and held her fiercely to his chest. Mom put her arms around both of them. Bill and I looked at each other, shrugged, and joined the family hug.

"I'm hungry," Beth said. "Can I have a sandwich? And a glass of milk?" We went to the kitchen, and together we took sandwich fixings from the refrigerator. Beth kept up a running monologue while we slapped mustard and pickles and whatever we could find in the refrigerator on slices of bread.

"Mom, I was running home from school; and I would have got here early, but I saw an old woman fall on her porch. She was crying and asking for help, but she couldn't talk very loud. So I went up to her porch, and she kept telling me to help her, to help her get back inside her house. Mom, I had to help her get up; and then she had to lean on me all the way to her couch.

"She didn't have a phone, and she wouldn't let me leave. She was crying, Mom. So I told her I wouldn't leave her. She finally quit crying, but she wouldn't let go of my hand. I told her that I could go to the next house and get help, but she started crying again; and I couldn't leave her. She was old, Mom, like Grandma Chinn, really old.

"Her name is Mrs. Ralston, Dad. I told her all about our family and where you work and where Mom works and about Sissy and Bill. When she wasn't crying, she asked lots of questions about us. She has a boy, except he isn't a boy any more, that works at the foundry where you work, Daddy."

Dad nodded his head. "I know a Carl Ralston," he said.

"And that's why I didn't come home. Are you mad at me?"

Our parents answered at the same time. "No, we're not mad."

"We were scared, Beth. We didn't know where you were, and no one had seen you: so we were really scared," Mom explained. "Didn't anyone from the school office tell you that Sissy and Bill were coming to get you?" Beth shook her head.

"Nope. I looked for your car, but I didn't see it. I thought that you probably had to work; so I just started running home."

We sat up late that night. I think we were reluctant to lose sight of one another. The families of the poor little murder victims were not as fortunate as we were. I know that my parents had to be thinking about them, as I was. For the second time in two weeks, my parents took turns gazing at the sleeping form of their youngest child, just to reassure themselves that she was safe.

The only light in the living room came from the Christmas tree. The four of us watched the bubble-lights send up multicolored bubbles, while the silver tinsel reflected every light and sent cascading prisms with the slightest movement of air. Yet, happy as I was that my little sister had returned safely and that we were all together, a huge sadness filled my heart.

The moment that Dad had picked up Beth and held her like he would never let her go, something twisted inside my chest. It wasn't jealousy. I knew how that felt. It was something else, a great, heavy sadness that wouldn't turn me loose.

Long after the lights were out and everyone was in bed, I lay awake, thinking about the day. There was a familiarity about it, a sense of déjà vu that wouldn't go away. Then, all at once, a montage of pictures came back to me. An incident I hadn't thought about for years came flooding my mind and my senses. Another dark, winter evening flashed upon the screen of my memory; and it was like watching a movie unfold before me....

For a short time in the late nineteen forties, my Uncle Dan and Aunt Pearline lived in Redbud Grove, about six blocks north of us on Pine Street. It was the only time we had relatives living in the same town we did. They had two little boys, both a few years younger than I.

One January morning in nineteen forty-eight, just as I was going out the door for the long, cold trek to school, my mother stopped me. I was almost eight years old, and I was in the second grade. I was no longer afraid to walk to school alone. I felt like a big girl.

"Go to Uncle Dan's house after school today, Sissy. I'm taking Buddy and the baby up there this afternoon, and our house will be locked. In case you forget, you can go to Sharon's house until we come home."

"Okay, Mom." It's a shame that mothers are not equipped with x-ray vision, although they do sometimes come close. If my mom could have seen the wheels turning inside my head that morning, both of us could have been spared a lot of anguish. Before I closed the door behind me, I knew that I was going to "forget" to go to Uncle Dan's house.

It was no fun to play with more little boys. One lived in my house, and I played with him all the time. I'd much rather go to the house of one of my friend's, and there were several to consider.

Wish I May, Wish I Might...

I spent the day working out the plan in my head. I had been to Sharon's house many times, probably more than any other, because she lived right behind me. So I thought that I should branch out a little, maybe go where I had not yet been.

I knew where Ellen Kay lived, but I hadn't been to her house. She lived just two blocks north of Sharon, on Locust Street. Coming home from Ellen's, I could walk past Sharon's house and turn onto Alley Street, which led right to my house. It would look as if I had come from Sharon's, and my mom would never know the difference. The machinations of an almost-eight-year-old mind can be an awesome thing.

My plan worked perfectly. School dismissed at three-thirty, and Ellen Kay and I walked to her house, a big, light yellow, two-storied house with a wrap-around covered porch. I didn't make up an elaborate story to tell Ellen Kay's mother. I had merely come to play with her daughter.

We had a marvelous time. Mrs. Cunningham made a snack for us and served it in the living room. Ellen and I played simple board games and played with her dolls. I had made a good choice. Unfortunately, I had kept no track of time; nor had I given to Mrs. Cunningham a time that I must leave.

"Sissy, it's getting dark outside. Don't you think you should go home, before it gets darker?" Mrs. Cunningham sounded concerned. I nodded, put on my coat, picked up my books, and headed for home.

It wasn't a long walk, but it was darker than I wanted it to be. The tall maple trees along the streets took on grotesque forms in the deepening dusk. A cold, winter wind kicked up, and I pulled the collar of my coat higher around my neck. A dog barked from the porch of a nearby house, and I started to run. My adventure had lost its appeal.

I hurried across Route 133, and ran past Sharon's house. When I turned left on Alley, I could see that all the houses on Pine Street, across from the park, had lights shining in the windows. The lights were on in my house, too.

Just as I turned into the back yard, my dad's car pulled in from Pine Street. I assumed that he was coming from work, for it was always dark when he came home. I opened the back door, the words of my "forgetting" story on my lips. I closed the door, took two steps into the kitchen, and I heard the front door slam.

My dad strode into the kitchen, and I knew that I was in serious trouble. I had never seen him so angry. His blue eyes were flashing fire, and he was breathing hard.

"Where have you been, Young Lady?" he demanded. All lies fell away from me. I looked up, way up, into a face that I scarcely recognized.

"A-at Ellen Kay's," I stuttered.

"Didn't your mommy tell you to go to Dan's house?"

"Yes." I nodded.

"And if you forgot, you were supposed to go to Sharon's house?"

"Yes." I nodded again.

Dad grabbed my left arm, and my books fell to the kitchen floor. He swung me around, bent me across one of his knees, and delivered the worst spanking I ever received. More than a spanking, it was a beating that I thought would never end. It was the only time I was thankful to be wearing the heavy, red snow pants. Without them, I don't know how I would have survived. It was the first and only time my dad ever raised a hand to me.

"Daddy, no, Daddy, no, Daddy, Daddy!" I screamed. He wouldn't stop hitting me. Through my tears I could see the geometric pattern on the linoleum, fuzzy and blurred. I stopped struggling. I felt my body go limp against his leg, and I couldn't catch my breath. My father finally stopped delivering the punishing blows. He dropped my arm; and without another word, he left the house. He was still wearing his coat.

Sobbing, I stood where he had left me. I was dazed, hurt, and humiliated. From the corner of my eye, I could see my little brother, who was going to celebrate his sixth birthday the following week. He stood just inside the door that led to the front room. His eyes were big, and tears of sympathy and fear rolled down his face.

Eighteen-month-old Bethy was quiet. I could see her, too, where she sat on the couch. She clutched a stuffed, rag doll in her arms. Her big blue eyes stared at me, and she looked as if she were afraid to move.

"Did Daddy whip you?" My mother came from the back bedroom. Tears ran down her face, too. I had no idea why she was crying. I was the one with a throbbing, aching behind.

"Ye-e-e-s," I hiccupped. I couldn't stop the sobs.

"Well, if he hadn't, I was going to!" she told me. "Sissy, you scared us to death! What were you thinking?"

"I just w-wanted to p-play with Ellen K-k-kay!"

"Go change your clothes. I've got to make supper." I could see that no sympathy would come from that quarter. I did as she told me. I discovered that I had wet myself during the whipping, adding additional shame to my state of disgrace. Big girls didn't wet themselves.

I stayed in the bedroom that my brother and I shared. I sat, gingerly, upon the bed and stayed there until Mom called me to come to supper. It was late, after seven. We always had supper no later than six o'clock. Not only had I upset the whole family, I was responsible for disrupting the dinner hour.

Dad had not yet returned. Grateful for that small blessing, I sat down at the kitchen table. My skinny buttocks and thighs hurt with every movement, so I tried not to squirm on the wood chair. I don't remember what my mother made for supper. I know that she put something on my plate and told me to eat, but I had a hard time trying to swallow.

"Mommy, I'm not hungry. Can I go to the bedroom?" I asked. My mother nodded. Carefully, I moved from the chair. I had taken no more than two steps when the kitchen door opened, and my dad came into the room. I kept my eyes down and hurried, painfully, out of his presence.

I don't remember much about the next few days and weeks. I recall that I tried to stay away from my dad, as much as possible. He never referred to that horrible evening, but I had a hard time regaining my sense of ease around him. It was weeks before I could look at him, and I think that he was uncomfortable with me for a while. Gradually, we re-established a relationship; but for a long time, I was afraid of what he might do should I displease him. That had never before been an issue.

Some time later, I asked my mother why my dad had whipped me like he did. Tears formed in her eyes. It was several seconds before she answered me.

"Sissy, just a week or so before that happened, a little girl in Chicago was kidnapped. Her body was found a few days later, cut up in pieces and stuffed into a city garbage can. Her last name was Grimes, and she was six years old. They hadn't found the man who killed her.

"When you didn't come home, your daddy went to every house we could think of, where you might be. He went to the Romine's, Cathy's, Sheila's, Sharon's, Shirley's, even drove into the country to Patty's house. No one had seen you. Then someone told him that they thought you had walked home with Ellen Kay. By the time your dad got to the Cunningham's house, you had already left.

"Sissy, your daddy was nearly crazy. He was afraid that someone had kidnapped you, and that we would never see you again. Can you understand why he was so upset, why we were all so scared?" I nodded. Young as I was, I began to understand the magnitude of pain my parents had suffered because of my deceit.

Even so, I never understood why my dad, who was my protector, who was supposed to keep me from harm, had beaten me as severely as he had. I forgave him, as children do; but still, something had been broken, something precious....

I couldn't sleep. I wished that the memory had stayed buried. It was hard enough to cope with the fear of the last several hours, without dealing with something so painful from the past. I threw off the covers and crept downstairs. The light above the kitchen sink illuminated the hall that led to Beth's room. Carefully, I tiptoed to her door and looked into her room. I could see the small mound of her body beneath the covers on her bed. Tears formed in my eyes again. I was overwhelmed with gratitude that my little sister was safely in her room, warm beneath the hand-stitched quilts.

I went back to the kitchen, thinking that a glass of milk might make me sleepy. Dad sat at the table, dressed in his khaki pants and an undershirt. His hair was disheveled, and I could see dark stubble on his face. He looked terrible.

"Can't sleep, Sissy?" I shook my head.

"I just wanted to look at Bethy," I told him. Dad smiled.

"Yeah, me too."

"Is Mom asleep?"

"Finally. She's been up several times."

"Do you want a glass of milk or something, Dad?"

"I don't really like it, but I'll take a glass." I filled two glasses with milk and joined him at the table. We sat quietly while we sipped, both lost in our own thoughts.

"Dad, why did you beat me?" I was as surprised at the question that came from my mouth as my dad was, probably more so. "When Beth came home tonight, you grabbed her and hugged her. You were so glad to see her, just glad that she was home; but that time I didn't come home like I was supposed to, you beat me.

" Dad, you *beat* me! It wasn't a spanking. I probably deserved a spanking, but I don't think I deserved what you did to me. I was a month from being eight years old, Daddy; and I *was* little! It was days before I could sit down without hurting." Tears seemed to be the order of the night. They rolled down my face, as if there were a never-ending supply.

Dad rubbed his hand across his face. He looked haggard. For the first time, I saw what he would look like when he grew old.

"Sissy, it's late; and I'm tired. Can we talk about this another time?"

I stood up, put my glass in the sink, and turned back to my father.

"We don't have to talk about it at all, Dad. It's been nine years, over half my life; but I guess it's not a big deal, is it?" I headed for the front hall.

"Sissy, you're right. I shouldn't have whipped you like I did. I had spent an hour trying to find you, imagining all kinds of horrible things, afraid that you were lying somewhere in the cold, hurt or worse. I was crazy with fear, Sissy, just like tonight." Dad stood up, too.

"Honey, don't you see the difference between what happened with Beth and what happened with you? When I saw you walking toward our house like nothing was out of the ordinary, I was so glad to see you that I was nearly sick. And then I got mad. I was so mad at the worry and fear you had caused your mom and me, and the whole neighborhood. I know I was crazy. I shouldn't have hurt you like that, and I'm sorry.

"But, Sissy, Beth didn't do anything wrong. She didn't try to deceive anyone; in fact, she was helping a woman who was in trouble. She doesn't deserve punishment. Don't you see the difference?" Dad held out both hands to me.

I knew that he was right. Beth had simply done what her gentle, kind heart told her to do. On the other hand, my actions had caused needless worry and the kind of fear and agony that only parents of a missing child can know. I knew all that. Still, I knew that what I had done didn't deserve the kind of punishment I had received.

"Did you learn anything that night, Sissy?" Dad asked.

"I learned that I didn't want any more whippings from you. I was afraid of you for a long time," I told him.

"I know you were, but it didn't last forever. Remember the other time that you disappeared? The day you rode your bike out to the Thompson farm? Your fear of me didn't keep you from deceiving your mother about where you were going, did it? That little trick nearly got you killed, Sissy; but I didn't spank you then, did I? I never spanked you again."

"I had a broken ankle," I muttered. I dropped my eyes. I hadn't thought about my crush on Frank Thompson for a long time. My dad was right. I *had* misled my mother about where I was going that March afternoon. Shame brought a flush to my face. I recalled how my dad had taken me from Frank's arms, and how closely he had held me while the heavy snow swirled around us.

"I know, Dad. You're right. I had a hard time following the rules sometimes. I didn't stop to think about what I was doing. I just wanted to do things my own way, I guess." Dad grinned.

"I don't think that's changed much." Dad ran his hand through his hair again. "I was wrong, Sissy," he continued. "The day you went to Ellen Kay's, I took out my anger on you. I wish I had handled it better than I did. You'd be surprised at the times I've remembered the fear on your little face. I'm sorry, Honey. I'm sorry that I hurt you." I knew that he meant it.

I went to my dad and put my arms around his waist. He hugged me, tightly, as he had hugged Beth. It felt good.

"If I could do it over, I would hug you and tell you that I was glad you were safe." He smiled. "And then I would have spanked you like you deserved, not the way that I did."

"It's okay, Dad. I was just so little…."

"Oh, but, Sissy; you still knew right from wrong. You planned it, and you deliberately set out to deceive your mom and me."

He had me there. I nodded.

"Yep, I did, Dad. I'm sorry."

"I am, too, Sissy, every day of my life." He kissed my forehead. "Now can we please go to bed? I'm exhausted, and I've got to go to work in a couple of hours."

"Good night, Dad. I love you." Well, now. That wasn't something we said to each other every day, not even once a year. Dad cleared his throat.

"I love you, too, Sissy."

I left Dad to turn out the kitchen light. In the hallway, I glanced toward Beth's room; and there stood my mother, just outside the bedroom door. She leaned against the wall. Exhaustion was apparent in her sagging shoulders. She raised her head, looked at me, and gave me the sweetest smile I had ever seen on her face. Slow tears ran down her cheeks, and I knew that she had heard the conversation between my father and me. I knew that she understood.

I hurried up the stairs and jumped into bed. The sheets were cold again, but I felt warm and cozy. A nine-year-old tear in my heart had just been mended. My little sister was safe and my family, intact for the night, slept beneath one roof. For us, it was going to be a wonderful holiday season.

As it turned out, all families in Kanawha County breathed more easily. Three days before Christmas, another little girl managed to escape from the man who tried to pull her into his car. She was able to

Wish I May, Wish I Might...

give a description of him and his car, and he was apprehended within hours. An item of clothing from each of his victims was found in the vehicle, so there was no doubt that he was the killer of children.

We celebrated Christmas with a newly found appreciation for each other. Just repeating the ages-old phrase, "Merry Christmas," was like saying a blessing. There was a sense of sadness just below the surface, an awareness of how tragic the holiday was for the families whose little girls had been so brutally snatched from them. For those mothers and fathers, Christmas would never be the same, not for as long as they lived.

Their lives would always be over shadowed with brokenness.

Unmendable broken pieces.

Still Waters

My senior year at Dixon High followed a summer that had been filled with good times and good friends. Karen Courtney and I had reestablished our friendship following the birth of her daughter, whom they named Mona Gail. Motherhood brought a great happiness to Karen that I had not anticipated; and I'm not certain that Karen had, either.

Karen's skin actually radiated glowing health and contentment. There was a softness about her, a maturity that made me wistful. While I didn't envy the responsibility of a baby at our age, I recognized the joy that a baby generated between loving parents.

There was no doubt that Karen and Matt adored their baby and each other. Perhaps my wistfulness was the result of observing the closeness between them, as much or more than watching them with their little girl. I hoped to experience what I saw in their lives, but not too soon.

Inevitably, whenever I spent time with Karen, she asked about Jack McCoy. In her mind, Jack and I remained a couple. He still sent notes to me from the University of Illinois. He had not returned home that summer, choosing to stay in Urbana and work as a clerk in a law firm. In one of his letters he had told me about the firm, how his father had pulled some strings to secure the position for him. I had no doubt that Jack would do well on his own, regardless of how he had edged into the company.

In spite of myself, I sometimes longed to see him. I didn't know why. Perhaps it was his physical appearance, his charm, his manner in public. Occasionally, I thought about the way he had kissed me and held me; and, to be honest with myself, I had to admit that I sometimes missed that feeling, too. Still, I suspected that an ugly self-centeredness resided in the soul of Jack McCoy; and that scared me.

In moments of weakness, I sent short notes to Jack. I kept them impersonal, for the most part. I related local events to him, without giving details of my day-to-day life. I was having too good a time with my freedom and a third or fourth-hand car that my dad was helping me to buy. Although Jack and I were no longer dating, I hesitated to anger him.

When I drove my brother to school the first day of my senior year, I felt that life just couldn't get much better. I was seventeen, working enough to supply my personal needs, and driving my own car—well, mine as long as Dad and I made the payments. I looked forward to all my classes, two of which were electives and both passions to me—Art and Creative Writing.

The guidance counselor told me that I should concentrate upon one or the other, but I couldn't let go of either one. Both subjects brought such pleasure to me. I enjoyed the process of creating, of delving into my own mind to find the right words for a story, as much as receiving a good grade for the finished article. The same process applied to painting. I loved the way paint mounded on the pallet when I squeezed the tubes. Watching my own painting develop beneath the brushes, sometimes with surprise at the results, was as exciting as beholding the completed canvas. I dreamed of the day that I would have a career in one or both fields.

No other students in high school move with the same cockiness and confidence as senior boys. In the fall of nineteen fifty-seven, most boys sported flattop haircuts; but some of the more trend-conscious let their hair grow. The ducktail style seemed to cause an increased swagger in the jaunty senior stroll.

Summer vacation had not cooled student interest in the handsome new teacher and coach, Lucas Esmond. More than a few senior girls suffered heart palpitations at the mere thought of the coach. Poor Miss Seabrook was so smitten that she was an embarrassment to the students and staff. Mr. Esmond seemed not to notice.

It was my good fortune to find myself enrolled in his World Geography class. I had taken the course as a certain A, risking the possibility of being assigned to Mrs. Worley's classroom. Near retirement age, Mrs. Worley was a bit absent-minded and prone to taking short, spontaneous naps at her desk. I was overjoyed to see Mr. Esmond's name listed as my instructor.

Within the class were many of the first friends I had acquired in Dixon: among them Jerry, Beverly, Judy, Wes, Jimmy, Gary and Rowena. We had maintained our gang friendship, widening the circle to include new people, one of which, of course, was Ginger Bellini. Laura Dunham was another.

Laura and I had been in a few classes together during the past three years. There was a calm, self-contained air about her that could have bordered upon aloofness, except for her friendly, soft brown eyes. The amber-y flecks in their light brown depths seemed to glow when Laura smiled.

Slender to the point of thinness, Laura moved with a grace acquired from her study of ballet, in which she excelled. Her performance from "Swan Lake" at the previous annual Variety Show had stunned the audience. Ignorant of the finer points of the dance, I could still recognize the beauty and poignancy of Laura's interpretation.

Laura maintained a straight A average. She was a shoo-in for valedictorian, a position I had occasionally half-heartedly pursued. I would be content should I graduate within the upper five percent of the class. However, there was nothing half-hearted about Laura's pursuit of her goals. I had no doubt that she would attain each one.

I was glad to see her come into Mr. Esmond's class. I motioned for her to join us where we sat in adjoining rows of seats. She smiled in greeting and sat in the desk across and two up from me.

"Hi, Sissy," she said. The boys perked up immediately. More than one of them had asked Laura out, but she didn't date at all. Although she seemed to have no time for boys, they hadn't stopped their pursuit of her.

"Find a seat, People." Without preamble, Mr. Esmond entered the classroom and took command. "I don't care where you sit, as long as you stay there, once you've decided," he said. There was a noisy shifting of desks while places were chosen.

Mr. Esmond half-leaned, half-stood against the front of his desk. He crossed his arms, which strained the fabric of his shirt. He watched the slow maneuvering for back-seat positions among the boys, moving nothing but his dark brown eyes.

"I don't have many rules, but I'm serious about the ones I do have. When I talk, you listen. There won't be much homework..." A loud cheer emanated from the back of the room. "...because I'll give you enough class time to complete most assignments." Mr. Esmond paused. "If you don't turn in assigned work, it's an automatic F for the day. I won't remind you of assignments that are due. I'm not your daddy."

Chuckles filled the room. The shift from dread to anticipation was almost palpable. This was going to be different from the usual classroom.

"If you want to chew gum, chew it. If you crack it, you're out of here. If you stick it underneath your desk, I'll personally kick you out of the room." For the first time since Mr. Esmond entered the room, a smile hovered upon his lips. "There will be spot checks."

He stood up and sauntered around his desk. I looked at Beverly, who looked at Rowena, who looked at Ginger, who looked back at me. We all rolled our eyes in appreciation of the muscular specimen of manhood who would be presiding over a boring geography class for the next nine months.

I glanced at Laura. There was nothing upon her pretty face but a pleasant smile. For a moment I wondered if she were human. I leaned across the aisle and whispered to her.

"Isn't he handsome?"

"Do you have a question?" I looked up to find Mr. Esmond looking directly at me. "Your name is...?" he asked. He wasn't smiling.

"Sissy Bannister," I murmured.

"Well, Sissy Bannister, would you like to enlighten the rest of the class?"

"Uh, no," I said.

"Uh, well then, perhaps we can get on with why we're here." His mockery of my stupid stutter stung. He looked away from me, and I felt as dismissed as if I no longer existed. I could feel my face growing warm. I glanced at Laura, who smiled at me and mouthed one word: *Yes*. I felt better. It seemed that Laura Dunham was as susceptible as the rest of us to the teacher's handsome face.

In the weeks that followed, Lucas Esmond's class became the highlight of our days. World geography was not a subject that grabbed the imagination, but he managed to insert some interesting current event or tidbit into the discussions. While a lot of teachers seemed to favor leaning against the front of their desks as they discoursed, Mr Esmon's favorite "stance" seemed to be the reclining position.

At some point in every session, he leaned back in his swivel chair and deposited his feet upon his desk, the perfect picture of an in-charge CEO. A yellow or red grading pencil often rested behind his ear, and sometimes he chewed gum. I don't know if he were as relaxed in all his classes. We had him the last period of the day, which could have been a factor.

Wish I May, Wish I Might...

One warm, lazy October afternoon, the whole class seemed half asleep, including Mr. Esmond. The subject was South America, specifically Brazil, a place none of us ever expected to explore. Some of the boys sat at their desks, heads upon their arms, as near to dozing as it's possible to get without going to sleep. Others looked out the window. My left elbow rested upon the top of my desk, and my head rested upon my hand. With my right, I drew squiggles and stars on notebook paper. After what had been a long pause, Mr. Esmond continued with the lesson.

"Who can tell us some of the more important products of Brassiere?" he asked. For the space of five seconds, there was utter silence. I exchanged glances with Laura. Heads popped up from desktops and swiveled, disbelieving eyes meeting other disbelieving eyes. Suddenly an explosion of laughter to rival the eruption of Mount Vesuvius filled the room. In nineteen fifty-seven, women's unmentionables were just that: unmentionables.

Mr. Esmond simply closed his eyes and grimaced in painful embarrassment while a wave of red traveled from his shirt collar, all the way to the roots of his reddish chestnut hair. Pandemonium reigned. Our delighted laughter drowned out the bell that signaled the end of class. With a gigantic sigh, Mr. Esmond lowered his feet and pushed his chair away from his desk. He stood up and made an elaborate bow.

"Class dismissed," he said.

We discussed Mr. Esmond's faux pas and decided that he was probably more preoccupied with winning football games than with mundane facts about agricultural products of a foreign country. Who could blame him? He was a dedicated coach.

For the first time in years, the Dixon High School football team showed promise. By the end of his first year, the Dixon Wildcats had won several games; and Mr. Esmond's second season as football coach created a lot of optimism among students and fans. The tantalizing scent of a winning team, no matter how sweaty, was in the air.

Most of the seniors gathered at the football games that fall. We realized that it was our last autumn together; and there was a sense of poignancy as well as excitement in the crisp, mountain air. We bundled up in our warm coats and cheered and booed and clapped like the maniacal fans that we were.

Lucas Esmond lived up to his reputation. Game after game fell to the Wildcats, and the team advanced to the state championship playoffs. They lost by a small margin, but second place in the state was cause for jubilation. The ten senior boys on the team were justly proud of their efforts.

The romance between Ginger and Jerry had burned itself out sometime before school started that year. Neither of them seemed upset about it. If anything, Jerry looked happier; and Ginger was as ebullient as ever, perhaps more so.

Ginger's sweaters looked a little tighter, and her skirts fit awfully close to her hips. She hadn't gained any weight. She was still petite and physically fit. There was something a little different about her that raised girls' eyebrows and boys' hopes.

Ginger lingered often in Mr. Esmond's class after the bell rang. At first, I didn't think much about it, but one day it dawned upon me that Ginger was actually flirting with the teacher. A smile is one thing; a seductive crossing of shapely legs is another. Had I not looked over my shoulder one day, I would not have witnessed Ginger's performance. I could think of no other word to describe it.

At the end of class, under the guise of asking about an assignment, Ginger placed her books on the desk right in front of Mr. Esmond's. Slowly, she scooted into the seat, wriggling much more than was necessary. Slowly, Ginger raised her right leg and draped it carefully over her left knee, exposing more than a generous amount of thigh.

Coyly, she pretended to pull the hem of her plaid skirt down a fraction. A sudden upsweep of lashes and a soft smile from red lips should have caused some kind of reaction in any red-blooded American male. From the doorway, I glanced at Mr. Esmond. He seemed totally unimpressed. Grinning, I turned away. It appeared to me that Ginger had just made a fool of herself.

I called Ginger that evening. "Want to come down and do homework with me?"

"Sure," she answered. Ginger came down the path that her cousin and I had beaten into our back yard. We took glasses of iced tea and a plateful of cookies up to my room. Homework wasn't on my mind.

"Are you flirting with Mr. Esmond?" I asked.

"Why not?" she asked.

"Well, gee, I don't know. He's a *teacher*! You can't date him or anything. Even if he weren't, he's ten or eleven years older than you are. When you're twenty, he'll be *thirty*! He'll be old!"

"Oh, Sissy, grow up! I don't want to marry him. I'm just having a little fun. I bet you I can get him to ask me out as soon as we graduate. I'm warming him up a little. Besides, I'll be eighteen in a few weeks."

"Ginger, you could get him into real trouble! Teachers can't date students. What if Mr. Sheffield finds out what you're doing?" Ginger laughed.

"Who's going to tell him? Besides, he's so old he probably doesn't remember what flirting is." Ginger threw back her head and laughed.

"You really do look like Marilyn Monroe sometimes," I said. Ginger looked pleased.

"Only sometimes?" She turned her sideways, flirty, impish grin on me; and I had to laugh. Mr. Esmond didn't have a chance!

A flurry of celebration and activity surrounded Christmas. The band performance was better than ever, but the highlight of the season was the presentation of the entire "Nutcracker Suite." Night practices had been grueling and long, and both the band and choral departments had worked diligently. Mothers and other seamstresses had designed and made the costumes.

Several grade school children, including Beth, had parts in the musical. As a member of the chorus, all I had to do was sing; but I was excited about that, too. Anticipation filled the cast and backstage crew, most of whom were teachers. Mr. Esmond's brawny arms were in charge of the curtains, and even he seemed to be impressed with the production.

The Dixon High School band played as professionally as any group of musicians, and the characters had every line perfected. However, the single most impressive number was "The Dance of the Sugar Plum Fairy" by Laura Dunham. She seemed to float across the floor, gliding as effortlessly as a lark upon the wind. I had thought that Suzy Kirk's interpretation of the same dance three years previously was unmatched, but Laura's was one of the most beautiful things I ever saw.

Instead of the classic tutu, Laura wore a longer skirt, fashioned of sheer, shimmering organza strips, diaphanous and ethereal. Her shiny hair, piled atop her head, dripped with sparkling crystals, while wispy tendrils curled at her neckline and forehead. Laura Dunham was dazzling, both in appearance and movement. Theater make-up enhanced the bone structure of her face and made her look older.

At the end of Laura's dance, Mr. Esmond was supposed to pull the curtains, but they remained open. Laura held her pose, unmoving, for a long moment. I glanced backstage, where Mr. Esmond stood with one hand on the pull. As though mesmerized, he stared at Laura.

Someone nudged him, and he sprang into action, jerking the pulls so hard that the curtains fairly scooted across the stage. I wasn't surprised to see Ginger, who had no part in the production, sidle along side Mr. Esmond. She brushed against his arm, as if by accident, which led to a smiling apology from her. She touched his shoulder. He looked down at her, but only briefly, as one would glance at a mild distraction, before his attention refocused upon the beautiful ballerina.

Laura ran gracefully off-stage, right by Mr. Esmond and Ginger. Mr. Esmond grasped Laura's upper arm, then dropped it just as quickly. Startled, Laura looked up at him.

"Your dance was beautiful," Mr. Esmond whispered, mindful of the audience just beyond the curtain. From my position, I could read his lips. I couldn't see Laura's face, but she answered briefly and hurried away. Mr. Esmond watched Laura. Ginger watched Mr. Esmond. I watched all three of them. I grinned at the small pout that formed on Ginger's red mouth. Her alluring powers seemed ineffective and totally wasted on the object of her affection.

"What's so funny?" whispered the soprano beside me.

"I'm just happy that the program is so good," I whispered back to her. There was no time for further repartee. On cue, the curtains parted smoothly; and the program resumed. I stole a quick glance at Mr. Esmond, where he leaned nonchalantly against the backstage wall. For a moment I thought that I had imagined the intensity of his attention to Laura's dance. I turned my head a fraction, and I knew that I wasn't imagining the angry face of Ginger Bellini before she turned and disappeared from view.

The next day of school was the last before Christmas vacation began. Classes were cut to half periods, and most of the teachers, including Mr. Esmond, assigned no homework. Relaxed as ever, he sat upon his desk, muscle-y arms braced upon the desktop, muscle-y legs dangling. He laughed and joked with the boys, teased the girls, and merely raised an eyebrow when someone loudly popped chewing gum. He paid special attention to Ginger, who responded with her usual sensuality. Ginger cast one veiled glance at me that as much as said, "See? I told you that I could get him!" Mr. Esmond didn't even speak to Laura Dunham.

I felt foolish.

"Sissy, I think that I'm going to marry Lucas Esmond," Ginger whispered. Had we not been watching a movie in a dark theater, my reaction would have been loud and long. All I could do was stare at her. Ginger smiled in the darkness, glanced sideways at me, and tossed popcorn into her red mouth.

"You're crazy," I whispered back.

"No, I'm not. I'm confident. I know he likes me, and I think that I can get him to *really* like me, as in *love* like."

"Ginger, he likes Laura, too."

"He does not!" Ginger had forgotten to whisper.

"SSSSHHHHH!" Several people glared and hissed at us like a bunch of angry snakes.

"He does not," Ginger repeated in a fierce whisper. "That wimpy, skinny little thing wouldn't appeal to a man like Mr. Esmond! She barely has breasts! He could *never* go for someone like her!" I thought that Ginger might be right, but I couldn't forget the expression on the teacher's face as he had watched Laura dance. On the other hand, I suspected that Ginger, unleashed and determined, could be a mighty force.

By mid-spring, Ginger's frontal attack upon the affections of our geography teacher was the talk of the class. Mr. Esmond, good-natured and tolerant as he was, seemed more amused than threatened. He took in Ginger's provocative style of dress, sometimes with a raised eyebrow, sometimes with a lewd grin, sometimes with a shake of his head. Nonplused, Ginger responded with sultry smiles and languid, lowered lashes.

On an afternoon that Ginger lingered, again, after class, I followed Laura Dunham into the corridor. Although Laura often ate in the cafeteria with our group of friends, she never joined into any conversation or speculation about Ginger and the teacher. I was curious about her feelings.

"What do you think about Ginger and Mr. Esmond?" I asked.

"What about them?" Laura answered.

"Well, do you think that they'll date after graduation? Ginger just turned eighteen, so she's old enough." We walked for several seconds before Laura answered.

"I feel sorry for Ginger," she said.

"Why would you feel sorry for Ginger?"

"Because I think that she's setting herself up for a big disappointment. I don't believe that Mr. Esmond is interested in Ginger at all, not in that way. I'm sorry, Sissy. I've got to meet my mother in front of the school now. I'll talk to you later." Laura waved to me and ran gracefully down the hall.

Laura's opinion surprised me. I think that the boys had bets on how long after graduation it would be before Ginger and the football coach became an item. The girls openly discussed the possibility, with Ginger's encouragement. No one, besides Laura, had suggested that Mr. Esmond wasn't in the least interested in Ginger. I decided that Laura was just too unworldly about the facts of life. My bet was with the boys.

With spring came the realization that graduation and real life lay only weeks away. As expected, Laura was named valedictorian. I was happy with my rank of number seven in the class. Not even my dad's feigned disappointment in me could hamper my little glow of self-satisfaction.

"How come you didn't get number one?" he asked. Neither of my parents had attended high school, and I knew that they were both proud of me. Dad couldn't hide the teasing twinkle of pride in his eyes.

We had discussed where I would attend college. There was never a doubt in my mind that I would go, and there were several possibilities. Scholarships were offered. After looking at several schools and weighing all my options, we decided that I would attend the university in Charleston. Some of my friends made the same choice.

Dixon was close enough to Charleston that I could drive my little second-hand car to classes every day. I could also keep my job at the A&W and perhaps find a second part time job. It was an exciting time.

Jerry Davis was accepted at the University of Illinois, where Jack McCoy would be a junior in the autumn. I was happy for Jerry, but I found it ironic that he would be living only thirty miles from Redbud Grove, the little town that held such a huge place in my heart. I had sent for an application. I filled it out, but I didn't mail it. Even with scholarships and student loans, the cost was too great. With two other children to care for, my parents simply couldn't afford an out-of-state university.

As graduation approached, Ginger Bellini's excitement grew with every passing day. She was convinced that Lucas Esmond was the love of her life, and the only thing that prevented him from claiming her was her status as a student. Ginger actually sizzled with anticipation. Her skin glowed; her bright blue eyes sparkled; she emanated confidence.

By contrast, Laura Dunham, who sat behind Ginger in Mr. Esmond's class, seemed to become more demure. Her soft pink lipstick was the only color in her face. At times Laura looked sad, contemplative, even distracted. Then one day, during our final exam, I discovered the source of Laura's preoccupation.

With a sigh of relief, I put down my pencil and flexed my hands. I had just completed the last test I would take in Dixon High. I glanced at Laura, prepared to smile in commiseration. Laura was finished with her test, too; and she sat very still, both hands on her desk. She was looking at Mr. Esmond.

The longing on her face could have meant only one thing: *Laura was in love with Mr. Esmond!* I barely kept my mouth from falling open in amazement. My eyes shifted to our teacher. He was looking at Laura, and his brown eyes conveyed the same soft, intimate yearning as Laura's. I felt as if I had stumbled into a foreign land, one where I knew not word of the language.

Quickly, I dropped my eyes to the test paper. My mind swirled with the ramifications. What was Ginger going to do? Even better, what was *I* going to do? Should I warn Ginger, talk to Laura, or keep my mouth shut and stay completely out of the potentially messy situation? I knew that the latter was the smartest, but how could I let Ginger go on believing in something that would never happen?

I worried needlessly. Perhaps in passing my eighteenth birthday, I had acquired a bit more discretion than I had previously shown. I said nothing to Ginger about my suspicions, choosing to let events play out as they would. It was one of my better decisions.

Graduation ceremonies were held on a warm evening in late May. The gymnasium was filled with family and friends of the graduates, as well as alumni, one of whom was Jackson McCoy. Following the traditional tossing of graduation caps into the air, Ginger grasped my arm.

"Sissy, look! There's Jack! Oh, Sissy, he is *so* handsome! Don't you want to just go hug him or something?" I looked where Ginger pointed. She was right. Jack was coming toward us, and he was even more handsome than I'd remembered. My heart did a little tap dance at the sight of him. I hadn't seen him for a year, although he had come home for all the holidays. In fact, I had been a little miffed when I hadn't heard from him. My mother had called me a "dog in the manger" when I'd voiced my complaints.

"You don't want him, but you don't want him to stop wanting *you!*" she had told me. Her words had irritated me because I knew that she was right. I didn't want to think that I might be easily forgotten.

"Sissy, are you sure you don't want to date Jack anymore?" Ginger whispered. I hesitated only a moment.

"I'm sure," I replied.

"Good! Then I think I'll date him, myself!"

"What? Ginger, you've been planning to go after Mr. Esmond for months!"

"I know, but I've changed my mind. He really is too old, and Jack is just so handsome!" Ginger nearly squealed, but she managed to suppress it with a bright smile for Jack.

"Jack! How lovely to see you again!" Ginger's breathless voice accompanied a wide smile, and she grasped Jack's arm with both hands.

"Hi, Ginger," Jack smiled down at her. His brown eyes took in Ginger's charms, unhidden even by the green graduation gown, which Ginger quickly removed and draped over one arm. "How are you, Sissy?"

"Fine," I muttered. "Just fine."

"That's good," Jack smiled. I took a deep breath. In spite of myself, my heart fluttered even more at Jack's nearness. Memories of his kisses warmed my cheeks. I glanced up at him; and I knew that he was remembering, too. The kiss was in his eyes.

"Do you have plans for the evening?" he asked. Ginger replied before I could.

"Oh, there's just a stupid graduation party at Dooby's," she said, "nothing I can't get out of. Would you like to go somewhere else?" Jack smiled at her, much like one would smile at an engaging child.

"I don't know," Jack laughed. "Sissy, would you like to skip the party, too?"

"No, Sissy already has plans," Ginger said. She still clung to Jack's arm. "We'll see you later, Sissy. Okay? Let's go, Jack!" Jack bit his lower lip, and I knew that he wanted to laugh. He waved his free hand as they turned away.

Jack will see through her. Jack won't be fooled. What do I care, anyway? I don't want Jackson McCoy. I'm going to college. I don't want any boy. He sure looks good. What do I care? Ginger can have him. No, she can't have him. Jack McCoy has never wanted anyone but me. I wonder where they're going? And what is Ginger going to do with Jack! Ginger doesn't know how to care about any one but herself! Jack McCoy, what are you doing with Ginger Bellini?

Thoroughly disgusted with the thoughts that rattled through my head, I went to the graduation party at Dooby's, the last party we would have there as high school students. Little by little, couples drifted away, until only those who were not dating remained. I took part in the chatter about the approaching summer, about college in the fall, about those girls who were already planning their weddings.

I just couldn't shake the nagging little irritation that Ginger was out with Jack. He didn't call me before he went back to his summer job in Illinois. That really irritated me! I could barely stand to look at Ginger.

A few weeks after graduation, Ginger's mother decided that she had punished her unfaithful husband long enough. Overnight, she made plans to go back to California, taking Ginger with her. I was prepared to support Ginger in her sorrow at leaving friendships she had formed, but that wasn't necessary.

"Oh, I can't wait to get back to the beach!" Ginger exclaimed. "There's this boy I knew out there, and I've already written to him that I'm coming back. I know that he's going to just flip out! Sissy, you'll have to come and see me! You will love California!"

Like a whirlwind in the desert that sucks up everything in its path and then dissipates, the Bellinis were gone. I missed Ginger. I missed her exuberance, her cockiness, her belief that she was irresistible to boys and men, alike. From what I had seen, she had good reason to feel as she did. I wondered what life would hold for Ginger Bellini. One thing that I didn't want her life to hold was Jack McCoy.

Summer passed quietly, except for one remarkable, some even said scandalous, event. Laura Dunham and Lucas Esmond were quietly married. They told no one, not even her parents, until the ceremony had been performed. There was one faction that wanted the school board to fire Mr. Esmond, but no just cause could be found. Laura was of age, and there was no proof that any contact between the two had taken place before graduation.

I had thought that my mother might be upset over the wedding, but she merely smiled. Had I been the one to drop college plans for a husband, I'm sure that her reaction would have been less benign. About Laura, she simply quoted one of her old axioms, one of the many I heard her repeat over the years.

"Still waters run deep," she said, "deep and dark."

"Like the New River Gorge, huh, Mom?" I suggested. My mother nodded and smiled, then added:

"You never know what they may hide."

#

Dad

As in many homes during the fifties, the hub of our house was the kitchen. Even though my mother continued to work at the hospital, with seniority she was able to spend most of our dinner hours at home. Mom loved cooking in what she called her new kitchen. Somehow, Dad had found time to replace the kitchen linoleum with red and white checkerboard tiles, chosen by Mom. Thrilled with her new floor, she splurged on new kitchen towels and red pottery dishes.

That led to new paint for the cabinets, new curtains for the three windows, and a new dinette set, complete with six cushioned, vinyl-covered chairs. The pride of her kitchen was a new refrigerator, which featured a freezer compartment big enough to hold several ice trays and as many frozen packages as she could cram into it.

It was wonderful to come into a house filled with the good smells of supper cooking on the stove. I had missed those aromas while my mother was going to school and when she worked the three-to-eleven shift. It was more than just knowing that a good meal was in progress. I felt a sense of security when I came home from school to find my mother in the house, whether I was eight or eighteen. Nothing could replace the feelings of togetherness we experienced when the five of us gathered in the kitchen around the rectangular, Formica-covered table for supper. Those evenings provided the perfect ending for the day.

The first time my dad went into a mine, he told us about it at the supper table. For reasons I could never understand, coalmines fascinated him. My mother didn't understand, either; and she didn't hesitate to let my dad know that she didn't want him to go into the mines. I suppose that we had grown used to the pervasive odor of the fine dust that hung in the air, but a strong whiff sometimes reminded me that I didn't like it. After a while, we stop noticing things we can't change; or perhaps we just push it to the backs of our minds.

During the four years we had lived in Dixon, there had been no mine cave-ins or explosions. Some of my friends, who were born and lived their whole lives in Dixon, remembered one bad cave-in and smaller, less tragic occurrences. Sadly, some of them had lost relatives in the depths of the mountain.

"Jackie, it's unbelievable!" Dad said. "There's a network of tunnels and paths and rails that goes back for miles into the mountain. Wires are hung up along the way, with bare bulbs lighting the tunnels. The men wear headgear with lamps that are really bright. Did you know that they don't look at each other directly? That's so they don't shine the light in someone's eyes."

"Mark Watson's dad died in a cave-in," I told him. "Maybe you should stay out of the mines." Dad shrugged his shoulders.

"It's much safer now," he said. "The tunnels are shored up and reinforced and there are more safety measures. I've talked to some of the officials about that."

"Do those officials go into the mines?" Mom asked.

"I'm sure they do, Jackie. There are inspections and regulations that have to be followed." Dad slathered more butter on a warm biscuit. "Sissy, I've talked to a retired miner named Watson. He's one of the oldest miners who worked in the Number Seven. I think someone said that his son had died in the mine. Maybe he's a relative of your friend." Dad laughed. "Some of the guys tell funny stories about him, but he's a nice old fellow. Seems he had a terrible temper in his younger days. He had a brother, and they had some kind of falling out. For fifteen years, they worked side by side in the mine and never spoke a word to each other. Now, that's what I call a grudge."

"Dad, can I go with you to the mine the next time you go?" my brother asked. Before my dad could answer, my mother issued one of her RULES.

"You absolutely will not go into that mine the next time your dad goes or any other time," she said. The fact that Mom didn't raise her voice gave additional weight to her words. In fact, she almost whispered. "Do you understand me, Bill? I can't keep your dad out of those black pits, but you will not go into them, not one." My brother dropped his eyes to his plate.

"Yes, Ma'am." Bill, like Beth and me, had picked up the colloquial manner of speaking to our elders. We kind of slipped into the practice, just as we had acquired an accent without realizing it.

Even though Dad showered before he came home from the foundry, Mom always knew when he had been inside the mine. He wasn't able to get all the coal dust from behind his ears. She finally accepted that he wasn't going to stop his forays into the mine, no matter how much she objected. Tongue in cheek, he told her that he had to inspect the coal that fired the foundry's furnaces. She pinned him with the look that threatened to lower the room's temperature by twenty degrees, and he found something to do elsewhere.

Mark Watson, the boy whose father had died in the mine, asked me out the summer after graduation. Tall and lean, Mark was a shy, soft-spoken boy with a pronounced drawl that was more sweet than slow. Dark, curly lashes lined his blue eyes. He combed his thick, dark brown hair back from his forehead; but it managed to fall in a deep wave to one side. Mark was a handsome boy, not magazine-model handsome, like Jack, but second-glance handsome.

We had spoken to each other at ball games and other school functions, but Mark, like many others, had considered me Jack McCoy's girl. Someone had told me about his father's death in the horrendous mine explosion that had taken the lives of thirty-seven men. Only ten years old at the time, it was said that Mark had vivid memories of the disaster. I supposed it wasn't something he would casually mention.

Instead of a movie, Mark took me to a family picnic at his grandfather's home in the hills. Perched on the side of a steep slope, the house was small, but well built. Dozens of people swarmed around the house, up and down the slope, lolled upon the sturdy porch rails, and meandered in and out of the woods that surrounded the place. My first cousins numbered over sixty, and I had fourteen blood uncles and aunts; but this family outnumbered mine.

Mark introduced me to so many people that I lost count. Some of them made lasting impressions upon me. One of his aunts, a large, black-eyed woman with a mound of black hair twisted into a massive bun, was the picture of a stolid Indian woman. Mark told me later that he had an Indian ancestor only a couple of generations back.

A tall, lean man with streaks of gray in his black hair came onto the porch. His eyes were the most incredible shade of blue, framed with sooty lashes. I knew immediately from whom Mark had inherited his beautiful eyes. High cheekbones and lined, leathery skin were further evidence of the family's heritage. The man shifted a small twig from one side of his wide mouth to the other. Mark told me that the twig was a substitute for the chewing tobacco his grandpa had given up, but still missed.

"Sissy, this is my Grandpa Watson," Mark said. "He has just about raised me. Grandpa, this is Sissy Bannister, a friend from school." Mr. Watson extended his hand, and I placed mine inside his firm grasp. His hand was warm, and his skin a bit on the rough side.

"I'm glad to m-m-m-meet you," he said. "M-m-m-make yourself at h-h-h-home."

"I'm going to take Sissy up to the spring, Grandpa," Mark said; and his grandfather nodded. We spoke to several people, all Mark's relatives, on our way up the steep hillside. The climb made me breathless. Without warning, the ground leveled off; and I could hear the trickling sound of running water.

"Over here," Mark pointed. He led the way around some huge boulders, and suddenly we stood beside a lovely spring. Water bubbled from the ground and fell away into a crystal brook that meandered down the other side of the hill.

"This is beautiful!" I had seen no lovelier place in the Dixon area. Wordlessly, Mark and I gazed at the scenic glen for several moments. Children of all ages ran and played around the spring. One or two knelt and took a drink, exclaiming at the chill of the water before they ran away.

"Thanks for not laughing at my grandpa's stuttering," Mark said. "Sometimes he really is funny, but we don't laugh, at least, not while we're with him." Mark chuckled. "You should hear him swear. He doesn't stutter at all then. Grandpa's a great guy. He'll be eighty-eight his next birthday." Mark leaned against one of the big rocks. I climbed onto the one beside him and sat with my legs swinging.

"You said that he raised you?" I asked. Mark nodded.

"Pretty much. You've heard about the cave-in that killed so many miners eight years ago?"

"Yes, I have. My dad mentioned it just the other day. The foundry, where my dad works, gets its coal there. He's gone into the mine a few times. For some reason, he's fascinated with the mining process. I think it's the same one where your folks worked."

"Sissy, if I were you, I'd try to keep him out of there. You couldn't pay me to go inside that place, and there's not enough money in the world to make me work there," Mark told me.

"My mother got pretty upset with him when she found out, but he keeps going back."

"Grandpa and my dad were both at the mine when it caved in. My dad's shift had started about half an hour before the cave-in, just long enough for the men to be far back in the mine. Grandpa was getting off work. He got out of the mine a few minutes before it caved, and I guess he went nuts. People had to hold him to keep him from running back to find my dad. I was ten years old.

"Grandpa still goes to the mine sometimes. He likes to talk to the miners, and I think he has gone back inside, too. It's in his blood."

I shuddered. Just the thought of all those men, trapped in the black interior of that hole beneath the mountain, gave me chills. I didn't even want to think about what their last moments must have been like.

"It wasn't long before my mom married again, and I came up here to live with my grandpa. I never did care much for her new husband, and he didn't like me at all. I look too much like my dad. Mom and my step-dad have two little girls. He walked away from the cave-in that killed my dad. He was one of the lucky ones, but he isn't very smart. He still works in the mines."

"I'm sorry, Mark," I said. He shrugged.

"It was a long time ago."

"Do you remember your dad?"

"I remember playing catch with him. Most of the time he was too tired to play for very long. He worked long shifts in the mine, and the light hurt his eyes." Mark looked at the spring. "Even with the so-called safety measures, I don't think the mines are safe. They'll kill the strongest man, one way or another. Grandpa never went back to work, but he had been inside them long enough to get black lung. You can't work in that hole for very long without it hurting you." I could think of nothing to say. A lot of pain lay in Mark's words, regardless how matter-of-factly he spoke them. We watched the children play, and we listened to the comforting sounds of the spring-fed brook for several minutes.

"Are you going to school this fall?" I asked.

"I got a full scholarship to the University of Virginia," he said.

"In what?"

"Mathematics. It seems that I have a 'brilliant mathematical mind'." I could hear the quotes around the words as he said them.

"Wow," I said. "I'm impressed."

"You're supposed to be," Mark laughed. He held out his hand. "Come on. There's something else I want to show you." I let him clasp my fingers, and we held hands as we walked farther up the mountain. It was steep, but a worn path made the way a little easier, zigzagging as it did among the trees. About a quarter mile up the slope, a small, rugged building made of weathered slats peeked from within a mass of rhododendron.

"What is it?" I asked. Mark flashed an impish grin and walked ahead of me to open the cabin. He reached above the doorframe and took down a key. I expected the hinges to creak, but they made no sound when Mark pushed open the door.

"Come on," Mark urged. Hesitantly, I followed. A huge, iron-wrapped barrel, make of oak, lay on its side, well anchored to the base that held it. From a nail on the wall, Mark took a tin cup and held it beneath the spigot. Brown liquid flowed into the cup.

"What is that?" I demanded. Wordlessly, but with the same grin splitting his face, Mark held out the cup to me.

"Taste it." I looked at the contents of the cup. I wasn't at all certain that I wanted to taste it. Mark raised the cup to his mouth and swallowed once, twice, before he lowered it. His eyes dared me. Before I could change my mind, I took the cup and swallowed as he had.

"It's apple cider!" I think I expected it to be some kind of homespun liquor, which I had never tasted.

"Well, yes and no," Mark laughed. "It's Grandpa's apple cider, but it has a little kick to it." I lifted the cup to my mouth, but he grasped my wrist. "Better not," he said. "It's pretty strong, especially on an empty stomach. I just wanted to show it to you. All my cousins and I grew up sampling Grandpa's cider, so we're used to it." He drained the cup and put it back on the nail.

"You all use the same cup?" I asked. Mark laughed.

"There's enough alcohol in the cider to clean it each time," he said. "Germs can't survive in it. Let's go get something to eat."

The spread of food upon makeshift tables could have fed a small army, which, in a sense, it did. Well over a hundred people filled plates and scattered across the hillside to find comfortable seating, either on the ground or against a tree, or upon a boulder.

Mark's family treated me like one of them. After the meal, the children invited me to join in their games, which Mark and I did. We played Blind Man's Bluff, Hide and Seek, and Kick the Can, games that I had played at my own family gatherings and in schoolyards. As twilight came to the mountains, I sat with Mark on the grass and listened to the stories his aunts and uncles told, ones that I'm sure had been repeated many, many times.

Tales of bear-hunts and wildcats and moonshine raids, of relatives and friends long-gone, but still remembered, lasted long into the evening. When talk dwindled, Mark's Aunt Faith, the Indian-looking woman, began to sing. Deep and mellow, her voice pulled at my heartstrings.

Others joined her, and chills ran up and down my spine at the close family harmony:

"In the pines, In the pines, Where the sun never shines.....
And you shiver when the cold wind blows........"

They sang together, without instrumental accompaniment, for a long time. Mark didn't sing. He sat with his arms wrapped around his drawn-up knees, content to listen to the music. It was one of the most enjoyable, peaceful evenings I'd had in a long time.

The summer passed quickly. A friendship developed between Mark and me, a good, solid friendship without strings or romantic complications. We had no expectations about or from each other. We both had dreams of college and careers, and neither of us wanted to complicate those dreams with personal entanglements. That's not to say that I didn't want to meet someone who would sweep me off my feet some day, but not yet.

In spite of myself, I often thought about Jack McCoy, who seldom came back to Dixon. The same firm what had employed him after his freshman year had hired him a second summer. The brief chat Jack and I had shared at my graduation was the only contact I had with him for several months. It looked as if Jack had given up on me, and I should have been relieved. Somehow, I wasn't.

A new school semester approached. Going into his junior year, my brother was slated by Coach Esmond to play varsity football. Bill was a big guy, taller and heavier than our dad. He had the physique of Dad's brothers, all of whom were bigger than Dad. A bit of a swagger appeared in Bill's walk, and more than a hint of cockiness could be seen in the tilt of his head. From my lofty position as a college girl, I could afford to be benevolent about his attitude.

Beth, the little sister who had always liked to play with dolls and who seemed younger than her age, celebrated her twelfth birthday that August. Overnight, she began to blossom into a real beauty. Her glossy dark brown hair grew long, falling in lustrous waves over her shoulders. Her blue eyes lacked the gray that our father had passed on to me. Perhaps that's why her gaze was clear and free of melancholy.

Although Beth would only be in the seventh grade, a couple of high school freshman boys had already telephoned the Bannister house, asking to speak to her. It didn't take Dad long to squelch their ardor, much to Mom's delight and Beth's dismay. It looked as if Dad was going to be just as protective of Beth as he had been of me, possibly more so. She was his baby.

The drive to classes in Charleston every day was a joy. Scenic views, each more lovely than the last, waited around every curve in the highway. The campus was beautiful, and I loved the courses. I became eighteen in February; but for the first time, I thought of myself as an adult. I suspect that, like my brother, I had developed my own little swagger.

New friends and experiences awaited me at the university. Among them was Penny Olson, who shared two classes with me that fall. From South Dakota, Penny found the West Virginia drawl as fascinating as I had when we'd first come from Illinois. The accent that had seeped into my words was not as thick as that of native-born south-easterners, but Penny was delighted with it.

"You sound so cute!" she told me. I didn't want to sound "cute." Sophisticated, perhaps, or worldly, certainly not cute. As time went by, I was delighted to hear little snippets of southern accent creep into her speech, too.

Of strong Scandinavian stock, Penny Olson was a big, raw-boned girl with long hair reminiscent of flaxen-blond peasant girls from German paintings. Her skin radiated good health, and her eyes were the blue of summer skies. Penny smiled often, revealing not only a pleasant personality, but also a set of big, white teeth. She looked like what she was: a big farm girl who trusted every one to be as honest as she believed them to be.

"Why did you choose this school?" I asked her.

"Well, mostly because my Aunt Penelope lives here. I live with her, which saves me the cost of housing. She has no children; and I'm her favorite niece, as well as her namesake. My aunt is my dad's sister, never married, and she's got a ton of money. She's the one who suggested that I apply here; so when I was accepted, she invited me to stay with her." She flashed her big-as-the-world grin.

Penny Olson was responsible for igniting in me an interest in genealogy. She could rattle off the names and dates of births and deaths of several generations of her ancestors. She knew in which Scandinavian country they originated, when they immigrated to the United States, and how many children each had begat. I knew the names of my grandparents and their offspring on both sides, but nothing farther back than that. One evening after supper I questioned my dad.

"Dad, did you know your grandparents? On both sides, I mean?" My dad looked surprised, but pleased that I had asked.

"Sure, I did," he said. "My dad's parents lived only a couple of miles down the road from us, and I spent a lot time with them. My grandpa

Bannister had two families. His first wife died, leaving him with two kids at home. He remarried and had four more, and one of them was my dad. They even took in Grandpa's brother's twin girls and raised them. Grandma Bannister died not long after my mom did." He looked pensive

"What was your mother like, Dad?" I didn't recall having ever asked that question.

"She was a good woman, Sissy."

"Do any of us look like her?"

"Not much. My mom had sharp, brown eyes that could pin us to the wall. Her hair was dark, too. She was a little heavy from all that good home cooking and having all those babies, but I guess she looked as good as any other woman in Ripley County." Dad grew pensive. "I wish I'd paid more attention. She died when I was fourteen, and I know I took her for granted."

"What did she like to do? I mean, did she sew or sing?"

"She played the organ in two churches. I think she passed her love of music to most of us. You kids and several of your cousins have her love of music in you. She taught your Aunt Blanch to play the old pump organ we had."

"What about the guitar? Did she teach you how to play it?"

Dad grinned. "No, Sis, I picked that up myself, the same way your Uncle Clarence picked up the harmonica. You play the piano a lot by ear, just by picking out and remembering the sounds. That's the way I learned to play."

"Still, that desire to play must have come from your mother," I said.

"It probably did."

"I wish I could have known her," I told him.

"I wish you could have, too," he said.

After that conversation, I felt closer to my dad. I realized that he still missed his mother, after nearly twenty-five years. I was able to see in him the little boy who had lived and run and played and been spanked, much as my siblings and I lived. It was then that I began to see Will Bannister as a person other than just my dad.

I had a greater knowledge of my mother's genealogy because of all the stories she had related as I was growing up. She, too, missed her mother, not as a person, but as a vital presence in her life, a protector, someone to stand between her and the evil that lived inside her father. It gave me a sense of continuity and gratitude that both my parents were still in my life. Some of my friends had lost parents, and I couldn't get my mind around even the possibility of life without either of mine.

The weeks and months seemed to fly. Suddenly the soft greens of spring covered the mountainsides again, following the vanity of lush, blooming dogwood and redbud trees. I never grew tired of the splendor of the changing seasons around Charleston, West Virginia. The morning and evening commutes continued to be a source of pleasure and relaxation for me.

Late one lovely afternoon, I drove along the winding road from Charleston to Dixon, thinking more about the day than driving. The car ahead of me braked suddenly. Had my reaction been a fraction of a second slower, my car would have plowed into his trunk. After a few moments, he pulled away; and I was able to see why he had stopped so quickly. An older car, barely off the highway, had just blown a tire; and it was still smoking. I pulled off the highway, right behind the disabled vehicle, which had a Mississippi license plate. A young black man stepped from the driver's side. I could see a young woman on the passenger's side, but the car was too close to the hill to open that door.

I let two cars pass before I got out of mine. "How can I help?" I asked.

The young man ran his fingers through his hair and shook his head. He frowned in frustration. "This is the second flat tire we've had today," he said. He backed away as I approached. He raised both hands. "Ma'am, I appreciate you wanting to help; but it would be better if you just drove away."

"The road is so narrow here," I said. "Let me drive you both into town and get a tow truck."

He shook his head again. "Ma'am, the best thing you can do is leave us. You're going to get me killed."

"What on earth do you mean? You stand a good chance being killed if you stay on this narrow road!"

"Ma'am, you're a young white girl standing here on the road with a black man. Too many folks will misunderstand. If you wouldn't mind, you could stop at a garage and send someone back for us. Please! *Please!* Just drive away!"

I stared into his desperate eyes, trying to understand his terror, which was very real. I turned from him and climbed into my car. "I'll send help," I called to him. He nodded his thanks, as I pulled onto the highway. As he asked, I stopped at the first garage I found that had a tow service.

I mulled over his words all the way home. As far as I was aware, there had been no racial confrontations or issues in our area for a long time. At the supper table that night, I told my family about the young couple and about his fear.

"Sissy, what on earth were you thinking?" my dad demanded. He was really angry. "Why would you stop like that, especially when you were alone?"

"Dad, they were in trouble! They needed help, and no one else stopped! You should be more upset about that!"

My dad frowned at me. He exhaled a long breath before he smiled ruefully at me. "I know your heart was in the right place, Sis; but you should have just driven into town and sent someone back. You shouldn't have stopped like that."

"I want to know why he was so scared that someone would see me there," I told him.

"Did you say he had a Mississippi plate?" my mother asked. I nodded. "Sissy, there's a lot of awful things going on down there these days. There are black men and boys being lynched and beaten, sometimes for no more than speaking to or smiling at white girls or women. That young man evidently thought that it's the same way here, in West Virginia."

"Is it?" I asked.

"I haven't heard of it," Dad said.

After I went to bed that night, I decided to find out for myself whether the scared young man had just cause to be afraid. That decision put me on the path that took a lot of years and a lot of research before I was satisfied with the answers.

Penny Olson occasionally came home with me for a weekend. Lutheran church bred, she wouldn't miss Sunday morning services. It would have been terribly impolite of me not to accompany her, so periodically I found myself enjoying the liturgy and formality of Martin Luther's legacy. My only experiences with church attendance had been inside the little First Baptist Church on Main Street in Redbud Grove, Illinois, and hit-and-miss Sunday school with Karen Courtney in the Methodist Church a few blocks down our street. I suppose I was an ecumenical attendee, somewhat on the eclectic side.

Penny was polite about my lack of instruction in the faith, but I think that she was also a little appalled. She spoke of her confirmation, which had taken place before she was twelve. I enjoyed listening to her, and I asked a lot of questions.

One day I told her about Lillie Faye and the snake handlers, and I thought that Penny was going to faint. She had no idea that such a movement existed. The astounding thing to me was that all those different denominations had grown from one common tenet. My mother's remark: "don't throw out the baby with the bath water," came to mind. I thought that I finally understood her thinking:

At the core of all denominations and beliefs and doctrines of the Christian faith, lies a belief in God, as the Supreme Creator of the universe and everything within it. They all teach that Jesus was the Son of God, and that He lived and died and was resurrected to provide the means of salvation for all. After that, they begin to diversify: means and methods of baptism, communion, confirmation or not, standards of dress, church attendance, what constitutes morality or lack thereof. For me, it was a light-bulb moment.

When the school year ended, Penny went back to South Dakota to spend the summer on her parents' farm. We planned to reconnect in the fall when we would be worldly college sophomores. Well, as worldly as it was possible to get with our upbringing. Like me, Penny wanted to work as many hours as she could to contribute to the cost of her education.

I was nineteen, a full-fledged adult living in my parents' house. I loved my room, loved my family and our little Schnauzer, Sophie. As much as all that meant to me, I longed for something more. Many of my friends were planning weddings. While I had no desire to get married, the thought of a steady boyfriend appealed to me. I had casually dated a few boys in high school and two or three at the university. None of them was "steady" material. It would be nice to have someone to depend upon, to share thoughts and ideas with, to eat and laugh with, someone to hold me when I needed comfort.

In July, Jackson McCoy came home for the Independence Day weekend. He called me; and when I heard his voice on the phone, my heartbeat quickened. "Hi, Sissy," he said. For a moment I couldn't answer.

"Hi, Jack. It's so good to hear your voice!" I couldn't believe the words that came out of my mouth. *Whoa!* I told myself. Jack laughed in pleased surprise.

"It's good to hear yours, too," he replied. "I wondered if you would let me take you to dinner one night while I'm home. Nothing elaborate," he sounded as if he thought I needed reassuring, "just casual."

"I'd like that," I answered. From somewhere far, far away, a warning bell pinged. I ignored it. I was going to go out with Jack McCoy, bell or no bell.

I hadn't seen him for over a year. When I opened the door to him the next evening, I was barely able to suppress the gasp that wanted to leap from my throat. Jack was the most beautiful man I had ever seen.

At twenty-one, his body had filled out a bit, and his bare arms were muscular and tanned. His next-to-platinum hair was sun-streaked and full, a perfect foil for his bronzed skin. It should have been illegal for anyone to have such light brown amber-y eyes, and for those eyes to look at me as if I were the most desirable girl in the world.

"Hi, Sissy." Jack's voice held magic in its depths.

"Hi, Jack." My own voice sounded husky to me. *What in the world is happening*, I thought. When Jack took my elbow, as he had always done, I almost shivered; but it was such a delicious shiver. I didn't know whether I was anticipating or dreading a wonderful time.

In our driveway sat a new car, a shiny, silver Mercedes convertible. Jack escorted me to the passenger side, opened the door, and assisted me into the soft, gray leather interior. It smelled brand new, which I was sure it had to be. Jack shrugged as he scooted beneath the steering wheel.

"My dad gave it to me for my birthday," he explained. "I suppose I could have declined, but that would have hurt his feelings." I laughed.

"Ever the considerate son," I said.

We did have a wonderful time. We laughed and talked over dinner, long after we had finished the meal. Jack wanted to know all about my year in college, the courses I took, my plans for the coming year and whether I was seeing someone. I asked him much the same questions.

"Would you like to go for a drive?" he asked. "It's a hot night, but nice in the convertible." The bell pinged faintly.

"Maybe a short drive," I answered. I told myself that I would make Jack take me home should he even turn in the direction of the grove where we had parked when we were in high school. He turned in the opposite direction, and we ended up near the reservoir, where the fireworks display would take place the following evening.

"Do you feel like taking a walk?" Jack asked.

"Sure." I opened the car door, forestalling any assistance. Jack turned up the soft music that played on the radio. Strains of current popular tunes lifted into the night air.

"It's beautiful here," I said. Not touching, we strolled toward the water line, where it seemed degrees cooler. The sky was filled with a glorious array of stars that reflected like shimmering diamonds in the water. The sounds of night creatures blended into the music from the radio, forming a background concert as we walked in the summer grass, already damp with dew.

Quietly, Jack stepped behind me and placed his arms gently around my waist. I leaned against him. He felt good. His breath stirred the hair at my temple. I looked up at the starlit sky, and I felt as if I were a part of it. *"Star light, star bright, First star I see tonight; I wish I may, I wish I might..."* It had been a long time since I'd uttered my childhood mantra.

"What do you wish, Sissy?" Jack whispered.

"I don't know," I replied. "I've been wishing on those stars ever since I was a little girl, but I never did voice a wish." Jack's arms tightened, ever so slightly.

"I know what I would wish," he said.

"What?" Gently, he turned me to face him. His eyes glittered as brightly as the stars. His hands cupped my face, and he slowly lowered his head. As soft and sweet as spun sugar, his lips touched mine once, twice, three times. I could feel myself melting against him like warm butter on hot toast.

"Sissy, Sissy..." Between kisses that threatened to ignite an early display of fireworks, Jack whispered my name, over and over. I forgot where I was, even who I was. I held his head in my hands, and I kissed him as I had never kissed anyone except Victor Delacourt. This time I wasn't a child. As on that other night, the voice of Elvis came from the car radio... *"...when I hold you close, and I want to kiss you, Baby, don't say don't..."*

Jack drew me closer to him. His arms tightened, and he buried his face in the curve of my shoulder. "Sissy..." Through my blouse I could feel Jack's heart beating, at least I thought that it was his. It could have been my own heart pounding against my ribs in a cadence that left me weak-kneed with longing. No lucid thought found its way to my brain. All I knew was that the most handsome man in the world held me in his arms, but it wasn't close enough.

Without warning, Jack pushed me away from him. His hands gripped my upper arms so tightly that I knew there would be bruises. "What's wrong?" I asked. Jack expelled a long breath that ended in a shaky chuckle.

"Nothing is wrong," he said. "For the first time in years, everything is right." I tried to move back into his arms, but he wouldn't let me.

"I don't understand," I told him. The night air held a sudden chill, and I shivered.

"Sissy, I love you. I have loved you since you were fifteen years old. Right now, what I want most in this world is to lay in this grass with you and make love to you until morning." Jack took a deep, ragged breath. "But I won't. I want things to be right for us. I want to marry you. I'd marry you tomorrow, if you'd agree. Will you, Sissy? Will you marry me?"

Jack's voice was like cold water on a hot fire. With his words came sanity. I was so embarrassed by my behavior that I couldn't look at him. Briefly, I thought of Karen Courtney; and I understood how she had become overwhelmed with her feelings for Matt. I pulled away from Jack. I looked up at the stars, still just as sparkling and brilliant as they had been moments ago; but now they held a brittle, hard edge.

"Sissy, don't pull away from me," Jack begged. "Don't go back into that place that always left me out! You just showed me a glimpse of the passion in you, a passion you feel for *me*! Baby, don't...don't..." Jack pulled me to him, and I let him hold me. He shook with the force of his feelings. For the first time, I realized just how much he cared for me—to use his own words—his love for me. I was humbled and more than a little scared. I didn't know what to do or say.

"It's all right, Sissy," Jack murmured against my forehead. "We have lots of time. I won't rush you; but please, *please*, Sissy, keep yourself only for me! I know that you care about me. You couldn't have kissed me like that if you didn't. I know you, Sissy. I know you better than you know yourself, and I've been waiting for you all this time."

Jack's soft, urgent words were hypnotic. Interspersed with soft kisses against my face, they were compelling. *Maybe Jack is right. Maybe I really do love him, and I've just been afraid to admit it. Maybe I'm afraid of how he makes me feel. Maybe....* I shook my head, hoping to clear my thoughts. I listened for the warning bell, but it was silent.

"Sissy?" Jack whispered against my hair. "I'm serious about getting married. Will you think about it?" I didn't answer. Jack began to move to the music from the radio. Pat Boone crooned something about "the wind and the rain in your hair." I let Jack lead me in a slow dance through the moonlight, while my head rested against his chest. I opened my eyes, and I could see the stars glittering in the blackness above the hilltops. I shivered. "Are you cold?" I shouldn't have been cold. It was only moments from being the Fourth of July.

Jack held me closer. His arms encircled me tightly against the warmth of his body, but it was different from before. It wasn't passion that emanated from him; it was gentleness and reassurance. In that moment, I felt as secure as I ever had in my whole life.

"I'll think about it," I whispered. Jack tilted my chin upward and kissed me. It was a sweet kiss, filled with promise and a touch of something else. I think it was a touch of triumph.

As I promised, I did think about Jack's proposal. I thought about it all through August. Jack called me two or three times a week, not to pressure me, but to tell me how much he had enjoyed our time together over the Fourth. It was a different side of Jack that I saw that summer. I thought I recognized in him what I had first seen four years previously.

Labor Day passed, and I began my sophomore year at the university in Charleston. Penny Olson and I reconnected. Her Nordic skin had acquired a faint burnished hue, and delightful freckles frolicked across her nose. Her whole being projected "Wholesome!" I felt good, just being in her presence.

Penny went home for Thanksgiving. Like her, as much as I enjoyed my classes, I looked forward to four days away from them. Aside from my mother's annual Thanksgiving Day feast, other events in Dixon called for my attention. Now in the eighth grade, my little sister was a cheerleader for the junior high varsity basketball team; and she was excited about her school's upcoming tournament. My presence was mandatory for at least one game.

Jack was coming home. I was certain that he was going to ask for an answer to his proposal, and I was fairly certain what that answer would be. I had thought about him—a lot; and I missed him.

"I have something to tell you, Sissy." Jack's last phone conversation had been enigmatic. I had pressed him, but he successfully evaded giving me even a hint. "I'll tell you when I can see you. I'll have dinner with my family Thursday, and then I'll pick you up, if that's all right." Hmmm. Another positive attribute in Jack was that he no longer issued dictums. I liked it.

Living with my family while I went to college prevented me from noticing how gradually the family was changing. At Thanksgiving dinner, I looked at all of them with new eyes, perhaps because of my upcoming meeting with Jack. Beth had blossomed into a stunning eighth-grader. Mom allowed her to wear the same modest shade of pink lipstick that I had worn at her age, but it looked to me as if the pink had a bit more pigment.

Bill had grown taller and a lot stockier than our Dad, and he played varsity football. A high school senior, Bill dated a cute little red-haired girl, one year younger than he was. Predictably, she was a cheerleader. I had already heard overtones of jealousy when she and Bill talked about Bill's attending college the following autumn. It would be interesting to watch his life change, as I knew it would.

My mother seemed happy. She worked regular hours at the hospital, and she had earned several promotions, the most recent one, as head nurse on her floor. Her salary had escalated to the point that she made a little more than my dad, although the subject was never discussed. Dad seemed a little sensitive about that.

Looking at her objectively, I thought that my mom was attractive, for an older woman. At thirty-nine, awfully close to forty, she maintained her trim figure. She still wore her light brown hair cut short, and there were a few strands of gray; but her skin was clear, with a minimum of lines. She was a lovely woman.

I looked at my dad. On November twenty-second, just two days before Thanksgiving, Dad had become forty-one years old. Always thin, he looked thinner to me. Perhaps I just hadn't taken the time to look at him for a while. The lines that formed grooves on either side of his mouth were more pronounced. A deep furrow creased his forehead, and his hairline had receded a bit. I was dismayed to see how gray were his temples. To me, he looked older that just past forty; but my perspective was from just short of twenty.

"Dad, do you feel okay?"

"Sure," Dad said. "Don't I look okay?" He grinned at me, and I felt better.

"I think you look a little tired." I told him.

"Well, I guess maybe I am. The foundry got a government contract, and we're working longer hours to fill it."

"What's the rush?" Bill asked. "What're you making?" Dad looked at his plate and took a bite of turkey and dressing before he answered.

"I can't tell you what we're making," Dad answered.

"Uh, oh. Dad's working with secret stuff!" Bill teased.

"Not so secret, maybe just a little sensitive."

The moment passed, and my perusal of the family dissipated. After the cleanup, I hurried upstairs to get ready for Jack. My heart beat a little faster. It felt good to be filled with anticipation. Jack had not been home since Labor Day weekend, possibly a planned strategy, testing the absence-makes-the-heart-grow-fonder theory. If so, it had worked.

The moment I opened the door to his knock, it felt right to go into Jack's outstretched arms. He hadn't told me where we were going, and I was surprised when he drove up the winding driveway to the home of his parents. The one and only time I had been inside the house was not one of my pleasant memories, but it was a beautiful place. Even in the dismal November twilight, the mansion glowed with lights and color.

"My family went to visit my dad's sister across the river," Jack told me. "I thought that it might be nice to have a warm place to talk without interruption. Would you rather go somewhere else?" I looked at Jack.

"No," I said. "This is fine." As we got out of the car, snowflakes began to filter through the deepening dusk. The taste of snow had been in the air all day, so the lazy white flakes were not a surprise. Inside, a fire burned softly in the huge fireplace. I knew that at least one servant lingered inside the house.

The room was much as I remembered. Jack led me to a brocaded loveseat, where we sat closely together. He took my hands between his. "Well?" he asked. "I can't wait any longer, Sissy. You've got to tell me what you want to do." I looked into his beautiful eyes. I couldn't resist.

"What do you want me to do?" I asked. He blinked.

"Sissy, for the love of—!" I smiled. A light came into his eyes. He grasped my shoulders and kissed me like he was never going to stop. "Tell me," he finally whispered. "Tell me that you'll marry me. Tell me now."

"Yes. Yes, Jack, I'll marry you," I whispered against his mouth. Jack drew in his breath and held it for a long moment before he completely enveloped me with his arms. He trembled.

"I was so afraid that you wouldn't." He reached into his pocket. "But just in case, I brought this." With a flick of his thumb, Jack opened the small velvet-covered box. It was my turn to gasp. He took the ring from the box and picked up my left hand. As if standing outside myself, I watched him slip the emerald-cut solitaire diamond onto my finger. The stone looked huge to me, and the ring was cold on my hand. From far, far away that stubborn little bell pinged; but the tone was barely discernible. I ignored it.

"Now there's something I have to tell you." Jack sounded so somber. "I've been drafted."

"What do you mean?" Jack brought my hand to his lips and kissed it.

"I mean that I've been drafted. I have some choices, but I still have to serve some time in the military, somewhere. They'll let me graduate in the spring, and then I'm going into the Air Force."

"For how long?" I asked. Jack kissed my hand again.

"Four years." I didn't know what to say. I had just become officially engaged and learned that my fiancé was committed to at least four years away from me. I bit my lower lip. "Don't worry, Sissy. We can be married next summer, after I graduate, and you can go with me, wherever I go."

"Next summer? But, Jack, I'm going to school. I'll have two more years after this year. I can't just quit."

Wish I May, Wish I Might...

"You can still go to school, just not in Charleston. You can enroll wherever I'm stationed. I'd never stand in the way of your getting a degree." Jack pulled me against his shoulder. "Don't worry, Sweetheart. It will work out just fine. I promise." I wanted to believe him, so I did.

We sat in front of the fire for a long time. Nestled within the circle of Jack's arms, I watched the flames flicker and dance. Not even the unobtrusive appearance of the manservant disturbed my reverie. He spoke deferentially to Jack, placed a small log on the fire, and disappeared. Jack's chin rested upon the top of my head. I could feel the steady beat of his heart beneath my cheek, and being there with him felt right.

"Well, good evening," Jack's father said. Startled, I sat up straight. Had Jack not held on to me, I would have scooted away from him.

"Hi, Dad, Mother," he said. He stood then. He extended his hand to me and drew me to my feet. "We have something to tell you." *Oh, no!* I wanted to tell my parents first, but it was too late. "I've asked Sissy to marry me." A small sound escaped from his mother's mouth. I couldn't decide if it were pleasant surprise or shocked dismay. "We're going to be married." Jack made the announcement with full confidence that his news would be accepted.

"Congratulations, Son!" Mr. McCoy extended his hand to Jack, but the handshake became a quick embrace, which engulfed me, too. "Welcome to our family, My Dear," he said to me. Mrs. McCoy approached. She shrugged off her coat and tossed it onto a chair.

"My best wishes to both of you," she said. She kissed Jack's cheek, gave me a perfunctory embrace, not quite touching my face, and stepped away from us. Mrs. McCoy looked elegant, as I would have expected. Her dark green woolen dress whispered that it had been purchased in an exclusive shop.

"Where's Deanna?" Jack asked.

"She stopped to see the dogs," his father said. "She'll be here right away, I'm sure."

"Dogs?" I asked.

"The kennels are at the back of the house," Jack explained. "Dad has two Brittany spaniels."

"How about a toast to celebrate your good news." Mr. McCoy stated, rather than asked.

"Sure, Dad." Jack followed his father to the far end of the wide room. I hadn't been in the house enough to notice that a wet bar stood below the mullioned windows. Mr. McCoy pressed a lever, and wood panels parted on both sides of the windows to reveal stocked wine racks and glass shelves, filled with bottles of various liquors. He selected a bottle from a small, refrigerated unit, while Jack took narrow fluted glasses from a shelf. They chuckled together when the cork popped from the bottle.

Uneasy, I wasn't certain how to conduct myself. I glanced nervously at Jack's mother, who stared pensively into the crackling fire. I was not yet of legal age to drink, and I had no desire for alcohol, no matter my age. Jack and his father returned to us, each of them carrying two filled champagne flutes. Jack handed one to me, while his mother took one from her husband.

"To Jack and Sissy and a long, happy life with lots of little McCoys!" Jack and his dad drained their glasses. Mrs. McCoy lifted hers to her lips and took a tiny sip. I lifted the glass, but I didn't drink. No one seemed to notice. "Well, Son, I think this calls for a *real* drink! Care to join me?"

"John, perhaps..." Mrs. McCoy murmured. Her husband focused all of his attention upon her lovely face.

"Yes, Cynthia?" Mr. McCoy's warm, West Virginia accent couldn't conceal the cold undercurrent beneath the surface of his words.

Jack slanted a quick glance at me. I met his eyes, a long, level gaze. I'll never know whether or not he saw doubt in my eyes, but I saw something flicker in his. "No, thanks, Dad. Sissy and I need to go tell our good news to her parents." He put his glass upon the cocktail table and picked up my coat.

I didn't speak all the way down the hillside. Two revelations had just unfolded before me inside the McCoy mansion, the first being that all was not well between Jack's parents. The second being that I had to face the possibility Jack drank too easily. Early in my teens I had seen what alcohol could do to people's lives, and I had decided that it would have no part in mine. "Jack, I don't drink. I will never drink, and I won't live with someone who does." There. I had said it.

"Did the toast upset you, Sweetheart?" he asked. There was nothing in his voice but concern for my feelings. "I'm sorry. No, I don't drink, except for an occasional beer at the frat house. I'll only be living there a few more months. I didn't want to offend my dad, so I drank the champagne."

"Does your dad drink a lot?" I asked. "My dad sometimes has a beer with his friends after work, but I wish he didn't. I hate the smell of it."

"My father drinks socially, I suppose. I've never really thought about it. Sit close to me, Sissy." As easily as that, Jack changed the subject; and I moved across the seat to be closer to him. I decided that I had been too quick to judge.

I didn't expect either of my parents to be shocked, but I thought that they would be surprised. After the Fourth of July, I had told them that Jack and I had resumed our relationship, but that I wasn't sure what might develop. Dad was more accepting than my mother, probably the baseball factor. I hadn't told them at that time about his marriage proposal.

When Jack and I entered the house, my family sat in the living room in front of the television set. Dad recovered first. "Well," he said. He cleared his throat and stood up, reaching for Jack's hand. "Well. Jack." He turned to me. "Well. Sissy, are you sure?" I nodded, and Dad opened his arms. I felt a pang when he hugged me. There were tears in his eyes when he released me.

My mother looked at me long and hard before she opened her arms to me. She whispered in my ear, so only I could hear her. "Sissy, what are you doing?" I hugged her.

"Look, Mom." I held out my hand, and the light bounced off the stone.

"Wow!" Beth ran to me and took my hand. "Sissy, it's huge!" Even my brother was impressed with the ring.

"When are you planning to get married?" my mother asked. Jack and I exchanged glances.

"Next summer, after Jack graduates," I said.

"What about *your* school? Where will you live?" she pressed me.

"Mrs. Bannister, I'll see that Sissy finishes school. It's important to her, and to me."

"The two of you can't possibly make that much money, Jack," Mom said. I knew that look. My mother had dug in her heels. His charming self, Jack smiled at her.

"You don't have to worry about your daughter," he said. "I have a trust fund. It became available to me on my twenty-first birthday, last summer. Sissy will be well taken care of, I promise." Mom closed her eyes, exhaled and looked at me. She seemed more heartsick than relieved at the promise.

"Well," she said. "I hope that you both know what you're doing. I want you to be happy, more than anything, Sissy." She blinked hard. No tears spilled, but they lingered in her eyes.

The Monday after Thanksgiving brought more snow. Jack left early, wanting to get back to school in Illinois. I had only one class that day, and it wasn't until late afternoon. I offered to drive Beth to school, and I smiled at her chatter all the way to the junior high building. She was growing and changing so fast, and it made me sad to know that my little sister had left her childhood behind.

"Sissy, when are you and Jack going to get married? Do you think that I could be your bridesmaid? Some of my friends have been junior bridesmaids at their brothers' and sisters' weddings." Beth sounded so excited that I had to tell her that she could be an attendant. I hadn't consulted Jack, but I didn't think that he would mind.

When I got back home, my brother stood at the foot of the stairs. "There's no school today," he said. "Something on the furnace broke, so I get an extra day of vacation. I'm going back to bed." He took the stairs in four bounds and disappeared into the confines of his bedroom.

I cleared away the breakfast clutter and washed the dishes. Sophie whined to be let out at the back door, and it was just as I stepped onto the back porch that I heard the siren. My breath caught in my throat. Although I had never before heard it, I knew what it meant. Something was wrong at the Number Seven mine.

Bill came running down the stairs. "Sissy, what is that?"

"It's the mine! Something's happened at the mine!"

"Let's go!" Bill had pulled on his jeans. He sat on the bottom stair and quickly drew on his socks and shoes.

"I don't think we should go out there," I told him. "We'd just be in the way."

"Sissy, we've got to go! Dad told me that he was going to the mine today, and Mom doesn't know! We've got to go now!" I felt the blood drain from my face at the implication of his words and the desperation in his voice. By the time I had grabbed a coat, he was already out the front door and halfway to my car.

The streets were snow-packed and lined with cars. When we reached the perimeter of the Number Seven, cars lined the road some distance from the mine's entrance. We drove into the first spot between two cars that we could find. There was barely room for the three ambulances to drive between the lines of frantic people who ran beside the parked vehicles, desperate to discover the fate of relatives and friends who worked in the mine. A cloud of thick, black, coal smoke and dust spewed from the hole in the side of the mountain. Screams and moans of despair rose with the smoke, and my throat closed with mind-numbing fear.

"Sissy, Dad's in there!" Bill cried. We ran as fast as the snow and the crowd of frantic people would allow us. Bill grabbed my hand and pulled me through the throng. A line of policemen and other mine employees formed a barrier between the rescue workers and us. So many of them milled around the area in helpless frustration. Firemen threw a heavy stream of water into the dark hole, only to be forced back when another belch of thick smoke erupted.

"Bill, maybe Dad's not here," I said. "Maybe he wasn't coming until later today."

"He's in there," Bill said. Tears ran down his face. "I know that he's in there." My little brother, who towered over me, put his arm around my shoulders. We stood, united, hoping with all our souls that our father had not come to the mine, or if he had, that he had not gone to the interior.

A crew of rescuers entered the shaft about an hour after we arrived. With two-way radios, they communicated with their counterparts on the outside world. Except for an occasional muffled sob, those of us who waited were frightfully silent, lost in our own prayers and pleas for mercy. Two hours passed, then three. The waiting was agony.

"They've found them!" A loud spontaneous cheer greeted those three words. A mine official stood upon the platform that led to his office and repeated what was told to him from those inside the mine. "Fifty-seven men are in the area of the cave-in. Some are alive!" Another cheer rose into the air, until he raised his hand for quiet. "Some are still trapped under rocks." The man dropped his head. "Unfortunately, there are some who didn't survive."

My brother squeezed my shoulder. I tried to swallow, but my mouth was too dry. There was nothing to do but wait. Snowflakes began to filter through the air, gradually becoming as big as windborne feathers. I pulled up the hood of my jacket, and Bill withdrew a knit cap from his coat pocket. By the time figures emerged from the mine's entrance, all of us who waited were covered with snow.

Bill and I were not close enough to identify the first men brought from the mine. On stretchers, their faces were all black. Some waved feebly to the crowd, and others called out their names to let their identity be known. Others lay very still, eyes closed.

I kept looking for a glimpse of Dad's jacket, hoping both to see it and not to see it. Made of a unique dark blue and black plaid, it was heavy and warm, one of his favorite coats. I couldn't remember a time when he hadn't worn it, so it had to be at least sixteen or seventeen years old. No matter how many coats and jackets Mom bought for Dad, his favorite was the blue plaid. The blue matched the color of his eyes.

"Sissy, look!" Bill pointed. He saw the coat before I did. We pushed our way through the mass of people. "Dad! Dad!" my brother called.

The dark face above the blue plaid did not respond. "Wait!" Bill yelled. "That's our dad! Wait!"

The ambulance attendant looked at us. He shook his head. "We've got to get him to a hospital," he said. "He's hurt real bad." In horror I watched bright red blood seep slowly onto the sheet that covered my dad's chest. "Meet us at the hospital as soon as you can, but we've got to go now." With that, he slammed the door and jumped into the ambulance.

"Come on, Sissy! Run! We can't let Mom find out like this!" Bill grabbed my hand, and we ran through the falling snow as fast as we could. The ambulance was far ahead of us by the time we got to our car and headed to the hospital, where our mother worked. Neither of us spoke.

A crowd had formed outside the hospital. I double-parked, not caring if my car were towed away or if I were fined. Bill and I, along with other scared people, ran into the emergency entrance. We stopped at the desk, where the receptionist spoke to us.

"Hi," she said. "It's not a good time to visit with your mom, Sissy," she said. "There's been a mine..."

"I know, Mrs. Cahn; but we really need to see her! It's an emergency!" Mrs. Cahn shook her head.

"Kids, I'm truly sorry; but she's working with injured miners."

"Mrs. Cahn, our dad was in the mine! He's one of the men brought here, and we don't want her to find out about it like this!"

"Oh, I'm so sorry! Go on through that door. You'll find her in one of the cubicles, I'm sure. I'm so sorry," she repeated. Without taking time to answer, Bill and I hurried down the corridor. We had scarcely cleared the door when we heard our mother.

"Will! Oh, Will, no!" Four cubicles down, we pulled aside the drapery. We were too late to prepare her. Mom's ashen face spoke more eloquently than her stricken cry. A doctor barked orders and two nurses worked quickly to fill them. Dad's blue plaid coat lay in strips on the floor.

"Mrs. Bannister, you shouldn't be in here now," one of the nurses said. She looked at Bill. "Take your mother to the waiting room."

"No! I've got to help! Bill, Sissy, you wait outside! Go!" Reluctantly, we turned away. Our mother would not leave Dad's side. His eyes were closed, and he lay horribly still. I bit my lip. The doctor slipped an oxygen mask over my dad's mouth and nose. A nurse closed the curtains.

Together, Bill and I stumbled to the waiting area, where dozens of other relatives and friends of the injured huddled in separate little islands within a sea of abject fear. I didn't recognize anyone. Some rocked back and forth in their anguish. Others stared at the floor. I had never before heard such horrible silence.

Bill and I sat side by side in straight chairs. From far away, I was aware of the clinical sounds and smells of the hospital. Each time a white-clad nurse or doctor came into the room, my hopes soared, only to dissolve as other names were called. Again, I looked at the round clock on the wall. It was nearly three-thirty. I couldn't believe that so many hours had passed.

"Bill, we've got to pick up Beth!"

"But we can't leave until we know about Dad," he countered.

"You go get her, and I'll stay here," I said. "Just be careful!" My brother shook his head. *"Buddy, please just go!"* Tears I had been holding at bay threatened to spill. Bill touched my shoulder and hurried down the corridor and out the door. I don't like to think of how fast he must have driven. It seemed like a very short time before he came back with our little sister in tow.

"Sissy!" she wailed. I opened my arms and she came into them. Her beautiful little body shook with sobs.

"Shhhh," I murmured. "Bethy, Daddy will be okay. Mom is with him, and she'll come get us just as soon as she can. Shhhh." The words were barely out of my mouth before a nurse approached us.

"Are you the Bannister children?" she asked. We nodded. "Come with me, please. Your mother is with your dad."

"How is he?" Bill asked.

"The doctor and your mother will answer all your questions." The nurse led us past the emergency room cubicles to an elevator, which took us up several floors. "Right this way. Your mother will be out in just a moment." Across the width of the double doors were big letters that read: INTENSIVE CARE. The nurse indicated chairs where we should wait, and she went through the doors.

I put my arm around Beth, probably drawing more comfort from her closeness than I gave back to her. Bill paced back and forth, hands in his pockets. He had the stature of a man, but his face revealed a scared little boy who adored his dad.

"Mom! How's Daddy!" All three of us pressed around our mother as soon as she stepped through the restrictive doors. She looked terrible.

"Let's sit down," she said. Beth and I sat on either side of her, while Bill squatted in front of her. "I'm not going to lie to you, Kids. Daddy is hurt. He was pinned beneath heavy rock, and his chest was just about crushed. All his ribs are broken, and one of his lungs is punctured." Mom's lower lip trembled. "The doctor had to remove his spleen, and there's damage to his liver."

"Mom, is Daddy going to die?" Beth voiced the words, but the question had hovered above us for hours. Tears spilled from Mom's eyes and trickled slowly down her cheeks. She seemed unaware of them.

"He might, Sweetie," she said. "The doctors are doing all they can to save him, but we don't know yet."

"Can we see him?" Bill asked. Mom shook her head.

"Not now, Honey. He's still recovering from surgery. He'll be asleep for a while. I want the three of you to go home. There's nothing you can do here, and you need to let Sophie in and get some supper. I'll stay here with Daddy."

"But, Mom…"

"No buts," she said. A sad little smile touched her lips. "I need you to listen to me. You'll help more by doing what I tell you. Beth, get started on your homework while Sissy makes something for supper. Okay, Sissy? Beth? Bill?" Slowly, we nodded. "Come back around seven. Dad should be awake by then, and maybe you can see him."

Reluctantly, we did as she asked, for the most part. We ate leftovers, but homework wasn't even mentioned. Instead of books, Beth held Sophie on her lap, something the cold little dog appreciated. Adequate shelter in the fenced yard kept her dry, but she had never before been left outside so long. Beth clung to Sophie, finding comfort in the closeness.

We drove back to the hospital well before seven. The elevators were full of visitors, some happy, some somber. Others waited in the lobby on the intensive care floor. We were not alone in our fear. We were eager to see our mother; but dread of what she might tell us made us reluctant, as well. When she came through the door, I was not reassured.

"Your dad is awake, but he's on strong pain medicine. You can only come in one at a time." She touched Beth's hair. "Beth, they'll let you come in, but only for a minute. They agreed to let you see your daddy, even though you won't be fourteen until August. Who wants to come first?" I shook my head.

"Take Beth first."

"Yeah, go ahead," Bill agreed. Neither of us could sit while we waited, which didn't take very long. The visits were limited to five minutes. Beth looked so scared when Mom brought her back. My heart ached for her, for all of us.

"Bill, you go see Dad. I'll wait with Beth," I said. "Let's sit over there." Beth brushed her face with her hands, but she couldn't stop the tears.

"Sissy, Daddy looks awful! He's all bandaged and swollen and there are tubes everywhere! And his face is so black!"

"That's from the coal dust. They probably couldn't get it all off of him while he's so sick, but he'll look better tomorrow. Don't worry." I felt like such a hypocrite and coward. I was afraid to see what the accident had done to my dad.

"Sissy." My mother stood in the door. I looked at my brother's face, hoping to find something there that would soothe my fears. His lip trembled, and he shook his head. A place inside my soul grew cold.

"Sissy." At the doors, my mother stopped me. She looked into my eyes, and what I saw in hers made the cold place grow bigger. "Honey, your dad is...your dad's injuries are really bad. I don't want to scare you, but I don't want you to get your hopes up..." I blinked.

"Daddy's going to be fine, Mom. You'll see. He'll be fine." I clenched my teeth, willing my words to be true. My mother led the way to a room halfway down the large, well-staffed area.

"Will? Sissy's here." I must have entered a dream-like state. I heard Mom's words, and I saw the man on the bed. I knew that he was my father, but I didn't recognize anything about him. As Beth had warned me, tubes ran from his sides, his arms, even one of his legs. Bandages encased his body from his armpits to his hips. Traces of coal dust lingered on his face, but the black and blue masses on his shoulders and arms were bruises. The man turned his head slightly and opened his eyes. It was only then that I saw my dad.

"Hi, Daddy."

"Sissy," he whispered. "Sissy." I knew that he was saying my name with his lips, but the rasping sound of escaping air didn't come from his mouth. Horrified, I saw that the oxygen mask rested upon his throat, covering the hole there that was surrounded by white gauze. My dad was breathing through that hole, and his breaths exhaled before air reached his vocal chords.

"Oh, Daddy," I whispered.

"Love you," his lips said, but the tracheotomy only hissed. "Love you," he said again. I looked at my mother, but she was looking at her husband. I had never before seen such sadness on anyone's face.

"Can I kiss him, Mom?" She nodded. I leaned over my dad, careful not to touch anything that might cause him additional pain. Efforts had been made to cleanse the black dust from his face, but much of it clung to his skin. I kissed his forehead, which was as cold as any ice could be.

"I love you, Daddy," I told him. He closed his eyes once, opened them, looked up at me and tried to smile.

"Be good…Sissy." He closed his eyes again.

"He needs to rest now, Honey," my mother said. At the door, I looked back at my dad. He lay so still, and he looked so small. Neither Mom nor I spoke until we left intensive care.

"Mom, I'm not leaving," I announced.

"I'm not, either," said Bill.

"Me, too." Beth folded her arms. Mom tried her best to smile at us.

"Okay," she said. She pointed to the chairs and sofas in the waiting room. "There are your beds." They turned out to be just that. Somehow, we dozed, leaning against each other for several hours.

"Sissy." I opened my eyes. My mother knelt in front of me. "Sissy, Honey…." I blinked. I seemed to be caught in some kind of bad dream. I was dreaming that my dad had been hurt in an accident, and someone was trying to tell me that he was going to die. I closed my eyes and tried to go back to sleep. "Sissy, wake up." The apparition that pretended to be my mother wouldn't go away. "Sissy, please…" The sob woke me completely.

"Mom? Mom, how's dad?" My mother laid her head in my lap. Sobs of despair and exhaustion shook her body. "Mom? Mommy?" She raised her head, and I saw in her face the words she could not say. "Oh, Mom, no!" I wailed. My brother and sister sat up.

"What is it?" Bill struggled from sleep. Mom gathered all of us into her arms right there on the floor.

"I'm sorry," she sobbed. "Your dad woke up; and I was sitting beside him, talking to him. He said all your names, and I told him that you were in the lobby, that you were waiting to see him again. He smiled at me and squeezed my hand. Then he told me that he was sorry."

For a long time we cried together, and then Mom cleared her throat. Her voice grew stronger. "Your dad knew that he was going to leave us. He told me to put him beside Johnny, and then he closed his eyes. He was gone. So quickly, he was gone."

We huddled together on the floor of the intensive care waiting room, holding onto each other, each of us wanting to wake from the nightmare that held us. I knew a moment of extreme anger at my dad, anger that he hadn't listened to my mom, anger that he had gone back to that damnable Number Seven coalmine. As quickly as it had come, the anger dissipated. Sorrow and grief such as I had never imagined possible swept over me in waves. I thought that I could not bear it.

Word of my dad's death spread quickly. He was one of sixteen men who lost their lives in the mine. We were only one of the grieving families in the area. Jack called me the following day, as soon as his mother had notified him.

"Oh, Sweetheart, I'm so sorry," he said. "I wish I could be there with you."

"I wish you could, too, Jack," I sobbed. With all my heart, I wanted Jack's arms around me. I knew that he had just returned to the university and that he couldn't cut classes so close to the end of a semester. My head knew that, but my heart wanted him to fly to my side and share my grief. He couldn't.

Somehow, we got through the funeral. When the casket was closed for the final time, an ache began inside my chest that threatened to overwhelm me. The little click of closure sounded like a sledgehammer to me, pounding home the knowledge that I would never see my father again in this life.

The trip back to Southern Illinois, where my baby brother had been buried, was a long, hard one. Bill and I took turns driving the car. Ordinarily, that would have made our mother nervous. Lost in her grief, she hardly spoke. We followed the hearse, stopping when it stopped. The gray day matched our somber spirits.

We arrived at our destination very late. Relatives waited for us at my aunt's house. Mid-morning the next day, a large gathering stood beside the open hole that would be my dad's final resting place. At the far side of the plot, a tiny white headstone marked the spot where his second son lay.

Following the short service, seven war veterans fired their weapons three times, a traditional twenty-one gun salute to honor my dad's participation in World War II. The flag that had draped his casket was folded and given to my mother, who stoically received it. Sorrow left no room for pride upon her face.

Very early the next morning, the four of us started the journey back to Dixon, back to a house that would never be the same, to lives that would forever be diminished by the loss of a good man. There would be happy times again, and there would be laughter in the house again, but it would be forever different. Life and the passing years would be marked by "before Dad died" and "after Dad died."

I had thought that I could not bear the loss, but I did.

It wasn't a matter of choice.

#

Through A Glass, Darkly

Like a snowball that gathers momentum on a downhill run, the weeks and months passed swiftly; and like a jet-propelled snowball creates an avalanche, it seemed that I was being swept along by events over which I had little, if any, control. My family exchanged gifts, but Christmas Day was more somber than joyous for us. Mom insisted that we put up a tree, and we went through all the motions. It was one of many firsts, all those special days and events that would take place without my dad.

Dad's life insurance included a clause that paid off the mortgage on their house. That was one burden off my mother's shoulders. She assured me that she was going to be just fine, that her job and the insurance money would be adequate to take care of her and Beth. Bill's scholarship, already a sure thing, would cover much of his college costs the next fall. He worked part time, as well.

In late February, I spent my twentieth birthday with Penny Olson and some of my high school friends. Karen Courtney, pregnant again, radiated good health and contentment. She passed around pictures of her three-year-old daughter, Mona. Beverly Bodine had married and was the mother of a two-month-old son. Only a couple of the girls, besides me, had not yet married. Eighteen or nineteen seemed to be the requisite age to become a bride at that time. Not many girls went to college.

"Oh, Sissy, I heard from Ginger last week. You do remember Ginger?" Karen asked.

"How could I forget?" I asked. The girls laughed fondly at the memory of Ginger. Penny raised her eyebrows.

"Was Ginger special?" she asked. Several pair of eyebrows rose, and we nodded in unison.

"How is Ginger?" I asked.

"She got a part in a movie last summer, something that was being shot on the beach. A producer or writer or some movie person saw her and asked if she'd like to be in it. Of course, she did!" I clapped my hands. I wasn't a bit surprised.

Before the party broke up, the girls planned a bridal shower for me. I listened to the chatter and gaiety around me, to the planning and the...*stuff* that bounced around my head; and I felt absolute panic. *What was I thinking? I couldn't imagine myself as a wife, much less a potential mother! What did I know about choosing linens and china and silverware? That was the domain of Jack's mother!*

When Penny and I returned home after the party, I discovered that a dozen red roses in a crystal vase, along with a small package had been left for me. The card with the flowers read simply: "Jack." Inside the package was another box, embossed with the emblem of a local jeweler. I expected jewelry to be inside it, but I wasn't prepared for the contents.

Upon the satin lining lay a strand of perfectly matched pearls so lustrous they looked like captured moonbeams. Where in the world would I wear such an elegant thing? I would rather have received a simple bangle bracelet. The ring on my hand sparkled, a perfect complement to the diamond-encrusted clasp on the pearls. Beautiful, yes; but practical? I knew that Jack meant to please me, but such expensive jewelry made me uncomfortable. The pearls looked like something that Jack's mother would wear. I wondered if Mrs. McCoy had chosen them.

"Wow! Are those real pearls?" Penny asked.

"I'm afraid so." I smiled at her. At that moment, I would have felt better with a trinket from a box of Cracker Jacks. One of two things would have to happen to make Jack and me more compatible: He would have to accept me as I was, or I would have to change. I didn't see either one of those options happening easily.

Jack came home every weekend that he could. Between studying for finals and discovering what the Air Force had in store for him, he and I made wedding plans. Jack's parents wanted to pay for the wedding, even my gown; but neither of us wanted an elaborate ceremony. We set the date for August tenth and decided upon a simple service in the park near the reservoir, where Jack had proposed. As the days passed, my excitement and anticipation grew exponentially. The only thing that kept me from being perfectly happy was the absence of my dad.

At some point after the Fourth of July the previous summer, I had fallen in love with the person that Jack had become. More than the physical attraction that had hit me with the force of a ten on the Richter scale, I felt a tenderness for Jack that deepened each time we were together. My focus changed. I began to look at scary things, like linens and china and silverware, with a different perspective. I saw them as desirable items with which to make a home for Jack and me.

The wedding was everything I could have desired. My heart melted when I saw Jackson McCoy waiting for me beneath the flower-covered bower in the park. I know that the same expression on his face was reflected in mine. His features were a bit blurred, seen through my veil; but I could still read his amber-y eyes.

Beautiful in her soft pink dress, Beth preceded me up the unrolled white fabric path. My brother escorted me. I walked proudly beside him, as the tea-length white chiffon moved around my ankles. I felt as beautiful in the gown my mother had made for me as I would have felt in the most expensive designer dress. The scent of the pink roses I carried wafted through my veil.

When the minister asked who gave the bride in marriage, Bill replied, "Our mother and I." I was aware of so many things: the cleric's words; the touch of Jack's arm; songs of birds in the trees; the faraway drone of an overhead airplane; muted laughter of children beside the lake. Superimposed upon the sights and sounds that mingled behind my eyes, well hidden behind the veil, was the face of Victor Delacourt. Faint at first, the likeness became sharper, until he was all I could see. He seemed to look right at me, and a smile hovered upon his lips. *Sis-s-s-y-y-y-y...*

"Sissy." Jack's whisper focused my attention. "It's time to answer." The image of Victor dissipated, and my eyes flew to the minister's face. "Say 'I will,' Sissy," Jack whispered.

"I will." For a second or two, I wasn't certain that I would. The ceremony ended, Jack lifted my veil, and I kissed my new husband. The adoration on his face at that moment was a sight that I would always remember.

My mother hugged me. "Be happy, Sissy," she whispered.

"I will, Mom. I wish Daddy..."

"I know, Sweetie."

The McCoys had their way with the reception. Our wedding may have been small, but it seemed to me that half of Dixon turned out for the reception at the country club. People I didn't know hugged me, kissed me, enveloped me, until I felt like a puppet, pushed and pulled in all directions. It was so noisy. Laughter, the sound of clinking glasses, people all talking at once, music—it all ran together.

Long tables set with lavish arrangements of white flowers held china and crystal settings, complete with name cards. Ice sculptures bookended a massive six-tiered wedding cake. The room looked like pages torn from decorating magazines, each one competing with the next

We cut the cake and observed all those traditional rituals, as outlined and scheduled by Jack's mother. Elegant in her pale yellow brocade dress, Mrs. McCoy portrayed the perfect hostess of a perfect social event. Her lovely face was never without a perfect smile, but I wondered what really lay behind the beautiful mask. I had the feeling that it covered a great sadness. I smiled until my face hurt, said "Thank you" until the words were meaningless, and generally wanted nothing more than to flee with Jack.

He must have read the feelings on my face. Shortly after we were seated for dinner, he leaned close to me and whispered. "It won't be long, Sissy. We'll leave right after the first dance." Dismay filled me. Jack and I had danced at Dooby's together, but never formally and never as the only couple on the floor. I would have to trust him to lead me.

I should have remembered how accomplished Jack was at everything he did. He swept me into his arms and we moved across the polished floor as easily as if we danced together every evening. I rested my head upon his chest, and his arms tightened around me. Everything felt like a dream. I caught glimpses of my mother and my sister, but I didn't see my brother.

"Okay, Angel," Jack murmured. "It's time to go." Skillfully, he maneuvered me between the dancing couples. In moments, he danced me out the open doors and onto the patio, where we stopped. He held me close and looked into my eyes. "I love you, Sissy. You've made me the happiest man in the world."

"I love you, too, Jack." Why had I fought him for so long? There wasn't a doubt in my mind that he told me the truth. I knew that he loved me, that he had always loved me. There was something different in his kiss, something that held not only passion and desire, but possession. I was breathless with the promises his lips conveyed. I opened my eyes.

In the moonlight, Jack's eyes glittered with an expression of smug, self-satisfied victory. I felt a chill of unreasonable, absolute fear. What had I done! I closed my eyes, dizzy with the onslaught of doubt and dread that darkened my mind.

Wish I May, Wish I Might...

"Sissy? Honey, are you all right?" Jack's arms held me, supported me against the dizziness. I looked up at him, and the only emotion on his face was tender concern for me. I nodded. There was no trace of what I thought I had seen. It must have been a trick of the moonlight.

"I think I'm just tired, Jack. It's been a long day."

"Come with me." Jack took my hand and pulled me along the patio to the driveway. He motioned with his hand. A parking attendant nodded, and within a short time he brought the convertible to us. Jack opened the door for me and helped me maneuver the skirt of my gown. "Wait here," he said.

I rested my head against the cool leather seat and closed my eyes. So many emotions warred inside my head and heart. *I love Jack! I do!* I told myself. I knew that we would have a good life together, that he would love and protect and all those other things that were said in the vows. I had stumbled over the "obey" that was in the list of things to which I had agreed, but I could manage all the rest. My parents' relationship had been a good example.

My eyes closed. I went back over the events of the day, and I could honestly say that they had been good. I didn't know why the image of Victor Delacourt had intruded into my wedding, but I dismissed it as a fluke, perhaps a last-ditch effort to hold onto my childhood. I was ready to put that childhood behind me, and I intended to be a good wife to Jack.

Anticipation and nervousness held a wrestling match over the evening ahead for Jack and me. Anticipation won. By the time Jack returned to the car, I was eager to feel his arms around me. I welcomed the kiss he gave me, and I returned it with all the passion that was now legally and morally mine to give.

"Sissy, Sissy," Jack chuckled around my name. He started the car. He pulled me close to his side, and we exited the parking lot of the Dixon Country Club. So complete was our get-a-way that no one had a chance to paint and decorate the convertible with "Just Married" signs and tin cans, which was all right with me.

"Where are we going?" I asked.

"I reserved a suite for us at a hotel in Charleston," Jack told me. "Tomorrow we'll drive to the coast and take a ship to Bermuda. We can stay as long as we want, for I don't have to report to the base until mid-September."

Bermuda! I couldn't imagine it. I had thought that Jack would probably take me to Niagara Falls or the Poconos, something traditional. Island resorts had not crossed my mind.

"Jack, can we go by my house? I'd like to change out of this dress and get some of my things."

"Sure, Honey. You won't have to take much with you, though. We'll get new stuff as we need it." He planted a quick kiss on my forehead.

I changed clothes and selected toiletries and personal things from the room that had been my retreat for seven years. As a wedding gift, my mother had given new luggage to me. I filled a small bag with summer clothing. From the window, I could see the star-filled sky above the mountain. It had been a long time since I'd wished upon a star. I whispered the little verse that had been such a part of my growing up: "Star light, Star bright, First star I see tonight; I wish I may, I wish I might, Have the wish I wish tonight."

"Sissy? Are you ready?" Jack called from the stairway. I took one last look around the room and hurried to him.

"Give me just a minute, Jack," I said. I made a quick trip through the living room. The scent of my dad still lingered in the house. I stood beside his chair and touched the place where his head had indented the back. More than anything I wanted him to know how happy I was and how much I missed him. I blinked away tears. This was my wedding night, and I wanted to have only happy thoughts. "I'm ready," I told my new husband.

The hotel was much more than I expected. Jack hadn't told me that he'd reserved the honeymoon suite. It looked like pictures from a bridal magazine, all gold and white and burgundy. I was embarrassed at the wink the bellboy surreptitiously gave to Jack. My face turned warm, and I retreated to the bathroom.

A huge white, gold-veined-marble bathtub greeted me. I had never seen such opulence in a bathroom. Gold satin draped the double windows. The vanity stool, covered in tufted white velvet, sat in front of a low dressing table that held fancy jars of creams and lotions. I opened a closet door and found two fluffy white robes, marked His and Hers.

I heard the outer door close. I peeked from the bathroom door, to make certain that the bellboy had gone. A linen-covered cart, filled with covered silver dishes, a bouquet of roses and a champagne bottle in ice stood in the center of the room. Jack, shirtsleeves opened and rolled back at his wrists, picked up the bottle and tore away the foil.

"I thought that you might be hungry," he said. "Do you want something to eat?"

"Maybe, yes," I answered. He popped the cork and quickly poured the pale, bubbly liquid into a tall, stemmed glass. He took a sip from the glass, looked at me, and drained it. I blinked, stupidly. After the conversation we'd had about drinking, I was more than a little surprised at his actions. He filled his glass again and poured some into another, which he held out to me.

"Jack, you know I don't drink," I told him. He laughed.

"This isn't drinking, Sissy. This is a toast to us, to our wedding night and to all the years ahead. Here, take it." Gingerly, I took the glass from him. Knowing that the Bannisters had bred their share of alcoholics, I had opted never to take the chance that I might become one. Some of my friends, although not yet twenty-one, had begun to drink with their older friends and family; but I had not been tempted.

Rather than make an issue of it this special night, and to please Jack, I took a tiny sip from the glass. "Come on," he said. "Drink it. It won't hurt you." He held his glass out to me, motioning that I should do the same. He touched my glass, and there was a tiny ping when the crystal goblets met. "To us, Sissy. To this night and all the nights to come. I love you, Sissy." He lifted the glass to his lips, but waited until I had done the same. I took two small swallows before I put the glass back on the table. Jack drank all of his.

"Look, Sissy." He raised one of the silver covers from the table. Beautifully cut fruit lay on a crystal platter. Jack lifted a strawberry and held it out to me. "Open," he said. I smiled at the teasing sparkle in his eyes and opened my mouth. I bit into the berry and felt a trickle of juice upon my chin. Jack tossed the berry onto the tray and gathered me into his arms. He kissed away the dripping juice.

Slowly, he walked me backwards until my legs touched the huge bed. Before I could say a word, Jack lifted me onto the bed and bent over me. "You're mine, Sissy. Finally and forever, you are mine." With frantic fingers, he began to unbutton my clothing.

"Jack, wait," I said. "I have a nightgown, something special. I want..." He stopped my words with a kiss. I knew a moment of fear, uncertain what to expect; but Jack's mouth was doing incredible things, telling me that he loved me, moving from my throat to my lips to skin that had never before been touched by any man.

I put my arms around him and gave in to the marvelous sensations he created, to the unbelievable fire of arousal he stirred within me; in essence, Jack McCoy brought to me the knowledge of what love could be between a man and a woman. I was an eager pupil. Between the hours of ten o'clock that night and dawn the next morning, the beautiful nightgown that I had chosen for my wedding night was never taken from the suitcase. Somehow, it didn't matter.

I woke to the sound of the shower running in the bathroom. I stretched languorously, reveling in my new state as a married woman. I looked at the rings on my finger, and I smiled. I probably looked like a satiated cat that had just found the creamery. The silky sheets tangled around my legs. On a whim, still wrapped in the sheet, I tiptoed to the bathroom, thinking to surprise Jack.

Steam filled the luxurious room. I slipped to the door of the shower; but before I could open it, Jack slid it open, jerked the sheet from me, and pulled me beneath the warm water. "Jack!" I sputtered. He laughed, but suddenly his laughter turned to a soft moan of desire and he pulled me into his arms. It was a very long, hot shower.

Looking back, those first few weeks were the happiest time of my first twenty years of life. Insatiable, yet gentle and patient, Jack brought new meaning to the word, "lover." We spent two weeks in Bermuda, and we toured much of the island. There were times that we stood upon a wooded hilltop, or strolled along a sandy beach, or walked together in moonlit parks, when a sudden, undeniable spark would be ignited by a glance, a touch, an innocent kiss. More than once, there was grass in my hair when we returned to the hotel.

Life cannot be sustained at such a fevered pitch. I didn't expect a fairy tale existence, but neither did I expect to be living in the home of Jack's parents. I had assumed that we would find a small apartment when we returned to Dixon. Jack had other plans, which I discovered on the drive back from the coast.

"Honey, it makes no sense for us to rent a place for such a short time. There's lots of room in my dad's house, and we can have as much privacy as we want. It will only be for two or three weeks, four at the most. As soon as I get to Lackland, I'll find a place and you can join me."

"Jack, you'll be in basic training for at least two months. I'll go back to my mother's house until we can find something off the base. I'm not going to stay with your folks when you aren't there," I stated. Jack frowned.

"You're my wife, Sissy. You can't go back to your old home. You belong with me and my family now."

"If you're not here, what would it matter?" I watched the play of emotions on Jack's face. It was the closest thing to an argument we'd had, something I didn't want; but on this issue, I was just as adamant as he was. He turned away from me. I watched his fingers drum impatiently on the steering wheel.

"Let's just see how things turn out," he said. "It might be that you can join me right away." I nodded in agreement, knowing that it would be weeks before that could happen. He took my hand and brought it to his lips. Nothing had been decided. I had sense enough to know that he had not given in nor given up, but neither had I.

My mother cried when Jack and I entered the house. Bill hadn't returned from Charleston, where he was enrolled as a freshman at the university; but Beth ran to me and threw her arms around my waist. Jack embraced my mother, and planted a kiss on her forehead, something he had never done. I followed closely behind. Tears filled my eyes, too, when Mom drew me to her.

"Are you happy, Sissy?" she whispered. She took my face in both her hands and traced my features with her eyes. What she saw there must have reassured her, for she smiled through her tears.

"Yes, Mama, I'm very happy. Jack is wonderful to me."

"You disappeared so quickly from your reception. I didn't get to tell you goodbye or wish you a happy honeymoon," Mom said. "You were just suddenly...gone."

"Sissy was tired, Mrs. Bannister. I thought that it would be better if we left early." My mother nodded slowly.

"You're probably right, Jack. Well, what are your plans for tonight? Can you stay for supper? Or overnight? Sissy, I cleaned your room and it's ready for you." She smiled.

"I'm sorry, Mrs. Bannister," Jack spoke before I could open my mouth. "We've made plans to stay at my parents for this evening."

"Oh, I see." I thought that my mother probably did see, all too well.

"I'll run upstairs and get some more of my things, Jack. Mom, will you come help me?"

"Can I come, too?" Beth asked.

"Sure. Come on, Bethy," I grinned at the fleeting indignant expression on her face at my use of her childhood name. At fourteen, she rejected all things she considered childish. It would be awhile before she realized how precious child-like things are, and what a short period of time childhood holds in our lives.

Great news greeted us at the McCoy house: his parents had taken his sister on a trip to Washington, D.C. We learned later that the trip was to make up for Deanna not being an attendant at the wedding. It seemed that she was furious that my sister had been awarded that honor. In retrospect, I should probably have included her; but I wanted to keep down the cost of the wedding, which my mother had insisted upon paying.

The days passed swiftly. Jack's orders came sooner than he expected. "Lackland, Texas," he said. "That's where they told me it would be, but I was hoping for Chanute. I have to report in one week." I took a deep breath.

"Will I be able to stay near you?" I asked. Jack shook his head.

"Not during basic," he said, "but as soon as that's over, we'll find a place in town. Sissy, I don't know how I'm going to get along without you." I think that Jack had known all along that we couldn't be together at Lackland until he was out of basic training. He just hated not being in control.

Tears filled my eyes. I had already grown so accustomed to falling asleep in Jack's arms, to waking in the night to find his arm tucked around my waist, and to seeing his handsome face first thing every morning. The brief irritation I had felt toward him vanished. He was my husband, and I was going to miss him.

I put aside my aversion to the McCoy mansion, determined to make Jack's last days in the house before his departure as peaceful as possible. Still, every day I moved something in the house, just a little. Beautifully decorated, each piece of glass, figurine or painting fit into the grand design of color, texture and style. One day I shifted a porcelain vase about two inches. The next day, I moved a small crystal bird from a shelf to an end table.

I should have known better. I'm certain that no one saw me, but the pieces were back in their original spots within twenty-four hours. I gave up the childish game, ashamed that I had been so petty at a time when I should have been focused only on Jack.

In spite of Jack's original objections, we decided that the sensible thing for me to do was to live with my mother until he completed basic training. I would begin my junior year at the university in Charleston and transfer when I could join him. Two days before he had to leave, Jack gave me a small, gift-wrapped box. He loved to give me jewelry, something I could live without; but instead of an expensive trinket, the box held a set of keys.

"What's this?" I asked. Jack drew me close, locking his arms behind my back.

"I want you to be as safe as possible while I'm gone," he said. "These keys will make sure you don't have car trouble to and from Charleston."

He grinned, and my heart melted at the sweetness of his smile. He kissed the tip of my nose. "Let's go outside."

Parked beneath the porte cochere, gleaming with what looked like acres of chrome, was a cream-colored Pontiac Chieftain. I didn't know what to say or do. My parents had never owned a new car, and I had driven the same little Chevy since high school. "Oh, Jack," I breathed. "But you didn't have to buy this! I can drive my old car, and…"

"Hush," he said. "Come upstairs and show me how grateful you are." His smile took away the sting of what could have been an insult. "My parents will be home tonight; but for now, we have the house to ourselves." *Well,* I thought, *except for the hidden members of the household staff.*

Four days later Jack boarded a train bound for Lackland Air Force Base. I moved into my old room, went back to school in Charleston, and lived much as I had before I became Mrs. Jackson McCoy. However, I was no longer the girl who had occupied that room for seven years. At night I missed my husband. I longed for the sound of his voice, for his touch, for the closeness we had shared.

When the day came that he sent for me, weeks later, I was more than ready to join him. Not only had there been basic training, Jack was a candidate for flight school, which took many more weeks. I knew that I would miss my family, but it was time for me to leave the Bannister house. There was no way that I could know how soon or how much I would long to be back within the safety of its walls.

From Lackland, Texas, Jack was transferred to Grand Forks, North Dakota. I found a two-roomed apartment in the city, and Jack joined me every weekend that he could get a pass. I couldn't decide if the Air Force was changing Jack or if he were just becoming more of what he had always been. He was often short of patience with me and short-tempered at red lights, at slow drivers, at inadequate television reception.

I made excuses for him in my mind, telling myself that the changes were the result of pressures of flight training school and life in the barracks. I tried to be as understanding and compassionate as I could be, without knowing the real causes of Jack's problems. Most of the time, he was still a gentle lover; but there were occasions when I felt that my feelings didn't matter to him.

One hot, Saturday afternoon I came into the apartment with a bag of groceries, planning to prepare some of Jack's favorites for dinner.

He had gone fishing with some of his buddies in the Red River that morning, and I didn't expect him to return until early evening. I placed the bag on the counter.

"Jack! You scared me!" I put my hand to my throat, startled at his sudden appearance from the bedroom.

"Did I?" I knew that something wasn't right; and then I saw the beer bottle in his hand. I hated the smell and taste of beer, which Jack knew.

"Oh, Jack," I groaned. "Beer?" I couldn't hide the disgust in my voice.

"Aren't you glad to see me?" he asked. "Come and give me a kiss, Sweetheart." His words were slurred, and I felt a shudder of revulsion at the thought of kissing a beery-mouth. He had obviously been drinking for some time. This was a Jack I had never seen, and one that I didn't like.

"What happened?" I asked. "I thought that you were going to be fishing with your buddies until later." I turned from Jack and busied myself with the groceries. I couldn't bear to look at him. Hard and trim from months of strenuous training, he was in better physical condition than he had ever been. Although military-short, his silvery blond hair still shone with care and good health. His handsome face was tanned and his teeth were brilliant against the bronze of his skin, but coldness glittered in his gold-flecked brown eyes.

"The party broke up early," Jack said. "The fish were invited, but they didn't come." He laughed loudly at his joke. "So we sat around and drank some beer, and then we drank some more beer." He laughed again. "And then, Sweet Sissy, I decided to come home and invite my beautiful wife to the party. Let's party, Honey."

Jack pressed close to me and slipped his arms around my waist. The bottle in his hand clinked against the counter. I grabbed it and poured the contents down the sink. "I think you've had enough, Jack." I moved away from him, wanting to put as much distance between us as possible. I heard him take a big breath and release it in a sigh.

"You shouldn't have done that," he said. His voice was a near whisper. "A good wife does what her husband tells her to do. Be a good wife, Sissy."

"Jack, you're drunk." I couldn't hide the disgust I felt. I turned toward the bedroom. In two giant steps, Jack was beside me. He grasped my upper arm with one hand. With the other hand, he hit me, back-handed across my face. Before the slap had registered, he hit me again, open-palmed. I staggered and would have fallen, had he not still held my arm.

Too shocked to cry out, I could only stare at Jack McCoy, my husband, the beautiful man I had married less than a year ago. I tasted blood. A warm trickle ran down my chin, and my cheeks throbbed from the force of the blows. The thought that I must surely be in a nightmare was the only thing that made sense. Jack looked at me with eyes I didn't recognize.

"Go clean yourself up," he said. "You're a mess." He released my arm and turned away from me. Without another glance at me, he stretched upon the couch. I heard him begin to snore before I got to the tiny bathroom. In the shower, my tears mingled with the water. Over and over the same words filled my head: *My husband hit me. The man who had promised to love and cherish me had hit me.* For the first time since I was eight years old, someone I loved had struck me. It was only the first of many, many times.

When Jack's four-year stint was over, he decided to make a career of the Air Force. He was a pilot, and he loved being in the air. He was happiest just before he flew, and I grew to long for those times as much as he did. I could completely relax only when he was gone. In spite of military transfers, during the months I was alone, I had managed to earn a bachelor's degree in journalism. At that point, I was uncertain what I would or could do toward earning a living in that field; but at least I had the degree.

Jack had not consulted me about his decision. I would rather have been able to stay in one place, to put down roots and make a home like my parents had done. On the other hand, traveling gave me a wonderful perspective as a would-be writer.

Overnight, it seemed, the United States became involved in a military action in a little, unheard-of country on the far side of the world, Viet Nam. Excitement filled Jack's voice when he told me that he would be flying missions to secret destinations. He couldn't wait to be shipped to Viet Nam.

"Sissy, this little fracas won't amount to much; but it will give me the chance to earn a lot of decorations. You just watch. Before I'm finished, I'll be a general." In his anticipation, he sounded like the old Jack, the Jack I had loved. His eyes sparkled, and he looked at me with the nearest thing to tenderness that I had seen for a long time. I saw the desire in his eyes, and I tried to respond when he kissed me. It's hard to feel loving toward someone who can become abusive at the slightest provocation.

Although Jack never connected with him, my friend, Jerry Davis, had also enlisted in the Air Force. Our mothers exchanged our addresses, and our first letters to each other crossed in the mail. It was good to hear from him. A few of my high school friends and I corresponded for a while, but eventually we lost touch, dwindling down to Christmas cards.

By that time, Jack was stationed at Shaw Air Force Base in South Carolina. I had made several friends among other military wives, where we were all neighbors on the base. On the surface, Jack and I had the perfect marriage. He no longer hit me where marks would show, and I was too proud to let anyone know that Jack took out his anger and frustration on me. I had never confided in my mother or my siblings. I couldn't stand the thought that they would pity me, the independent, take-nothing-from-anybody Sissy Bannister.

Most of our friends had children of various ages. I had stopped suggesting that we should start a family. Jack's reaction was always the same.

"I don't want to share you with anyone," he had said the first time I approached the subject of a baby. "I don't want you to get fat and ugly." He had put his arms around me and run his hands along my waist. "This is only for me," he had said. "You belong only to me." It dawned upon me that bringing a child into a home where it was not wanted could not possibly be good for that child. I stopped talking about it, but the longing was still there.

The little fracas that Jack had predicted would amount to nothing became a drawn-out, ugly war. For two years he flew missions over the ravaged country, reveling in his successful record and many "kills." During that time, I made a decision. When the war was over or Jack returned home, whichever came first, I was going to file for divorce. I had found a job with a newspaper in Sumter, near the base, and I loved the feeling of independence that it gave me.

Living alone didn't scare me. I was safe within my own home. I regained a sense of who I was, so that I felt empowered to carry out the decision I had made. I would no longer live with someone who hurt me.

On a cloudy morning in late October of nineteen sixty-eight, I opened the door of my house, eager to get to work. Walking with military strides toward me were two men in Air Force blues, carrying their hats. One wore a stark white collar, indicating that he was a chaplain. I frowned. *They must want directions,* I thought.

"Can I help you?" I asked.

"Mrs. McCoy? Mrs. Jack McCoy?" the younger man asked. I nodded.

"Yes, I'm Mrs. McCoy."

"May we come inside and speak with you?"

"Of course." I stepped back and held the door open for them.

"Ma,am, we're sorry to inform you that your husband's plane was shot down in Viet Nam two days ago. The plane exploded and there are no survivors. We are so very sorry." Unshed tears filled the young man's eyes. I frowned. The words registered in my ears, but they made no sense to me. It was almost as if he spoke a foreign language.

"Mrs. McCoy, perhaps you should sit down," the chaplain said. I allowed him to lead me to a chair. When I just stood there, he gently pushed me down until I was seated. "I know that this is a terrible shock to you, and I'm so sorry for your loss. Is there someone we can call for you, a minister perhaps, or a friend?"

"What?" I frowned again. "Oh, no thank you. No." Quizzically, I examined the younger airman's face. He had the bluest eyes. I wondered if he looked like his mother or his father. His face held such concern. From him, I turned to the chaplain, an older man with silver temples and crow's feet around his hazel eyes. Hmmm, I thought. He's about the age of my dad. I wondered if my dad's hair would have been that silvery by now.

The chaplain said something, but the words came from far away and I couldn't understand what he was saying. His voice became more blurred. The faint hum in my ears became a roar, and the chaplain's face faded away to nothing. From a great distance, I heard him call my name. Then there was nothing.

One of the most difficult things I had to do was call my mother. About six months before Jack was killed, my mom had remarried. She hadn't told Bill or me about her plans. She hadn't even told Beth, the child to whom she was closest. Perhaps she hadn't wanted to take away any of the spotlight from Beth, who had married her fiancé only three weeks before our mother virtually eloped.

"Oh, Sissy, no!" Mom cried when I told her. "Not Jack! Oh, Honey, I'm so sorry! I never wanted you to go through what I did when your daddy died!" For a moment, I was speechless. Our situations were so different. I had never told my mother or anyone else how Jack had treated me.

"It's going to be all right, Mom. I'm doing all right," I assured her.

"Oh, Sweetie, how can you be all right? I *know* how you feel!"

"Mom, there are arrangements to make; and I have to call Jack's parents. I'll be home in a few days, but I'll call first to let you know a definite time." I hesitated. "Is Russell okay?"

"He's fine," Mom told me. At the mention of her new husband's name, her voice brightened. She sounded happy. I was glad that she had found a good man to share her life. Even after eight years, it would be a while before I could accept the fact that he was living in my dad's house. "You be careful, Honey. I love you."

After we hung up, I took a short walk around the base. I walked fast, but I couldn't out-walk my demons. The call to Jack's parents would have to be made; and much as I dreaded it, I couldn't put it off any longer.

"We'll take care of everything, Sissy," Mr. McCoy told me. "I've already notified the State Department that we want Jack's remains, should there be any, shipped to Dixon." His voice broke. He cleared his throat and continued. "Of course, you will have to sign the papers, which I'm sure will be no problem." I assured him that I would do so.

"This shouldn't have happened," he continued. "Jack was the best and the brightest of the McCoys. He could have become a general and done great things for his country." I clenched my jaw. If hitting his wife was a prerequisite of greatness, Jack had been on the right track. "I wish that you hadn't refused to have children, Sissy. Jack told me that you didn't want babies, but I wish that you had borne at least one. Now his line has ended." Though his tone was deceptively gentle, Mr. McCoy's reproof cut like a knife.

"Mr. McCoy..." A quick denial hovered upon my lips. I heard the sob in Jack's father's voice, and I choked back the words that I wanted to throw at him. He had just lost his only son, and parents are not supposed to outlive their children. It isn't in the natural order of things. I would let him keep his illusions about his son. Mine had died a painful death years earlier.

"Whatever is left of Jack will be buried in the McCoy plot outside of Dixon," he continued. "We'll see you when you return, Sissy. Goodbye." He broke the connection.

The human mind and body can be amazingly separate from each other. For the next few days, my mind was numb; but my body functioned normally. So many procedures and documents and so much *stuff* had to be taken care of, giving me no time to think during the daylight hours. The nights, however, were another matter.

I lay awake for hours, often not moving, lying in the darkness. I felt no grief. The strongest emotion I experienced was guilt, guilt that I had already emotionally walked away from Jack, guilt that I had decided to end a marriage that brought me nothing but fear and pain, guilt that I was more relieved than sorry that he wouldn't be coming back.

I pulled up memories of the first few months we were married. I wanted to remember the nights that I thought had been filled with magic, to recall the sensation of being loved and cherished by my husband; but I couldn't connect with the pictures I saw in my head. It was like watching someone else's home movies. I missed the man I had thought Jack was, the man I wanted him to be, not the man he had been.

One night when sleep eluded me, I pulled boxes from the small closets and began to go through the contents. A bit of a pack rack, I still kept letters and mementos of trips and special events, much as I had done when I was a girl. I opened one of the boxes, thinking that I would begin to sort the throw-a-ways from the keepers.

It was not the box I wanted. I started to close it, but I caught a glimpse of a bundle of letters. Although the handwriting was not Jack's, I recognized it. I pulled an envelope from the rubber band. I smiled briefly when I looked at the return address: J Davis, Cedar Hall, University of Illinois. The postmark was nineteen sixty-one, the year after Jack and I got married. There weren't many from Jerry, but I had kept all of them. It had given me a connection to home, one I had sometimes desperately needed.

Dear Sissy,
Congratulations on your wedding! How did ole Jack finally persuade you? My mom didn't send me any details—she just wrote that you got married, and that Jack had joined the Air Force. Where is he stationed?

Mom told me that you're still living at home and taking classes at the university in Charleston. I guess you'll join Jack when he gets settled? No kidding, I hope that the two of you are very happy.

I haven't settled on one girl yet. There are so many and only one of me! Believe it or not, I really am working hard. Drop a line and let me know where Jack goes.

Jerry

I was hooked. I took the little stack of Jerry's letters, opened and read each one. A short history emerged from the pages. It was like watching a mini-movie take form through the words, brief as they were. Jerry hadn't come home the summer Jack and I got married. I hadn't seen him since his freshman year in college, and these letters were like renewing an old friendship.

June 1963

Hi Sissy and Jack,
How's life down there in Texas? I got your note saying that you were at Lackland. How's the Air Force treating you, Jack? Is it what you expected? Write back and tell me what you can. I've got to make some decisions pretty soon. I have three more years of vet school, that is, if I don't get drafted.
Sissy, I've met a really cute girl. Her name is Marilyn. She's a little bit of a girl—kind of a cross between a pixie and a terrier—cute and feisty. I like her a lot....

Jerry

#

September 1964

Dear Sissy and Jack,
Well, I finally had to make that decision! I got a draft deferment by promising to enter the Air Force after I graduate from Veterinary School. Who knows? Maybe I'll end up at the same base as you. That's still two more years, though; and there's no telling where you'll be by then. Do you have any idea where you'll be going from there?
Marilyn and I are still dating. It seems like I've known her all my life.
Take care of each other.

Jerry

#

October 1966

Hey Sissy!
You're not going to believe this: Marilyn and I got married last month. I'm not joking! On my way from Sheppard AFB in Texas to Seymour-Johnson AFB, in North Carolina, I swung by Champaign. It turns out she missed me as much as I missed her! (Those lovely nurses I dated at Sheppard during the last four months don't count! I still thought about Marilyn!) Anyway, I asked her to marry me, and she said "YES!" We were married two days later in a chapel at Chanute AFB, near Rantoul.

We didn't have much time. I had to report to my new job about forty-eight hours after the wedding. Those attending our wedding included the chaplain, Marilyn, me, and two witnesses we hailed from the street outside!

Are you doing all right? How's Jack? Don't worry, Sissy. I'm sure he'll keep his head down. A lot of guys I know have been shipped to Viet Nam, too.

We really like it here in North Carolina. I'll write more later...wish you could meet Marilyn. You'd like her.

Jerry

#

June 1967

Dear Sissy,
How's it going? I got a note from Jack last week. He didn't say much, but then I guess he can't. Try not to worry about him. Those planes get in and out pretty fast. He'll be okay.

My wing commander is Colonel Chuck Yeager. Do you remember hearing about him when we were in school? He's the pilot who first flew faster than the speed of sound. He is really something! He likes to hunt, so I've been dove hunting with him in the fields on weekends. We take my black Labrador, Ebony. We call her "Ebbie." I think that dog loves Colonel Yeager as much as, if not more than, she loves me!

The Colonel sits on his can (no, really, he sits on an upturned five gallon can!), and Ebbie brings to him every dove he bags. His peripheral vision and visual acuity are incredible. He can "eye" doves long before the other hunters in the field; and he shoots with unmatched precision and accuracy. It's as if he has eyes in the back of his head!

The same was obviously true as he sat in the seats of fighter jets during WW II and the Korean War. Colonel Yeager is among the few pilots that have earned the title "ACE." I never dreamed that I would actually meet the man, much less have him as my wing commander. He has given me a high performance rating, and I've been promoted to Captain! How 'bout that?

There's much I could tell you, and some that I can't. Chin up, Sissy! Jack will be home before you know it.

Jerry
#

I let the letter drop to my lap. I picked up the last envelope, postmarked only a few weeks before Jack was killed

September 1968

Dear Sissy,

If you've been watching the news, as I'm sure you have, you know that North Korea captured the USS Pueblo. The 4th Tactical Fighter Wing at Seymour-Johnson was deployed to Korea. My job was to provide veterinary care for the 150 or so sentry dogs at three different bases in South Korea: Taegu, Kunsan, and Kwangu. Every other day, I traveled from base to base in an Air Force C-47, attending to the animals, some of which had been injured by North Korean infiltrators attempting to break through the perimeter security forces surrounding the bases. The dogs can detect an enemy long before the guards, especially at night.

I was allowed to fly in the back seat of an F-4D Phantom fighter jet on two separate reconnaissance missions near the DMZ. The sight of scores of Russian-built MIGs, parked just north of the demarcation line, sent chills down my spine. That was quite an experience for this Southern Illinois/West Virginia farm boy! I'm glad that the North Koreans finally released the ship and that we didn't have to go to war there—again. It seems to me that we've got our hands full in Viet Nam. I'll be glad to get back to North Carolina.

Do you hear from Jack often? Do you have any idea when he's coming home? His tour should be over pretty soon, shouldn't it? Be sure to let me know where he is, if you can. Take care.

Jerry

I placed the letters back into the box and closed the lid. For the first time since the notification, I felt sleepy. My bed looked inviting. I left the boxes in the floor and climbed into the bed, clothes and all. Within minutes, I went to sleep.

The next morning, I answered a knock on the door to find five military wives, all acquaintances of mine, from neighboring housing. In their arms they carried coffeecakes and fruit; one of them held an electric coffee pot. Another carried folded boxes.

"Just sit down, Sissy, and let us help you," Tammy Curtis told me. She pushed me into a chair at the kitchen table. I watched the women scurry around the house while I sipped good coffee and ate their food. They picked up clutter, cleaned the bathroom and packed my bags.

"Sissy, I'm putting everything that was on your desk in one box. You'll want to take it with you. Just tell us where you want the rest shipped, and we'll take care of it." She hesitated. "Would you like for us to pack up Jack's things or...?" I put my head on the table and began to cry for the first time since the Air Force had notified me of Jack's death. I sobbed and blubbered and sobbed some more. I cried for myself, for the McCoys, for Jack, for the other pilot who had been lost, for all the miserable soldiers in a miserable place in a miserable war. I cried until I hiccupped. Tammy stood beside me and patted my shoulder, crooning words of comfort that I heard, but didn't understand.

When the flood of tears had ebbed, I felt better, cleaner and stronger. "No," I told Tammy. "I'll take care of Jack's things."

I drove Jack's nineteen sixty-five red Corvette, much too fast, from the base in South Carolina to Dixon in one day. The sky threatened rain all day, but held off until I drove into my mother's driveway late that night. She was still up, waiting for me in the living room. She didn't say a word when I, looking like a drowned daughter, opened the door and stepped into the hall. She held wide her arms and took me inside, soaked clothes and all.

"Your room is ready for you, Honey. Why don't you go on up and get out of those wet things? There's a robe in the closet." I did as she suggested. Mindful of the noise, I didn't run a bath. I just stripped off my wet clothes and shrugged into an old chenille robe, left over from high school. Weary to the bone, I crawled into my old bed, in my old room, and snuggled beneath quilts made by my Great-grandmother Chinn. I had come home.

The next days were like a slow-motion bad dream from which it was impossible to awaken or escape. A week passed before a flag-draped casket, escorted by men in dress blues, was brought to a local funeral home. The casket would not be opened. I learned later, from a cousin who had been such an escort, that quite often nothing was in the casket but dog tags or bits of uniform, sometimes not even that. The escorts were under orders that no one, not family, friends, nor funeral directors would be allowed to open the casket, not under any circumstances. The escort was armed, in order to carry out those orders.

The memorial service, held in the gray-stoned Presbyterian church where local members of the McCoy family attended, was impressive. While the speaker extolled the virtues of the deceased McCoy heir, I gazed at the huge, round, stained-glass-window, wherein Christ in the garden of Gethsemane was depicted. When I wasn't looking at it, I gazed at my gloved hands. In the pew behind me sat my mother and her husband. Bill and Beth, with their spouses, sat next to them. I could feel their support through the heavy oak pew.

Mr. McCoy insisted that I ride with them and Jack's sister, Deanna, to the cemetery. It was the correct protocol, I suppose. Although I knew that it was part of the service, I was startled when three rounds from seven rifles discharged in a twenty-one-gun salute. Only when the plaintive, haunting melody of Taps was sounded, did tears fall from my eyes. The ceremony was nearly identical to the one that had been performed at my dad's burial, except that this time, the flag that was removed from the casket was given to me.

The service ended. A chilly, November sun shone briefly upon the face of Jack's father before it slipped behind its cover. "All of you are invited back to our home for refreshments and a time to comfort each other. Please come."

"Wait for me," I told my mother. "I want to ride with you, but I need to speak to Mrs. McCoy. I'll be right back." I approached Jack's mother, whose face behind the stylish veil looked haggard. Deanna clung to her mother's arm.

Tears stained Deanna's face. She had never been as pretty as Jack, which was a shame. Her facial features seemed mismatched, not quite made for each other, whereas everything about Jack had been perfect. Unlike her mother, Deanna was stocky and built more like her father. Whereas Jack's blond hair had been shiny and his skin smooth, his sister's hair was mousy brown, her skin prone to acne. Jack's flaws had not been physical.

Deanna and Beth were the same age, twenty-two. Although they had been in the same class from the time we came to Dixon, the two had never been friends. My marriage to Jack hadn't influenced the girls to like each other.

"Deanna is such a baby," Beth had said. "If things don't go her way, she pouts. She actually runs her lip out and *pouts* like a little kid! And she's a snob, too. I don't like her." As far as Beth was concerned, that was the end of it.

Deanna stepped aside as I drew near. "Mrs. McCoy, I'd like for you to have this." I held out the folded flag. With the saddest eyes I had ever seen, she gazed at me for several moments before she took the flag from me.

"Thank you, Sissy." Impulsively, I hugged her. She seemed startled, but then she lifted her arms and returned the hug. I had to bite my lip to keep from apologizing to her for marrying her son. Somewhere in the back of my mind lay the thought that Jack might still be alive had I listened to that bothersome, pinging bell of intuition. Guilt is a terribly useless emotion, I thought. It doesn't fix anything; it just keeps one emotionally off balance and clinging to "what-ifs."

My family and I spent a reasonably polite amount of time before we left the reception. It was the first and only occasion that any of them had been inside the mansion. I suspected that it was the topic of conversation in my brother's car. My mother didn't have much to say about the house, but I knew that it had impressed her with its size, if not its warmth.

"I don't like November." Mom's statement took me completely by surprise. "My three-week-old baby boy died in my arms on the eleventh of November. Will went into the army the following November. My half-brother's mother died in November, leaving five kids to live in a house with a man unfit to have children." She turned to look at me where I sat in the back seat of her car. "Your daddy died in November, the week after Thanksgiving; and now Jack."

"You're being superstitious," Russell told her. "There's no connection. It's all coincidence." I felt like a cat whose fur had been rubbed the wrong way. I bit back the quick retort that I wanted to spit at Russell Dunbar. He had completely missed my mother's point. I thought that he had just been extremely insensitive.

I looked closely at my mother. At forty-eight, she was still an attractive woman. When I was younger, I hadn't realized how pretty she was. She was just "Mom." Cut short and fashionable, as well as practical for her nurse's cap, her brown hair had no gray. A few lines around her eyes and mouth spoke more of stress than age. Sadness had always made her look vulnerable, as she did that day.

My eyes shifted to Russell. I didn't really know him, so I tried to reserve judgment; but I couldn't understand what my mother saw in him. Nine years her senior, the man would soon be sixty years old. His iron-gray hair had a tendency to stand up in spikes, due to his short, out-of-style haircut. He stood at least six feet five inches tall. At five feet two, my mother came to just above his belt buckle, which may be a slight exaggeration.

Russell had a pronounced look of Lincoln about him, except that his lips were thin, not full. Light blue eyes peered from behind dark-rimmed glasses that sat upon a long, narrow nose. Given the opportunity, I might like him; but that opportunity had not yet knocked.

"How is your daughter?" I asked. I barely remembered Betty Ann Dunbar. She had been a freshman when I was a senior, and very tall for fourteen. I did remember when her mother had died unexpectedly that year.

"She's fine," Russell said. I waited for additional family data, but none was forthcoming. I could mark off "brilliant conversationalist" from the list of his attributes. For the remainder of the ride to my mother's house, I retreated into my own thoughts.

I stayed in Dixon for a week before returning to Shaw AFB. My friends had boxed up everything except my clothes, so there wasn't much packing to do. I donated Jack's personal things to the Salvation Army. The only things I set aside were pictures and his medals, which I shipped to his parents. The few pieces of furniture that I had chosen during our marriage included a desk, an armless chair, and the small dinette table with two chairs, all of which I kept. Everything else, including the bed, went to a second-hand furniture store.

The Air Force sent a respectable life insurance check to me. With my salary, the insurance money, and the small widow's pension from the government, I would be solvent enough to maintain independence from Jack's trust fund. I was relieved to sign a paper relinquishing all claims to it.

In Sumter I found a one-room apartment with a bathroom. It was big enough for my needs, and it was near the newspaper office. I loved my job. For the first time in the eight years since I left Dixon, I was independent, doing something I loved, and I wasn't afraid.

I thought a lot about Jack, trying to figure out how I could have been so wrong about him. During those weeks and months, I realized that my sense of something not right with him had always been there. I had just stopped listening to the ping of the little warning bell inside my head that had first sounded when I was sixteen years old. What I thought had been a change in Jack had merely been his camouflage.

It was as if Jack had held up a glass, a dark, smoky glass that had allowed me to see only what he wanted me to see. The times of confusion had occurred when the glass had slipped, and I was able to see what I had glimpsed when Jack was only eighteen. Unfortunately for me, Jack had broken the dark glass soon after I married him. It seemed that once he had attained possession of me in marriage, he no longer had to maintain the façade.

On Christmas Eve I drove back to Dixon. It was a long trip to stay for only a couple of days, but I had missed several holidays at home when Jack was stationed so far from West Virginia. The rest of my family was there, and I enjoyed being with my brother's two little boys, Willie and David, who where the ages of three and one.

Being there for that short time allowed me to see what my mother saw in Russell Dunbar. He was a gentle man, and he adored Bill's boys. I will always carry in my mind the picture of those two little boys on Russell's knees, looking up at their new Grandpa's face. Russell's countenance actually glowed with love for the children. It became easier for me to accept the new recliner that sat in the spot that had held my dad's overstuffed easy chair.

On the way back to Sumter, South Carolina, the day after Christmas, I thought a lot about my dad and the months just after his death. I wondered if I might not have married at all, had Dad survived the mine cave-in. He had always been in my life, a strong, dependable, and protective force. Perhaps I had thought that Jack would embody those same qualities, providing for me a stable continuity of family life.

During that long drive, I realized that losing my dad had taught me many things. I had learned that life goes on, even when we think it's impossible. We are strong enough to survive pain and loneliness and despair, which can be worse than death. Day by day we grow stronger through adversity, but only if we don't give in to those negative emotions that can weigh us down, if we allow it. By the time I arrived back at Sumter, I was ready to begin a new life.

I worked hard at the paper. Tom Byars, the editor, gave me a byline on several articles, and I was gratified by the feedback from readers. When I presented an idea for a weekly column, Tom agreed to run it for a month. Reception was good, so he ran it for another four weeks and then another. My column, "Roundabout," covered Sumter and the surrounding area and eventually branched into the outlying countryside and beyond. That column opened other doors and possibilities beyond my imagination.

During the next few years, I realized that my mother had done a good thing when she remarried. My sister and her handsome husband, Eric Malone, relocated to California, where they built an exciting life together. My brother and his red-haired wife, Lainie, had another little boy, whom they named John.

Me?

I moved to New York City.

#

Epilogue

I closed the front door of my apartment and dropped the keys onto the foyer table. A cursory glance revealed that the small stack of envelopes I had just taken from the mailbox contained very little of interest: a utility bill, a travel brochure, and a hefty letter from my mother, which I retrieved. Nothing else merited my immediate attention. I hooked my wet umbrella and damp coat upon a wall peg, kicked off my shoes, and collapsed against the soft sofa cushions.

It had been a tiring month, culminating in a hectic day of juggling appointments and meeting with editors. I had met my deadlines, but only barely. I should never have taken on three assignments at the same time; but since I had gone freelance, I couldn't afford to renege on any accepted proposal.

All three extensive articles had turned out well. The magazine editors seemed pleased, and each one had spoken of additional commissions they might have for me. It wouldn't hurt my resume to have pieces in three prominent magazines within weeks of each other. Still, the long hours and little sleep had taken their toll, both mentally and physically. I was tired.

A brief onslaught of early-April sleet pelted the window. I pitied my co-New Yorkers on the street below, and I was grateful that I had arrived home before the rain turned to ice. Thoughts of my sister, lounging beside her swimming pool, enjoying a tall, cool drink in the California sun beckoned like a mirage on a desert isle. However, the only sand within my proximity was that scattered to prevent falls on the icy streets.

The break I had long been promising myself seemed very desirable. During the five years I had lived in New York, I had not taken a real vacation. All the locations throughout the country, even various parts of the world that I had covered, were all work-related. As I opened the letter from my mother, I thought about the travel brochures in a desk drawer, just waiting for me to choose a destination from their colorful pages. Perhaps after dinner I would make that choice.

Mom's letter was thicker than usual. When I opened the pages, a newspaper clipping fell out. Actually more than a clipping, it was the whole front page of a newspaper. My heart twisted in surprise. I hadn't seen a copy of that paper since I was a child. The banner read: **Redbud Grove Record-Herald.** I quickly scanned the paper before I turned to the letter.

Committee Votes to Hold All-School Reunion, stated the headline. I hadn't heard from any of my old friends in Redbud Grove since my sophomore year in high school, in nineteen fifty-five. I did a quick calculation: twenty-three years. My eyes hurried over the page, trying to take in all the information.

The various reunion committees had joined forces, and a massive undertaking was being planned. The town was issuing an invitation to anyone who had ever attended any of the Redbud Grove, Illinois, schools. The reunion was scheduled for the next Labor Day Weekend. Unless the town had grown substantially, I saw no way that it could accommodate so many people. It would take all the motels within a hundred mile radius to house them.

I turned to Mom's letter. I skipped through the usual stuff, hoping to find more about the reunion. The letter contained personal news that I skimmed through quickly, planning to reread later.

"...so I thought you would be interested in the reunion. I don't know who sent the paper. The return address just had "Reunion Committee" and a box number. Someone you knew must still have our address. It was sent to you, here in Dixon. Do you think you might go? It would be a good chance to reconnect with your friends. Maybe you could find Sharon and all the girls you knew. What were their names? Melissa, Sheila, Shirley, Cathy...who else? I can't remember all of them. I've passed the news on to Bill and Beth, but they haven't said whether or not they're interested.

"I'm working part time now. Russ wants to start traveling more, since he's retired. Who knows? I might just retire, too. Well..."

I let the letter fall to my lap. People and places I hadn't thought about for years tumbled through my mind. Through memory's eyes, I saw our little house, the park, my schools, our neighbors, and my friends. A pang of nostalgia shot through me, and I knew that I would return to Redbud Grove. I was as certain of it as I was that the redbud trees still bloomed there every spring, and that the far banks of the Embarras River still looked like a pink carpet when the trees dropped their blooms.

I could hardly wait.

Readers' Reviews of Starlight, Starbright...

I actually found myself between tears and laughing out loud while reading Barbara Elliott Carpenter's book, Starlight, Starbright... The characters in the story seem to resonate with a life force of their own, and they live in the reader's imagination and heart after the last page is finished. Reading this book felt as good as a journey back to Little House on the Prairie and Stand By Me. No one should miss reading Starlight, Starbright...! I'm looking forward to the sequel.

~ G. Boda
California

I took a copy of Starlight, Starbright... with me on vacation to Las Vegas for a poolside read and nearly burned myself to a crisp! Now I understand why another avid reader stayed awake all night to finish reading Sissy's story. The author must have a very romantic love interest in her life. When she described Miss Kate's kiss, I felt it all the way to my toes! Barbara Elliott Carpenter has succeeded in sprinkling this book with so many small treasures....moments of utter bliss to ponder later, and enjoy all over again!

~ J. Miscinski
Chicago

I have just read my new favorite book, <u>Starlight, Starbright</u>.... I absolutely absorbed it! With outstanding scenery description and intriguing characters, it is a MUST READ! I am recommending it to everyone I know. I can't wait for the sequel. Barbara Elliott Carpenter's book will whisk you back to a familiar, complicated time in a young girl's life. You can't help but fall in love with Sissy and her family. Finally, without grossly exaggerated details of life's hardships, here is a completely believable story, from beginning to end. I think it rates right up there with <u>To Kill a Mockingbird.</u> A true gem!

~ J. Cape
Illinois

In <u>Starlight, Starbright...</u>, Barbara Elliott Carpenter turns delightful phrases throughout the pages of a story of the loss of innocence of a young girl. Coming of age in the post World War II era, Sissy brilliantly learns to face her fears in a mysterious world as it touches her and the reader, through the clear and descriptive writing of the author. Carpenter has created a vividly animated personality in Sissy, who endears herself to the residents of Redbud Grove, the fictional small, rural community in the Midwest. The reader is treated to vignettes of Sissy's memories as she journeys from early childhood to high school. I found myself identifying with the era, and Sissy is a character I would have picked as a best friend when I was her age. I was reluctant to lay the book aside after reading the last page.

~l. Bengelsdorf
Virginia

Barbara Elliott Carpenter, author of <u>Starlight, Starbright...</u>, has written a magnificent novel, mixing her warm love for humanity with great story-telling power, giving readers a close, in-depth look into young Sissy Bannister's life. The characters leap from the pages, weaving a magic that captures the essence of mid-America during the Forties.

~b. Smith
Arkansas

Starlight, Starbright... took me back to my childhood. The characters in the book are as vivid as if seeing them upon the silver screen. Seldom have I caught myself laughing out loud while reading a book, as I did as I read this one. I was reading so quickly to see what was coming next that I literally had to force myself to slow down! Besides falling in love with Sissy, her family, and other characters in the story, the book brought back memories of my childhood that I thought were gone forever. This story reflects a time when it was safe for children to ride their bikes and play outside, of stay-at-home mothers, home-cooked meals, and neighbors looking out for each other. I so look forward to Barbara Elliott Carpenter's sequel to Starlight.........no doubt it will be another delightful MUST READ!

~k. Baker
Texas

Barbara Elliott Carpenter's book, *Starlight, Starbright...*, triggered memories from my own childhood. The characters come to life on the pages. I fell in love with Sissy and the Bannister family. Carpenter could become my all-time favorite author.

~j. Stallings
Illinois

Dear Barbara:
I have just finished reading your novel, Starlight, Starbright...; and this letter is a FAN MAIL! I enjoyed reading your book so much. It is cleverly written, held my attention to the very end; and I am waiting for its sequel, "Wish I May, Wish I Might." Your book is a story that all readers would enjoy. We'd love to see it in a movie!

~ M. Beal
Illinois

Barbara~
I just wanted to let you know how immensely I enjoyed Starlight, Starbright.... You really know how to paint a picture with words. I can't wait for your next book--please let me know when it comes out!

~s. Hester
Illinois

Barbara:
Your book is the reason my quilts won't be ready for the quilt show! I couldn't put it down! This is the best book I've read for a long, long time! Put me on your "to notify" list for your next book!

~p. Foutch
Illinois

After I read Starlight, Starbright...,I began to wonder if I had read a book or if I had actually been witness to the events in the stories, especially the chapter, "Rebecca." The characters are so real, and the descriptions are so vivid, it was as if I knew the people and had seen the town.... I can hardly wait for the sequel....

~ M. Davis
Illinois

INTERESTED IN A GOOD BOOK?

I tend to shy away from writing book and movie reviews in this space, but there can always be exceptions to the rule....No, this is not a book written by famous millionaire author J.K. Rowling, Stephen King or John Grisham, but by Barbara Elliott Carpenter. Carpenter has written "Starlight, Starbright..."and, while fictional, the characters in her book are based on her memorable and joyful experiences while living in Arcola as a girl. In a recent interview with this writer, Carpenter spoke glowingly of her five years living in Arcola...and those experiences are brought to life in her book.... If you're interested in a book about a slower-paced and perhaps more carefree time from the early 1950s, this is the one for you.

~ Chris Slack, Owner/editor, Arcola Record-herald
Illinois

About The Author

Award-winning author and poet Barbara Elliott Carpenter has been writing for pleasure most of her life. She describes her view of writing as "a love affair with the written word." Her first novel, <u>Starlight, Starbright...</u>, the first in a series of three, was released in the summer of 2003. <u>Wish I May, Wish I Might...</u>, eagerly awaited by Sissy's fans, is the second; and the third, <u>The Wish I Wish Tonight,</u> will be released in the spring of 2006. The third book will not only complete the saga of Sissy Bannister and her family, it will resolve the mysteries and unanswered questions from the first novel.

Painting with oils and acrylics, quilting, gardening and travel are among the author's interests. She enjoys keeping in touch with classmates from the schools she attended, and she maintains friendships with people from all areas and walks of life. Readers' comments and reviews are welcome. Her website address is: <u>www.barbaraelliottcarpenter.com</u> . Email address is: <u>bjlogger2@aol.com</u>

Barbara and her husband, Glenn, have been married for forty-six years and live in a wooded area beside a small lake in South Central Illinois. They have two children and four grandchildren.